A Gift for the Sovereign

Sophia Akiva

A Gift for the Sovereign

Olympia Publishers
London

www.olympiapublishers.com
OLYMPIA PAPERBACK EDITION

A CIP catalogue record for this title is
available from the British Library.

ISBN: 978-1-78830-732-1

First Published in 2021

Olympia Publishers
Tallis House
2 Tallis Street
London
EC4Y 0AB

Printed in Great Britain

Prologue

"They say we are betrothed now," spoke the boy, brilliant midday sun reflecting in his walnut-brown eyes.

"Aye, to be wedded in but two summers from now," Adelaide smiled back at him, gently brushing her hand over the soft green grass. They sat together atop a cliff, savouring the crisp seafront breeze. The winds have changed in the recent weeks, bringing the first sheltering gusts of summer.

"A daughter and her father's apprentice, one to take up the trade and build a house for them both, right here, right by the sea. And on the morrow, we would step out into the light and walk up to the church and bid 'Good morrow!' to our neighbours. And here we shall raise a family; a son to take after me and a daughter to be wedded to a noble prince one day," he spoke playfully, looking out into the blue horizon. She saw his vision and knew that she would be as fortunate as a girl can be to live a protected life in their beautiful coastal homestead, surrounded by friends and family who she grew up with and a loving husband she befriended as a child, yet one thought weighed heavy on her heart.

"Jon, d'ya think there's more than this?" Adelaide yearned for him to understand, but his expression remained blank. She started again, "Have you not heard tales of magic and adventure, tales of brave knights fighting dragons, evil mages ruling kingdoms, sailors finding distant lands? Have you not wondered what it is like, out there? It's nearing my thirteenth summer here, and not once have I seen beyond these fields."

After a moment of thought he replied, "The land that lies out there is full of danger, but here you will live without a worry." The boy smiled comfortingly and turned his face up to the gentle sun, closing his eyes.

His words did not put her worries at rest. Being the only child born to a potter and his wife, Adelaide knew that she would never have the chance to see outside this kingdom, nor to live in one of the big cities near the king's castle, nor to see the fascinating artefacts foreign merchants brought to the markets. Envy held onto her soul with that subtle but ever-strengthening grip.

Adelaide could often see trading ships in the distance, but the waters near her village were too shallow for them to dock and the bay was surrounded by a tall cliff with but a single steep path leading up, used only by the local fishermen and children who were curious enough to venture down to the water. The rock of the cliff was soft and crumbled often, piling up at the bottom, where harsh grass roots sprouted from the displaced soil.

"We should return to the village. Father may need you," said the girl, jumping to her feet and brushing out the folds in her skirt. Jon stayed seated for a little longer gazing into the distant waters, trying hold on to his own daydreams. Releasing a deep breath, he lazily rose to his feet. His shirt and breeches were caked in dirt. The edge of the cliff caught his eye and he cautiously walked up to it and looked down at the shore. Adelaide gasped when he got close to the edge and he turned and flashed a confident boyish smile. He went to her and together they headed back towards the tiny mud houses in the distance.

The fields they walked through were still empty, but in a few months, they would be alive with farmers and crops. The sun which was growing hotter with each passing day had dried the soil, making it soft on their bare feet. When she glanced back, Adelaide could see the dust stirred by their steps linger in the still air, turning lightly in the vortices the two kids left behind them, and then slowly settle back on the ground.

"Could it not have been the sun?" Jon asked after staring at her for a while.

"The sun?" She looked at him inquisitively.

"Aye, for your braids to go charmed." She realised that he was referring to the two white locks in her hair which framed her face. They adorned her head for as long as she could recall and greatly stood out from her night black hair. Many have wondered about this abnormality and often blamed superstition, so she kept them braided in and tied back.

"My father told me of how his father's hair turned white from working in the sun all summer."

"Aye, it could be," she concurred quietly.

"The baker's wife said, that if you weren't from our village, and if she didn't know your mother and father, she would have sworn you bore the devil's mark."

"It's not!" she exclaimed, "I have no sin, no unholy act to be marked for!"

"I dare not accuse you. I know that a heart so pure shall ne'er be marked by such an ungodly fault."

Adelaide knew that his words were intended to flatter but she was grateful for the kindness nonetheless. Blushing, she slowed her step. The midday sun shined brightly above them, warming their skin, the breeze gently moving their hair. They were suspended in time. She wondered if perhaps she was too preoccupied with the wonders that lie beyond this little patch of paradise.

Their moment was broken by the loud calls that erupted in the distance. They both turned curiously towards the huts. At first nothing appeared out of the ordinary. As they looked on, commotion and chaos began to break out in the streets. Distant shapes hurried from hut to hut.

"Who in devil's blood is that?" Jon muttered under his breath.

"Can't you see? They aren't no good people from our village! Those are bandits!" Adelaide cried.

Part 1

The Thief

Chapter 1

Silent Fields

Adelaide sprinted towards the village. As she got closer, she began to see the streets clearer. She saw one of her neighbours dragged out of her house by the hair and made to kneel on the ground. The woman's husband ran outside with a meat knife but was stabbed instantly by one of the strangers who now filled every little dirt road. Three of them stood around the woman, taunting her, mocking her, and then one moved behind her, hooked his arm around her neck and pressed a dagger to her throat. A young boy ran out of the house with a fire poker and rushed to help his mother. She screamed at him to run and moved to point him away from the village, but the man holding her pulled her back and laughed. The little boy relentlessly swung the fire poker at one of the outlaws and caught him in the shin, piercing his flesh. Their laughter stopped abruptly as one of them grabbed the boy and ripped the poker from his small hands, throwing it across the road. He then held the boy in front of his mother and forced him to watch as his accomplice cut her throat. The little one screamed and struggled, fighting the man who held him, but his efforts were futile as the bandits threw him on the ground and drove a sword though his little chest. Their chocking hyena-like laughter was distinguishable amongst the roar of the village.

Adelaide was still running towards them when a hand grabbed her elbow and sharply pulled her to a stop. Jon stepped in front of her, holding her in place. He glanced quickly towards the houses and then glared at her darkly.

"Have you gone mad?" he hissed, "they will slice your throat if you take one step in there, if not worse!"

She tried to rip out of his grasp. "But Mother and Father…"

"Dead! Already dead!"

Adelaide stopped struggling and stared at him. She opened her mouth to protest but he interrupted.

"Look at them!" He twisted her so she was facing the village, "They've got their swords and they swing them at all in their path! There won't be a good man alive in the village upon the sunset, and if one is, they shall be forced to stray from the Lord's path. Go! There's nothing more to be done here! Go!"

The truth of it hit her. Her parents were dead, slaughtered by filthy bandits. Everything she ever knew was gone. Everything was destroyed. Her heart was racing; she could hear it in her ears. Her skin was hot from running and sweat dripped from her brow. She gasped for breath, trying to think of what to do, what to say.

Jon's hands let go of her and he turned towards the village.

She wanted desperately to ask him what he was doing, but too many thoughts were fighting in her head. All she could do was to silently reach after him.

"But for me, there is more to do," he said and turned back towards her. In his eyes, she could see so much fear, so much devastation, but also a hint of reckless bravery.

"When Father first heard of bandits bothering good men and women, he said that if misfortune ever brought them upon our family we would protect the young ones. They were told to go hide beneath the floor of the house where they dug a hole many summers ago. 'Tis not in eye's sight unless you've seen it before, so those soiled fleabags will likely look past it. But my brothers and sisters will be safe there hidden. I must find them, for if there is any hope they are still well, I cannot leave." He looked down at the ground and closed his eyes in sorrow. "I know that our mothers and fathers may well be dead, but I must return for what family I have left."

Adelaide realised that this was their final goodbye, even if Jon and his siblings were to make it out alive. When he looked up, she saw that he knew it too.

"We must part. I pray that one day I shall see you again," he spoke gently. "Farewell Addie."

"Aye…" was all that left her lips.

There was so much she wanted to say but she just froze and stared at him as he gestured her away from the village before he turned and ran. They were close to the houses now and a number of the outlaws had caught sight of them. Jon had noticed this too, so instead of heading straight into the village he went around it in search of a safe way in. There were dozens of bandits, they crawled in like roaches, filling every street and every house, but the village was surrounded by flat ground and empty fields leaving Jon nowhere to hide. They arrived suddenly so they must have been on horseback, leaving him with little hope of outrunning them. It would truly be a miracle if he survived and, in her desperation, Adelaide clung to the hope of this miracle.

When they saw him run, some chased after him on foot while others went to fetch their horses. Many stood around laughing knowing that he was set for death. They must have already killed the majority of the residents and were now going around the houses looting. The previously dusty little streets were red with the blood of the villagers. Corpses lay in front of their raided homes, constantly kicked and trodden on by the bandits going in and out. One of them was still alive, still moving. He held his hand against his chest, instinctively covering a gashing wound and with the last of his strength reached towards the body of his wife. Bandits stood around him, laughing at his misery as one of them placed his foot over the man's hand and pressed it into the moist ground.

Adelaide was held motionless by the sheer terror of the events that were unfolding before her eyes. These scenes forever carved themselves into her memory as she watched on, unable to look away. Although most of the bandits who saw them went after Jon, there was still one looking at her maliciously and when their eyes met, he turned and walked towards the nearest horse. The shock that held her before was turning to blind panic. The girl knew that she had to run if she stood the slightest chance of seeing another sunrise.

Yet, she could not stop herself from quickly glancing back at her dearest friend. She could see him in the distance, still running. This would be the final time they would meet in this mortal realm.

She turned and ran as fast as she could. The movement brought her into reality. She prayed and prayed that this was just a bad dream and that she would wake up and everything would return to the way it was before but deep in her heart she knew that it would not. She was panicking, gasping for breath, forcing her legs to move rapidly. There was a sharp pain in her chest. Was it the terror that made her want to collapse on the ground and cry? Or was it the dust that cloaked itself around her throat as she panted, weighing on her chest, making it almost impossible to breathe.

The soft ground beneath her feet no longer made for a pleasant terrain. Instead, she sank into it with every step, making her progress slow and exhausting. She had not been running for long yet she could already hear the stomping hooves that were gradually getting closer. Adelaide pushed her muscles to contract faster, but she could barely breathe. Her vision was getting hazy and the hot sun on her head was playing tricks with her mind.

She was getting further and further away from the village and the tended farmland was losing ground to unkempt wilderness. The soil had toughened and lost its bounce. Through it, she could feel the vibrations made by the animal, whose rider was right behind her now. Sharp rocks ripped at her bare feet but the solid ground made it easier for her to run. Overwhelmed by the emotion and physical exhaustion, her mind began to fade and just as she got to the top of a small hill, her eyes closed and balance left her body. She fell, half-conscious, and rolled all the way down. Her arms flopped about uncontrollably and caught beneath her as Adelaide was made victim to gravity, tugging at the joints in her shoulders.

Adelaide laid there, her head spinning, her eyes opened, but not seeing. Panic still filled her body. She could no longer move. She was helpless and vulnerable. When the rider caught up to her, she would be dead. Adelaide knew that he was not far behind her when she fell. The sudden realisation that he must already be here shot a jolt of terror through her body. She gasped for breath, only to inhale the dry soil on which her head had crashed, and sat up, leaning on one elbow, coughing.

Looking up, she saw a horse and a darkly clothed rider standing atop the hill. Frozen by fear, she could only stare. He simply watched her, unsure of how to proceed now that he finally caught up to his prey. She could see him clearly in the light of the sun that peaked over his shoulder, with his worn stained shirt and dark leather tunic, his brown hair tied back and his face that was no more than a few years older than her own. He studied her with his malicious gaze, but she could see the sorrow lingering in his eyes. He slowly raised his sword preparing to ride down and strike her. The sun shined brightly off it, blinding her momentarily. Closing her eyes, Adelaide braced herself for death.

She pitied herself. She would never see those distant lands or the towers of the king's castle. The travelling merchants would never haggle with her for their goods. Even the prospect of a humble village life was out of her grasp. In that moment, she was finally honest with herself in how much she despised the thought of being bound to the insignificant duties of a family home. It sickened her to accept that this chase was the most excitement she had ever had. In that moment, right before her death, she felt exhilarated.

"Oh hell!" She heard from above and opened her eyes to see him slide the sword back into his scabbard. He turned his horse and harshly called down to her, "They're all dead. Don't bother coming back." And with that the rider galloped back to the place which had once been her home.

Dirt engulfed her hand as the girl pressed it into the thawing ground, the other still shielding her face from the attacker who never made his move. Sunlight pierced through her fingers, painting rainbow rings on her veil of tears. The ground vibrated beneath her body as the merciful bandit departed. Her lungs were aching from the run, but she was almost too frightened to take a breath, fearing that the moment she does would bring her back to the horror she was facing.

Lowering her defensive arm, Adelaide looked up. Blue skies overhead, dust blowing down the hill in the breeze, having been shaken up from the ground by the galloping beast. Such a peaceful sight. Tears began their torrent down her cheeks as the unyielding hysteria sent her small fatigued form into uncontrollable convulsions on the ground.

The world stood silent around her. No birds to sing their songs, no animals to hide beneath the cold rocks, no trees to play their flutes in the wind. The once-fertile field was just awakening from its winter slumber only to discover that it had been abandoned by its patrons. Never again will their feet walk through its soil or their tools forge this hard land into a source of life-sustaining food. This year it will stand alone, overgrown and chaotic yet in its isolation it will blossom. The nutrients will enrich the ground and life of all forms will emerge, unhindered by controlling hand of man. Of the people who had governed it, only one remains. A fragile snivelling creature who now laid in its icy embrace. Screams of agony burst forth from her throat and she clutched to the soil like a child to the skirts of her mother. Yet, this child will find no sympathy in the idle arms of nature.

The land that had once brought life was now collecting its debts. It swallowed the moisture of her tears as this broken soul lay weeping. When at last this being was able to move once again, she found herself on the verge of unconsciousness. Her skin was scraped and red all over and her dry cracked lips were hanging apart as she desperately sucked in air through her teeth. The throbbing in her head made her sway from side to side as she stumbled through the dirt away from the village that she could no longer return to.

Adelaide would often collapse during her journey under the weight of her trauma; yet, each time, she would find the will to stand and walk once again. For many hours, she gazed at the unforgiving earth beneath her feet through half closed eyes, reluctant to raise her heavy lids and watch the light of day retreating from the heavens, surrendering its post to the twinkling harbingers of darkness.

Cold water touched her bare toes, startling the child. Before her was a small puddle, the surface of its murky water sparking in the twilight. Collapsing heavily to her knees she sunk her trembling hands into the dirty liquid. Such a delightful sensation. Scooping this newfound treasure with both hands she brought it to her lips and gulped greedily. The putrid taste was of no concern to the girl as she drank more and more, feeling the water soothe her dry throat. She drank until her shrivelled stomach could take no more and contracted, causing her to spew the filthy water back into the puddle. Exhausted and weakened further by the pain, Adelaide's trembling body fell unconscious into the dirt.

***

Silence.

The lifeless wasteland stretched out to clash with the heavy grey clouds on the horizon. Their battlefield faded, obstructed by indistinguishable shapes. A bitter taste on the tongue, a lump stuck deep in the throat. The smell of sickness. The heavy air that sapped body heat through the droplets of sweat on the skin.

Adelaide lazily opened her eyes. Murky water was before her, laced with blood that trailed to her lips. A murder of crows hopping about on the soil, inching closer to their motionless target, pecking curiously at her clothes. The girl rolled onto her back and the birds shot up into the sky, a great cone of them scattering in all directions. Upon trying to inhale deeply, her crusted windpipe rejected the moving air and she twisted in a coughing fit. Her insides felt as if they were being torn apart. Desperate for hydration, she once again reached into the puddle, but his time her twitching fingers did not obey their impulse. They merely moved rigidly through the water, feeling the cold sensation. With all her might, she pulled her hand from the moistness and pushed herself to her knees.

Her head thrown back, the girl looked around. The view was the same in every direction; brown and dirty. She fought back the images that flushed before her eyes, shutting them off even though she longed to see them fully. Her mother's face she could remember clearly. Those kind azure eyes, the thin lips that often stretched into a delicate smile, the patterned cloth that always held back her hair. Her father, the local potter, a man famous for his healthy appetite and light-hearted words. His grey eyes were just the same shade as the ones that now stared hopelessly, blinking away the dust in the air. How must those faces look now…

Her sweetest Jon. Did he truly have a plan or did his brave heart send him into certain doom? Will she ever stand before him again?

What had they done? Those innocent people, children, farmers, humble craftsmen had lived their lives in peaceful seclusion. They led honest lives, spending their days in work and prayer. They had not travelled through dangerous waters or bargained with corrupt merchants. What could have brought this curse upon them? What could they have done to deserve a fate such as this?

The poor girl could not help but wonder if anyone else had made it out with their lives. Where would they be now? Would they help her or would they ask her to carry them upon her shoulders? She would oblige if they did. She would carry them until her legs would fail her. Yet, it seemed she was the only soul to seek safety in these fields and now she must rise and carry herself forward. She must find water and shelter.

And so the girl rose and stumbled forward, swaying as her muscles struggled to awaken. She must survive. She must push on.

For days, she walked aimlessly until at last an army of shaded trees rose out of the distance. They grew closer until, eventually, Adelaide was surrounded by their tall shapes. In summer, this would be a dense forest filled with life, but now it stood silent. Adelaide hovered in the shadow of the trees, finally relieved of the blazing sun.

The branches appeared dead but as she looked closer, she saw little buds, the first young leaves emerging from them. The woods were arising from their winter rest and the grass was beginning to appear on the dry ground. Looking up, Adelaide imagined being here when they are in bloom, standing under the green canopies, breathing in the luscious scent of the woods, hearing the animals trot gently across a carpet of grass and tasting the early morning dew.

The thought of water dragged her back to reality as her thirst was becoming unbearable. Taking careful steps, she wandered deeper into the woods. Darkness embraced her with just an occasional ray of light to illuminate her path. The world she walked into was far more eerie than she first perceived. There was a rustle here and there, but no animals crossed her path, the birds sung high up in the trees, but closer to the ground, their songs echoed, sounding mocking and sinister.

Adelaide moved through the trees as swiftly as she could, glancing behind every now and then. Each time she saw nothing, but the feeling of someone following her never faded, sending shivers down her spine.

She must have been walking for hours, through the sharp branches that caught her hair and over the rough bumpy ground till she saw a light in the distance. Rushing towards it, Adelaide came to a beautiful lake, surrounded by colossal trees that seemed to gaze down on her. The water was still, undisrupted and like a giant mirror it reflected the sun's rays.

After momentarily admiring the beauty before her, Adelaide ran towards the lake and jumped in, blissfully engulfed by the cool water which rippled and sparkled in the sunlight. Swimming back towards the shore, she stopped when the water was shallow enough for her to sit comfortably and cupped the water in her hand, gulping it down until she was sated.

Standing up, she peeled off her drenched dress and washed it, rinsing away the putrid smell which emanated from it. Crawling ashore, she found a patch of land that received the sunlight through the cover of trees and laid the dress out to dry as she lay next to it, arms and legs spread out wide, warming her skin. The scratches and lacerations that covered her from head to toe were like cracks in the weathered bodily shell she wore. She was due to ponder the events she had witnessed and worry about the uncertain future ahead, but the forest had a strangely tranquil atmosphere. It was one living, breathing organism that she had intruded upon; it was almost as if the forest wanted her gone, so it stayed quiet, leaving her in isolation.

Sitting up on her elbows she looked around, seeing only a wall of brown trees and the endless darkness between them. There was no life here, no plants to gather and no animals she could hunt. The branches could be dried in the sun but there was no flint to light a fire with. Surviving here will not be easy.

When her dress had dried, she put it on again and walked along the bank of the lake, afraid to venture too far from it. Everywhere she walked, there was always the same lifeless scenery until, to her disbelief; she saw a single mushroom hidden in the roots of a tree. Kneeling beside it, the girl brushed through the nearby soil to reveal more of them. She picked up as many as she could carry in her arms and brought them back to the water to clean the caps.

After staring at the moist fungus for a few minutes, she finally convinced herself to eat them raw, knowing she would starve without them. It was good to be able to eat something again, but the soggy mushrooms were all but delectable. She forced herself to eat them all and drowned out the horrible taste with water. Leaning against a small hill by the water, she began to think up a plan.

Chapter 2

The Sailor

Adelaide knew she had to leave the woods. There was barely any food here this time of year and if she walked through open land, she was more likely to come across people. Supposing that all the trees depended on the lake for water, it would be the centre of the forest and it only took her a few hours to get here so it would not take much longer to get back to the fields on the other side. It was dusk now, too late to begin the walk, for she could barely see her path in sunlight, so she planned to sleep by the lake overnight and travel again at dawn. Making herself comfortable she closed her eyes.

Yet, sleep refused to welcome her as if something urged her to stay awake. The sun was setting in the distance and the sky overhead was burning red. Looking around, the world began to look different to her. The tree bark was no longer brown; it had shades of black and purple winding through it like serpents. The pebbles beneath her turned to colourful crystals and she found herself sinking into a pool of them. Hastily climbing out, she ran to higher ground, away from the water to hide in the roots of a tree.

Adelaide jumped over one of those roots and crouched behind it. The world stood still again for a moment and the ground was solid beneath her feet. Beginning to relax she peered out.

"If them winds don't change, we'll ne'er get to the Isle o' Cato on time, eh lass?"

Adelaide staggered to her feet, tripping over the roots and quickly getting up to face the old man who stood leaning leisurely on the tree before her.

"Din't mean to startle ya," he laughed and stretched out his tanned wrinkled hand, "Roger."

The girl stared at him with mute astonishment. His old brown hat covered the upper part of his face and from behind his ears long loose strands of grey hair twisted down and cloaked his shoulders. The old man wore a simple shirt beneath a plain leather coat; an attire common among the poorer mercenaries who relied on their own inexperienced tanning skills to produce low quality leather that would serve as both clothing and rudimentary armour. On one leg, he wore a boot; the other was missing, replaced by a wooden peg.

"Who are you?" she demanded.

"What the devil got into ye, I just told ye me name, lass!" he drew his hand back, looking somewhat hurt.

"How d'ya get 'ere?" she didn't soften her tone.

"Arrived by sea not long ago."

"Which sea?"

"The one right there, yer mad wench!" he said pointing towards the lake.

When she turned, she indeed saw a sea before her; there were no longer any brown-barked trees on the other bank, or pebbled ground that she had once walked upon. The water was now endless, reaching out to the horizon. Confused and terrified, she spun around to ask Roger where she was but the man who stood before her now was no longer the friendly old sailor but, instead, the bandit with the malicious gaze who chased her away from her village.

"Thought ya could ran away?" he grabbed her by the arms and stared darkly at her, the grin never leaving his face. "You'll never get away!"

"You let me go!" she struggled, but his grip was like metal chains that dug into her bruised flesh.

"Aye, but only to savour your death later," he hissed. Those dark eyes seemed inhuman; the whites being almost completely overtaken by blackness. It was as if two obsidian stones rested in his eye sockets. The creature intended to kill her, and in the most grotesque way.

Despite him standing right before her, she could not make out much of his face, other than those cold dark eyes that she saw in the fields. It was almost as if she was looking at a reflection of him, his image distorted, fading. The darkness was no longer in his eyes, but spreading from him, like smoke from a fire, like a black mist that cloaked the ground, surrounded her.

"Why?" she screamed at him.

"Because I will never stop hunting you!" his voice changed. It sounded deeper, louder. "Because on every cold night you spend alone, in every dark corner of this world, in every nightmare, I will be there! I will always be there! Even when you think I am gone, forgotten, lost, I will not leave you alone till the day that you die!"

His limbs have turned into the very darkness that surrounded him. What stood before her now was no man, no beast but a monster made of vapour, a murky black shape with a barely distinguishable face peering from its sinister form.

Adelaide spun around and ran from it as fast as her legs would carry her, but trees moved before her, blocked her way. Their roots were reaching up, winding themselves around her legs till she could no longer break free. They pulled her underground. The soil she was dragged through was rough, filled with sharp rocks that scratched at her and caught her hair, yet the roots pulled her down quickly, not giving her a moment to grab onto the walls of the tunnel. The earthly tentacles did not let up. Her screams were hopeless, instantly muted by the soil that blocked her throat. She coughed and choked yet she could not breathe.

Just when her mind began to fade, the rocky tunnel came to an end and she could feel herself falling. Opening her eyes, she caught a glimpse of tall grey walls but, in an instant, her body fell into a pool of icy water. She quickly rose to the surface, gasping for breath.

Adelaide now found herself in a vast cavern that was filled with water except for several small stone elevations that acted as islands. A small campfire flickered on one of these islands, illuminating the cavern by casting dancing patches of light onto the walls and ceiling. A slouching figure was sitting beside it. The girl swam towards him in hope of an explanation. Clambering out of the water, she rushed towards the warmth of the fire and at closer sight recognised the man next to it.

"Roger!" she called. Her voice echoed deafeningly through the cavern.

"Eh, lass," he responded, looking up from under his hat.

"What are you doing here?" She sat next to him, close to the fire.

"Waiting." He stared into the flames. The wood crackled gently.

"What for?"

"What for does a man wait? A day when one can be free to live his life as one wishes, a day when a good and fair king wouldst take the land, a day when famines end and men stop dying needlessly, a day when peace rules this world."

Adelaide was unsatisfied with such a vague response. There was so much she wanted to ask, but the questions would not form a logical structure in her head. Finally, she mustered a simple question, accepting the deviation from present events, perhaps even welcoming it somewhat.

"Is the king not good?"

Laughing, the man replied, "One can tell that you lived in a village, lass. No king is ever good, none can end the wars or give us simpletons a chance at fortune."

Curious, she continued her line of questioning, "Have you seen the royal city?"

"The capital, aye, and it's no pretty sight! Why d'ye ask?"

"I oft wondered what it's like. Are there many merchants and knights and ladies in beautiful frocks?"

"Aye, and the thieves and the drunken brawlers and the guards that pound you for merely looking at them wrong, but let those fool-born bastards run free."

"Because of this, you have taken to sea?"

"Aye, there be nothing like the open waters for me. The creaking masts, the winds that carry ye forward and the calls of the gulls when ye be close to land."

"And then you would return home?" she inquired.

The man squinted into the flames. "Nay, folk like us got no home to return to. The sea is our hearth and the rum is our bread."

Adelaide found his sadness easy to relate to. "Nor do I anymore."

They sat in silence for a while, two lonely travellers lost in a world of ignorance and cruelty. There were no sounds but the soothing crackling of the timber that echoed through the cavern. Roger looked up at her through his white hair.

"You will find little peace in the towns of this land."

"You do not know what I search for," she replied defensively, "how could you, when even I don't?"

"I know more than one would think, lass."

"I believe there be more for me in the towns. There is little I can do here, but there I can find work or maybe help from a kind soul…"

"You will find neither!" the man croaked. "People there are little like ones ye've met. Heartless sinners, they be! Go to a village, to a farm, but not to the towns."

"Very well," she responded quietly, with no intention of taking his advice.

Adelaide looked around the cavern. It was enclosed in tall grey stone walls that reached higher than any building. The other dry platforms of rock were deserted, and the rest of the cavern floor was hidden under an extensive pool of water that stretched further than the light of the fire would allow them to see, hiding in little caves in the walls and possibly continuing into other caverns. The surface of the water was calm, undisturbed, perfectly reflecting the walls and ceiling, which appeared to be made of solid rock. Adelaide looked up and could see no tunnel or passageway above her.

"Roger," the girl was starting to challenge her vision, "where did I fall through?"

He looked up and studied the cavern for a few moments.

"Up…" he replied, pointing aimlessly in the direction he was looking.

"But there be no break in the rock. The burrow I was dragged through was made of soil, I swear it!"

"This be a strange world." He returned to gazing sadly into the flames.

"And how did you come to be here? How did you bring the firewood to this place and light it?" she demanded loudly, getting up to her feet. Her voice echoed eerily. Roger simply looked up at her and smiled.

She began to sense a threat, something haunting, dark was coming towards her. The old pirate continued to stare, as if looking through her. She spun around to see if there was anything behind her but was met with the endless pool of water. When she turned back, he was gone, as was

24

the fire. The stone platform began to disappear, as if swallowed by the pool and soon Adelaide was in the icy water once again with nothing beneath her feet.

The cavern was pitch black now and the water began to move around her, pulling her down, pushing her side to side. She could hear waves splashing around her but there was no echo of the sound.

Her muscles felt numb as she desperately struggled to keep her head above water. Coughing and choking she fought for air, but eventually the dark forces pulled her under.

Chapter 3

A Warm Welcome

Still splashing her arms, Adelaide discovered solid rock beneath them and pushed up. At once, she found herself above water. Opening her eyes, she looked around, instantly recognising the pebbled beach she walked on the day before, the huge rock she fell asleep against and the familiar lake with brown trees on the other bank. Everything was back to the way it was before her meal of mysterious fungus.

She was sitting in the lake, close enough to the bank to be able to touch the lake bed, yet far enough to be almost fully submerged in water. Standing up, she walked out to dry land and simply stood there, admiring the late morning sunshine and trying to grasp what had happened to her.

Looking around, she chose a path and began her hike through the woods. The dark surroundings remained lifeless. Broken twigs cut into her feet, making every step agonising, so she ripped off two strips of fabric from the skirt of her dress and wrapped them around each foot. After that she continued steadily through the trees.

Eventually, the enormous trunks receded, giving way to small shrubs, beyond which lay endless brown fields. Adelaide glanced back occasionally at the mysterious woods as they disappeared into the distance, wondering what had happened to her there, yet knowing that she will never reach a full understanding.

She must have been walking for a full day as the colours began to dance in the sky. In the glow of the sinking sun, she saw a dark silhouette spanning the horizon. She hoped it was another forest to shelter her for the night. However, as she got closer, she began to distinguish a central peak rising over a level landscape. Her heart was racing and her steps turned to a sprint, fuelled by the excitement of finally seeing a settlement.

In the centre was a large castle, situated on top of the hill overlooking the rest of the town, which was surrounded by a tall stone wall. Many carts and carriages were entering and leaving the town through a huge gate. Above the gate were two guard posts and three armed guards stood on either side of the doors. Cautiously, Adelaide walked up to them.

"And what do we have here then?" one laughed.

"Please, my village was taken by bandits, I come here in search of work," she begged the man.

"I've got some work for you…" the guard muttered menacingly under his breath but looking to the others he gestured his hand into the distance and called out, "you won't find none of it here. Begone!"

"I beg you, kind sir…"

"Get out!" He drew his sword and Adelaide hastily stumbled back and rushed away from him. She could hear the guards laughing behind her. But she was not one to give up so easily.

She began to circle the city, looking for a way in. Every now and then there would be another watch post, but she crept close to the wall in the hopes they would not look down. Her fingers traced each stone, looking for a loose one or a small gap, but her search was fruitless. She heard children giggling in the distance. The noises from behind the wall were muffled and indistinguishable, yet the children sounded much clearer. Adelaide followed the sounds until she saw three boys playing outside the town.

"If Mother knew we were here…" One giggled.

The tallest one hushed the others.

"Shush! Can't you hear? That's the curfew bell!"

Adelaide heard it too.

"We must go back," the eldest ordered and despite the protests of the others, grabbed them by their collars and dragged them towards the wall. Adelaide watched carefully as he pushed his siblings into a hole in the ground and then crawled in himself.

She ran up to the burrow and after waiting for a few moments for the boys to leave, dived in. She was bigger than them so her progress was slow, further delayed by her memories of the night before, but eventually she climbed out the other side, coughing and covered in dirt.

Before her lay a city bigger than she could ever have imagined. Every narrow street was filled with people, their voices merging into one deep drone. The houses were not the little mud huts she grew up in, but tall buildings, some even with two or three levels, made of timber and thatch. Pigs wandered the streets, rummaging through the waste that piled before every house. Horses were led by their owners to the stables. Many people swore at the cats and dogs that ran between their feet, tripping them up, holding up the traffic of people. Everyone was walking, heading back home.

Adelaide admired the city for a while and then joined the flow of people, hoping it would lead her to a safe place to rest. Gradually, conversations died and the citizens dispersed, leaving her walking alone through the empty streets. The sun had set and the cold night breeze ran across her skin. She continued walking, studying the town.

The houses she passed were densely packed and the second floors often hung over the street. It would not be difficult to leap from one rooftop to another. Each had a timber frame with panels of woven twigs covered in straw and clay. The road beneath her feet, although made of stone, was very uneven, crumbling in places as the stones were unshaped and often did not fit closely together. Sewage lay on either side of the path, joined by piles of household waste. The stench of it was unbearable.

Adelaide reached what appeared to the town square, a large open area with closed market stalls and a stone well in the centre. A wide road was leading from it towards the castle. A group of people were assembled close to the well. Three armed men were dressed in uniform and stood facing the common civilians who were positioned into badly organised rows.

"You have all been selected to form this night's watch," announced one of the leaders in a nasal, unpleasant voice. "Are you aware of your orders?"

The men grumbled and nodded, clearly reluctant to partake.

Ignoring them, the leader recited a well-practiced order, "You will scour the streets for any scoundrels, and dispose of them. You shall possess a club, and no other weapon."

"So we 'ent gonna try an' kill you first?" called out one of the men, laughing. The others sniggered. The leader slowly walked up to him, trying to maintain his authority. Upon reaching the man, he held his nose high and clasped his hands behind his back to mimic a stance of superiority that he himself seemed unfamiliar with. The insubordinate townsman straightened his back, revealing he was about five inches taller that the snobbish constable. The other men watched grinning and even the two constables cracked a smile at the awkward confrontation, but quickly looked away as not to encourage the civilians. Growing more enraged, the leader raised his hand and slapped the man across the face, then hastily returned to his spot between the other constables.

"No man is to be found in the streets, unless with an exceptional cause. If a filthy miscreant be found with no stolen goods, throw him out the gates nonetheless, they all steal eventually." Upon realising the lack of interest in his words by the group, he cleared his throat and gestured the men away, who instantly began talking and laughing among themselves.

Adelaide rushed back through the streets, away from the square, looking for a place to hide. She hurried around a corner and leaned her back against the wall, catching her breath. There were no footsteps in her direction and she relaxed a little until she heard a rustling in the shrubs. Curious, she ventured closer. An elderly woman suddenly emerged, making Adelaide jump back a step. The woman was dressed in filthy rags. Her hands, despite being wrapped in cloth, were covered in cuts and many large moles plagued her face.

"Eh, how big the watch be this night?" she hissed, revealing both of her teeth.

"No more than twenty men and three constables."

The old woman smiled madly and rubbed her hands together. "Good, good." She scurried away through the bushes but glanced back.

"Ya got some place to stay?"

Adelaide shook her head.

"Come, come then!" And she disappeared under a fence.

After a moment of hesitation, Adelaide followed. She made her way through the bushes and under the fence, just in time to see the old woman rush behind a large wooden cart. Cautiously walking around it, Adelaide saw a group of other people, all dressed in rags. Most of them were under ten years of age. They all turned to face her as she stood before them. The adults glared at the old woman who led Adelaide there while the children looked curiously at the newcomer.

"What ya bring her 'ere for?" a man scolded the elderly woman. His dark hair reached past his shoulders and scraps of cloth covered his hands and feet.

"She got no place to go," the woman explained.

"Should have left her be. How'd ya know she 'ent with the watch?"

"She be running from 'em when I see her. She says there an't no more than twenty men this night."

The man smiled, "Twenty, eh? Twenty cannot look over the whole town. They soldiers?" he addressed Adelaide.

"Nay, men."

"They care not for the town. They walk through the main streets as the constables tell 'em to, but not around 'ere."

The children were already sitting on the ground huddled together against the city wall and the adults joined them, forming a circle of people. The old woman grumbled as she sat down but moved to the side, inviting Adelaide to join them. The adults were still hostile towards her.

"How'd ya end up 'ere?" the man asked.

"Bandits took mine village." There were gasps among the children.

"This close to Aeraworth?" the man looked concerned.

"Is that where I am?"

"Aye, the grand city of Aeraworth. The king's cousin himself is up in that castle there. You come from one of the villages by the sea?" Adelaide nodded. "Upon the morrow, go see the one of the fish traders in the market, he should know someone from your home; the old man with a green cloak."

"Father told me there be no cities near our village," Adelaide thought aloud. "Why would he keep it from me?"

"To stop ye from coming up this way. It be no good place for us simple folk," the man replied.

"Then why do ye stay?"

There was a silence among the adults.

"We got no other place to go."

"How did ye end up in the streets?"

"Why's it any concern of yours?" the man snapped, "we took ye here, away from the watch, so be grateful ye little cur."

Adelaide sat in uncertain silence among the beggars. The children were falling asleep, snuggling together for warmth as the adults murmured quietly among themselves. She subtly studied them, wondering who they were and how they ended up in rags. After the previous few days, she was glad to finally have some company and although she didn't even know their names, she was nonetheless enjoying being in the presence of other people. Leaning close to the old woman to avoid any attention from the others, she quietly asked a question that had been on her mind since she first arrived.

"What is the watch?"

"Just some folk that the constables choose to guard the cities from criminals. They make sure there are no souls in the streets after curfew and if they find us, they'll throw us out the gates. Those who fight back will hang from the gallows upon the sunrise."

"So there were more of you once?"

"Aye, many more! A few leave, a few come, even the little ones. It's easy in the day, the crowds are large and the people are busy, but at night we gotta hide. They en't checked around 'ere before and God forbid they start now. It's the constables ye gotta watch, they get coins for every one of us they find." The woman produced a horrific snort and lay down on the ground "Ye should get some sleep while ye can."

Adelaide closed her eyes. She knew that the times ahead were going to be hard, but for the first time since she left her home, she was surrounded by people who may not have welcomed her, but spoke to her and stood watch over the group now, and for the moment Adelaide felt safe.

Chapter 4

Coin

Adelaide woke up to see the sun rising in the distance and as colour stretched over the sky, life embraced the city once more. Voices reached her from the street; angry calls, laughter and conversations, yet one seemed closer than others. Looking in the direction of the voice she saw a man walk up to one of the carts leading a horse. He was mumbling something to the animal, stroking its mane, but stopped when he saw Adelaide.

"What ye doing 'ere all by yerself?" he asked her, as he began to fasten the horse to a cart. His tone was friendly and he wore a genuine smile on his face.

She glanced around to find that her new companions had abandoned her. A little hurt, but determined not to cause suspicion, she quickly jumped up and brushed the dirt off her dress.

"I dropped a coin."

"Is that so? Perhaps you should invest in a belt pouch to store yon coins in," he said, without even glancing up at her.

A little threatened, she quickly replied, "I only carried one coin, to the market to get bread for my mother."

He looked at her, eyebrows raised, still smiling. "Through here? I don't think any of these carts are gonna get ye to the market any quicker."

Adelaide babbled incoherently, internally praying to God that he wouldn't take her to the constables. Her heart was pounding as her brain worked furiously to come up with an explanation, an excuse but the string of words leaving her lips could barely be called a sentence. Did he really know she was a stranger in this town, or was he just making conversation? The all-too-familiar sensation of panic began to return. She took a few steps back, slouching and looking at the ground, gripping her hands together.

When she eventually collected the courage to look up, expecting to see the accusing eyes of an angry citizen, she met his gaze and was surprised to see understanding in place of judgement. He had an aura of peace about him as he gently brushed his horse.

Reaching into his belt pouch, the strange man tossed her a coin. "I hope that covers yer loss. Go get some bread, child." And with that, he departed, walking alongside his horse as it pulled along a small wooden cart.

Adelaide stared after him for a moment, holding the little coin with both hands. She silently sent her heartfelt gratitude after him.

She followed the path she took the night before; under the fence and through the bushes to the street, which was busy once more. There were farmers leading their horses to the city gates and towards the fields. Some were pulling empty carts, others had tools and metal in them, one or two had children and dogs climb into them, laughing and playing. Women were talking in the streets, carrying their infants. Children were running around, pushing past people and climbing fences. Many were walking back towards their houses carrying buckets of water from the well.

Adelaide joined the flow of people towards the market. Her unknowing guides took the path through the interconnecting little streets and eventually merged into the crowds of the town square. There were more people there than she had ever seen. The wooden stalls stood out above the crowd, with painted signs advertising their goods. Merchants were calling out, grabbing people by their clothes, blocking their way. People stood around the well, conversing and laughing. In the distance, Adelaide could see the city wall, and the guards positioned at their posts. She glanced around and spotted one of the constables leaning on the wall of a nearby house, overlooking the gathering, but she knew that during the day she was safe from them. In the bustle of the markets, no one would know who was a stranger in this city and who was a citizen, who had a home and who did not.

There was one sign Adelaide was looking for: the fishmonger. She made her way through the people, being shoved by rushing citizens and tripping over a few children until, eventually, she stood facing the fisherman. Somehow, even the stench of fish was pleasing to her, bringing back the memories of her village. The man that stood before her was leaning on the wooden counter with one arm, sipping from a costrel with the other. His hair and beard were grey and over his shoulders lay a green cloak. This was the man she came searching for. A disgruntled citizen who was walking away from the stall shouted at him in anger.

"And yer mother is a bawdy glutton!" the merchant called back, closing his costrel.

Upon noticing Adelaide, he instantly gestured towards the fish, "What takes yer fancy? I have minnow from up north and…"

"I mean only to ask you a question," the girl interrupted impatiently.

Looking disappointed he leaned on the counter again, "what's bothering ye?"

Shouting over the noise of the market she proceeded, "I heard that you trade with a fishing village, not far from here, by the sea."

"There're many fishing villages near the sea," he laughed, "all destroyed by bandits now I'm afraid."

Taken aback, she inquired, "All of them?"

"Aye, they swept along the coast, taking all in their sight. They must have seen some value in them. Now tradesmen like me must to travel south in hopes of finding supply. Got to get rid of all this first though, else I will have no coin for travel. Why'd'ye ask?"

"I was from one of those villages and I found that it was only a few days walk to here. My father never told me we were this close to a city. I am curious to find out why?"

"A few days walk…" the man repeated thoughtfully, "ahh I see…" he clicked his fingers at her, trying to recall a name, "…you must know Geoffrey!"

"Aye, he was a neighbour of mine!" she clapped her hands. She knew that this man would hold no answer to her family's secret or bring them back, but it was a consolation to her to meet a person who knew her village, her neighbours. After the trauma and madness of the previous few days, she once again held the fond memory of her home.

"Great man, reliable and resourceful, he was!" the man said smiling.

"My name's Godwin, by the way, don't know if he had ever spoken of me."

"Adelaide," she introduced herself, "and they had never spoken of anything outside the village."

"I see. And now…" he took on a sombre tone, "a real pity… so many good men… lost to the barbarians."

Adelaide nodded.

"So ye got away?" Godwin inquired.

"Aye, I was in the fields when they took it."

"And now ye be here, with nothing?"

"Aye." She gazed down.

"How have the watch not found ya yet?" he asked in a surprised tone.

"I've only been here one night. I ran to the woods when the bandits chased me out. It took me a day to find this city from there."

After a moment of thought, Godwin spoke, "Listen, I knew yon village, I know they were good people, so for their sakes, I can offer you some help. If you can help me sell this fish before the end of this day, I will give you some coin and a room at the inn?"

"I'll do my best!" Adelaide nodded with a smile.

They spent a day trading. Adelaide was sent out to find more customers and each time she brought back a wife looking to feed her children or a man too poor for meat. She quickly figured out just what to say to each person and they succumbed to her persuasions. Perhaps it's a skill she always had, but never had a chance to employ and, by the end of the day, the stall stood empty and Godwin held a hearty purse in his hand.

The beams of light shined over the castle as the sun was beginning to sink behind the stone walls and the market square was glowing in shades of burnt ochre. Most of the crowd had dispersed hours before and the last few merchants were packing their goods and drawing the covers of their stalls. The town constables were enforcing curfew and rushing them to leave. One walked slowly over to Godwin and Adelaide. She recognised him as one of the men subordinate to the vertically deficient constable she saw on the previous night. He was a young man, dressed very formally with a sword resting in its sheath. There was a calm atmosphere about him as he leaned on a stall near them in the dimming sunlight.

"It's dusk now, you should get going," he instructed gently.

"Aye, we're on our way," Godwin nodded, "just need to take down the sign as I won't be back next week I'm afraid."

He attempted to climb up the stall but after a few humiliating tries instead gestured for Adelaide to get the sign.

"Me back's not what it used to be," he justified to the constable, who nodded slowly, working to maintain a solemn face.

A few moments later, she jumped down, the wooden sign in her hand.

Godwin threw his bag over his shoulder. "Farewell!" he called to the constable.

"May the Lord guide your path," the man replied, and leisurely strolled back towards the other constables.

"To the inn we go!" Godwin said to Adelaide enthusiastically.

She walked with him through the streets towards a large house, one of the few in the city that had a chimney. The door creaked as they entered and the sudden warmth and smell of cooked food embraced them both. Adelaide realised her hunger and glanced towards Godwin, who was already conversing with the owner of the inn. Soon, he walked over to a table and took a seat, gesturing Adelaide to join him. She sat nervously on a small wooden stool.

"Never been to an inn before?" he asked, swirling the mead around his clay mug. An identical one stood before Adelaide but she just looked at it, waiting for permission to drink.

"Oh, go on then." He smiled at her, "it's for you."

She gulped from the mug. The startling sweetness was a little heavy, but it finally quenched her thirst.

Godwin leaned back against the wooden beam behind them, "This little house is doing well; every market day all the merchants come and stay here, and with King Bohemond's cousin himself living in that castle up there, more and more local villagers come here just to admire the city."

A girl not much older than Adelaide came over to their table and threw down two plates of food. This was the first proper meal Adelaide had since she left her home.

She looked around the inn as she ate. It wasn't busy; several tables were taken, but most stood free. Smoke was creeping in from behind a small wooden door. That must be the kitchen. Adelaide wondered how much food must be stored there. They would stock up just before market days to prepare for the peak in demand. Unknowingly, Adelaide found herself storing that observation in her mind. She turned away from the door. The ceiling hung low, supported by wooden beams that bent under the weight of the roof. Through the smoke, she could see a group of people standing in the corner, talking quietly while sipping from their mugs. They were all working men, exhausted from a hard day's labour yet reluctant to return home to their wives. One of them must have made a joke as the others laughed, yet their joy lingered, as if they savoured every smile, every silly pun. They must not see much merriment in their lives, but who would in a city like this? Adelaide realised she was wrong to come here; she should have stayed away, as even the woods seemed more welcoming to her now. But more than anything, she wished to return home. The thought of it filled her eyes with tears.

"What weighs on your heart, child?" She glanced up to meet Godwin's concerned eyes.

"What am I to do here? I have nothing to trade, nothing to offer…"

"Nor did I at one time. But things will come, maybe in ways you would ne'er have thought. I ne'er thought to become a fishmonger, but travelling through this very city I was, as a young lad, and a man comes up to me and asks for my help. That very day, we thought up a deal; he would spend all his time fishing and I will spend all my time selling, saved the time on travel ye know, gets ye more done and then I went to another village and began to trade with 'em too. After that, things became easy! Work on market days, sleep the rest of the week!"

Adelaide smiled at the cheerful old man.

"That's how you met Geoffrey?"

"Aye, and the other lads from yon village. Masters they were, to get up a cliff like that!"

"Aye, I've gone down to the water many a time, it's a quest to get back!"

They laughed and talked for some time, till their plates were clean and their mugs empty. Then Godwin rose from his seat with a loud groan, rubbing his aching back. Adelaide slid off her stool and patiently waited for further instructions from her elderly companion. He brought out a few coins and handed them to her as she accepted them gratefully.

"Thank you for your work today," they began to walk through the inn, "ne'er would've sold all that fish without you. You got a real gift with words you know, people listen to ya. And now I've enough coin to travel down south towards Tarrynsdew, to find new stock and trade in new villages…"

"Are you not afraid?"

"Afraid? No! Of course not! I have nothing here, nothing to leave behind, but only the Lord knows what awaits me there. What adventures!" he joked.

They reached a corridor with half a dozen doors on either side.

"Alas, I'm afraid this is farewell. On the morrow, I must leave to get an early start on my journey. It was a joy to meet you, Adelaide, and I wish you the very best in your own adventures. May the good Lord guide you!"

"Thank you for your kindness and may you have good trade in the south. I hope one day we shall meet again."

With that, they parted. Adelaide never did meet him again.

Chapter 5

Opportunist

A piercing call of a cockerel sounded outside the inn, bringing Adelaide out of her slumber. Her hands brushed the rough spun fabric of the bed as she sat up and looked around. The small chamber was simply furnished with a wooden chair and table, on which stood an empty candle holder. The room was cloaked in darkness except for a few beams of morning sunlight slicing through the panels of the window.

Rising from her bed, Adelaide lifted the pillow and took the coins that she hid underneath it the night before. Holding these somewhat circular lumps of shining metal in the palm of her hand she stared at them for a few moments then clasped them and walked outside with a renewed sense of hope.

She followed the sound of the bells to a small church and slid in carefully onto the back pew. Once everyone had settled down, the sermon began. The priest's deep voice boomed through the otherwise silent room as he spoke of sin and eternal damnation, shaking the hearts of the citizens, smithing their morals in the flame of fear.

Adelaide could see the faces of the men and women who shared her pew. They were hypnotised by his words, overwhelmed by their power. She could see it in their eyes, this limitless devotion to the church, their surrender to the greater power.

Adelaide too had faith, yet despite that she resisted the influence of the sermon. His words flowed through her. She heard the meaning behind them but was not pulled into the trance that held the others.

Thinking back to the small mud hut that served as church in her village, Adelaide remembered the old priest that took a different approach. He consoled the people, gave them advise and peace of mind in times of trouble. He did not resort to intimidation to retain his authority, instead it came to him naturally. Adelaide closed her eyes at the pain of the realisation that he too was brutally slaughtered at the hands of those barbarians.

And so she sat there, sliding the coins between her fingers, desperately trying not to think of the life she once had until the voice of the priest abruptly hushed, replaced by the sound of people shuffling as they left the church. Adelaide joined them, realising that she had stopped paying attention to the sermon quite some time ago.

Once outside, the girl scoured the streets until she saw the shop she was looking for. The small sign hung above the door indicating this was the tannery. The door creaked open as Adelaide stepped inside and the foul acidic stench instantly made her gag.

"I should open a window perhaps. We here get used to the smell, ye see, and it does not bother us, but I forget we get men and women coming in sometimes," a woman muttered as she opened the shutters. She wore a felted woollen dress with a hood that covered her head, but beneath it was a gentle mature face. Adelaide leaned on the door, keeping it open with her weight while at the same time gasping for fresh air from outside.

"Whatever can produce such a stench?" Adelaide demanded.

"'Tis because we soak our skins in piss for days! That's why our leather is the best in the city," the woman replied, smiling proudly. "Now whatever were you seeking, child?"

After a moment of disgusted hesitation, Adelaide replied, "A purse. A coin purse."

"Ah, lovely!" the woman exclaimed. "Please, come."

Adelaide followed her into a different room that was filled with barrels. She glanced into one of them to see what resembled a rabbit skin soaking in a mysterious liquid and looked suspiciously towards the woman.

"That is just salt water," she laughed and led Adelaide to a table, on which lay a large sack. Opening it, she took out various leather items.

"There's little left after yesterday's market, but here are some things that may interest you," said the woman, gesturing to the products.

Stepping closer to the table, Adelaide picked up a small leather pouch that she could attach to the string of her dress. It wasn't large, but there wasn't much she had to put in it. Her eyes drifted over the other items and stopped on some strapped shoes. She glanced down at the strips of cloth that covered her feet which were now soaked in the various fluids covering the city streets. Remembering back to her struggle in the woods, she decisively picked up the shoes and walked over to the woman who has been trying to catch a glance of the money Adelaide held in her hand.

"You new around here, aye?" the merchant began delicately.

"Aye," Adelaide was on her guard.

"Have ya… 'ave ya purchased much before in the city?"

"Spent a day trading at the market."

"Ah, and how much coin did ya earn?"

Adelaide clenched her money, knowing that she may not get any more for some time and was careful not to give away more than the product was worth. She subtly slipped most of the coins into her sleeve and held out the rest in the palm of her hand.

"Only this," she smiled innocently.

"Wonderful! This is just the right amount!" the woman snatched the money as soon as she saw it but after counting it she silently reprimanded Adelaide a disappointed look, "is this all?"

"Afraid so."

"Very well, I guess this is better than not selling it at all."

Adelaide nodded politely at the merchant and left the room.

"Wait, what ya need a coin purse for now?" the woman called after her, but by then Adelaide was long gone.

The following few weeks went easily for her, sleeping at the inn at night and finding ways to occupy herself in the day. She spoke to a several merchants, helped them out however she could for a little coin and could even afford herself a clean new dress. The rough mahogany coloured fabric was thinner and weighed much less than the thick wool of the dress she once made herself under the careful instruction of her mother. The light urban design was better suited for the oncoming warmth of May.

Eventually, Adelaide's coin purse began to feel lighter and no more work came her way. It was while she was searching the streets for anything of value that she stumbled across the sight of a local hunter lying face down in a small alleyway. He was a notorious drunk but she had never seen him in such pathetic a state. Walking over to check on him, Adelaide could hear his heavy breathing and having been assured that he was still alive, she began to walk away. Yet, something caught her eye.

In the light of the setting sun, something glistened. Standing still for a moment, Adelaide contemplated her actions but curiosity overwhelmed her and she snuck carefully towards him. Her heart was beating rapidly as she gently moved his hand with her foot, revealing a small pile of bronze coins. He stirred. She froze still, watching for any other movement. Her mind was working quickly thinking of an excuse, wondering if he would believe that she was simply making sure he was well.

To her relief, he moved no more and his eyes remained closed shut. Adelaide glanced around. People were walking past the alleyway, but no one turned in. Panic was brewing in her and she quickly reached down and snatched the coins almost without thought. The realisation of her crime struck her and her legs began to move past him and to the other end of the alley, away from the main street. As she moved, Adelaide glanced back in fear that someone had witnessed her actions but her eyes fell on the small knife that was sheathed in the hunter's belt. She rushed back to him and removed it as delicately as she could with her trembling fingers, trying to listen out for any footsteps nearby, but all she could hear were the palpitations of her heart as they resonated in her ears.

Once the knife was in her hand, she sprinted from the scene of her crime and when she gained enough distance, she collapsed against the foundations a nearby house. The city wall was right before her now and she knew not many people would be walking through these dirty side-streets. Adelaide was glad nobody saw her run when she looked down and discovered that the knife was held visibly in her hand.

The sudden ringing of the curfew bell made her jump to her feet. Adelaide knew she had to get inside, but wondered how she could hide the dagger. A man wearing a deer hide tunic with a scabbard perfectly sized for a hunter's knife may not have raised suspicion but a young girl carrying a blade in her hand would certainly provoke more attention.

She stuck the knife into the underskirt of her dress but, as she tried walking, it cut at her leg so she pushed it through the other way like a pin and walked hastily to the inn. The innkeeper greeted her with a smile of familiarity. Nodding politely, she dropped a few coins in his hand and rushed to the room where she had been living for the last few weeks. When inside, she slammed the door shut, immediately chastising herself for her lack of caution and leaned her back heavily on it, relieved that no one had noticed the strange folding of her skirt.

Rushing to the windows, Adelaide closed the shutters and sat down on her bed. Taking out the knife, she studied it. It was a simple make, with an iron blade and a grip wrapped in a strip of soft leather. She brushed her finger along the metal edge and tested the sharpness with her thumb. With a slight push it drew blood that ran down her hand and dripped onto her underskirt. The weight of the knife must have pushed it down as she ran because the fabric of her pretty new skirt was already tattered. If she was to continue carrying the knife around, she would have to find a more secure way of hiding it, some form of a simple scabbard that she could craft herself.

Being taught how to sew from a young age, Adelaide knew it would not cause her difficulty, if only she could find a durable enough fabric. The hunter sheathed it in thick leather, but that would be difficult to acquire. Any thinner leather, such that was used in making purses could easily be cut through.

Realisation of an opportunity struck her like a blow to the face.

Quickly, she brought out her purse and made a small cut in the top. Although it required some effort, the knife went through. Fortunately, some people carried their coins in fabric pouches, which could be far easier to access.

A smile lit up her face. This was the answer to her struggles. It would not be easy, but it could certainly turn out profitable.

That night Adelaide rested well, calm with hope.

The next morning, she attended the morning mass, as every other day, hiding the knife as best she could. Having listened to the sermon on the dangers of sin, she went shopping in preparation for committing said sin.

With all the required items ready, Adelaide found a secluded street and began her work. The sun moved steadily across the sky, shifting the shadows, peeking out from the clouds. A tree sparrow hopped along the ground nearby. This was not an uncommon sight this far north. The little bird looked lost, isolated from its host, hungry and looking for seeds on the ground only to find that there were none. No nest could be seen in the barren trees, no birdsong was heard. With no other resource available, the little sparrow had only one hope. It hopped over to the wall of a house and killed a spider that had been hiding there. A hideous thing it was, likely to have been killed by any human who saw it, yet a fuel for the survival of the little sparrow. The world had always been so cruelly beautiful in this way, the death of one for the life of another. An innocent murder of one that was already set for death.

Adelaide stood up and admired the new modifications of her dress. A short layer of fabric was added over her skirt beneath which was hidden a slit. The layers of her dress were separated by a loose leather belt into which the blade would easily fit. Picking up the knife, Adelaide slid it through the slit and under the belt. The hilt remained outside, covered by the new layer of fabric, making it both hidden from sight and easy to grab when necessary.

After proudly admiring her handiwork, Adelaide went back towards the busy streets to look for a chance to use her newly acquired tool.

Behind her, a house cat was greedily consuming the grisly remains of the little tree sparrow.

Chapter 6

An Offer of Employment

The sun would be high up in its midday post would it not have been for the disc of dark clouds that has formed over Aeraworth. The unusual weather formation centred over the city and dissipated within a mile or so in radius. Several cold droplets of rain landed on Adelaide's skin and she hurried inside a nearby tavern seeking shelter. The crescendo of their patter echoed through the small wooden building as Adelaide found a seat in the corner and began to assess the few people that were here in the middle of a workday.

An elderly man sat alone at a table, staring deeply into his mug of ale. His wrinkled face had a look of sorrow that he so desperately tried to drink away. His clothes were well made, with fur and a dash of rich colour. He was a well-off merchant perhaps, who had come here in search of new customers yet by his feet lay a sack full of goods. Unsuccessful in his attempts, he would have little coin to his name and would be leaving Aeraworth with an empty purse.

At another table sat a group of people. All but one, were dressed as scholars, with skin so pale and sickly it made Adelaide glad she sat some distance away. Their hollow eyes were locked on the floor, their hands shaking with either cold or fear of the man who sat with them. This central figure wore a coat fit for a nobleman. It was sewn from a luxurious fabric and dyed an unnatural deep black. Large black feathers adorned the lapels of the collar and followed the front hem past its silver buttons. The hair on this stranger's head was the same raven shade as these feathers and flowed down his back like a silken scarf all the way to the seat of the chair, upon which he lounged complacently. His skin, although pale, had a sunny tint to it. This traveller must be from a distant southern land where these forsaken clouds frequented the skies in fewer number. He met her gaze with eyes of striking celestial blue. He was the most handsome man Adelaide had ever seen, but in his youthful features hid a dispassionate condescension. Adelaide realised that she had been caught staring and quickly averted her eyes as her heart pounded in her chest.

She continued to wait in the tavern, listening to the gentle drumming of raindrops against the shutters. To her surprise, a man rose from another table, previously concealed by the shadows of the poorly lit room. He stumbled drunkenly towards the door, tripping over a chair on his way, and fell out into the street. All the eyes in the tavern were turned towards him. The merchant glared at the drunkard for disturbing his silent self-pity, the mysterious foreigner appeared bemused and the owners of the tavern mumbled between themselves until one eventually shuffled to the man's table and collected his mugs.

The man had most likely drunk away any coin he had, but this opportunity was simply too good for Adelaide to pass by. Waiting a few more minutes to avoid suspicion, she quietly rose from her chair and slipped out through the door, instantly being struck by several icy droplets. The clouds remained dense over the city but the eye of this storm hovered right above her now.

There were few people in the streets, just a lone child running errands for her mother and a merchant closing his stall, but through the fog, Adelaide saw a stumbling figure. She hurried after him, but as she got closer, her pace slowed and her feet moved more carefully. He leaned heavily on a corner of a house and doubled over retching. Adelaide knew that this was her chance. His coin pouch was tied to his belt, right in front of her. All she had to do was take it.

Her heartbeat echoed against her eardrum. Her hand trembled as she reached for the hilt of the knife. Despite the chilling rain, her flesh felt like it was burning beneath her skin and cold sweat broke out from her pores. Adelaide brushed the water off her face and her hand tightened around the grip of the knife, pulling it out from her hidden belt. She glanced around cautiously but saw no movement nearby, no shutters open, no eyes watching her actions. What if she was caught? They would throw her out the gates if she was lucky, but if not…

No, she must do this, she must reach out and slice through the thin leather, Adelaide told herself. It would be no different to taking the coins from the hunter. Except he was asleep and his small treasure lay on the ground. This man was somewhat more aware of his surroundings, albeit barely so. Yet, he was too occupied with releasing the contents of his stomach onto the ground, he was vulnerable; he would not notice the slight drop in the weight of his belt.

Taking a deep breath, Adelaide reached out with her shaking hand and pressed the knife to the leather purse. With a quick pull she sliced through it and caught the coins in the palm of her hand. Relief overwhelmed her as she stood in the pouring rain looking down at her prize. The gold seemed to shine brighter than any other metal would.

The man straightened his back and looked over his shoulder only to see mist stretching far into the street. Swearing under his breath, he walked slowly home. Adelaide stood hidden between two nearby houses, still admiring her success. She leaned her back on the wall and looked up. There she stood, a lonely lost child in a huge city, with a knife in her belt and stolen money in the palm of her hand. At that moment, in the cold rain, beneath dark looming clouds, Adelaide realised that she had finally found her purpose. In this dangerous hostile city, surrounded by liars, thieves and drunkards, she felt that same familiar pang of excitement.

Grinning proudly, Adelaide made her way back to the inn. Her feet squelched in the mud, her wet hair clung to her neck yet even the discomfort she felt could not hinder her joy. With a smile on her face she entered the inn. The inn keeper was wiping the counter, but his eyes shot up as she stepped inside. Cheerfully, she reached into her purse and dropped two coins in his already outstretched hand, as she had always done before, but this time she was no longer greeted with his polite nod. The keeper's eyes were dark and full of suspicion. He was no more than thirty years of age, yet the strain on his face wrinkled his brow. He glanced down at the coins she gave him, moved them around and looked up at her. He parted his lips to speak, but then sighed in defeat and returned to scrubbing the already clean counter.

"See ya 'morrow, lass," he mumbled monotonously.

Adelaide hesitated for a moment and then walked slowly to her usual room, attributing his change in mood to a bad day and starting to worry about a potential increase in prices.

The inn keeper watched her as she walked up the stairs and put down his cloth. His steps were silent as he made his way to the front door and, after a quick glance back, stepped out.

Adelaide sat on her bed thinking over the events of this hectic day. She had changed from a helpless child into a woman with a purpose, she had discovered a way to earn money and although it was neither righteous nor easy, it was sufficient to support her. Would her parents be proud of her, she wondered? Perhaps not, but she had long ago accepted the finality of their lives. As much as she hoped to deny it, deep inside Adelaide knew she was alone and no one in this damned city cared if she had a bed for the night or a meal in her belly.

As quickly as she found her way in this world, it could just as quickly be taken away. The inn keeper had perhaps suspected something. Adelaide tried to shake off her nervousness as mere paranoia, triggered by the risks she had taken. If he did figure it out, however, would he tell the watch or confront her alone? Needless worry or not, she would have to be prepared for both outcomes. Yet, if he had intended to confront her, why had he not done so earlier?

Questions ran through her head, plans of escape formed until she could think no more and sleep lifted her into its gentle realm where she dreamt of riches, of freedom and of further success in her endeavours.

In the morning, Adelaide awoke to the sound of knocking on her door. Cautiously, she walked up to it and listened. She could hear a man cursing on the other side, muttering to himself, but he was alone so Adelaide slowly opened the door and peeked out.

"Ahh there ye are!" the innkeeper exclaimed and pushed her door open. Adelaide stumbled back.

"Aye. Is a reason for me to leave?"

"Perhaps," he said menacingly and reached out as if to grab her by the arm but paused and instead gestured for her to follow.

"This way, lass, there's much for us to discuss."

He began to walk but stopped and waited until she was by his side before leading her downstairs, past the counter and into the inn cellar. Damn, Adelaide thought to herself, maybe I should have run away in the night.

The cellar contained three items of furniture; a small wooden table that resembled the ones by the bar, but with the addition of a hole knocked through the surface on one side, and two chairs with poorly repaired broken legs. The only source of light was a pre-lit candle balanced on this table and the darkness expanded far into the length of the room, being contributed to by the large barrels of ale that blocked the meagre candlelight. As Adelaide and the innkeeper sat down, dust rose up in a cloud and clogged her throat. Once they were both done coughing, the man looked up at her.

"I do apologize for the conditions, but I'm afraid there can be no other place for a conversation such as this."

Adelaide began to play with her fingers and nervously kick at the straw that covered the floor.

"Firstly," the innkeeper began, "the blade." He tapped the table.

Adelaide stared at him wide eyed.

"The blade!" he insisted. Growing increasingly scared, Adelaide lifted the knife from her belt and laid it slowly on the table, close to her, reluctant to let go.

"It was in your possession for no more than two days, I believe?"

Adelaide nodded, her eyes still locked on the knife.

"And how did it come to you?"

"I bought it. It's for making purses and shoes. I have been working for the tannery."

"I think we both know that is a lie," the man hissed.

"Nay, I've the needle here too if you need to see it!"

The man sat silent for a moment, then reached down to a nearby barrel. As soon as his head was turned Adelaide went for the knife.

"Don't ye dare," the keeper said calmly, without looking up. He faced her again and put a mug of ale in front of her.

"It 'ent poisoned, if that's what y'er thinking," he took a big gulp from his own mug. Adelaide reached out and drank carefully.

"What do ye know?" she began inquisitively.

"Me? I know that ye've been staying in my inn for the last few weeks. At first, ye turned up with that merchant, so I assumed ye was doing work for him but he ne'er returned and ye always had more coin in that purse. Sometimes ye would come back in the middle of day, and what girl with a job can afford to do that? Nay. I know there is a job or two in the city that would need a youngster, but that would ne'er give one the money ye had nor all this free time ya seem to have found. And then, all of a sudden, ye turn up with a knife! And tried to hide it too! Probably fooled all the men in the streets but ye can't fool me."

"What makes you so much better than the rest of 'em?" Adelaide probed.

The innkeeper laughed, "Ye can't best a thief at his own game."

Now she understood.

"So ye won't tell the watch?"

"Perhaps I will, perhaps I won't."

Adelaide glanced down at the knife. The hilt was closer to her than to him. If she could just grab it, he would have no chance to escape.

"You couldn't do it. Ye may steal a coin or two, but ye could ne'er kill a man." He grinned confidently, "And if ye were to kill me, ye would ne'er hear my offer."

"I'm listening."

"There is a job that needs to be done, and for it I need someone just like ye."

"Why me?"

"Young, sneaky and terrified of being found out." He leaned back. All Adelaide could think about was how much she'd like to slap that cocky grin right off his face.

"There is gain in it for ye too," he continued, "that room in my inn will be yours for free and I'll pay ye."

"All right," Adelaide leaned on the table, "what's the job?"

"So ye agree? Good. Every market day, more and more merchants choose to go and stay at The Knight's Head inn instead of here. I am close to becoming bankrupt and I ain't going back to living in the streets again. So I'll need ye to break into their inn, steal their gold and burn them down."

"You wish for me to start a fire? But what about all the innocent people? What about the nearby houses?"

"I don't give a shit about the innocent people! They can burn for all I care!" he said bitterly.

"You chose the wrong person for this." Adelaide backed up her chair. "I cannot do as you ask." With that she dashed for the door, but the innkeeper grabbed her by the neck and pushed her against a wall, her own knife to her throat.

"Ye asked me if I will tell the watch," he hissed in her ear, "well, I won't. I'll just cut you down right here, ye ungrateful little bitch!"

Adelaide whimpered in terror, her hands desperately trying to reach for the knife, to pry it out of his hands but her efforts were futile.

"I'll do it! I'll do it!" she croaked.

He released her and stepped away, yet her knife remained in his hand.

"But I've only stolen twice, and the first time he was face down in the street," Adelaide warned him.

"Ulric the hunter? So that's where you got the knife, eh? He had it coming, that crude bastard." The inn keeper laughed, tossing the knife in his hand. "And although you may not have much history in this art, I can teach ya a thing or two."

"Why not just do the thing yourself?" Adelaide grumbled, one hand leaning on the wall, still recovering from the shock of his threat. The maniacal grin momentarily disappeared off the man's face.

"That's not for you to know, child, just do as you are bid and get yon gold and get the hell out."

They both stood in silence for a while, watching the dust settle back on the table and chairs. The flickering light of the candle sent shadows dancing around the cellar. Adelaide looked back towards the innkeeper. He stood with his arms crossed, still gripping the knife, waiting for her to speak. His deep-set eyes made his face look even older and with the light so close to it, she could see a scar across his neck. She remained silent, simply staring at him.

"Go now, think about my offer. If you wish to return, do so soon, and if not... they'll see you hang at the gallows before dusk," the keeper spoke calmly.

Adelaide turned and dashed out of the cellar, up the stairs and into the street. She inhaled deeply and felt fresh air fill her lungs. The cold chilled her skin but she savoured it, allowed it to soothe her. The dark clouds still hovered over Aeraworth, but she chose to stay outside nonetheless. She always did find it easier to think when not enclosed by walls. A child ran by and shoved her to the side. Wanting to be left alone with her thoughts, Adelaide wandered towards the river.

Chapter 7

Sleight of Hand

The water was refreshing against her skin, flowing from the icy mountain peaks towards the eastern sea. The river passed close to the castle, and the local children often came to this spot to gaze up at those imposing stone walls, playfully guessing what treasures lied inside. Adelaide sat on the grassy bank with her back resting against the cold city wall. To her right, a rusted iron gate served to guard the city below the water level, guiding the river underneath the wall and out into the surrounding farmlands. Twigs and larger debris that were swept up by the current upstream were too wide to pass through the bars of the gate and were trapped on the inside, catching smaller detritus and forming a blockade of rotting flora. In the village where she grew up, the water was so clear that one could see the fish that foolishly swam into the fishing bay, whereas here in the city the river was murky, tinted by the dirt and shit of the population. This realisation caused Adelaide to hurriedly shuffle away from the water.

After spending all morning alone, she was prepared to return to the inn to face her task. After all, if she were to pursue her newfound dream of being a cutpurse, it would do her no harm to learn a thing or two. Standing up, she brushed the dirt off her dress and stretched, feeling the effects of sitting still for so long. On her way, she stopped off at the bakery and shortly after, while chewing on a cheap loaf of stale bread, she opened the door of the inn.

The inn keeper stepped out of the cellar with a barrel of ale in his arms but, upon seeing her, he placed it on the floor and straightened up.

"Smart girl!" the man smiled cheerfully.

"You knew I would return?" Adelaide delicately walked closer to him.

"Of course. You are more afraid of the gallows than of me." He laughed.

"You promised to teach me."

"I see. The girl seeks knowledge more than coin. You should speak to those scholars that are passing through Aeraworth. Alas, they are resting at The Knight's Head, so if they stay too long, they may not be leaving." A cruel laugh erupted from him. "First, I must test how light your hand is."

He placed her knife on the counter. Adelaide quickly snatched it and placed it back into her belt.

"Return to me tonight with no less than thirty coins."

"Gold coins?" she yelled in amazement.

"Gold, silver, what do I care? Just fifty coins to show that thou can do a simple job without getting caught," he instructed.

"But what if I do get caught?"

"Then I never heard of ya. Now away with you." He picked up the barrel of ale and carried on with his daily duties.

Adelaide stood in the inn for a while. She had stolen before, but how many men would go wondering the streets in a drunken state? No, today she could not rely on pure luck. Stepping outside she began her search.

The town square was busy with women and children fetching water from the well or bargaining with the wealthy shop owners who could afford a house in such a central district. The pebbled road reached from the city gate to the castle, circling the well. Any tradesman or messenger who came to the city would walk through here, so the houses on this street matched the importance of the men who occupied them. The walls stood strong, thickened by the layers of straw that kept them warm in the bitter winter, the large windows opened straight onto the town square so the merchants could sell their goods on market days without stepping outside. These rare extravagant houses could even boast the luxury of a brick chimney.

All that Adelaide knew was that these men had money, which they so proudly carried in large pouches on their belts for everyone to see and envy. Alas, the constables followed them around like hounds and any who dared steal from them would find their hands cut brutally off, right there in the street. Yet it was not the merchants themselves that Adelaide was after.

"Oh, forgive me!" a young girl exclaimed after bumping into a man in the street. She was a servant girl in one of the rich houses, not much younger than Adelaide herself, but nervous and terrified of her master. She scurried to the bakery, fetching food for the household's evening meal. In her shaking hand, she carried a small purse. It was the merchant's money and Adelaide could see that the girl hated the responsibility of being entrusted with such a task, rushing to get it done.

Adelaide followed her like a hungry stray cat on a hunt. The girl was muttering to herself, nervously playing with the purse in her skeletally thin hands. A group of children ran through the streets and Adelaide joined them, running past the servant girl, almost pushing her to the ground. When they were gone, the poor girl desperately looked around, searching for the purse that had disappeared from her hands, whimpering about the beating she would get for losing the master's coins.

Adelaide looked down at the small leather pouch that she now held with pride, but her admiration of her work was rudely interrupted by the children that continued running. From their shouts, Adelaide could tell they were siblings, running errands for their mother. As the others made it around a corner, the youngest boy was following behind, struggling to catch up. He was running past Adelaide when she stuck out her foot and tripped him up. Kicking dirt into his eyes to conceal her identity, she reached down and heartlessly ripped two copper coins from his little hand. When the boy sat up, coughing and rubbing his eyes, Adelaide was gone.

The rest of the day was spent cutting purses, stealing coins from shop owners when their backs were turned and tricking people into giving up their money with a few clever words. The delicate sleight of hand came easier to her now. It began to feel natural to take what was not hers. By the time dusk crept up on the city, Adelaide held more coin in her hand that she had ever dared to hope for. With joyful, proud strides she entered the inn.

A dark interior welcomed her, cloaking her in the shadows. The only rays of light that illuminated the house were peeking in through the open window and with them came the humid warmth of a spring evening. The inn keeper stood by the counter, leaning heavily on it. Upon seeing Adelaide, he nodded his head towards the cellar door. Even the notion of stepping back into that filthy little room filled Adelaide with dread, but hearing coughs from a shadowed corner of the room, she knew that their business could not be discussed in the open.

"I trust ye would not show up here without coin?" the man spoke as soon as they entered the cellar.

"I would not."

"Hand it over then," he demanded.

Adelaide stood unmoving, staring defiantly at him but a single glare from his dark eyes and she buckled, dropping her loot on the table. The man stood over it, counting the coins as they sparkled in the candle light. Pleased, he turned to her with uncharacteristic sincerity.

"Nice job, girl! And I thought I'd have to give ya up to the watch."

Adelaide lingered close to the money. The inn keeper picked out the largest gold coins for himself and nodded towards the remaining pile.

"Take it back then," he commanded, sitting down leisurely. She quickly swiped the coins off the table and into the several various hidden purses that she had already constructed for herself previously. Feeling less threatened, she sat down, struggling to balance her weight on the poorly repaired chair.

"Not leaving it all in one place, eh?" he laughed.

"Nay. Don't know how many there are like me."

"What, thieves?" The man sighed heavily. "More than ye think. Many don't last long. Some end up on the gallows, most just lose their hand. And a few... end up floating face down in the river."

"For mere theft?" Adelaide gasped.

"It's never just theft though, lass. When a man gets caught, he gets scared. He fights or he runs. Let's just say that the one that fights dies a quicker death."

As she looked at him now, she began to uncover his secret. Leaning back in his chair, that arrogant mask plastered on his face, his eyes were filled with sorrow that he could not disguise.

"Who was it?" Adelaide began.

He glanced at her inquisitively but upon seeing her expression looked up at the splintered ceiling, staring into a distant memory.

"My brother. My dearest friend." Was his reply.

"Was he hung?"

"Aye."

"But why would you steal when ye have this inn…?"

"We… I didn't always. You see, our… oh, I shan't bother ye with this." He stood up again, that irritating grin back on his face, "So, do ya want to learn or not?"

"Was the coin I gathered today not the start of my learning?"

The keeper raised his brows.

"Sure, why not. But coin will not always be there, in plain sight, just waiting for ye to take it and when ye get to The Knight's Head, they won't welcome ye with open arms, ya know."

"I see." Adelaide followed him as he led her further into the cellar towards a pile of hay. Brushing it off, he revealed a small metal safe box.

Hours were spent there, talking about the correct tools, getting used to their feel and Adelaide's endless attempts to break the lock on the box, all of which ended in disappointment. They would go from laughing to him shouting at her for breaking the tools to eventually them both giving up and sitting in the hay drinking cloudy honey ale. They talked and talked about the richest houses in the city, the castle and the lord, about the wild woodlands, even the inn and the boy who was left to look after the customers when the keeper was down in the cellar. As the night darkened, they both grew tired and vowed to resume training at daybreak.

"I big ye a good night, Adelaide," her new friend called to her as he locked up the inn.

"And ye…" she paused.

"Deacon." For the first time, he smiled a genuine smile.

"And ye, Deacon." She smiled back and returned to her chambers.

Chapter 8

Companion

Several days into her training, Adelaide was awoken in the early morning by the sound of raised voices. Creeping out of her room, she found Deacon fighting off the accusations of a local woman, who believed the innkeeper to be responsible for her husband's drinking problem. Preoccupied with this confrontation, Deacon half-heartedly waved Adelaide outside, muttering that she should stay out of the way until the matter was resolved. Pleased to have the morning to herself, the young thief embarked on a springtime stroll through the city. The streets looked different to her somehow and the weight of the knife in her belt added confidence to her step. The houses she passed were now known to her in great detail, along with their inhabitants. There was the horse trainer who made a poor decision to live in the city instead of outside the wall and then blamed his wife for it relentlessly. Then the bungalow of the greedy and spiteful old Ulma who was made so by the constant whispers and accusations of witchcraft that so often bore their presence around her.

Adelaide continued, letting her mind wander until she reached the church. Placing her hand on the iron ring, she began to push but a dark thought stopped her in her tracks. Her fingers brushed over the grooves in the metal ring and down over the aged oak timber of the door. The deep cracks in it were filled with spider webs and dirt. Time and weather had damaged the wood irreparably, yet the thickness and natural rigor of it persevered. Adelaide removed her hand, feeling unworthy to touch the sacred building. With a heart heavy with guilt, she timidly entered the small church.

Sitting on a pew among the villagers, she looked around and wondered how many of them had too committed crimes? A man sat by his wife as she moved her headscarf to cover the bruises on her face, a skinny old man hid his hands under his rags, young children scanned the room with their sharp eyes. Was this world full of sinners like herself, with not a single good heart to keep them at bay? Yet they all sat here, under the watchful eye of the almighty, aware of their unholy ways yet with no intention of changing. Was there truly no good in this world or was it simply hidden too far under the desperation and greed of the common folk to show itself?

The monotonous voice of the priest as he continued his sermon lulled her into deeper contemplation of the morals of her actions and her lips moved with a silent prayer for forgiveness, for a guiding light. Once the priest has completed his duty, the crowd rose and exited the church. Adelaide stayed seated, watching them as they went past. She studied their faces, their clothes, their complexions. But it was no longer curiosity that made her observant, it was her newfound employment. For each familiar face, Adelaide constructed a model of their profession, their family, their income that could help her better gauge between the poor and the very poor.

Tearing her guilty eyes away, she too rose to her feet and slyly left the place of worship. The morning sunshine contrasted immeasurably with the dark interior of the church and Adelaide blinked away the brightness that momentarily blinded her. A warm breeze brushed her skin and she savoured the feeling, deeply inhaling the musky aroma of spring.

The villagers set about their daily duties. The servants ventured out into the streets in search of food and goods for their masters; the carpenters set out their tables and sharpened their tools; the hounds master cradled two puppies in his arms as he carried them up to the castle and the grocer set out her stock. Turning her back for a brief moment to lift another tray of produce onto the counters, she missed the mischievous children as they dashed past, snatching up what they could. A passer-by caught one of them by his collar, ready to scold him but the youth stealthily manoeuvred out of his captor's grasp and sprinted off through the crowd, dropping his loot. The man turned back in hopes of salvaging what was dropped and returning it to the grocer but the dirt road was empty and anything that was dropped was instantly collected by the less righteous. Adelaide walked away from the scene biting into a fresh turnip.

When she had half devoured her prize, she sat down by the well and thought with pleasure about the comfortable turn her life has taken. A stray mutt walked timidly up to her and let out a heart wrenching whine. Adelaide tossed the rest of the turnip towards the dog and he swallowed it in one.

The poor thing was starving. Its dry grey skin was covered in patches of brown fur and clumps of mud that could not conceal the multitude of bruises and scrapes on its flesh. The mutt's ribs stuck out so far, they all but pierced through their wasting blanket. The hound cautiously stepped closer to Adelaide and sniffed around. Upon finding no gifts by her side, he turned his deep brown eyes to her face and gazed upon her with such sincere plead that she turned away and quickly got back on her feet.

She hurried away from the dog, swallowing back the desperate pity, but the beast tailed her through the streets. Adelaide could no longer ignore the animal and, stopping briefly by the rat catcher, returned to her grateful follower with three small rodents in hand. The dog stared at her with eyes full of wonder and awe. He moved his paws side to side with anticipation and even its tail began to weakly wag. Adelaide laid the rats in front of the dog, who rushed forward and greedily devoured her offering. She squatted, watching him eat and when the rats were consumed, the dog walked delicately up to her and rested his head on her knee.

Adelaide reached out and stoked the mutts head, playing with his floppy ears. He happily barked at her and jumped up to lick her face. Losing her balance, the girl rolled backwards and her furry friend nuzzled up to her side as she lay in the dirt. Laughing, she rubbed his fur, trying to pick the clumps of mud from it.

The animal stayed by her side for the duration of the day and when the stars began to shine in the darkening sky, Adelaide led him to the inn. She walked around the building, looking for a way to stealthily help her companion into her room without the host finding out. Standing out in an adjacent alleyway looking towards her window, she was surprised by her recent acquaintance.

"What're you doing?" Deacon inquired with a tone of mild irritation.

"I was just…" Adelaide stuttered in response.

"No. Keep that filth out of my inn," he replied sternly, walking past them both towards a shed.

The dog sat by Adelaide's feet and watched the conversation with his curious eyes.

"I will not have it going around that my tavern is infested with fleas. And look at him, he's as good as dead by now," the innkeeper spoke against her demanding gaze.

"Is there no storage room, no empty space for him to rest inside? I will stay with him and not let him out of my sight nor my grasp. He will not wander through the tavern, he will stay with me," Adelaide begged.

Deacon returned from the shed with a bucket in his hands and, seeing two pairs of pleading eyes, paused with a defeated sigh.

"To hell with it, get some straw from the cellar and take rest under the stairs if you so desperately wish. And since you're here anyway, be a good lass and run down to the well for me."

With that he thrust the dusty bucket into her hands and strolled back towards the door. Adelaide looked down at her pet and lovingly brushed her fingers against his scalp as he leant against her for support. Together they wondered up towards the well and fetched the water. Upon their return, Adelaide obeyed her host and laid out a small pile of straw under the stairs, on which she took her place. The animal laid his frail body next to her and together they rested on their makeshift mattress, listening to the conversations that filled the tavern. Adelaide's hand was loosely placed on his belly and she felt his broken ribcage rise slightly with every painful breath. She looked skyward at the underside of the steps and let a whisper of a prayer escape her lips. A man walked up to the second floor and dirt from his shoes fell onto her head. The girl brushed it off her face and turned her gaze downwards towards the snoozing mutt.

Deacon stood behind his counters and watched his two stair dwellers with a hint of compassion in his dark eyes. Disappearing quickly into the cellar, he returned with two large wooden bowls in hand. Setting them down by Adelaide, he squatted next to her and patted the mutt. The dog jumped up at the scent of food and greedily emptied one of the bowls.

"It was the food that had gone spoilt. I usually leave it and feed it to

George's pigs in the morning, and he gives me a few coins off the meat. Should be good enough for this one. There's water in the other bowl." Deacon spoke with an unusually gentle tone but, quickly regaining his exterior, he continued. "But don't ye go and expect charity from me. For yourself, you gotta pay just as the rest of these bastards."

"Then I will," Adelaide replied softly, refusing to abandon the fact that even his cold heart could not stand to see the poor creature suffer.

Embarrassed, he returned to his post but every now and then he would glance back towards the hound with tender pity. Adelaide ate her own meal and sat with her gentle beast until the crowds dispersed and the tavern quietened. They were left alone together in the dark, with nothing to illuminate them aside from the moonlight that crept in through the gaps in the panels of the window shutters. Adelaide hugged the dog the way a child would hug a younger sibling. They rested together in absolute tranquillity, listening to the whispers of the wind outside and the gentle sound of one another's quiet breathing.

When Adelaide opened her eyes the next morning, she saw in her arms a peaceful being, a beautiful corpse.

Chapter 9

The Majestic City

Weeks had passed and the hot humid air of summer now cloaked Aeraworth. The mysterious dark clouds that had once hovered over the stone walls were long gone, replaced by the unforgiving sun that cooked the rotting filth in the streets, the stench of which was spreading all through the city. Due to the frequent rains, the waste flowed into the river, and the animals that wandered the streets drank from it, contracting diseases and later spreading them onto the people. The rich citizens kept to their houses during this time of sickness. The poorest members of the population suffered early exposure and when they got too sick to work, were left in the streets to die. Their corpses added to the rotting filth of this majestic city.

People were afraid to drink water even from the central well, yet the shortage of the life-giving fluid was not the only threat. Crops had not yet bloomed and food was in short supply. Many of the animals were too diseased to be eaten and had to be abandoned. This annual summertime plague led to chaos and people had surrendered to it in their desperation. Pestilence and famine ruled the streets.

"They say they'll burn all this, before it ravages the city," Deacon said to Adelaide as they walked through the putrid pathways.

"That why they're collecting the bodies?" she pointed at a cart full of corpses.

"Aye, they're taking them to the town square. The fire will start tonight, at dusk. A few hours later, The Knight's Head will go up in flames. The folk will blame it on the wind that had carried the flame from the square. This has all worked out rather wall, has it not?" He smirked proudly to himself.

"But, surely, the fire would reach the nearest buildings first, not just that one," Adelaide pointed out.

"Perhaps. Ye can go and burn those down too if it bothers ye," he barked in response.

"Why do you care so little for human life?"

"Look around. None of these bastards do!" He gestured towards the people.

Adelaide could not refute the ignorance of the citizens. Gladly, they reached the inn and stepped inside. Being in the house made her feel protected from the disease of the city, yet the windows were wide open, and the stench had filled the rectangular dining space that spanned the ground floor. People were sitting at the tables, coughing and snorting. She sat down as far away from others as she could find. Deacon joined her with two mugs of ale.

"There are more men and women in here than before," Adelaide mumbled.

"Aye, ale is all they can drink without getting sick."

"Maybe with the coin coming in, we need not burn anyone down?" she delicately proposed in a hushed tone.

"Don't even try it. The thing must be done."

"Still, is it not a little harsh? To kill innocent people for nothing more than a few more coins in your pocket at the end of each month? In the end, there are more inns in Aeraworth; not every man that needs a room will come here," Adelaide was desperately trying to reason with him.

Deacon sat silent for a few moments.

"No man in this God forsaken world is innocent. And perhaps my methods are more brutal than need be, but don't ye try to make me feel pity for these bastards. Not one man felt pity for my brother," he hissed.

"I have lost my loved ones too. I know your pain…"

"Ye know nothing. I made a promise to myself that I will use the money we made to live the life of an honest man, to never end up in the streets again! The inn is named after him for this very reason! This is the least I can do, after all, he would still be alive were it not for me!" he spoke passionately.

"For you?"

The man stared into the distance for a while, contemplating whether or not to tell his tale. Sighing heavily, he turned to Adelaide and began.

"Our father was a simple farmer, a terrible drunkard, a bad man. We were told mother died of an illness when we were young, but we always knew that he had killed her himself. He was cruel, so when my brother got old enough, he ran away, taking me with 'im. He always watched over me. He learned to steal and got good at it, so he taught me too. For many years, we had it all: the freedom to go wherever with nothing holding us down and all the wealth and food we could steal. The coin we had was spent on warm rooms, sweet ale and pretty girls. A few years ago, we got to the city of Morrihold, south of here. It was great for thieves. Houses were richer than here. Merchants came from distant lands, bringing things I had never seen before. One summer day, just like this one, I tried to sneak a golden flagon from a foreign merchant's stall and got caught. They were ready to cut my hand off right there. My brother saw, came running and stabbed the merchant with a lock pick. Told me to run so I did, but I could hear them, dragging 'im to the gallows."

Deacon finished his ale and departed gravely. Adelaide stared after him, watching as he disappeared into the cellar. She stayed in the tavern and waited for her tutor to return. Only when the sun began to sink into the distance and the sky glowed like a sea of embers did the small wooden door finally open.

"Come, lass. Do you not want to see the flame?" he said with a friendly smirk.

"What for? Must we not prepare?"

"Nah, we have some time yet," he spoke as he walked past her. Adelaide quickly followed.

The streets were filled with sorrowful joy. Many people were grieving for the dead, whether they knew them or not, yet many were celebrating the end to the disease that plagued the city. Any animals that were caught in the streets had their throats slit and their bodies thrown onto the gruesome pile of flesh that stood in the middle of the town square. The stones on the ground were red with blood as it could not soak into the wet ground fast enough. The townsfolk stood around with torches in their hands, dancing in the glistening dark red liquid. As Adelaide and Deacon joined the crowd, the people began to chant. The power of their deep, united voices sent shivers down Adelaide's back.

Away from the citizens, on the wide road towards the castle, large cushioned chairs were placed for the more noble viewers. On them sat the Lord of Aeraworth, the king's cousin. Around him were members of his court and officials from the capital.

"It's no surprise King Bohemond himself hadn't the courage to turn up," Deacon whispered scornfully.

"Ye do not hold much respect for the king?" Adelaide replied, shocked at his words.

"Nah, the king just sits in his castle, drinks his wine and marries one woman after another while the common folk get none of that. Ya know the news of all these deaths had reached the capital, else none of these bastards would be here now. I bet it weren't even the king that thought up to burn the bodies."

"Who then?" Adelaide prompted.

"Ya see then man standing over there? The merchants that come to the inn from the capital all say he's the one that whispers in the king's ear."

Adelaide looked in the direction he was pointing. Behind the soft cushioned chairs stood a man dressed in a manner that was humbly formal. His skin was a shade darker than most and his black hair was tied back with a ribbon. He held the posture of authority yet nodded politely whenever the obnoxious lord shouted at him. Adelaide could not hear him from this distance but she could see that the man addressed the constables in a calm manner, gesturing towards the crowd. When the orders were given, he returned to looking intently around, searching for any other issues that needed his attention. He was a man who was accustomed to holding responsibility for both his own actions and those of his superiors.

"Who is he?" Adelaide whispered.

"Darius. They say he's the king's advisor," Deacon replied.

Their conversation was brought to an end by the cheering of the crowd as a torch was carried towards the grotesque pile. Straw was added to the pyre to help it catch light, but many of the bodies were in the early stages of decay and still oozing fluid. After several attempts, the constables finally started a small fire. The flame spread slowly and clouds of smoke engulfed the city. The air was thick and difficult to inhale as smoke buried the onlookers. The embers burnt their skin, yet they continued to rejoice as the disease that poisoned their city was finally eradicated, burnt in this gruesome bonfire. They thought the deaths would stop, but Adelaide knew otherwise as Deacon pulled her out of the crowd and back towards the inn through the shrouded streets.

As they stepped inside, he dashed into the cellar and returned with a leather satchel.

"Inside is all ye'll need. Go now, while they are all out gawking at that fire," he hissed.

She nodded and turned to leave.

"And good luck, lass! Don't get caught," he cheered after her as the young protégé departed.

Chapter 10

Fish on a Hook

The stars above Aeraworth hid from the pillar of smoke that reached to the heavens. The huge flame now danced happily in the town square, as did the people around it. The air was denser than before, it dried her eyes and made her dizzy. Adelaide checked the satchel to ensure that all of the tools she used during training were there and content with them she made her way through the alleyways towards the target building. The route she took had been practiced many times, so she could find her way in the poor visibility and avoid the streets where she would be seen.

The inn appeared right before her. The building had only stood a few years and the wooden panels were strong, not yet withered by rain and frost. Blue flowers bloomed near the main door, bringing colour to the entrance and a welcoming sign hung over the street. The inn seemed so inviting, so friendly that Adelaide once again questioned her motives. Despite the guilt, she knew that she had a job to complete.

The streets were empty so she quickly picked up her tools and with some effort forced open the lock. The little door creaked as she stepped inside. The interior was calm and heavily shaded yet Adelaide found herself holding her breath, scared to take another step. Summoning all her courage, she continued through the building towards the door that she believed would lead her to the owners' quarters. In the weeks she spent training for this, Adelaide had visited this inn many times to study every aspect of the building, but she had to remain in the visitors' section to avoid arousing suspicion and could only guess the layout of the private rooms.

Breaking the lock to this secret door, the girl breathed a sigh of relief when she found a room decorated so much nicer than the visitors' that it could only belong to the innkeepers. The light peeking in through the shutters barely allowed her to see but she could not risk opening them further and Adelaide dug through her satchel for a small candle. With this delicate flame, she searched the room and found a decorated wooden box with an engraving that she could not read. Her heart racing, Adelaide struggled to force the lock with trembling hands. No words could describe her joy when the seal finally gave. Inside this miniature treasure chest lay more gold coins than she had ever seen, along with a delicately crafted silver brooch.

After hastily scooping her prize into the satchel, Adelaide rushed out of the room and towards the cellar. The door was unlocked and having descended down the stairs, Adelaide stood before a small room filled with sacks of straw and barrels of ale. If the fire was to be lit down here, it would burn through the wooden barrels and the ale would extinguish it in no time. 'Maybe I should do that', she thought to herself, 'then I can tell Deacon I had lit it, but it put itself out'. But she was too afraid of being given up to the watch. All the inhabitants of the inn were out watching the bonfire so no lives will be lost, the reluctant criminal reasoned with herself.

Adelaide picked up a bag of straw and spread it up the stairs and into the entrance room. She held the candle over it, her heart beating so hard she feared it may break her ribcage, as the light flickered in her shaking hands. Cold sweat covered her skin and, with a deep breath, she braced herself to release the candle.

Moments passed as the light of the candle trembled above the flammable trail. Wax dripped down. The fragile strands of straw snapped under the impact. The room was chilling to behold, its empty chairs and unattended bar giving it the look of an old abandoned building. But it was pristinely clean, far more so than Deacon's tavern. The wooden panels of the floor were barely scratched. Such immaculate isolation further enhanced the eerie atmosphere. This place began to scare Adelaide and her fingers loosened their grip on the small waxy mode of destruction.

A hand seized her from behind. The unknown assailant harshly

69

dragged her outside and threw her to the ground. Adelaide looked up in terror to see one of the owners of The Knight's Head. He was glaring down at her in rage.

"Why?" he yelled at her. She could only stare back in petrified silence. Realisation dawned in his fierce eyes and he picked her up by her neck.

"It was Deacon that sent ya, weren't it? That wicked bastard finally did it. I knew he would strike at me some time. It was that greedy fool weren't it? Weren't it?" he screamed in her face.

"What's this?" a woman spoke as she approached them.

"A little gift from that maggot Deacon," the man explained.

"Do ye know for sure?" the woman asked.

"Nay, the quailing wench won't speak."

"I'll fetch the constables," the woman hurried away.

The man threw Adelaide to the ground again and she gasped for breath, wiping tears from her face. In fear and panic, she desperately tried to crawl away but his boot quickly met her ribs and she curled up in pain. After several agonising hits, the man stepped away as two pairs of hands grabbed Adelaide and dragged her through the streets. She struggled to breathe through the blood-soaked hair that broke free from her bonnet and clung to her face, suffocating her. The leather sandals that covered her feet were ripped off by the sharp stones on the ground, which then attacked her feet, slashing at her skin. The pain continued for what seemed like an eternity until her toes felt steps beneath them. The hot red air from the fire, that hovered like a fog all through the city, was replaced by the darkness of the dungeon. As they descended deeper into the ground, the air grew colder and the stale putrid smell of decay filled Adelaide's lungs.

The men that were carrying her threw her into a cell and she hastily backed into a corner. Beneath her hands, Adelaide felt a moist substance that stretched across the floor and walls of the dungeon. Looking up through her hair she saw three men standing by her enclosure.

"I'm telling ye, Deacon sent her!" the owner of The Knight's Head yelled at the two constables. Them, she recognised. One was the obnoxious little man that struggled to maintain his authority even around common citizens and the other was the gentle constable she met when she was working at the market with Godwin.

The men mumbled among themselves and then the young, kinder officer crouched beside her. Adelaide quickly shuffled away, but he held out his empty palms.

"Listen, lass, I only wish to speak with you. Are you aware that the crime of plotting murder and burning down a man's house will put you on the gallows?"

Adelaide glared at him, blinking away the blood that tickled her eye.

"We offer you your life, all you have to do is confess. So tell, who sent you?"

Sobbing, Adelaide whispered her mentor's name. The second constable and the furious innkeeper both dashed for the stairs. The gentle man rose before her and slowly walked out of the cell, locking it behind himself. Before leaving, he gave her a pitying glace as his hand rested on the cold metal bars of the gate.

They left her there, alone, in a wet dungeon cell, with nothing but a single flame to illuminate her surroundings. In the flickering light, she could see metal shackles hanging from the wall. Beneath them, the wall was stained black, tainted by the blood of prisoners.

Adelaide hugged her knees and rocked gently back and forth, whimpering softly to herself. The dark brown fabric of her dress disguised the blood well, as did her hair, but her pale skin revealed the severity of her wounds, even in the poor light. There was a number of deep lacerations on her arms and small rocks were embedded in the flesh of her feet and knees. Eventually the light died, leaving Adelaide in absolute darkness. Every breath, every tiny movement echoed in the empty open space of the dungeon. The sound of cockroaches scrambling along the mossy floor seemed to be especially overwhelming. Finally, Adelaide could no longer fight her exhaustion and rolled to the side, curled up and passed out.

***

The metal gate of the cell smashed against the bars and not a moment later two hands grabbed Adelaide and dragged her out of the dungeon. The bright morning sunlight burnt her eyes and the taunting calls of the townsfolk struck her ears. She was horrified to catch a glimpse of a worm crawling in her crusted hair. Despite her struggles, the two constables holding her refused to let go until they reached the town square, where they let her straighten up to face the gallows, upon which stood the man she betrayed.

His dark eyes looked at Adelaide. The anger and betrayed she expected to receive through his gaze did not make its appearance. He was calm and had seemingly accepted his fate. Deacon was always a fighter, either through physical intimidation or emotional manipulation he was relentlessly trying to get his own way, yet looking at him now she failed to see the ruthlessness that he had always displayed. As he stood with a noose around his neck and his hands tied behind his back, he had the look of a man who had lost his war.

Despite the insults and the rotten food that was being thrown her way, Adelaide was unable to take her eyes away from him. She knew that she was to blame for his death but he expressed no accusation. From his sombre face shined the gentle eyes of a mentor, of a friend.

The rope was pulled. The man continued kicking for what seemed like an eternity until his struggles ended and his lifeless body dangled from the rope. He met the same end as his brother once did before him.

Adelaide stood motionless, staring intensely at the body with a look of horror and devastation yet not a tear ran from her eye. She felt numb. She was hollow.

"Right, your turn," the short constable said as he grabbed her arm.

"You promised me my life!" she called out, struggling.

"Aye, but we didn't say nothing about yer hand. You commit a theft — you lose a hand. Especially as you caused this ruckus on the day when the officials were visiting from the capital. Now they gonna tell the king that Aeraworth is a city of criminal scum and that 'ent good for none of us."

As the constable placed the blade against her wrist, she kicked with all her might and broke away from their grasp.

Seizing the opportunity, Adelaide pushed past the other observers of the hanging and sprinted through the streets. Within seconds, the entire town was after her but to her own surprise she managed to dodge their grasps and lead them to the narrow backstreets near the city wall. As they could not all pursue her at once, some instead spread out, surrounding the area. The heavy weapons carried by the constables slowed them down and soon Adelaide managed to escape their line of sight, snaking between the houses with catlike agility. The voices of the townsfolk sounded close behind the girl and her heart dropped when she reached a dead end, surrounded from all directions. The city wall glared down at her as its stone blocks stood impenetrable and the current of the river cut off her escape.

"A way out," Adelaide's lips whispered with psychotic desperation, "a way out."

The voices were closing in and she could almost feel the icy blade against her wrist, against her throat. 'Those who fight die a faster death', Deacon had told her, and soon her life will meet its abrupt end. No, she refused to surrender so easily. With a deep breath, she dived into the river.

The water had just met the city and was as pure as when it left its source high up in the mountains. It was not yet tainted by the filth that the girl had often observed at the exit gate on the other side of Aeraworth. The current slammed into Adelaide with a force much more powerful than she anticipated but she just about managed to grab onto the metal bars of the gate. With all her strength, she struggled to hold on as the water smashed against her damaged starved body, pushing her under, robbing her of breath. Adelaide felt around the slimy bars only to find that there was no gap big enough for her to fit through. After a moment of hesitation, she pulled herself forwards and kicked. The rusted bar shifted. She continued to kick tenaciously until, to her relief, a single metal bar finally broke and bent outwards.

Aware that her pursuers were gaining on her, she quickly tried to swim through the gap but as she was halfway through, she realised with frustration that it was too narrow. Adelaide desperately tried to move back only to suffer unimaginable agony as the sharp metal bar pierced into her body and impaled itself under her ribs, trapping her like a fish on a hook. She was panicking, kicking and splashing, gasping for breath, but the powerful current only forced her further back and the metal dug deeper into her flesh. With a sharp yelp, she grabbed onto the nearby bars and pushed her body through the narrow gap, enduring the pain as it scraped layers off her skin.

Upon reaching the other side, she rushed towards the shore and crawled out of the river, coughing and gasping. With the city wall between her and the angry mob, she took a moment to assess her wound. Although deep and vigorously bleeding, it was clean. Even the rusted metal has been washed out of it by the current and Adelaide took a moment to thank every saint she knew that she ended up at this gate, rather than the one flowing out of the city, for if she had to swim through dirty water, she would have surely died. Slowly picking herself up off the ground, she stumbled away from the majestic city of Aeraworth.

Adelaide had waited her entire childhood to visit a grand city and, in the end, she got her wish. She walked in a lost and scared child with nothing to her name and now she left, months later, with no material gain, other than a wet, blood soaked brown dress, but with skills and knowledge that would serve her well. As she hobbled away, pressing her wound shut to stop the ferocious bleeding, she felt intense relief and pride. How many others have escaped the knives of the constables? How many thieves got to keep their hands? She was different. She was better. As the grand city sunk behind the horizon, she whispered a prayer for Deacon and walked away to new lands and new adventures.

Chapter 11

Brooch

Five years had passed since Adelaide left the city of Aeraworth but she had not forgotten the tricks of the trade she had learned within its stone walls. She sat alone in a tavern, in a small southern village that served as her current temporary home. From beneath the hood of her cloak, she watched as the village folk danced and drank on this jolly autumn eve. A handsome young man with luxurious blonde hair leaned on her table.

"Lucretio," she murmured.

"Aye, lass."

"How's the hunt?"

"There's good game just east of here." He nodded at a small group of men who spoke quietly among themselves.

"They're on guard, not easy to get close to."

"Aye, they're merchants from the city, here to look at the harvest, see what they fancy. We 'ent get their type 'round 'ere oft and they know not to trust the taverns but if a pretty lass like ye give 'em an ale or two, they be dancing 'fore the sun sets," Lucretio encouraged his friend.

"Merchants, eh? Ye sure they've not spent their coin yet?" Adelaide was still doubtful.

"They would be far more cheerful if they had, no?" he laughed.

She leaned forward decisively, taking her feet off the table.

"I need ye to bring me a tray of ales, and don't forget to drop a toad's tear in each mug, just to make sure our dear guests are merry enough. Then, sing us a jolly song." Adelaide dropped a handful of coins into his hand and he vanished into the crowd.

Standing up, she removed her cloak and folded it over the seat of the wooden stool. She now stood dressed as a humble barmaid, with a linen blouse beneath a badly dyed kirtle. Her dark hair was tied in a bun with a blue ribbon but loose white curls still hung around her face. She stretched out her hand and Lucretio handed her a tray. They had been performing their well-choreographed routine since the start of harvest.

"Go now," he urged her, "the other barmaids won't see ye."

He then rushed across the tavern, grabbed a lute and leapt gracefully onto the little stage. While the bard played his joyful melody, Adelaide handed out the ale as compliments from the tavern's owner and later, as the drunken merchants danced to the playful sound of the lute, one by one their purses, rings, brooches and other valuables disappeared from their persons. Before the night was over, a hooded figure silently crept out of the tavern and into the moonlight.

Adelaide returned to the tavern the next morning. She was greeted by half the village gathering in the little building, cheering and shouting.

"Lucretio!" She searched for the familiar face in the crowd. He appeared in front of her, a girl on each arm. "What calls for such festivities?" Adelaide quizzed, somewhat disoriented.

"'Tis be the day of the Royal wedding! Our king has taken himself yet another lovely wife! Lylith is her name. They say she is the most beautiful woman in all the land!" Lucretio looked to the girls he was with. "Apart from ye, my dear. And ye."

The girls giggled as the lovable minstrel charmingly lead them towards some secluded corner of the tavern. This is to be a day of joy and celebration, which will inevitably end with a lot of drinking and a lot of people vulnerable to theft. A twisted smile lit up Adelaide's face. Let the hunt begin!

She sat strategically at her usual table, disguised by her dark cloak, and observed the crowd. Most were just peasants and simple workers that were allowed to have a free day due to the happy occasion. But words were spoken of wealthy foreign merchants passing through the village on their way to the capital who were willing to open their stalls on this special day to let the village folk marvel at the exquisite trinkets that only the rich could afford.

Five large mugs of a potent local brew later, Adelaide stood up, holding onto the wooden table for balance. She drunkenly stumbled towards the door, but was pushed to the side by a large and angry man that stormed into the tavern.

"Ye filthy scoundrel!" the man yelled across the tavern and dragged Lucretio out of the crowd by his hair. "Ye were said to marry my daughter!"

The bard fought his way out of the man's grasp.

"That foolish girl fell in love with ye! And here ye are, finding more wenches to lead astray," the disgruntled father continued to yell.

"Your daughter was a lovely lass but having had my way with her I must say, I've had better," Lucretio replied with a taunting laugh. The tavern fell silent.

With a single punch, the man sent the boisterous bard through a nearby table.

"Ye roguish dog!" The raging man stormed towards the remains of the table, but Lucretio had picked himself up and dodged the second punch. The crowd retreated from the fighting duo but as the brawl continued, cheers started to erupt from the onlookers. Adelaide joined in, drunkenly shouting words of encouragement at her accomplice. Many punches later, the bard was on his knees. His fair hair, his skin, his clothes were all dripping in blood. He was breathing heavily, exhausted from the fight. The angry father reached down, grabbed the fatigued troublemaker and dragged him out of the tavern. That was Lucretio's last dance.

As the excitement of the fight died down, Adelaide stumbled out of the tavern. She was saddened by the loss of her accomplice but in the past five years she had said many farewells. Travelling from city to city, stealing what she could and escaping by the hair of her neck was a lonely life but it became the only life she knew. Every now and then, on a forlorn drunken night, she would think back to Deacon and many others like him, whom she befriended, learned from and eventually lost to this cruel world. Then she would just drink more ale and move onto a new town. At times, she would be successful and have many trinkets in her satchel and many shining coins in her purse but other times she would be sat in the filthy streets of some town, waiting for the baker to look away so she could steal a loaf to savour for a week. Nevertheless, she survived, which is more than could be said for the people she associated with.

While wandering the streets contemplating this matter, Adelaide found herself near the village market, which was now full of merchants in beautiful coloured frocks. She hazily approached the stalls and studied the items. There were gilded flagons, sparkling jewels, rugs with mysterious designs and pendants that shined as bright as the eyes of a phoenix. Hypnotised by the splendour of what she saw, Adelaide continued around the stalls until something rather special caught her eye. A delicately crafted emerald brooch lay on a velvet cushion. It was the most breath-taking piece of jewellery she had ever laid eyes on. In her drunken state, Adelaide reached out to touch the wondrous decoration, to caress its tantalizing design and before she knew it, her fingers instinctively curled around the tiny treasure and her feet was hastily distancing her from the stall.

"Thief!" The cry of the merchant pierced her delirious state.

Brought suddenly back to reality, she sprinted through the streets, shoving people out of her way, until she made it to the outskirts of the town and into the farmers' fields. The crops had been harvested recently and the empty ground was easy to run on, but her feet felt the heavy echo of hooves on the ground. That all-too-familiar vibration resonated through her very soul. That day almost six years before, when she was just a young daughter of a potter, running for her life, chased from her home, orphaned. The girl stumbled as her body seized up at the traumatic memory.

Adelaide fought against it and continued to run, pushing the horrific flashback deeper into her mind, focusing on the chaos she was currently in. In the distance, she saw the woods. Many tales have been told about this region. People said that the woods were enchanted, haunted by the spirits of the poor souls who lost their lives there. Hesitant, Adelaide ran towards the deciduous trees. She could not outrun a horse in the open, but the villagers would not dare follow her into the damned forest.

The horses were gaining on her, she could hear the calls of the riders, she could see them, galloping towards her. With all her might, Adelaide sprinted towards the approaching trees. Yet when she reached them, she stopped in her tracks.

What if the woods truly were enchanted? Turning back, she saw the riders approaching. The fate that awaited her in the woods could not be as dreadful as what she would meet back in the village. Still indecisive, she glanced towards the forest again. Squinting into the shadows, she struggled to make out a dark silhouette that was standing beneath a tree. It extended one arm, gesturing deeper into the woods. As if compelled, she followed this mysterious instruction and fought through the underbrush towards the black tree trunks. Climbing over the exposed roots of an ancient and imposing tree, Adelaide hid beneath them, entrusting her life to the protection of this earthly colossus.

Peeking over the roots, she could no longer see the dark figure that had led her there and seemingly neither could the riders. The horses paced nervously and reared when led too close to the shadows cast by the towering trees. The riders hovered outside the perimeter of the forest and eventually, defeated, turned back. Adelaide almost cried out with joy. She did it again! Escaped at the last second, both her hands intact!

After resting in the roots for some time, she clambered out and walked deeper into the woodland that had saved her. Her experiences in the woods had not always been the most pleasant and she much preferred the stone walls and dirty streets of towns and cities, but what surrounded her now left her breathless. This was not the dark menacing forest she ran to from her plundered village, but rather a vibrant and bustling environment. Birdsong was heard from all directions and sunlight pierced the green canopy, illuminating the mossy ground. Colourful insects stood on giant amber leaves like thespians on a platformed stage.

Captivated by the surrounding beauty, Adelaide continued to wander deeper into the woods. She planned on leaving once the villagers stopped searching for her but until then she would have to hide out here and somehow that prospect brought her intense joy. Adelaide spent the day admiring the woodland, the little emerald brooch pinned to her cloak, until exhausted but tranquil she once again burrowed into the roots of a tree and, safely cocooned in her cloak, fell into a deep sleep.

Part 2

The Apprentice

Chapter 12

A Single Arrow

Awakened by the morning sunlight, Adelaide sat up. The woods were just as breath-taking as the day before. Droplets of dew fell onto her face from the canopies above. Rising from the mossy ground, she wiped the cold water from her skin and picked off the moist leaves that clung to her clothes. Drenched to the bone, the girl shivered and carefully climbed over the nearby tree roots towards a patch of forest floor that was bathed in sunlight. Throwing back her heavy cloak, Adelaide basked in the warmth, closing her eyes against the brightness. Through the birdsong, she caught the sound of running water and, following it through the trees, reached a small stream. Kneeling beside it, Adelaide washed her face in the cold clear water and drank until quenched.

A young deer approached the stream. The animal gracefully bent down its head and drank. Adelaide admired the delicate creature with great curiosity, never having seen one up close before. Its fur was short and rough but it clung close to its body, making the animal streamlined so it could tear through the woodlands with great speed and agility. Its dark eyes stared at the water unfocused and unblinking. Flapping its ear against the insects, the deer raised its head, ready to gallop away.

An arrow pierced through the air and, before Adelaide knew it, the deer was lying dead in the stream, the previously clear water now running a deepening crimson. The tranquillity Adelaide experienced was so brutally ripped apart that she quickly jumped to her feet, bracing herself for whatever dangers she was about to face in this enchanted forest.

A man stepped out from the shadows of a large oak tree, holding a bow. From his aged face, two bright green eyes were locked on Adelaide like a barn owl looking at an unexpected intruder. A greying blonde beard covered his jaw. A beautifully crafted cloak rested on his shoulders, held together by a delicate silver brooch, yet the clothes beneath it were no different to those of a beggar. Walking towards her cautiously, he moved not like an old man, but with the confident strong stride of a warrior.

"What's your business in these woods?" he questioned in a calm but stern tone. His voice carried an unfamiliar accent.

Hesitant, Adelaide replied, "I was chased... by bandits."

"There are no bandits in this region," he stated confidently. After studying her for a moment, he spoke again, "You're a thief. You stole that brooch and were chased by the villagers till the only place for you to go were these woods. Yet, you have heard tales of this forest being haunted and did not wish to step onto this ground but a hooded man told you to enter and now, here you are."

Adelaide stepped back. What if this man was a witch?

"How did you know?" she called, completely unprepared to get into a fight with the supernatural.

"That brooch is clearly worth more than everything else you own put together," he replied calmly, walking towards the deer.

"And the hooded man?"

"You wouldn't be the first to be led here by him," the man replied with a grim laugh.

"Who is he? Why is he here? Why are ye here?" Adelaide threw her barrage of questions at the stranger.

The man picked up the deer and threw it over his shoulder.

"My name's Gabriel. I live here," he said nonchalantly and looking at the white strands in her hair, continued, "you remind me of my daughter. You may join me for a meal and some mead if you so choose."

"Ye won't take me back to the village to be punished for my crime?" she asked, surprised.

"The matters of that village don't concern me. Just watch that you don't steal anything from me because if you do, I will know," he spoke sternly and walked off into the woods.

Adelaide hesitated and, remembering the fate that awaited her back among civilisation, chose to follow the mysterious man. There were no pathways or trails and the forest appeared as though completely free from the interference of man until a small wooden cabin appeared in a clearing. Right in front of the porch was a burnt-out fire surrounded by a semicircle of large logs crafted into crude benches. Tentatively approaching the camp, Adelaide found it endearing how cosy the little house looked sheltered beneath these grand trees. On the other side of the clearing was another shimmering stream with insects hovering over the cool water. Gabriel dropped the deer near the logs and placed the bow on the ground. Adelaide glanced at it and was surprised to see that the weapon was very finely crafted, with an intricate design covering the metal.

"It's not from these lands," said Gabriel, noticing her fascination with the bow.

"It's made of metal!"

"Aye, and not just any metal but a rare alloy, made by a master craftsman," he explained further.

"And ye do not carry a quiver," she pointed out.

"I only needed one arrow," the mysterious man replied, looking around for firewood.

"How did ye know ye won't miss?"

"I never miss," he stated factually. It was evident that he did not keep much human company and appeared to have forgotten about the limitations of normal folk. Remembering his manners, he asked her, "Now do you have a name, my dear?"

"Adelaide."

"Well, Adelaide, go gather some firewood," he then sat down with a tanning knife and started skinning the deer.

Adelaide hesitantly walked away and returned later, holding all the firewood she could carry in her arms. The deer was perfectly prepared, ready to be cooked.

"Well, hurry, child! We don't have all the time in the world," Gabriel rushed her as she started the fire. After shooting him a frustrated glance, she continued to strike the pieces of flint together until a tiny spark was born. The light spread through the wood and the entire campfire came to life. She moved away from the flames and placed herself upon one of the log benches. The pool of heat that was now before her illuminated the surroundings more than the light from the sun, which had cowardly retreated behind clouds. She heard a cackling laugh beside her.

"Your fire lighting talents will bring much amusement to the gods of these woods," Gabriel spoke like a parent teasing his child with a scary story.

"Ye speak of pagan idols!" Adelaide gasped.

"Idols? No," he replied, a crooked smile on his face, "ghosts, if you prefer."

A shiver ran down her back.

"Here?"

"Everywhere," he whispered ominously as he placed the meat onto a spit above the flames.

Adelaide had known much fear in the past five years. She feared the merchants would catch her hand stealthily reaching into their pockets, she feared the servants would awaken as she snuck into their masters' homes, she feared that one day she would be caught and lynched but nothing compared to the bloodcurdling fear that struck her now. In broad daylight, she was held motionless by the fear of the oncoming night and the terrors that would await her. Ghosts. Unholy restless souls that haunted the living were the greatest fear of any God-fearing man and woman. This insane loner lived comfortably among them and spoke of them with a smile on his face. He was the one she truly feared.

Gazing around, Adelaide planned her escape route. If only she could make her way to the edge of the woods, she could run east until she was safe in some nearby village. Panic urged her to start running, to get away before the skeletal hands of these fiends began to reach out towards her. All at once, even the trees began to appear threatening. Their crooked branches twisted in the wind, the yellowing leaves weighing down towards the barrier of thorny shrubs. Even in the light of day, this lonely little place appeared eerie.

Laugher erupted nearby. Turning to face the ranger, Adelaide saw him sitting leisurely on one of the logs with a boyish grin on his face.

"Will you not stay for the meal before you make your escape?" he questioned mockingly.

She stared at him, still surprised at his insight into her thoughts.

"Apologies, my dear, I do not often entertain guests. Would you enjoy an ale?" he stood up and headed towards the wooded cabin.

Nodding, Adelaide sat tight-lipped, perplexed by the strange world she found herself in. This man was a walking contradiction; he spoke with the eloquence of a lord, but his manner revealed a distaste towards socialisation. Gabriel returned moments later holding two gorgeous chalices. Handing her one, he sat back down on his bench. The chalice was silver, with colourful gems creating an elaborate pattern around its edge. The sparkling stones reflected the sunlight onto Adelaide's hand, and she stared wondrously at the kaleidoscopic design that danced on her skin. This one chalice was more valuable than any she had ever stolen. Yet one question weighed on her mind; how did a ranger come to acquire such precious items?

"Will you drink from it or marry it?" she heard Gabriel's childish words. Pressing the chalice to her lips, Adelaide took a sip. The plain ale tasted like nectar when served so beautifully.

"It does not seem like you were much of a thief, if a simple chalice startles you," Gabriel joked.

"This chalice is all but simple," Adelaide replied.

"A chalice is nought but a cup."

"Value does not come from the purpose of the thing but rather from the craftsmanship taken to make it," she explained, still fascinated by the gems.

"Wise words for a crook," he remarked.

Adelaide shook off his words.

"Any news from the village?" he continued.

"The king took himself a new wife," she replied excitedly.

"Ahh," Gabriel appeared disinterested, "which king is the fortunate one?"

Confused, Adelaide replied, "King Bohemond. The king of the Starkenhaart kingdom. Our beloved father and sovereign."

"I do not believe I have heard of this one," the ranger replied, thinking back.

"The seventh monarch of the Ryhall dynasty..." Adelaide continued in disbelief.

"Oh yes, them, I do remember," Gabriel exclaimed.

"How many summers have ye spent in these woods?" Adelaide began delicately.

"How many feathers are on a hawk? How many fish in a lake? How many stars in the sky?" he swerved her question facetiously.

Hushed by his reply, Adelaide sat silent for some time but curiosity got the best of her.

"Why eat a deer in the day? Most men eat their meal when the sun begins to set."

"How many men can eat deer when they please? Out here, we are not bound by their stone walls and their untrusting eyes. This is the life of freedom. Eat as you please, drink as you please," Gabriel responded contently.

"A man that can kill a deer with one arrow would become the wealthiest hunter in any city. Yer pockets would be full of gold," Adelaide pointed out.

"Aye, and then scoundrels like you would start following me through the streets. And what worth is gold to me? What would I need it for that I cannot find here, in the woods?" he replied.

"Is it not a lonely life?"

"Very much so." His voice was sincere.

"You said I remind you of your daughter. Does she also live in the woods?" Adelaide enquired further.

A dark look of grief struck his face. His fingers curled in as his hands tensed into fists. Gabriel shut his emerald-green eyes and turned his face away.

"No," he spoke in a deep voice and heavily walked towards the house to refill his chalice.

Chapter 13

The Ghost of the Enchanted Woods

The skies darkened as the first cold fingers of winter's grasp began to stretch over Starkenhaart. The winds ran through the woods, whistling in the canopies, waltzing with the fallen leaves. A flock of choughs fluttered their sleek black wings, rising from the branches upon which they resided, and followed the winds deeper into the woods. Animals shuffled in the dying grass, hastily returning to their burrows. The cold was soon to arrive, but the woods stood strong, unthreatened by the seasons, prepared for the winter, determined to survive.

The flames of the campfire stirred beneath the half-eaten remains of the deer.

"Never seen a lass eat like two men," Gabriel joked, sitting on the ground and leaning back against the logs, an empty chalice in his hand.

"Never had this much food to eat," Adelaide replied grinning, "but what will ye do with what remains?"

"Leave it on the ground. With the winter coming, the animals will clean it up before the sun sets."

"But they will return again and again, like strays, no?" Adelaide spoke, looking around to see what critters have been attracted by the smell of roasting meat.

"Aye. In the city, a man can have a dog or a pig, but here they are all mine to care for," Gabriel said, looking towards the trees.

From the shadows sounded a deep and prolonged growl. Jumping up, Adelaide rushed to the other side of the fire and stared into the darkness beneath the trees. A white wolf slowly emerged, in equal measure hostile and curious. It had a healthy summer coat which would only grow thicker in the coming months. This long fur was slowly wafting in the wind, shifting with each precise step. The animal walked carefully towards Adelaide, staring her in the eye and snarling whenever she shuffled away. Its ears were pressed back and its teeth were bared. Adelaide kept to the opposite side of the fire. She had never been this close to a wild, untamed beast before.

"Oh, get back, you," Gabriel called, throwing a large chunk of venison towards the trees. The wolf dashed back with its reward and disappeared into the shadows of the trees from whence it came.

Adelaide took a moment to calm her racing heart.

"Do you not fear that it might attack ye?" she asked, looking down at the glittering chalice in her still-trembling hands.

"Why would he?" Gabriel replied, puzzled by her fear.

Adelaide pondered her response and realising that he would not understand her concerns, sighed and sat back on the log. Gabriel remained sitting on the ground, staring into the fire. His face was ageless; wrinkled and greying, yet as bright and healthy as that of a child. He stood up and stretched with a loud yawn.

"You may stay in the house for the night, if the wolves bother you, but it hasn't seen many visitors so you may want to find some leaves to sleep on," he spoke, walking inside.

Adelaide got up and followed him to investigate the little cabin. Darkness greeted her as he opened the wooden door, the only source of light being a tiny rectangular window in the far corner of the room. Once her eyes adjusted, she looked around. The house appeared more spacious inside. A table stood in the middle, littered with scraps of leather, chalices, bowls, knives, shoes and various herbs. The wall on the left was covered in wide shelves that housed cast-iron pots and jars filled with seeds and sundried berries. Smoked fish hung from bolts in the wall and under the shelves stood several large barrels. Right opposite the door, past the table, was a small fireplace, the only stone formation in the otherwise wooden cabin. To the right was a narrow closet with a bolted door. The bolt was secured with a hefty metal padlock, which Adelaide found to be unexpected for a house that doesn't risk seeing many intruders. In the corner beside the hearth stood a bed on which Gabriel was now comfortably sitting. More shelves were secured above his bed, and these served to display an impressive collection of books and loose pages.

"You may set up anywhere on that side of the room," Gabriel said, pointing across the cabin.

Adelaide nodded happily, remembering all too well the types of places she had previously slept in. This wooden floor was far more appealing than a festering prison cell or wet ground under an overhanging roof. Grateful for the shelter, she set off in search of soft dry leaves. As her hand reached for the door, she caught sight of a sword placed against the wall with blood still glistening on its blade. Adelaide slowly turned around, staring suspiciously at the mysterious man that seemed lost in his thoughts, oblivious to her distress. Upon sensing her troubled gaze, he quickly caught on and unhurriedly walked over. Gabriel picked up the sword, throwing it playfully between his hands.

"This one needs a clean," he spoke and sat at the table, "and a sharpening," he mumbled to himself.

Adelaide remained by, hoping for a reassurance that it was the blood of an animal but Gabriel sat silent, lost to the task of tending the weapon. Having finally exited the cabin, she once again contemplated just making a break for it. A distant howl resonated through the woods and she quickly threw the idea from her head.

The two passed the rest of the day engaged in drinking and general chit-chat until the first stars started to glisten in the sky. The little cabin remained warm as the icy night-time winds began to dance in the dimming sunlight and Adelaide was grateful for the absence of any large windows. A strong wind in a city would send the shutters into a symphony that was about as pleasant to the ear as a small child taking a stick to a metal pan. The small rectangular hole in the wall of the cabin, that Gabriel loosely referred to as a window, was sealed with a cloth pinned to each corner. Adelaide plopped down onto her leafy mattress and closed her eyes. Gabriel's footsteps sounded around the house for some time then seized as he too took to sleep.

A noise brought Adelaide out of her slumber. She lay with her eyes closed, listening out for any commotion. It was nothing more than the wind whistling in the branches, she tried to convince herself yet the ghostly voice was clear. A whisper, calling her outside. Curiosity was pushing her to rise and investigate, but terror clasped her limbs and held her motionless, too scared of what she would see if she opened her eyes. Instead, she listened closely. The room was empty. Adelaide wondered if Gabriel was a part of this unholy disturbance or if he too was just another victim of the enchanted woods.

Taking a deep breath, Adelaide summoned her courage and quickly jumped to her feet. Standing with her back to the wall she struggled to see through the blackness of the night. She could barely make out the shape of the table before her. The whisper had stopped. Was she to follow it? She moved towards the door, constantly glancing back, terrified of what may be hiding in the shadows behind her.

The door opened. The clearing before the house stood calm. The scene looked as if in greyscale, stripped of all colour by the white moonlight. The spit had fallen from the fire and as Gabriel had predicted, not a scrap of meat nor bone remained un-eaten. Adelaide stepped further into the clearing. The air was heavy with mist that clung to her skin and clothes. She felt a sudden thirst, but would not dare go back into the dark house alone. A loud hoot erupted from the trees. The canopies swayed gently, like a child rolling over in his sleep.

In the shadows to her right, Adelaide saw movement. Cautiously, she approached the disturbance, clenching her skirt in her instinctively tensed hands. Using the talents she developed when thieving, she lowered herself silently into the brush and listened as the two figures spoke.

"...For far too long," an old man in a black hood finished his speech. An ancient twisted cane supported his frail body. The girl recognised the hunched figure that guided her into the woods.

"Not long enough for me to become reckless," Gabriel replied, undaunted by the apparition.

"Reckless? Nay, courageous," the man insisted.

Gabriel stood silent, unimpressed by the persuasions of the other.

"Dost thou not miss them?" the phantom continued.

"Haven't you seen enough of me to know?" Gabriel snapped back.

"Dost thou not grow tired?" the old man held out his hand.

"What do you expect of me?"

"I expect thou to make a choice in thine tormented mind. Once thou accept what is to come, ye will be free at last." And with those words the old man faded into the mist.

So the tales of spectres were true. Yet, the creature Adelaide witnessed did not seem threatening. He was old and crippled, and seemingly hoped to help the deranged swordsman. Many a time, while listening to one priest or another talk about the tormented spirits of those fated to walk the earth for eternity, Adelaide considered what she would do if she was ever to meet one. She supposed she would fight them, run or pray, but never could she have imagined that she would remain so unfazed. Indifference was kept back by mere curiosity.

Gabriel stood motionless, still looking at where the spectre had stood. For a brief moment, the girl thought that she saw him turn his head slightly, as if he heard her there, but she brushed the idea aside as a figment of paranoia. Knowing it was best to leave him with his thoughts, Adelaide crept back to the house. The darkness no longer struck fear into her heart and gently laying down on her organic bedding, she closed her eyes and embraced the deep wondrous sleep that suddenly claimed her.

Chapter 14

Wolfkiller

Days had passed since Adelaide witnessed the spectre and although it never appeared to her directly, she was awoken every night by Gabriel's voice as he argued with the ghostly figure. He allowed her to stay in the cabin for a while under the conditions that she would keep to her side of the room and under no circumstances touch the locked door in the corner. To her, it was a small price to pay for security and food. There were many items of immense value in the cabin; brooches of pure silver lay about collecting dust, Gabriel's beautiful green cloak, which was inscribed with symbols of an ancient language, suffered from a layer of dried mud along the base hem. Adelaide's conditioned thieving instincts were urging her to take all the goods and run. Nonetheless, her hand stayed away from the trinkets as in crossing Gabriel, she would surely lose the security he provided and, in these woods, surrounded by wolves and restless dead, she needed at least one friend.

They spoke a lot about Adelaide's past. She told him stories of her childhood, about the fishing village she used to live in, about Jon. Gabriel smiled and nodded but, when prompted to speak of his own life, he replied with only a few words, evading questions and changing topics. There was an aura of sadness about the peculiar man. He was heavily troubled by his burdens but there was a noble purity and a strong sense of honour in the way he conducted himself.

Dusk arrived quickly in the woods, with the dense foliage blocking the light of the sun in the final arc of its journey towards the horizon. Summer grew more distant and evenings started to arrive earlier as nights drew on for longer. The two residents of the "enchanted" forest were on the return journey from the snares, having acquired a hare for their night time meal. The path they struggled down was barely illuminated by the waning crescent of the moon that creeped sheepishly from behind the wisps of azure shaded clouds.

They were slowly making their way through the woods, talking aimlessly about the approach of winter. Gabriel stopped unexpectedly and gestured for Adelaide to be silent. He raised his face, listening out for something deeper into woods. Adelaide copied him, but heard nothing other than animals rustling in the leaves nearby. The swordsman turned a hawk-like gaze towards the perceived sound and moved silently towards it, tossing the hare into the undergrowth behind him. Using the catlike steps she taught herself over the years, Adelaide followed close behind. Her companion was broad-shouldered and well-built, but even she could not mimic the unexpected dexterity with which he moved in his advanced age. Gabriel stopped behind a wide trunk of a beech tree and looked out into the clearing ahead.

A group of five young men stopped there to rest for the night. They looked rugged, but in a way that was different to the common beggar. These strange men wore nothing but breeches, which was not only socially odd, but also unsuitable for the climate because even in the summer, temperatures would drop noticeably in the night. The limited attire they sported was soiled through and from their long, matted hair and beards it seemed as if they only recently emerged from some rancid underground burrow. Their disturbing appearance was further added to by their burly builds and utter indifference to the savage terrain of the forest against the soles of their bare feet. Collapsing by the stream, they gulped the cool water and washed the mud from their faces and hands. Adelaide squinted in the poor visibility. Not mud. Dried black blood was caked onto their skin. She glanced at Gabriel, but he was staring intently at the men. Noticing her distress, he gestured for her to come closer.

"Go back to the cabin," he commanded in a hushed tone. "Go back and push the table against the door. Don't light the fire. Don't make a sound. If they catch sight of you, you will die."

He gently shoved her in the general direction of the cabin and Adelaide set out towards shelter, but curiosity wouldn't let her retreat more than a hundred paces. She snuck around the clearing, keeping herself hidden from both her friend and the intruders. Huddled behind a shrub, the girl watched from her makeshift viewing booth as Gabriel walked out of the shadows with his hand tightly wrapped around the grip of a skinning knife. He walked with a light step, like a jester taunting a city guard, his head held up high and a cocky grin stretching his face. The five men were caught off guard and with instant hostility formed a circle around him.

"You just made a mistake, old man," one of them snarled while swaying from side to side and letting his long hair swing in clumps past his shoulders.

Gabriel remained dauntless. "I have seen your type before. And I have driven my sword through their hearts and they bled and they died just as any mortal man."

The gang of ruffians cackled.

"I don't believe you know our type," one called, falling into a crouch, his fingered digging into the ground.

"Oh, I do!" Gabriel replied with an excited grin as he twisted the knife in his hand.

What followed next was more horrific than Adelaide had ever seen in her nightmares. In a matter of moments, the filthy men crouched and bent their bodies in inhuman ways, their bones breaking and reforming. Their breeches were ripped off as they grew in size and their hair fused with their skin, covering them in dense black fur. Their fingers and toes elongated, and long sharp claws ripped forth from their nails. They snarled as their jaws stretched and teeth sharper than knives broke out from their gums. When the blood-curdling transformation was complete, all five stood around Gabriel, their massive bodies blocking him from view. They were a ghastly combination of human and wolf, standing tall on their hind legs, glaring down at the brave swordsman with their reflective yellow eyes. One pounced at Gabriel and his lycan blood splattered across the grass as the ranger effortlessly averted the attack and sliced through the werewolf's ribs.

Adelaide could watch no more. Terrified, she turned and sprinted as fast as she could towards the cabin. What if they heard her in the trees? What if they were chasing her? She made it to the clearing and leaped over the logs, rushed into the cabin and slammed the door behind her. Brushing the tears from her eyes she ran to the table and dragged it towards the door but a sudden realisation struck her heart. The old man was out there alone. He's surely dead by now, she thought, yet a spine-chilling cry of a werewolf sounded in the distance. In her travels, Adelaide heard many fables about these cursed beasts and their formidable strength and their invincibility to all but silver, yet this man, this remarkable man, had not only the courage but the skill to challenge them.

Pacing around the little house, she knew that she could not leave him out there to die. In her desperation, she searched the cabin. Swords and knives were littered everywhere, but not one weapon was grand enough to defeat those beasts. With the hilt of one sword, she smashed at the heavy lock on the forbidden door in the corner yet it would not give. After several relentless attempts, it finally broke and Adelaide pried the door open.

A closet. A mere closet filled with a pile of unknown items covered by a blanket. Adelaide yanked off the sheet and stared down at the most breath-taking weapon she had ever laid eyes on. The sword that lay resting in this tiny closet of this little hut was grander than any blade she had seen at the street markets of even the biggest of cities.

The hilt was intricately decorated with an inscription in a language she had never seen and images of dragons weaved in-between the letters. Such beauty! The blade itself was almost translucent, with a mystical glow surrounding it. It was as if the sword was forged from magic. Adelaide struggled to lift the weapon as it weighed more than she expected. The mystical sword was not the only item covered by blankets and Adelaide's imagination raced to imagine what other wonders were hidden there but she could not ponder it for long. With a step of certainty, she left the cabin.

Adelaide reached the clearing to find two of the werewolves lying decapitated with multiple deep gashes covering their massive bodies. Three others were still involved in a merciless dance with Gabriel. They were wounded and limping and blood poured through their fur. The man was fighting with such skill, such precision, that Adelaide stared in wonder for a moment before charging through the clearing. Gabriel's emerald eyes saw her from a distance and he instantaneously positioned himself between her and the werewolves.

"What are you doing?" he yelled at her, still fighting.

"I have come to help. I found this." She passed him the sword. He held it loosely, fingers tracing the design on the hilt. His lips formed silent words, but he swallowed back his feelings and looked towards his enemies with resolve.

"Then take this one," he gave her the knife, clenching the long-hidden sword in his hand, "and get out."

Moving with inhuman speed, Gabriel sliced through the skin of two of the wolves. The cuts were not deep, but the wolves howled in agony and retreated into the woods. The last one attacked Adelaide, pinning her to the ground. It stood over her on all fours, snarling and growling and as it opened its jaws to bite, saliva dripping from its twelve-inch canines, the beast froze motionless. Its yellow eyes stared aimlessly as its colossal legs surrendered to its weight, collapsing on top of her. She pulled herself out from underneath the dead wolf just in time to see Gabriel pull the sword from the beasts back.

They stood in silence for a moment staring at each over, both trying to catch their breath. A pained howl echoed through the trees.

"What about the others? Will they come back?" Adelaide panicked.

"No," Gabriel reassured. He tapped the blade of the magical sword with his finger. "Silver. Silver and plenty of other metals, crafted to kill any beast of darkness." He explained.

"All in one sword?" she tried to get a closer look at the material.

"Aye, but don't ask me how; only the alchemist knew that."

"The alchemist?"

"Ehh, I'll tell ya about him someday." With that, he turned and walked around rolling all the corpses into a pile at the centre of the clearing.

They stood and watched them burn.

"Whatever would ye burn them for?" Adelaide asked, turning to face the old man.

"So they don't rot and stink up the woods... and so they don't come back," he replied, lost in the dancing flames.

Adelaide knew it was best not to ask.

"Ye're covered in blood," she pointed out. He looked down at himself.

"So I am."

"Are you wounded?"

"No."

She remained by the fire, watching the wolves burn, watching their skin melt in the heat, as Gabriel walked away. After a while, she went back to the cabin. The ranger was sitting on a log outside, dripping wet, but no longer drenched in the blood of the werewolves. He swished ale around his chalice.

"I told you not to touch the door," he spoke quietly.

"I only meant to help." She sat near him.

"But you went back. With a sword. To face five werewolves," he said shaking his head, yet she could tell that he admired her courage. "You know each has the strength of five men?"

"No."

"Do you even know how to wield a sword?"

"No," she replied, looking at her feet.

"It's not hard, come on." He stood up, putting the chalice down by the logs.

Adelaide slowly rose to her feet. She picked up the simple sword that lay by her feet and held it out.

"You are holding it all wrong," Gabriel complained, correcting her.

He trained her by firelight late into the night. After that, they both slept peacefully, neither was again awakened by the spectral old man.

***

The weeks flew by and winter was getting closer. The trees had shed the last of their leaves and persistent rains flooded the woods. Gabriel had taught Adelaide to work leather and she made herself a crude cloak and boots, with hare fur on the inside. The swordsman was not troubled by the cold and continued to walk around in a dirty shirt and old breeches that were worn and ripped at the ends. Yet, the cold soggy ground bothered him as he boasted newly-fashioned boots with thick soles, coated in oil to repel water and fur lining to prepare for the oncoming frost. At times, he would throw his magnificent cloak over his shoulders, holding it together with some delicate silver brooch, a hood over his head. Other times he would stand silently in the rain, letting his clothes soak and his shoulder-length blonde hair flutter in the icy wind.

They sat in the cabin listening to the gentle patter of the rain when Gabriel suddenly jumped to his feet.

"Take a sword," he commanded.

"Now? There's a storm coming, I can hear the thunder," Adelaide protested.

"Take a sword," he persisted.

She reluctantly rose to her feet and looked longingly towards the beautiful translucent weapon.

"Not the Dragonslayer, but any other sword."

"The Dragonslayer?" she asked bewildered.

"Aye," he laughed, "guess how it got its name!" With that he turned and stepped out the door.

Adelaide stared at the mystical sword for a moment and then, quickly picking up another weapon, she followed Gabriel. The sky had grown dark and the winds had picked up.

"Have ye ever seen a dragon?" she called after the man.

"I have seen too many," he replied.

"And what of other fairy-tale beasts? They real too?"

"Aye, most of them."

They reached a clearing and Gabriel picked up a long heavy stick.

"Strike at me," he commanded her.

Hesitantly, she obeyed. In a flash she was on the ground.

"Get up and do it again," he ordered. She did, but with the same outcome.

"Again," he called.

Adelaide was getting frustrated. She picked herself up from the dirty sludge and infuriated, charged at him with the sword held firmly in front of her. He easily dodged the attack and swung the stick at her legs, smashing her in the shin. As the girl collapsed onto one knee, yelping in pain, he simply walked around her, swinging the stick in his hand.

"Never charge with your sword held out like that! Do you have no sense, child?"

"Ye told me nought on how to do it!" Adelaide yelled angrily.

"Think! Figure it out!"

"What are ya even training me for? I'm a girl. Girls aren't meant to fight."

"Girls aren't meant to steal either," he pointed out. "Do you have a father?"

"No…"

"Brothers?"

"No…"

"Husband?"

"No!"

"Then it appears you need to fight just as much as any man would," Gabriel said, pulling her to her feet by her cloak. "Do you not wish to learn?"

"I do," she replied grumpily, wiping rainwater from her eyes.

"Then strike!"

Adelaide took a deep breath and glared at the man. Her fingers grasped the sword firmly, twisting it in her hand to adapt to its weight. She straightened up and moved her legs to allow for better balance. The cold wind was biting at her skin, tearing at her cloak but she barely noticed it, so focused was she on formulating the perfect attack. Gabriel was watching her every move and through them he saw into her very thoughts. At times he would raise his brows in approval and at others he would flash a mocking smirk. After an eternal moment, Adelaide collected together every move she knew, every trick and every twist, considering his moves as well as her own. She moved instantly, planning to throw him off balance, but the sharp blade was met with that same old muddy stick and Adelaide found herself falling back into the sludge. She looked up to see Gabriel's laughing face.

"Wrong again, my dear. Yet, I must applaud your ability to break an old rotting stick in half. Maybe next time, we shall have you fighting the water in the nearby stream or perhaps even a living mouse!" he said, dropping the broken branch into the mud.

In a rage, Adelaide dug her fingers into the ground and launched a filthy handful of sludge at the sarcastic swordsman, only for him to dodge it effortlessly, laughing to himself at her feeble attempt.

She ran back towards the cabin and hung up her cloak outside, in what has now become a severe downpour, to wash the mud from it. Shutting the door, Adelaide went up to the table and lowered herself into a small wooden chair and there she sat in the cold darkened house, listening to the rain on the roof and the violent thunder in the distance. Upon hearing the door creak open, she raised her face from her hands. Gabriel walked in carrying an armful of wet branches and leaves. His heavy footsteps sounded through the little cabin as he made his way to the dying fire in the stone hearth and gently laid the new firewood near it to dry.

"Was ye trained to fight as ye train me now?" Adelaide demanded.

"No," replied the ranger, taking a seat near her, "but this is how I have learned to train others."

"How many have survived?" she laughed.

Gabriel smiled silently.

"I train you not only the skills of swordplay," he spoke again after a moment, "but also, more importantly, the ability to focus despite your fear, to see and think clearly in the darkness that is the world in which we must kill others to preserve our own cursed lives. As you'll see, there are few of those who will gather to spar in the training yards of some grand city, or those self-proclaimed knights that wave their blades around for the crowd at a village fair or take part in a game of jousting or two. No, the people you will face are not pretentious, but nor are they noble or just. The bandits... well, you have seen them for yourself, they are merciless fiends and yet they are far less malicious than others you may encounter."

Adelaide struggled to understand his meaning but did not dare interrupt.

"Werewolves and other such beasts lurk in the darkest parts of this wretched world, yet I have only ever seen one place that housed a creature far more malevolent. Even in death, she returned, brought back by a mad necromancer, to cause pain and suffering more potent than I had ever witnessed."

His voice began to tremble and he looked down at his shaking hands.

"Was she a demon?" Adelaide asked.

"Nay, she started her life as a creature of light. A light that soon faded."

"What happened to her?"

"She was defeated at last." Some distant memory was tearing Gabriel apart.

Moving gently around him, Adelaide poured ale into a chalice and silently handed it to him. As he looked up at her she could see the shattering despair in his eyes.

Lost for words, she stepped away and laid the dried branches into the fire.

And so, they sat in the warmth, drinking and listening to the frenzied storm as it passed through the woods.

Chapter 15

Fear

Many days had passed and Gabriel barely said a word to her. He often kept to himself, spontaneously walking out of the cabin at a ridiculous time of night and not coming back until the sun rose. Dark dreams haunted him but he refused to confide in Adelaide.

One crisp winter morning she was rudely awakened by Gabriel kicking at her feet.

"Get up! We have much to do," he hurried her on.

Barely awake, Adelaide stood from her mattress of old summertime cloaks layered with fur and rubbed her face with her hands. The rough fabric rags that covered them scratched at her skin and warmed her cheeks. She still wore her old brown dress, yet the outer layer of the skirt had been almost completely ripped off by branches, replaced with patches of fabric that she clumsily sewed together. A layer of mud covered her boots and she wrapped cloths around her feet to protect them from the bitter cold. Adelaide wore an old linen hat and used the strings to hold back her long hair.

Gabriel stood waiting impatiently by the door as Adelaide searched for her leather cloak. The poorly held seams were coming apart but a hood was added to keep her head warm. After she tied the strings with her numb fingers, she followed Gabriel outside. He walked ahead, calling her to walk faster as she scurried to catch up, his long dark green cloak fluttering dramatically in the wind.

"Where're ye going?" Adelaide called.

"More training, my dear," he flashed a familiar boyish grin. She feared he was in one of his eccentric moods.

They walked and walked, fighting their way through the dead branches. The trees protected them from what sounded like another gale sweeping through the woods. A loud crack resonated from a distance.

"Did ye hear that?" Adelaide asked, scared.

"Aye, it's just a tree breaking…" Gabriel replied indifferently.

"'Tis dangerous to be out in a storm like this," she mumbled to herself.

Gabriel only laughed. They walked for a long time until the dense trees receded and a large empty plain opened up before them. Barren fields stretched to the horizon in the west yet to the south they ended abruptly.

"What is this place?"

"Once a beautiful meadow. A lot time ago." Gabriel stopped and looked around, leaning into the wind to keep his balance. "The woods surround us. Can you see the trees in the distance?"

Adelaide looked but she could not, so strong was the gale raging around her.

"And that way, over the drop," Gabriel continued.

"The drop?"

Dark grey skies met the edge of the dead meadow. Gabriel walked towards it, gesturing Adelaide to follow. Reluctantly, she did until they both stood at the very edge. Before them was a tall cliff and at the bottom of it, a stunning gorge populated by a dense woodland that now stood black and empty in the cold. On the other side, the land rose again, forming a ridge that re-joined the woods in the distance. The gale surged through the trees below, passing through their barren canopies like a wave. The entire view was like a coal drawing of a grim artist, with no colour but the occasional glimpse of blue in the otherwise gloomy sky.

"Ye said we'll be training, but where are our swords?" Adelaide asked, turning towards the ranger.

He stared dispassionately into the distance for a while and then turned towards the girl, a twisted grin on his face. He walked away from the edge, his hands behind his back, and paced around. Suddenly, he stopped.

"We have spoken of fear before, have we not?" Gabriel began, "but do you know what fear means, my dear?"

Adelaide stood silent until she was struck by the realisation of his motives.

"Please don't push me off," she said quietly, stepping away from the drop.

"Put your feet back where they were!" she heard the authority in his voice and instantly obeyed.

"Now," he continued, "look down. Do you see the drop? Do you see the mist that shrouds those trees? Oh, how distant they look from up here. How beautiful! Yet think, one step, one powerful gust of wind and there you are, flying to your death. Do you know how many have been embraced by that mist? No? Me neither. So tell me, dear Adelaide, what do you feel?"

"Fear," she sobbed in response.

"Yes, fear. And what do you do? Weep? So what if someone was to, say, push you?" Gabriel nudged her, but Adelaide quickly recovered her balance, whimpering, yet her feet were now even closer to the edge.

"Keep looking. Do you see it?"

As Adelaide stared down, the height made her nauseous. Then, something glistened in the mist.

"Water?" she asked with a trembling voice.

"Indeed. A small but deep lake." Gabriel stopped pacing and stood next to the girl. "So what do we do when we are faced with fear?" His voice was gentler.

Adelaide stood silent, afraid of the answer.

"We fight it!" he answered on her behalf.

With that, Gabriel grabbed her and leaped into the drop. As they were falling, he let go of her and the gorge echoed with her frightened screams. The mist was rapidly approaching and the detail of the trees was becoming clearer. Adelaide struggled to see through the immense force of air that met her falling body yet her watering eyes finally caught a glimpse of the glistening water. The lake appeared too tiny for them both to land in. Her arms and legs were waving frantically, aimlessly grabbing at the empty space. The linen hat she wore had been ripped off and the strings of her cloak were digging into her throat. She struggled for breath, but was only met with a current that was too fast to inhale. Eventually, as her mind began to cloud and the surroundings faded, she only hoped for death to come quicker. Just when Adelaide gave up all hope, her body slammed into the water.

The sudden immersion rejuvenated her. Her head emerged from the icy lake and she hastily brushed her cold hair from her face, gasping instinctively. The heavy cloak was weighing her down and her limbs rapidly started to go numb. Gabriel's booming laughter sounded through the gorge as he splashed around near her, playing in the dangerously cold water like a child in a puddle.

Adelaide swam away from him and crawled out of the lake, shivering uncontrollably. Her body collapsed onto the hard ground. The swordsman stayed in the water for a while and then followed her onto land.

"You see? We survived!" he said cheerfully as he walked past her.

Before she knew it, a fire was roaring nearby. She lifted her head and gazed hatefully at the man who sat cross legged by the flames, watching her with an amused smile. He gestured for her to come closer, but Adelaide just looked away. Signing, he came over and dragged her by her arms until she was lying in the warmth. Closing her eyes, she drifted off into an exhausted slumber.

Adelaide awoke and looked around. The sky was as grey as before, but somehow the woods looked darker. The fire was still burning fiercely and Adelaide's clothes were mostly dry. She sat up painfully.

"This is why you always jump in feet first," Gabriel spoke from across the fire.

"I was afraid. I wasn't..." Adelaide cut off her sentence as she stretched her aching limbs.

"Are you afraid still?"

"Aye."

"Then we have more to learn."

"Ye're a cruel man," Adelaide said after a moment of silence.

"Oh, I'm aware," he responded nonchalantly. "Now let us go back. We won't find food here."

"What about those birds?"

"The choughs? Going to catch them with your bare hands, are you?" he joked, standing up.

Adelaide struggled to her feet and coughed until her eyes watered. Her head was throbbing and her lungs tickled with every shallow breath. Gabriel watched her closely.

"You've caught something," he pointed out.

"That may be from the icy water ye pushed me into," she snapped back.

He stood silently for a while, fidgeting and looking apologetic, then turned towards the fire and picked up a half-burning stick. He handed it to Adelaide and she carefully took it.

"It will provide some warmth. And it appears the night is soon to be upon us," Gabriel said, looking at the sky.

With that he kicked the fire out and began to walk.

"How far is there to go?" Adelaide asked quietly.

Gabriel's expression was enough to answer and Adelaide prepared herself for a long trek.

Chapter 16

The Most Valuable of all Treasures

The long walk back was a hazy dream. Adelaide barely remembered stumbling through the sharp dead branches of the woods, as the sun set and blue moonlight illuminated their path. She remembered feeling frail and dropping the heavy dim torch but Gabriel quickly picked it up and carried it close to her, to give her at least some warmth in the increasingly cold night. Adelaide couldn't remember how long the walk was or what time of day they finally reached the house.

She lazily opened her eyes. Mellow tongues of fire were dancing before her. Light bathed the little stone hearth. Beneath her body was a large fur rug and a heavy blanket was affectionately placed over her. Sunlight shone through the little window, but the fire was still burning strong, filling the house with golden light. Adelaide sat up, feeling very disorientated and sick. The room was empty but a mug of ale stood on the corner of the table. She grabbed it and gulped it down, suddenly realising her thirst. The door creaked open.

"Ahh, so you are awake!" Gabriel exclaimed upon his entry.

"What happened?"

"I guess, you city folk aren't the ones to go swimming in winter. You caught an illness." He stood at the door, looking guilty. "But by the time you finish training you will be jumping into the drop like a child jumps off a pier and coming back all well and healthy. And probably with game too! But now you must be hungry. I was unsure when you would awaken so I only have this I'm afraid."

He passed her the last smoked fish of a bundle hanging from a nail in the wall and opened a jar of pickles for her. Adelaide ate hastily and drank three more mugs of ale.

"How long was I asleep for?" she said with a full mouth.

"Two full days," Gabriel replied as he sat down at the table.

Adelaide paused her feast to think on it.

"Many people in the cities rested in bed for weeks if they got sick. The rich, I mean, the poor folk were left to die in the streets."

"You are not fully well yet, so stay under the blanket for a few more days." Gabriel smiled down at her. There was something gentler about him, more fatherly.

"And drink this," he gave her a small wooden bowl filled with a hot herbal mixture.

Adelaide tentatively brought the drink to her lips and sipped it. The bitter flavour shot through her, bringing tears to her eyes.

"Drink it all," Gabriel commanded, laughing.

"I remember this."

"I made you drink three bowls a day. The mixture really does cure any ailment."

She took a few more gulps and the sharp bitterness of sage, citrus and strong liquor sent a shiver through her. Finally, she finished the bowl and put it aside, grimacing. Adelaide shuffled around, removing her kirtle and freeing her legs from the tangles of her skirts.

"Rest now, child," Gabriel said as he lazily stood up and dragged one of the swords off the table, carrying it with him outside.

When Adelaide awoke later, he was back in the house, sitting on his bed with an old book in his hands. His eyes shot along the lines and he slowly turned the page, deeply concentrating on the writing.

"I didn't know that ye could read," Adelaide spoke, interrupting his thoughts.

"You think me to be a peasant?" Gabriel smirked with feigned offence.

Before she could contradict, he jumped up and sat down on the floor next to her.

"I thought you might have an interest in letters and words." He gave her the book.

The cover was barely decipherable and the pages had yellowed with age. Adelaide studied the symbol on the cover. It looked mystical, with three shapes delicately intertwined, portraying an image of some kind. Her fingers traced over the small black letters on the crinkled pages, following their curls and lines. Some were smudged, others faded, but most remained intact and, fortunately, those included the elaborately painted letters at the start of each page.

Gabriel pointed out each letter and some short words and by the time the sun began to set, Adelaide managed to make it through two complete pages. The book spoke of a time long ago, of a kingdom under the rule of a king long forgotten and a magical world full of wizards and magic. Adelaide was captivated by it.

"Who wrote this?" she asked.

"I don't know. I got it from a scholar who copied it from a book of another scholar who collected pieces of an old scroll from a distant land and translated it."

Adelaide continued to stare at the mysterious symbol on the front cover.

"Do you read but one tongue?" she asked, "or can ye translate from one to another?"

"I know four."

"Will ye teach me?"

"If you so wish."

She smiled to herself. Never before had she even held a book in her hands, never had she recognized their value. At times, in the markets of big cities, she would hear foreign merchants speak in their languages and she did not appreciate their splendour, she only knew how to exploit them. But soon she would understand it; she would read and speak in languages she did not even know existed. This unfamiliar intellectual excitement gave her hope.

Gabriel stretched out his left hand to take the book back. The sleeve of his shirt slid back, revealing black lines on his forearm. He realised she caught sight of them and quickly drew his hand back.

Adelaide was curious but didn't dare ask.

"They say it's a Gift from our Lord," he spoke while gazing sadly at the floor.

"What is?"

"The Rose."

With that, he pulled his sleeve up and exposed the full image. Into his skin was drawn the picture of a black dead rose. Its petals were withered and the stem stretched further up his arm. The thorns were so striking it was almost as if they were digging into his flesh. Adelaide had known many criminals in her time who would cut symbols into their skin and pour in ink, so it would leave a permanent mark on their body but it was a dangerous trick and many were left disfigured by it. Even when successful, it left them with miniscule symbol made of simplistic sloppy lines.

The rose that was on Gabriel's arm was very different. The flower and the pattern around it were so intricate, so beautiful that Adelaide would happily believe it was truly given to him by God himself. The rose was big yet every line, every curve was perfect with no scars or blemishes, almost as if it was his very skin that turned black with the lines. The picture had shading that brought it to life. It was not a symbol, but a work of art that even the greatest masters would take pride in.

Chapter 17

Archery Lesson

They spoke of the rose no more after that, but Adelaide remained curious. Gabriel had previously expressed his absolute lack of faith, yet he bore the message of God. How could he renounce the religion that chose him to be its prophet? A rose was such a beautiful flower, often a symbol of the king yet somehow too bright, too vivid to be chosen by God.

If Gabriel truly was the Lord's messenger, then why was he hiding away in the woods instead of inspiring the people? Was he here to purify the dark magic that Adelaide had witnessed and cure the land of the curse that has befallen it?

Or perhaps he was lying to her. The symbol of a dove or a cross would be expected of God, but a rose was not a mark of the divine. Maybe it was a spell crafted by a powerful warlock or a gift bestowed upon Gabriel by a magical being.

Adelaide shook those thoughts away. She trusted Gabriel and was willing to take his word on the matter yet more and more questions arose in her mind and although desperately curious to know the full truth she dared not ask.

Time went by and days grew colder as the dark hands of winter grasped the kingdom of Starkenhaart. Training was going well for Adelaide and she could wield a sword with precision and strength, or so she thought until Gabriel challenged her to a fight, equipped with nothing but his bare hands, and effortlessly disarmed her in seconds, mockingly tossing her sword between his hands as she tried to reclaim it.

They trained until Adelaide grew tired and her mentor got bored.

"Go, hunt," Gabriel ordered, suddenly turning to her. He looked at Adelaide with utter conviction. Never having been hunting alone before, she stuttered a broken reply.

"Yes, yes, today is as good a day as any to start," he shook off her objections and shoved a bow into her arms. She grabbed onto the cold metal of the weapon and just held it, protesting relentlessly.

"Here you have ten arrows. Come back with all ten or you will be making twenty more tomorrow." With that, he gave her the quiver and gently but sternly led her by the shoulder to the door. As soon as she was outside, a loud slam sounded behind her.

"It'll be getting dark!" Adelaide called through the door.

"Good, the animals will be sleeping." His voice had a note of amusement to it.

"The wolves won't be!"

"It's not the wolves you need to worry about. The bears have not gone into hibernation yet."

"Bears? … Bears? Gabriel, let me back in! Let me back in!" she banged her hands anxiously against the door. On the other side, she heard a very distinct laughter.

After persistently trying to get back into the cabin, her efforts proved to be in vain. With a sigh, she turned towards the dark trees. Loud cooing broke the eerie silence of the woods. Tightly gripping the bow, Adelaide began her walk away from the house. Dead branches cracked under her feet and the few remaining leaves rustled as she pushed past them. Cold winter wind ran through the trees and the girl shivered, wrapping her cloak tighter around her body. As she walked, she mumbled to herself about the injustice of her having to provide for them both while she could barely defend herself from what dangers may be out there. If the werewolves were to return this night, she would be dead the moment they catch her scent. And the white wolves that lurked in the shadows of these trees were as deadly as they were beautiful.

Adelaide had never even held a bow in her hands before. She studied the burdensome weapon and tested the tension with her finger. Taking an arrow from her quiver she placed in against the metal and pulled. The arrow slipped from her grip and fell to the leafy ground. Growing impatient, Adelaide picked it up and tried again and again until she finally held it in place. Aiming at the thick trunk of a nearby tree, she pulled the arrow back, balancing in against the metal with her finger. To her astonishment, the metal gave to the tension and recurved slightly with the pressure. She smiled to herself, knowing that by now she should no longer be surprised of seeing anything unusual or magical in these woods. Breathing slowly, she focused on the tree and let the arrow fly.

"Damn," Adelaide hissed under her breath as the arrow shot swiftly from the bow and flew past the tree into the brush behind it. Disappointed, she dragged her feet to where the arrow landed and started digging for it through the rotting leaves.

Through the rustling of the brush she suddenly heard a quiet undistinguishable noise. Adelaide paused in her search and listened. It sounded like a soft mumble.

"I knew ye wouldn't be so cruel as to send me out here alone!" she called out to Gabriel gratefully, rising from the bushes.

Yet, instead of seeing the old man, she was met with a dark emptiness.

"Gabriel?"

No reply. Just silence. Pure unmitigated silence.

Adelaide turned around, holding the longbow over the brush. She was not outside for long, but the skies darkened considerably. She struggled to see through the tall trees that surrounded her imposingly. The small gaps between them were filled with blackness.

The murmur was heard again from another direction. It was the voice of a woman. A gentle ghostly whisper that sounded sinister in the black night that had suddenly befallen the woods.

Unsure of what to do, Adelaide hesitantly followed it, secretly afraid of finding its source. Her steps rustled loudly but the mumble continued to sound, turning into a low-pitched drone that filled her head, deafening her until she could no longer hear anything else. The darkness of the trees swallowed her up and only then she began to realise the malevolent illusion of it.

The darkness came to an end, revealing a large burrow in the ground. The noise was emanating from far below the Earth's surface.

Adelaide turned back in hopes of seeing something, anything, but was met with an endless black veil. She knew that descending into the burrow would prove to be a frightening and dangerous experience, but she had to face the realisation that it was the only choice she had and whatever transcendental phantom was fuelling this illusion; it would not stop until it she was led to its origin.

By now she was certain that whatever dwelled beneath the ground was no mortal being, yet she gripped the bow tightly as she delicately climbed into the burrow. The dry soil crumbled beneath her feet and she fell, sliding down until the floor levelled out.

Adelaide stood up, finding herself in a deep underground tunnel the roof of which was just above her head. A stale smell of moss surrounded her. The tunnel was silent apart from her heavy breathing and the sound of dripping water that occasionally echoed in the distance. To her surprise, Adelaide was not immersed in utter darkness, for the bow in her hand had a faint purple glow. Holding it out before her, she took a brave step forward.

The silence of the tunnel shattered as the once gentle murmur erupted once more, striking her from all directions, urgently beckoning her further. With no choice but to obey, the girl continued through the tunnel with a firm step. Her heart was pounding in fear, but Adelaide was overpowered by an intense curiosity about the mythical events that were now unfolding.

She saw a purple glimmer in the distance. Rushing towards it she began to distinguish the end of the tunnel, which opened up into a large cavern filled with an ethereal purple light. The voice quietened, reducing to a soft whisper.

The floor of the cavern was immersed in a thin layer of clear water that stood undisturbed like a mirror. In disbelief at the image in the reflection, Adelaide turned her face up and was stunned by an affirmation of what the water showed her. Large crystals hung above her, shining like surreal chandeliers. They were held there by blue chords that stretched into the infinite darkness of the cavern. Delicately treading through the chilly water Adelaide continued to wonder at what surrounded her. Massive stalagmites stood grandiosely, some so tall they disappeared into the darkness. They were not formed from common rock but rather from some rare mineral that left them transparent like glass, with the only distortion being caused by the water that trickled down their surface.

As Adelaide continued on her path through the magnificent cavern, she was met by a waterfall that stood like a monumental gate. She looked up in search of its source but the water fell from the deep darkness above her, booming as it cascaded down. Splashing at her feet, the water disappeared into the ground.

There was no way around the waterfall and no other path in sight, yet Adelaide had still not met the magical being that summoned her here. She held out her hand, letting the water flow through her fingers. Although falling with great force, the width of this mass of water was unexpectedly narrow and it was not long before Adelaide felt cold air behind it. Reaching further, the girl followed her hand through the watery curtains, burying her face in her shoulder to hide from the crashing bombardment of icy droplets. Some slipped through her hair and ran down her back, sending an uncomfortable shudder through her body and causing her to jump forwards. Once Adelaide made it through the fantastical gate, she looked on to see the one who summoned her.

Chapter 18

Vision

The bow fell from her grip. Astounded, Adelaide collapsed to her knees. Before her was nothing other than an angel. She sat, majestic as any divine being, on a throne build of clear stalagmites that rose from the pool of inky water that filled this chamber. The walls did not stretch into the darkness but were visible, build from large blocks of glass, like an impenetrable wall of a beautiful dungeon. Large chains were thrown over the creature, binding her to the throne, to the very stone of the cavern. She turned her pale face towards Adelaide.

The angel's large all-black eyes looked sadly at the girl. Her ebony locks rested delicately on her shoulders. A humble robe covered her body and her bare feet moved sluggishly in the dark water. Mighty wings were broken and forced to fold uncomfortably behind her back yet the feathers that grew from them were neither white nor golden but as black as the feathers of a crow.

The fallen angel slowly lifted her shackled hand and held it gracefully out to Adelaide, beckoning her closer. Rising from the water, the girl obeyed but with every step the angel appeared more and more distorted. A spark of urgency flashed in her eyes and she reached out further to Adelaide but her chains tightened, pinning her fragile body to the throne, crushing her beautiful dark wings.

"The rose has thorns," the creature whispered. Her voice sounded as pure as a thousand divine harps. "Resist its lure for pure evil will await you beyond the black veil."

Darkness seeped in through the cracks in the walls, filling the room like a dense black smoke. It surrounded the creature until Adelaide could see her no more. The girl rushed towards the concealed celestial being but a hand roughly grabbed her arm and pulled her back.

Looking up she was met with the familiar face of the old man who was staring intensely into the dark cloud with an expression of uncontained fury. Behind him Adelaide saw dead branches. Trees surrounded them. The girl recognised the large oak she tried firing an arrow at not long before. The burrow, the tunnel, the cavern were nothing but illusions. Yet the darkness wasn't. Streams of black smoke slithered along the woodland floor, coalescing into a large stirring cloud.

Gabriel pushed Adelaide behind him and held out the Dragonslayer sword.

"No!" Adelaide screeched, trying to push him to the side, trying to break the blade from his hands. "It's an angel! Gabriel, it's an angel!"

He threw her to the ground, placing himself between his student and the stormy black cloud, the sword still firmly in his hand.

From the darkness emerged a horrifying beast with eyes that shined a hellish red. It stood on four legs, its massive clawed paws at the ready. The colossal hellhound was taller than Gabriel and its head alone was the size of a cart, equipped with jaws that could break through steel in one bite and fangs that stretched past its chin. The fur of this fiend was cloaked in fire and, as the stormy cloud from which it materialised faded, it sent embers flying in all directions. Such energy surrounded the being that it had a distorted aura about it, the way fire distorts the air above it.

"Begone!" Gabriel shouted at the enormous hound.

The creature looked at him then in a sudden surge leaped over both of them. It turned its massive head towards Adelaide and stared at her with its infernal eyes.

"Even as you walk through the valley of the shadow of death, you will fear no evil, for I am with you," the beast hissed in a human voice before it dissipated into nothingness.

Stunned, Adelaide stared after it from the ground until Gabriel helped her to her feet.

"An angel..." she whispered quietly.

"An illusion. They play tricks with your head, those beasts," Gabriel replied gravely.

"Why?"

Gabriel stood silent, looking into the darkness of the woods. He shared her feeling of betrayal. The deceit of the creature devastated them both.

"I thought a Godly vision appeared to me...." Adelaide muttered.

"There is no God," Gabriel interrupted harshly. "When she first came to me, all those years ago, I was overwhelmed with joy. I believed I was chosen by our Holy Father for a greater good. But then her disguise failed the creature and her true form was revealed to me. A demon! A filthy fiend!"

"Why does she come?"

"For the Rose."

"The rose upon your arm? Whatever for?" Adelaide was getting impatient.

"This Gift harbours more power that you could even begin to imagine. The fiend wants it contained, locked away from the people so they may never be saved by it."

"By why did she... it, come to me?"

"As my apprentice I have chosen you to be my heir." Gabriel looked her in the eye.

Adelaide stepped back, shocked by this revelation.

"You will wield the Dragonslayer and bear the mark of the Rose upon your arm," he clarified. "This is the honour I intended to bestow upon my daughter, but she did not survive to receive it."

"Thank you," the girl whispered.

"Yet there is a grand price for you to pay," Gabriel continued. "The hound will not leave you. It will haunt your dreams. It will torment you! At times, it will disguise itself as an angel but do not succumb to its lies."

Adelaide silently nodded her head.

"The bow," Gabriel commanded, holding out his hand. Adelaide sheepishly surrendered the weapon.

"It shone in the dark," she stated.

"Yes, it does that."

"What sorcery was it made from?"

"Honestly, I don't know. I never had an understanding of magic," Gabriel replied, studying the delicate design of the bow.

"Come now, let us return home. I need a drink after all this." He turned and walked away. Adelaide quietly followed.

Upon returning to the cabin, Adelaide found a rabbit roasting on the spit.

"I knew you would come back empty handed," Gabriel replied to her surprised gaze. "But I did not anticipate you would have such … an adventure."

"Ye have no faith in me!" Adelaide muttered hurtfully.

"But was I wrong?" the man replied laughing before entering the house. He returned a few moments later with two chalices.

Adelaide was sitting on a log with the quiver at her feet.

"And I only see nine arrows," he stated, handing her a chalice.

Suddenly remembering the lost arrow, Adelaide stuttered an excuse.

"Demonic apparition or not, you'll still be making twenty more tomorrow," he said, taking his place on one of the other logs.

With a yielding sigh Adelaide took a sip from her chalice. The unbearably bitter liquid stung her tongue and burned her throat.

"Rum?" she asked between coughs.

"No. This is moonshine I got from a merchant who was lost in these parts a few years back. Stronger than any rum you would find in the village. I thought you might need it to settle your nerves."

Adelaide looked doubtfully into the chalice, then shrugged and gulped down the entire thing.

"I wouldn't drink it all at once," Gabriel warned but by then the girl had already collapsed behind the logs.

Chapter 19

To See or to Listen

Adelaide raised the bow, aiming into the grey winter sky. Her hands were wrapped in rags and a thick fox-fur cloak rested on her shoulders.

"Now close your eyes," Gabriel spoke. She obeyed. All she could hear were his footsteps in the snow and birds calling in the distance. She moved to point the bow at the cooing.

"Good," the old man praised, "but listen closer."

Adelaide listened. A bird's call here, a flutter of wings over there. She moved the bow, trying to follow the sound but it was too inconsistent, too abrupt, and too distant.

In frustration, she lowered the weapon and turned around. Snow crunched beneath her feet.

"I can't do this."

"Do not surrender yet," Gabriel spoke. He was leaning leisurely against a barren elm. His dark green cloak looked striking against the white woodland that surrounded them. "It took you weeks to learn to shoot what you can see, but it may take you months to truly see what you can shoot."

"What does that even mean?" Adelaide cried after a moment of contemplation.

"I am not gifted with speaking wise words," he laughed, "but sight may only get you so far before you are left in the dark."

"Who would I need to fight in the dark?"

"I hope you will never have to find out," Gabriel relied sombrely.

"And what am I to do upon finishing training? Go out fighting beasts and destroying evil doers?"

"That I cannot tell you. You will go where the Rose guides you," he answered.

"Where did it guide you? To the woods. For what purpose?" Adelaide demanded.

"That is not for you to know!" Gabriel suppressed the interrogation. His voice sounded sharp and irritated. The girl looked down, ashamed to have overstepped a boundary.

The old man did not move a muscle. He continued to gaze emptily into the snow.

"I know that there is something great in you," he spoke again, "that you can accomplish what others only dream of."

"That I was chosen for something?"

"No, no! I'm not talking about all that fairy-tale nonsense. You are not gifted, at least not yet. But the mere mortal attributes you harbour are really quite extraordinary, yet it appears determination is not one of them."

"Attributes?"

"Qualities, traits. I chose you as my apprentice and heir for your courage, curiosity, ingenuity! Don't make me regret my decision, girl!"

"I do not mean to disappoint," Adelaide spoke timidly.

"Then turn around, listen out and shoot one of those cursed birds!" Gabriel encouraged with enthusiasm. Moving swiftly, Adelaide turned, aimed at the sounds of the distant birds, and fired the arrow.

It flew through the still winter air for what seemed like an eternity. Gabriel followed it with his eyes, straightening up. Adelaide held her breath in suspense.

The birds scattered in different directions as the arrow struck the trunk of a tree.

"Damn," Adelaide hissed under her breath.

"Well, you know my rule about arrows," Gabriel spoke, rubbing his cold hands together.

"Aye, ye shall have twenty more by the morrow," the girl replied.

"Let's get back inside now. Find some firewood on the way, will you."

Sighing, Adelaide followed.

"So tell me, what does the gift really do?" Adelaide asked as they sat by the hearth fire.

"Patience, child, you shall find out soon enough," the old man replied, chewing on a tough smoked fish they had saved up from autumn.

"But how soon?" she demanded.

"Once you finish training. Once you are ready."

And so, they continued training, though the cold months of winter and the mildly warmer months of spring, each grateful for the other's company. Adelaide got stronger, fought faster yet even as her skill developed, she could not hope to match that of the mysterious old man. He taught her to read and write and speak eloquently, as a proper lady should, rather than in the crude tongue of a peasant.

Chapter 20

Meadow Match

Adelaide stepped out into the brilliant morning sunshine. Smiling, she pulled her hood lower to cover her eyes from blinding brightness. The woods were truly alive that day, the birds singing their songs in the treetops, with the whistling of the warm summer breeze harmonising their melodies. Everything was bathed in light and the sun warmed her skin. The crickets, the bees, the rustling in the leaves, there was movement, there was life everywhere she looked.

Wooden bucket in hand, she made her way down the well-trodden path and through the trees to the stream. Throwing off her cloak and shoes, she put her feet in the water. It had not yet been warmed by the sunshine and still carried the chill of the night. Adelaide just sat there for a moment, looking around, admiring the forest in its pride. Her hand brushed over the kingcup flowers next to her, caressing their vibrant yellow petals. She felt the stream with her feet and found a smooth rock to stand on. Struggling to find her balance, she wobbled a little, arms flailing, until she could steady herself. Reaching down to grab the bucket caused a repeat of the less-than-impressive balancing act. After filling it with water, the girl stepped back onto the grass. To her, it felt softer than the most expensive carpets she remembered caressing in the village market; the colourful ones that were brought there by rich merchants from distant lands. She put her shoes on and threw her cloak over her arm, holding the bucket with both hands, and walked home.

The door creaked as usual and Adelaide paused when she stepped inside, as the house was so much darker and colder than the sunlit porch.

After a few moments, her eyes adjusted to the darkness and she deposited her bucket and cloak onto the table. The cabin was silent, and Gabriel was nowhere to be seen. Adelaide called out his name. No response. She walked around for a while, her normally quiet steps echoing through the otherwise silent house.

Adelaide went outside to look for him, first around the house, then through the nearby trees. She stopped and listened, but all she could hear were the chirps, squeaks and birdcalls that formed the familiar woodland symphony. Assuming that her mentor went hunting, she decided to go looking for wild berries to accompany the meal. During this season, they were aplenty near the meadow, so she made her way there. She still felt refreshed from standing in the chilly water and pranced through the brush with a light step. The meadow was not far from the cabin and soon she arrived to search for her prize. Adelaide had been trained to recognise which produce of the forest would sate her hunger and which must not be touched for any purpose other than the crafting of a poison most cruel. The maroon shade of the treats which were safe for consumption revealed their location from across the meadow and the girl leaped into the tall stalks of grass that engulfed the field, shifting in the breeze like waves of a calm ocean. She remembered training here in winter and wondered about how difficult it must be this time of year, when the flora near enough reached her waist. As she walked, Adelaide was thinking about her previous summers, many of which were spent in the streets. In this humid heat, food would rot within days, sewage and stray animals would fill the streets. But in the woods, it was more beautiful than ever. She was glad to be here, safe and free, away from the disease, from the violence, from the cruel people who populated the cities.

As she walked, lost in thought and enjoying the hot summer sunshine, she felt something hit her arm. It instantly brought her back to reality; she crouched and hid herself in the grass. She looked down to see a rock by her feet. Standing up again, Adelaide looked in the direction it came from, just as another hit her back. Startled, the girl looked behind as a third hit her from yet a new angle of attack. Her short temper could not withstand this. Adelaide picked up the stones, ready to throw them back but they kept hitting her and each time she searched for the source, another spawned elsewhere. Eventually, she started pelting them in random directions, hoping to hit the attacker. Her attempts were futile.

"One must not only know how to hit others, but also how to avoid being hit themselves."

"Gabriel? What are you doing?" No reply as the stones kept hitting her. "Stop this madness!"

"Then you must learn, child."

Adelaide started trying to dodge the rocks, but to no avail. After a few minutes, she heard him sigh in exasperation and he stepped out of the shadows of the canopies.

"This is very boring for me you know."

She awaited the instructions of this lesson. "Don't demand an explanation from me. You have to figure out for yourself how to avoid getting hit." He walked slowly around her. "You must sense even the smallest rocks around you. Be aware of your surroundings. Be aware of every potential danger. Sometimes you will know when a battle will begin and who your opponent is, but sometimes you may not. Be on your guard, at all times." Still walking around her, he stepped closer, his voice taking a deeper tone, becoming hypnotic. "Look up," he said. She obeyed. "Look up and what do you see? Do you see the spirit of the woods? In the trees… in their every leaf… In the skies above us. Do you hear his whispers in the wind? Do you feel his presence around you? Let him guide you. Let his ancient wisdom flow through you."

Adelaide resisted at first, struggled to open her mind, but that silky voice burrowed into her soul. She felt tranquil yet focused, she was conscious of nothing and everything. She could feel it, this calm strength in her. She turned to Gabriel and he knew that she understood him. She closed her eyes again, breathed slowly, prepared herself and when she looked again, he was gone. Now she was ready.

It was almost like she could feel the disturbance in the air and moved swiftly to the side, avoiding a rock. Another tremble of the atmosphere and another projectile missing its target. Again and again, Adelaide prevailed. It was like a dance with the woods, her movements were fast, precise and graceful. Jumping from foot to foot, hiding in the grass and then leaping out just in time. She spun, her arms held up high in the air, her head raised to the sky, smiling. There must have been twenty, thirty rocks. And then they stopped. Heaving, she placed her hands on her knees, bending over slightly, yet still grinning happily. Only then she realised that the meadow was silent. All the noise she heard before, all the birds, all the insects, were mute. Despite the bright sunshine, the meadow was filled with an atmosphere of suspense, as if nature were holding her breath. How long has it been like this?

"Well, now that you've grasped that, we shall move onto the next stage," spoke Gabriel as he walked out of the shadows again, only this time, he was holding a sword. He was striding towards her fast, raising the weapon. When she realised his intentions, all her calm focus vaporised and she froze in horror.

"Wait, I need a sword to defend myself with!" she screamed at him, jumping to the side just as he sliced through the air where she stood.

"One does not always have a blade in their hand!" he replied, slamming the sword down at her feet, which she moved just in time. "Your mind, your wisdom is your greatest weapon!"

Adelaide was on the ground, looking up at him, petrified, pushing herself away from him as fast as she could while he kept striding towards her. He caught up to her and raised the sword once more. She rolled to the side an instant before it crashed down with a thud.

"Stop this insanity!" she screeched at him, struggling to her feet. "They should tie you to a mast and let the winds carry you away for being a bloody madman!"

"And they did once, that's why I don't live with the villagers anymore," he said, that boyish smile plastered on his face while he kept swinging the sword in his apprentice's direction.

Barely dodging it every time, she tried running the other way, but the long grass made her progress slow. Fortunately, it slowed him too, but not by much. "This is no way to train someone!" she shouted over her shoulder. "This be a certain way to kill a man!"

"It is a dangerous craft you are learning, child, and it cannot always be taught through safe methods."

"Stop trying to cut my damn head off!" Adelaide was panicking and out of breath while he still seemed calm and full of energy.

"Remember the spirit of the woods!"

"Just stop trying to kill me for a bloody moment!"

"In battle, you shan't be given a moment. You must have stamina, both in body and mind. Especially in the mind! If not, you shall be blind to the spirit that guides you."

Adelaide couldn't quite follow the next few moments. All she could feel was a blade under her foot, the coarse grass as she fell into its embrace and the pain on her back as she hit the hard ground. Her eyes were half closed as she fell, but she could just see the sunlight reflect of the shiny blade as it rose above her head. Squeezing her eyes shut, she took one deep breath, suspecting that it may be her last, and held it. That moment was an eternity to her as her body lay frozen with fear, just waiting for the cold blade to pierce her skin. Hopefully, he would not cause a fatal wound, just a cut through her arm or leg, but with a man like Gabriel one can never be sure when they may lose their head.

After a few painfully long seconds, she realised that she was still alive and unharmed. Breathing out, she opened her eyes. What she saw made her flinch, as the blade was directly in front of her face, as if it went right through her neck. Gabriel stood there, with the usual mischievous grin, holding the hilt of the sword with only his thumb and two fingers, almost ready to drop it. The tip of the blade rested on the skin of her throat yet didn't draw a drop of blood.

Laughing, he tossed the sword up and caught it in mid-air, sliding it smoothly back into the leather scabbard.

"That wasn't really your best fight now, was it?" he said, offering his hand to help her up. She glared at him as she accepted his assistance and when upright she turned and stormed away.

"Aren't you forgetting something, my dear?" he called after her.

She looked back over her shoulder to see him holding out a small bunch of maroon berries. Snatching it from his hand, she turned and walked home. She could hear him walking behind her, giggling to himself.

"Oh, don't be like that, it was just a game!"

She walked back to the house in silence.

Chapter 21

The Swordsman's Burden

Upon their return, Adelaide collected her cloak and filled a flask with ale.

"You can't still be furious with me, can you?" said Gabriel as she stomped past him and out of the door. She walked towards the stream and followed it north, towards the mountains. She must have been walking for hours, and the previously pleasant warmth was beginning to become uncomfortable. She stopped for a moment and wiped the sweat from her forehead. Sipping the ale, she looked around. She must have walked through this part of the woods a thousand times now and knew the way to the lake like the back of her hand, yet she still struggled with the slope of the mountainous path. Looking back, she could see the full expanse of the woods that stretched to the snowy mountain peaks on the horizon.

Walking a little bit further, she finally reached the lake. The calm water seemed crimson in the light of the setting sun. Adelaide removed her clothes and stepped in. She walked further in and found a place where the water was deep enough to cover her up to her neck, but so that her feet could still touch the lakebed. Standing there in the water she looked around and admired the tranquillity of this place.

The spirit of the woods. She could see it now. Mysterious, powerful, mesmerising... it surrounded her. She breathed in deeply and felt the pressure of the water against her chest. She swam on her back for a while, just floating on the surface of the lake. There were birds and animals far in the distance, but around her it was quiet, except for the occasional splash of the water as Adelaide moved her hand to maintain her balance. She was looking up at the sky and could see the sparkle of the first star. It seemed so small, so insignificant compared to the vast blue pool around it.

Adelaide thought about all the people she had met, about her parents and childhood friends and how, after leaving her hometown, she was alone. She met dozens of new people each day, but they all just walked past her, fading into the shadows of other strangers. They were all ghosts to her, never truly existing in her life.

Except for Gabriel. She realised that despite all the jokes, despite all the mad, life-threatening actions, he was the only person who cared. He treated her like a daughter from the moment they met and all the danger he put her in had the purpose of teaching her, making her wiser and stronger.

Lost in thought, Adelaide did not notice how much time had passed and the skies were now draped in an inky cloak. She swam back to shore as quickly as she could and hurriedly got dressed. She looked back at the lake just one last time before she left, as the moonlight gently reflected off the shimmering water. Her walk back to the house seemed short due to the ease of heading downhill, and when she got close, she could see the smoke of the fire.

Adelaide was only a few feet away from fire when she heard Gabriel singing and she stopped behind one of the trees to listen. He was facing the fire, his hood covering his face, looking deeply into the flames as if seeing something else. His song was one that she had never heard before, but it sounded old, very old. His voice was strong yet gentle and she could hear his feelings, his emotions through it. The words he sung were ones of a lost love, of a time long gone and as he finished the last verse he said, without looking up, "It's warmer by the fire you know."

She walked towards him. In his hand was an empty chalice and she could smell rum in the air. He looked up and the light of the fire fell on his face. His beard looked whiter than usual and the wrinkles on his face stood out more. As she sat on a log opposite him, Adelaide wondered how old he truly was. Despite the drunken sparkle in his eyes, there was also wisdom there, and sorrow, as if they've seen too much of this earth.

"What is it that troubles you, Gabriel?" she asked gently.

He smiled again. "Talking to me now, are we?" But she could still hear the sadness in his voice.

"You cannot anger me for long." There was a silence. "So what is it?"

He looked into a fire for a few moments and closed his eyes. "How long are we to live on this earth, Adelaide? How long must we suffer?"

After a pause she replied, "I believe we each determine the paths of our lives, their worth and glee."

He looked up at her again and smiled mischievously. "A wise one you are."

"Our wisdom is our greatest weapon!" she playfully mocked the teachings of her mentor, one eyebrow raised.

He laughed and the boyish, innocent look returned to his face. "I have taught this one well!"

There was another silence.

"Have you trained many other squires?"

"You are no squire." His smile dropped again and the melancholic atmosphere restored. "And no. I am no teacher. I was a fighter, a killer!" He raised his voice. That voice carried authority and power despite the drunken slurring of the words. Adelaide recoiled slightly at his volume. "I won countless battles! I challenged countless opponents! I slayed countless beasts! I murdered and killed! I... I..." His head dropped and he relaxed again.

"Murdered and killed?" she repeated. She knew he was a dangerous madman, but it had never been stated so openly before. The girl knew that she herself was no innocent maiden, that her thefts had harmed people, that by stealing a man's last crumb of food she personally sentenced him to death, but she never took lives purposefully, only for her own survival.

As she looked at the man sitting opposite her now, covered by his dark cloak, a sword by his side and an empty chalice in his hand — a man filled with secrets and remorse — she wondered how many innocent lives were taken by his hand.

That is the burden that a swordsman must carry. Their art is not one of pure beauty, but rather of chaos and grief. It is a masterpiece, painted with the blood of their enemies, a graceful dance with the angels of death.

And Gabriel was a true artist, devoted to his craft, a master of the blade, a violent tortured shadow of unforgiven sins.

He looked her in the eyes, as if reading her thoughts. She could see so much in those sad green eyes; so much hurt and shame and above all else, guilt, too much for a person to bear. She wondered what he could have done to feel that way. After spending his life in combat, it was no surprise that he felt regret but she could sense it was more than that, as if he was responsible for something far more malicious.

He breathed in to say something, but a loud snap interrupted him and both he and Adelaide looked in the direction of the sound. A group of birds flew up; crows, or possibly choughs, it was hard to see them in the dark. Gabriel looked back at her and smiled innocently again.

They walked over to the rabbit trap and saw an unfortunate little one who got his hind leg caught. It was still alive and struggling to break free. Holding the animal by the neck, Gabriel opened the trap and picked up the hare, cradling it in his arms. It looked so small and vulnerable, kicking and trying to jump out, hind leg broken and bleeding heavily. It was defenceless.

A loud crack echoed through the trees as, in one smooth movement, Gabriel snapped the hare's neck. Adelaide saw the pity in his face as he walked past her to the house.

About an hour later, the girl returned to the fire, holding freshly found firewood, to find the hare roasting nicely in the flames. She deposited the firewood and sat down on a log. Taking in a deep breath of crisp cool air, she looked up at the stars that were still bright in the night sky.

"This is something you just don't find in the city," she mused.

Gabriel looked up over the fire, "A roasted hare?"

"No," she replied, "the smell of the oaks, the silent woods, and the freedom of having dinner in the early hours of the morning."

She heard a laugh.

"Why not?" he asked.

"The villages sleep at night, work in the day, over and over again," Adelaide explained.

"Oh, and do not forget the glorious habit of going to church every day o' the sun!" Gabriel added smirking. He was always so full of cynicism towards matters of faith.

She yawned.

"I will probably take to bed after the meal".

He nodded drowsily while sipping ale from his chalice.

"Why do you drink ale from silver chalices, Gabriel?"

"Why would I drink from mugs? Like a peasant."

"That's one of your quirks that I don't understand. You live in the woods, like a ranger, a huntsman, yet have silver weapons, trinkets, brooches and you drink out of chalices like a nobleman."

He stood up and went inside the house. He returned a few moments later, holding a clay mug. Walking up to Adelaide, he snatched the chalice out of her hands and shoved the mug at her. It was filled with the same ale. He drank all the ale in her chalice and sat back down. She took that as a hint to stop asking questions.

Chapter 22

Then I Looked and Saw a Pale Horse

Adelaide could feel the sun on her face as it ever so rudely slithered in through the moth-eaten rag covering her small slit of a window. She turned her back towards it, but the persistent ray rebounded off a carelessly dropped sword and attacked her eyes with amplified vigour. Sitting up with a soft groan, she looked around the tiny box that was her private quarters, which had once served as the weapons closet of her tutor. The condition of the room was perhaps somewhat less weathered than the rest of the cabin, mainly due to it having been untouched for those many long years. Muddy boot prints had dried into the cracked wooden floor by the entrance and had trampled over the loose items of clothing and weaponry that lay in disarray. Following their path, Adelaide sighed at herself in realisation that she had failed to remove her boots, as well as the rest of her outdoor gear, before collapsing atop her bed and that this filth had now crusted to the hairs of the deer skin that she used for a cover.

Her parched throat urged her to find a beverage, as did the acidic taste on her tongue. Adelaide rolled her aching body onto the floor, immediately regretting that decision, and stumbled to her feet. Her brain felt dry and shrunken inside her skull and yet she still retained some of the hazy dissociation caused by strong liquor. Adelaide shoved through the creaky door with the full weight of her body, cursing it for daring to make a startling noise. Mugs and chalices littered the floor, clanking as she made her way past. Several chairs appeared to be missing legs, which she discovered were sharpened into spikes and thrown at walls. At this point, the girl recalled a game that Gabriel had challenged her to: that whoever was able to strike somewhat or something with the greatest number of miniature wooden spears would win a price of some nature. Or perhaps it was Adelaide who set the challenge? She could not recall, nor was she willing to admit fault.

Adelaide dragged her feet towards a silver flagon, hoping to find it filled with water and instead found herself looking down at a small frog that was settled inside. Six empty bottles of foreign rum lay scattered among dirty chalices and mugs. She picked up the flagon belonging to the amphibian critter and made for the exit of the cabin. Humid summer heat flowed through the doorway and the girl grasped at the ties of her cloak until the bow untied and it fell heavily by her feet. As she stepped out, Adelaide was blinded by the striking midday sun but soon her eyes adjusted and she could see that some were not as phased by the light. Gabriel was sleeping peacefully, wrapped up in his cloak, right behind one of the wooden logs they sat on. The old man's senses must have been completely numbed by the copious drinking of the night before, as the only thing more intrusive than the light of the sun was the abominable snore that erupted from him every few seconds.

The fire had sizzled out long ago and a lone fox was scavenging among the bones that had been stripped bare. Upon seeing Adelaide emerge outside, the animal hunkered down, ready to take off at the first threat, but the girl stumbled along the perimeter of the campfire, leaving the fox to forage in peace. The young apprentice walked to the stream and plopped herself down heavily on the bank. She laid the flagon onto its side in the grass and after a few moments the frog jumped out. It sat for a while among the green blades and then made its way towards the water. Adelaide watched it slowly progress to the stream and onto the other side. When the curious creature disappeared from her sight, the girl rinsed out the flagon several times and drew the much-awaited water to her lips. The cold sensation on her tongue was invigorating and she gulped greedily until there was none left and then she filled it up and drunk again. The water filled up her dry withered stomach and briefly triggered the retching response through muscle memory of excessive alcohol consumption. Deciding, wisely, to let her poorly system settle, she filled the flagon up once more and walked back to the house. The scavenging visitor had departed and Gabriel was still sprawled out unconscious in the brush. Adelaide placed the flagon near him and retreated back into the comforting shadows of her room.

And so they carried on, drinking night after night, training day after day, and sneaking back to the nearby village on occasion to steal rum, until the trees started shedding their vibrant leaves and the summer warmth seeped out of the woods, being soon replaced by cold rains and dark skies. Demeter's reign came to an end once again.

It was one of those cold bitter days that the two forest dwellers were sitting by the fire, wrapped up in their cloaks, reminiscing about past adventures. Adelaide looked up to the skies. The tree canopies twisted wildly in the winds and the clouds wore a menacing, gloomy shade of grey. The long-eared owls had recently moved into this region and now they sat there, perched on the branches of a nearby tree, thoroughly surveying the ground with their unblinking yellow eyes.

Adelaide looked down towards the fire again. The wood crackled as it gradually turned black, then white. She studied the transition. The branches maintained their structure through this scaled inferno, but one touch would turn them into a pile of ash. The logs were cradled in a pool of blue flames, the almost unperceivable but most powerful form of combustion. Her eyes followed the flames up, admiring them as they performed their chaotic dance before her. Through the distorted pillar of grey smoke, she caught Gabriel's uninspired glare.

"Speak, child!" he ordered.

"On what matter?"

"Anything. We're already bored, cold and sober, may as well indulge in conversation."

"Ahh yes, why are you sober?"

After a pause, Gabriel reluctantly replied, "the rum ran out two days ago."

"And the ale..."

Looking at her guiltily he answered, "Last week."

She sighed and stared into the fire a moment longer. "We could return to the village? The peasants must be taking to their beds in a few hours."

"No, they will stay up longer during this time of year. There is no harvest for them to wake up for."

"They must still be celebrating the sizeable harvest. There will be lots o' ale around as they must be brewing more right about now, and finishing off the old."

"Indeed." He stood up and stretched his arms with that same flexibility that was uncommon for a man of his age, "and we could use more cloth, the weather is getting harsher now."

"I shall fetch the weapons!" The girl jumped up excitedly.

"Remember the poisoned berry flask!" he called after her as she eagerly galloped into the house.

Not a minute had passed and she came running out again, dressed in fox fur boots, with an old leather tunic over her dress and a second pair of breeches lest the weather turn sour during their journey. A dagger was placed into her right boot so that her skirt would cover it when she walked. It was a habit she preserved from Deacon's teachings. Her frost-numbed hands were struggling to fasten a leather girdle around her waist, a short-sword scabbard attached to it, with the hilt glimmering red in the light of the fire. There was a small flask of deadly concoction loosely strapped to the girdle beside the scabbard. On her other side, a second dagger was secured in place, beneath the tunic. In the dark, concealed by her cloak, she hoped to preserve these secret tools of the trade from a curious eye.

Adelaide handed Gabriel the other armed sheath and another dagger. When they were both suited for adventure and the fire was safely extinguished with collective stomps, they set off on a quest to find intoxicating treasure and exquisite gowns of hemp cloth. After a few hours of walking leisurely through the woods, they arrived before an abandoned farm. A few square acres of fields, overgrown with weeds and dying yellow grass, surrounded a nested stone shack. The visible outer walls were encased in dense vines and the neglected structure was struggling to hold up the weight of the slouching roof.

Adelaide eased ajar the creaking door and took a peek inside. She stepped over the threshold and the floorboards screamed beneath her feet.

"The walls won't hold!" called out Gabriel, watching the roof with increasing concern.

"I'll only take a hasty look inside!" replied the fearless apprentice, disappearing into the darkness of the house. Gabriel could hear her careful steps and held his breath, keeping an ever-watchful eye on the roof.

Adelaide stepped out. "Nothing valuable!" she exclaimed and headed towards a small path. He followed with a sign of relief. Some habits never die.

"So why do people stay away from the woods now? It seems they've lived this close before," said she, making conversation on the open road.

"The woods are enchanted," Gabriel muttered.

She was confused. "You don't truly believe that do you? You must have lived there for…"

"I have lived there for a very long time," he interrupted, "that is how I know."

Something was wrong. His perception of others was extraordinary but he lacked the same tact when disguising his own secrets and Adelaide had figured out his tell a long time ago.

"So what is it? What's haunting the woods?" No reply. "Tell me! I live there too now! If there is some beast or ghoul hiding out there, I should know too."

"There is a beast most foul," Gabriel said quietly, "me." Nonchalantly, he carried on down the path. Adelaide followed him in silence for a while but her curiosity got the best of her.

"Did you kill them? Did you kill the people that entered the woods?"

"No."

"Tell them stories of dragons and fiends?"

"There was no need to."

That's when it dawned on her. "You scared them. You controlled the spirit of the woods. You whispered threats and moved objects. You didn't tell them tales of magic, you made them create their own." He was still looking away, but she saw his smile and knew right then that her guess was correct.

"But why? Why not simply kill them?"

"It was better to let them live so they could spread the word of their fearsome travels. Killing them would only have tempted the brave ones to fight me."

"So why not kill them too?"

"If all the villagers were to die off, who would make me my ale?" he said with his mischievous grin, "and that's the village, there!" Adelaide saw the smog rising in the distance.

"Look at all that smoke from the fires!" she exclaimed. "One would think the whole village was ablaze!"

"This time o' year, it just might be."

***

They got closer and hid in the shadows of the houses, removing their hoods to blend in with the crowd and closing their cloaks to hide their weapons. The two glanced at each other and nodded. Adelaide stepped into the busy street first and Gabriel followed, and they made their way past the little wooden houses, dodging the drunkards and stepping over piles of waste, to reach the tavern. As they stepped inside, they were hit with the stench of cheap ale and manure. What little light was produced by the tiny candles was masked by the smoke from the villagers' pipes. There was a lot of noise, people calling one another, women giggling and men shouting.

Adelaide looked at Gabriel and saw his smile. They both knew this was perfect for their plan. She walked around, searching for the wealthiest men while Gabriel stood by the entrance and watched the people in the tavern. Many were men, fat and drunken peasants, or merchants, but there were women too — the unfortunate ones, desperately trying to charm the men into buying them a drink, or some food or giving them a place to stay in this cruel weather. There were other women, young girls, serving the drinks and cleaning up. They must be the daughters of the owner. They are the ones he focused on. They were walking around, going into different rooms in the tavern, but he saw two of them standing by a timeworn wooden door, unlocking it, talking.

"...Just bring more ale... the fat one has already drunk half a barrel..."

The younger of the two went through the door, with the key, and the other stood outside to stop people from entering. Now all Gabriel needed was to create a distraction, pull her away from her post. He walked up to Adelaide.

"By the maple tree to the north of the village," he whispered to her.

He saw her nod subtly and went towards a group of loud, boastful young peasants. There was one who was certainly more boisterous than the others, shouting about some pretty maiden he had supposedly known. Gabriel walked behind him, hitting the man with the hilt of his sword as he passed and slipped away just as the young man drunkenly spun around and punched a farmer sitting behind him, who instantly retaliated and a brawl broke out. Drinks were spilled and furniture was broken and the owner's daughter was instantly at the scene, trying to preserve as much of the taverns possessions as she could, leaving the small wooden door unattended as Gabriel silently snuck in.

He quickly hopped down a short flight of steps and was faced with a long underground corridor, five large wrought iron doors on either wall. The voices from the tavern were still thunderous but he tried to keep his steps quiet nonetheless. Hearing the bolt move on the one of the doors he stopped, and watched as the young girl stepped out, struggling to hold a heavy barrel. When she saw him, she froze, eyes wide open. Gabriel drew his sword and directed the girl away from the door. Inside was a small room filled with barrels of ale.

"Where's the rum?" he asked.

Tearing up with fear and clinging onto the barrel, the girl slowly walked towards another door and nodded at it. Opening it, he saw shelves filled with murky bottles. Gabriel grabbed an old hay sac that was conveniently lying by the door and filled it with the drinks. He stopped by the door, thinking.

"If there is another way out of here, it would be wise of you to tell me now."

"Aye," she led him down the corridor and towards another door. He opened it and looked out. She didn't trick him, it led into a passage beneath the street. Gabriel held the bag in one hand and, before she could respond, took the barrel of ale she was holding in the other. He was about to walk out but stopped and looked back at the girl with guilt and pity. Putting the barrel down momentarily, the generous thief picked off a piece of silver form his belt and held it out to the girl. She hesitated at first, but then snatched the silver pin from his hand and stepped away. Picking up the barrel again, he walked out.

Gabriel waited by the maple tree for some time, sipping the rum and mumbling to himself impatiently. He looked up at the night sky. It was beautiful. There were a million stars shining down on him, their gentle glow adding to the calm atmosphere of this place. He could still see the town and the vast cloud of smoke rising above it. The calls and shouts of the people have all blended into one deep drone.

He saw movement in the distance, but soon realised it was far bigger than a person. This huge dark shape was coming towards him, and fast. With no light but the stars to illuminate the path, he had no way to know what beast was approaching him now. Gabriel stood up in a flash and drew the sword, preparing for a fight.

The shape got closer and he could distinguish a horse with a rider yet his defence was still strong. Who would be riding around in the middle of the night and how did they know about this place? The horse got close and stopped right before him. The mysterious rider removed their hood and Adelaide gleamed down at him menacingly.

"I've not scared the fearless Gabriel, have I?" she laughed.

Putting the sword back in the scabbard, he answered, "One must always be on their guard. One can never know who might be riding around this time o' the night. How'd you get the beast?"

"The tradesman I was talking to was on business here, not a local. He needed a horse to get back and drunkenly told me what stable it was in. After a few drops from our berry flask, he needed it no more!"

"You killed a man for a horse?" asked Gabriel with disappointment.

"Nay!" she said proudly, holding up a small leather bag of coins. His shocked gaze wiped the arrogant smile from her face. She placed the bag into her boot and looked away.

There was a moment of silence as she sat on the horse and Gabriel stood near her, looking up. After studying her for a while, he leaned back and crossed his arms, grinning.

"Tell me, my dear, have you ridden a horse before?"

Adelaide understood why he looked so amused. "Nay," she answered, glancing away.

"How did you get on?"

"Told the stable boy it's me father's horse and he was too drunk to take it home. He helped me up."

"And how do you plan on getting off?" Gabriel's grin widened.

She did not respond. Before getting on, Adelaide assumed that she could jump off the animal with ease, but now that it was time to dismount, it dawned on her that the horse was taller than it first appeared. Yet, this should be no challenge for her, who spent her thieving years climbing up walls and sneaking into houses though windows and holes in the roofs. The horse whinnied and stamped its hoof causing Adelaide to instinctively grab onto the pommel of the saddle. She could hear Gabriel's laughter. Breathing in, she swung one leg over the horse, balancing on the stirrup on the other side. She then stretched that leg towards the ground, which was just out of her reach. As she tried to climb back up, her foot slipped and she fell into the dirt.

Feeling the empty saddle, the horse reared and Adelaide found herself beneath its stomping hooves. The girl squealed, which only startled the animal further. She tried to roll to the side but was horrified to discover that her cloak had become trapped under the horse's foot. As they were both trying to escape one another, Adelaide saw Gabriel holding his hand out in front of the animal's head. It was mad of a man to stand before an agitated creature of this weight, but Gabriel was the only man mad enough to do so. Yet in an instant the horse stopped and placed its forehead into his palm. He gently stroked the side of its head and stepped closer. The horse then rested its head against his chest, almost bowing to him.

Standing up, Adelaide stared in amazement.

"Tis a dangerous animal. Never underestimate it," said he without looking at her. "Why did you bring it here?"

Still awed by this display, Adelaide stuttered a response, "I thought it be faster to take the rum back by horse. With it being heavy and the walk being long."

"Aye, but with the weight of it, she can only take one rider."

"I can wait in the town. May try and find more loot."

Gabriel was hesitant. "All right, but try to avoid killing men for nothing more than a petty handful of coins."

"It may not be much to you but it's a decent prize for many others!"

"There'll be no use for gold in the woods."

"Aye, but if we return here..."

"Just don't kill innocent men," he interrupted.

"Aye." The authority in his voice frightened her. "When shall I return?"

Gabriel looked back in the direction of the woods and thought for a few moments. "Even with a horse this will still take time. There is one path that is suitable to pass through on horseback, but it would require caution. I haven't been down that way in many years." He thought in silence for a little longer. "Return here when the sun dawns."

"Aye."

Gabriel added his hay bag to the two others that were already tied to the saddle and swiftly jumped up onto the horse. He hesitated and looked back at her.

"I shall be as hasty as the horse allows." He paused. "Be wary of the guards." Another pause. "Avoid thieving those with weapons."

"I have travelled through towns better guarded than this one and got away," she boasted. "I shall see you here at dawn." The girl spun around on her heel and strutted towards the town.

"Aye," he said quietly. He knew that she was a strong fighter and a crafty thief but he still didn't feel right leaving her there. Yet Gabriel knew that he would not be gone for long so he took hold of the reins and galloped towards the woods.

Chapter 23

The First Taste

The streets were quieter than before, but there were still voices of people making their way home. Adelaide was snaking between houses and darting through narrow alleyways, trying to find more loot, when she saw a man lying still on the ground. She cautiously approached to check if he was breathing. When she got closer, she saw something reflecting the distant light but it didn't look like coins or metal. It was liquid... it was blood! She stepped back as soon as she realised, but curiosity pushed her to inspect closer.

His throat was sliced cleanly so it must have been done with a blade. There was nothing on his person that she deemed to be of value; he must have been robbed, as even the pin from his cloak was taken. She warily shifted his cloak with the tip of her foot. The unfortunate victim was wearing a rope belt, one that cannot support a scabbard so he couldn't have been a fighter, yet he looked wealthier than a peasant, a tradesman maybe. The perfect prey for robbers and thieves, she knew that herself. Maybe she wasn't the only prowler in this village tonight.

The cold breeze hit her and she wrapped her cloak tighter around her torso. Now Adelaide wished she was home in the woods, by the fire. She never imagined that she would grow to love the little cabin like she loved the house she grew up in. Adelaide was accustomed to spending nights in the streets of strange towns but now that she had a real home, somewhere to go to feel warm and safe, all she wanted was to be there again. She considered walking back by herself, as she was certain that Gabriel would travel along the same path as they arrived on and they will simply meet further away from the town. But she made a promise and so decided to wait it out until dawn. With resolve, she looked up from the cobbled walkway and made her way down the shadowy alleyway towards the town centre.

The taverns were closing and the guards were pushing drunkards out into the street. The girl watched them from the other side of the road and laughed as they danced and fell. The armour-clad guards mocked them, hit them and spat on them and when the men were lying motionless on the pebbled ground the guards laughed and walked away jeering. The silent men were those poor bastards who had drunk all their money away and were of no use to her and so she continued through the streets looking for more well-off folk.

Adelaide reached the small stone church. There was a fountain by the entryway and she rushed up to it and drank a few handfuls of its clear water. Looking up at the church, she thought about entering. Surely it must be warmer in there, away from the biting wind. But did she truly have the right to walk into a church? She was burdened with many sins and was certainly out of God's sight. Yet she hasn't been inside a church in a long time and was curious to see it.

The huge door creaked as she opened it, echoing ominously through the small building. Adelaide crept inside cautiously, looking around. There were two rows of dark wooden pews leading to an altar and a small pulpit. Right by the door was a stone basin filled with holy water. This was a modest, plain church, with indecipherable stained-glass patterns on the windows and aged wooden beams holding up the long-unmended roof.

She sauntered down the aisle, surveying the interior. There was just one other person in the church: a dark-haired man sobbing in one of the front pews. Curious but cautious she sat in the row behind him, on the other side of the church, and studied him. His dark brown cloak was coated in mud, as were his hands and face, his skin was covered with small cuts and tears sparked in the candlelight as they ran down his face. She wanted to find the cause of his despair, to console him, but she knew that he would not confide in her. So she sat there and stared silently at this wreck of a human.

Adelaide knew why people like him would go to church, looking for redemption, for a reason to continue their miserable lives; she encountered enough of them as a thief. She knew to avoid them, as all that was valuable had already been taken from them and with nothing more to their name than an old cloak, they were worthless to her. Like trying to eat soup from an empty bowl. She had experienced this herself, being so poor and lonely that her only reason for struggling on was the promise of salvation, the hope that one day she will have again what had been lost, a house, a family, an honest job. Adelaide wanted to be righteous, to follow the commandments, to live a good life but fate led her into the swamp of sin, and she could not find her way out.

A small door behind the altar opened and an elderly priest came out. Adelaide was happy to see him; thinking that he would restore the crying man's faith.

"Get out of here you filthy pigs!" His voice echoed through the building. Her surprise kept her frozen as the last glimmers of hope drained away.

"Go on! Go back to your taverns and brothels! There is no room for dogs like you in a place of God." She found herself walking hastily towards the door. She wanted to turn around and fight back, to defend herself but her legs kept walking, eyes down, like a scolded child. Once outside the church, she looked at the man who was now beside her. He was no longer crying but his face was cold, emotionless, drained as he stared into the night. Once again, she wanted to ask what troubled him, to comfort him but not a word left her lips. He turned and walked slowly away as the dark mist embraced him, surrounded him, till he was out of sight, gone as if he never existed.

Adelaide gawked after him for a few moments, wondering what will happen to him. But she could not stand there forever so she continued her way around the town. It was much colder than before as the icy wind was now joined by humid air, numbing her skin and clinging to her throat every time she inhaled. Pulling her hood up and wrapping her cloak tightly around herself, she walked closely to the houses. In the light from their windows, she saw a small cloud form around her face every time she exhaled. Looking up at the sky, she wondered how much longer she had to wait till dawn. The sky was black and the stars shined brightly, telling her that it was going to be a while.

Feeling tired, she contemplated going back to the tree now and falling asleep there, in the roots. She would be kept warm by the soil and Gabriel could just wake her up when he arrives. Pleased with her plan, she made her way there. Walking north past the last houses, she could feel the pebbles under her feet change to dust and knew that she was outside the perimeter of the village. Trying to see the maple tree in the distance, she heard a noise behind her and quickly turned around. A dark shape emerged from the shadows, followed by two others from different directions.

"Remove yer hood." The shape had a deep, commanding voice. This must be their leader. After not moving for a few moments Adelaide heard a sword being drawn.

"I said, remove yer damn hood!" This time she obeyed. She could hear her heartbeat hasten as fear gradually filled her. They must be the people who killed the old tradesman she saw in the alleyway. Realisation of how much danger she was in struck her like a dagger, leaving her frozen.

"Ahh, a lady we have here!" he laughed, stepping closer. She could see him now. Is hair was tied back and he wore the clothes of a peasant, except for a leather girdle with a scabbard. His sword shined in the moonlight.

"Aye, she be the one from the tavern earlier," chimed in another one. He was round cheeked and big bellied, but he too carried a sword.

"Stealing?" the leader asked him.

"Aye, she be with this merchant the whole time and when they leave, they not be back."

"So she is here, and he is… dead?" He faced her again.

Quickly summoning her courage, she replied, "Nay, he's waiting for me, he would wonder if I did not come back."

The leader looked at the fat one who shrugged, clearly confused. If they were truly this naïve, she could find a way out of this.

"Either way," the leader snapped, "he not be here to protect ye. So hand over all yer possessions or they will find ye here tomorrow. "

"I have nothing with me," she answered coldly.

A harsh, mocking laugh echoed around her. Still laughing, the leader stepped closer and pressed the blade of the sword against her throat.

When she tried to step back, the cold metal dug into her skin. She knew she was trapped, held motionless by her own terror.

"Is that so?" he asked scornfully.

"Aye," she whispered, scared to even breathe in.

"Where be all the loot you stole this night then?" called out the fat outlaw.

Without a moment of thought, she replied, "I took it back to the house."

"Where you walking to now then?" asked the leader menacingly. "A lone wander in the early hours of the morning? A young helpless thing like ye, all by yerself?"

Panicking, all she could summon was a quiet, "Aye."

As soon as the word left her lips, Adelaide closed her eyes, instantly knowing that they had her trapped. She tried to think of a plan, a way to escape that would lead her away from the empty fields and towards the town, where she could easily find a place to hide. She knew that the thieves standing before her now were not gifted with wit, yet she herself could not think of a way to outsmart them as the terror and chaos of the circumstances left her mind stumped. She tried to conjure a story to distract them, to say or do something that would buy her more time but nothing of the sort came to mind. Desperately, she considered just giving them the coins she hid in her boot and running away, but she knew they would not let her leave alive, not after she had seen their faces. She looked up to see the leader staring intently at her.

"Yer leave us no choice," he said, raising his sword.

Whatever happens, Adelaide knew she could not walk away from this confrontation alive and a recklessly brave spirit took over her.

"You dare not challenge me!" she yelled with a sudden jolt of courage.

She threw back her cloak and drew her sword. Both men stared at her for a moment and then erupted into a hyena-like cackle.

"A woman with a sword?" asked the fat one, "so ye think ye can fight us?" They laughed more.

"How did she find it?" called the third man, the one who stood silent in the shadows till now.

"I bet she stole it too!" replied the leader.

"A woman cannot know how to fight!" yelled the fat man mockingly.

Looking back at Adelaide maliciously, the leader whispered, "We shall see."

The dread that was blinding her before was now replaced by a clear vision and a focused mind, given to her by the realisation of her power. Fear was no longer in control of her. There was an inferno burning in her heart, a cruel bloodlust guiding her. She has been training for a year, now it was time to test her newfound knowledge.

Adelaide was gripping the sword with both hands, holding it out in front of her. She knew that if she made even the smallest mistake, she would not survive this fight. The leader of the thieves raised his blade. The metal shined brightly in the moonlight but, behind it, she saw the stars beginning to fade and the colour return to the sky. Dawn was creeping back.

The world stopped around her. She was not far from the maple tree, if Gabriel returned now, he would see this fight and he would save her. She quickly glanced up in the direction of the woods. That's when she saw it, a shadow of an animal stamping its majestic hooves, gloriously standing in front of the tree, their shadows merging. Hope filled her heart for she knew that now she was safe.

The animal lowered its head to graze and in the blue moonlight she saw the outline of its antlers. It was a deer. The disappointment brought her back to reality, reigniting her bloodlust. Adelaide was alone, and this was her battle.

The leader's sword swished down but, she blocked it, swiftly moving to the side. She now held her sword in one hand; the other one tensed for balance as she took a fighting stance, her legs crouched, ready to move at any moment. She heard the other two bandits draw their swords and struck for the nearest: the fat one. He blocked her and kicked her to the ground, raising his sword above her for a fatal hit. She kicked the flat side of the weapon away from herself and struck the man hard in the knee. When he too was on the ground, she twisted, bringing the sword over, aiming to slice his throat but he rolled to the side as her weapon hit the ground.

Adelaide tried to stand up, but something was holding her sword down. She looked up and saw the third, quieter man, his foot on her blade, looking to his leader. She tried to pull it back from under his weight, not wanting to let go, but one of them stomped on her hand, forcing her to release the sword.

Adelaide sat on the ground, alone and defenceless, surrounded by three tall shadows, blades pointing at her throat. But courage has not left her. In a flash, she grabbed one of the blades with her hands and kicked the man who was holding it, knocking him to the ground. In a swift move, she was upright, his sword in her bleeding hand, standing over him. She glanced down to see the leader staring up at her in shock. She slashed at the other two men, pushing them back momentarily and brought the blade down heavily, all her strength behind it, through the thief's chest.

The world froze around Adelaide again as she stared into the dying eyes of a man she killed. The pain she saw filled her with grief, with pity and with the horror of her act. She took a life, a human life. She did it to protect herself but still, the man was dead because of her.

Yet her disbelief faded and the disgust she felt turned into cruel pleasure. The sight of blood running from the body of her enemy brought her delight. She smiled to herself. He took many innocent souls for nothing more than a bag of coins. He deserved to die.

But she too had committed his sins. She too would go to any length to acquire even the smallest measure of wealth. So what differentiated them? What gave her the right to take his life? Still smiling to herself, she knew the answer. Her skill. Those who can find a way to survive and continue their sinful ways will do so, yet those who are weak, will be defeated. The judge and executioner shall be the one with the power to carry out the role.

Adelaide looked up at the other two men as they both struggled to accept the fall of their leader. The big bellied one moved first, striking at her. She prepared to block his attack, but to her distress found herself unable to move the sword in her hands. It must have wedged far into the ground beneath the dead man. She let go of it and moved to the side, barely avoiding the hit, but caught the fat man's wrist and smashed it against the hilt of her trapped sword. His bones cracked and the metal broke into his flesh, severing his tendons.

He screamed in agony, dropping his weapon and pulling back his crippled forearm. Adelaide stepped closer to him and drove his own sword through his neck. Now there was just one left. She looked at him, standing a short distance away, holding his own sword and the one that was previously hers.

They both stood motionless, waiting for the other to strike first. He gently stepped forward.

"It need not be this way," he said, lowering both weapons. "We both be thieves, fighters, we can work together."

"You would have gladly sliced my throat a few moments ago if your leader told you to."

"He did, but I did not." The man took another step forward.

"I see." She cautiously lowered her blade and stepped towards him.

"You can get more loot this way than you would alone." He now stood right in front of her. She could reach him.

Adelaide's laughter echoed through the fields.

"Did you honestly think I would accept your offer?" she said with maniacal joy, as she lashed out with great speed and wounded his right arm. He tried to strike her with his left, but she effortlessly blocked the hit and sliced his left arm too. She pushed him down on his knees and stood behind him, her blade on his throat.

She could feel the power pulsing through her, as he whimpered in terror. She was no longer the victim of his crime; she was the menace.

"Any last words?" she whispered in his ear.

He sobbed a reply and she drew the sword, slicing his throat.

Adelaide straightened her back and looked around. Three bloody corpses lay at her feet, showered in the delicate light of the young sun. Their blood was still warm on her face, dripping from her hair, from her clothes. Her own blood was pouring from her palm and down her sword onto the wet dew-covered ground. Her skin was hot from the fight, sweat running down her brow, but as she stood still, she could feel the icy air around her, biting at her skin, at her moist clothes. Every breath formed a cloud before her. It was just like it was back at the village, back before she was a murderer.

She looked up at the vivid colours of the morning sky. There was still dark blue in the distance but before her was a display of bright orange and yellow, almost blending with the dying fields around her.

Adelaide's admiration of the beautiful morning was interrupted by a loud shout to her right. She turned, facing the village and looked at the elderly man who was staring at her in disbelief, his eyes moving quickly from the bloodied blade in her hands to the dead men around her. He stumbled backwards and ran shouting back to the village.

"Of course they come now," she muttered to herself and picking up her sword, as well as keeping the outlaw's one that she was already holding, she sprinted up the hill, towards the woods. She knew she was at a disadvantage here, in the open fields, as the town guards will most likely follow her on horseback and without a place to hide, she was most vulnerable.

Just as she made it to the maple tree, her face lit up at the sight of a horse galloping towards her from the direction of the woods. After stopping for a moment to catch her breath, she ran towards it. As they got closer, she could see the shock on Gabriel's face. He stopped the horse and quickly jumped off, running up to her.

"Good God! Adelaide..." he held her by the shoulders, looking her over. His eyes stopped on the thief's sword. He looked her darkly in the eye with a furrowed brow and she could see that he was piecing together what happened.

"We must hurry, the guards will be here any moment," she croaked, her voice rough from running in the cold air. Raising his eyes towards the village at the mention of the guards, Gabriel nodded and rushed to the horse, which was waiting patiently for him. He swiftly jumped on and pulled Adelaide on behind him.

"They mustn't know that the forbidden woods are inhabitable," Gabriel called over his shoulder.

"They what?"

"We cannot let them know we live there."

The horse was galloping fast and the rapid wind made any communication almost impossible, so she just hid her face in the folds of his cloak and closed her eyes.

As they galloped away, neither of them looking back, a dark silhouette gazed upon them from a distance. A black hood covered his face and an old wooden cane held him upright. Yet he did not move, nor did he follow them. He simply watched the riders as they disappeared into the "enchanted" woods. Around him swarmed hundreds upon hundreds of red-billed black choughs.

Chapter 24

Forgiveness

They rode until the smoke that hovered above the town disappeared into the distance and the shadows of the enchanted woods swallowed them up once again. Gabriel slowed the horse, walked it delicately through the narrow remnant of a path that was now overgrown with weeds. The animal was hesitant to move. It reared and stomped its hooves, but the old man rested his hand on its neck and whispered into its ear and the horse calmed and walked on.

Once they neared the cabin, Gabriel jumped off and led the animal into the opening. He picked Adelaide off the horse's back and put her down. Silently, he stood there, looking at her.

"They were not innocent men…" she began.

"I know."

"Then why do ye gaze upon me with such hatred in your eyes?"

"No, not hatred, lass." His voice softened. "But relief."

Gabriel took the bandit's sword from her hand and walked into the house. She followed.

Inside, the hay bag was thrown on the table and the barrel stood on the floor. The old man tidied up, moving the bottles around and rolling the barrel into a corner. He then filled two mugs with ale and sat down at the table, gesturing Adelaide to join him.

"Here, but you look like you need something stronger." He placed one of the mugs in front of her and then quickly gulped down his own.

Adelaide stared at the ale.

"I'm proud of what you did," Gabriel spoke to her gently. "How many were there?"

"Three."

"Three bandits, eh?"

She remained silent.

"You enjoyed it, didn't you? You liked the way their blood glistened as it ran down your sword. You liked seeing their last breath leave their body," he spoke, staring her in the eye.

"No," Adelaide whispered in response.

"Don't lie. You cannot fool me."

"I could not help it! The feeling of success, of victory was..." The girl struggled for words.

"Overpowering?"

"Aye! I spent years in those streets, fearing them, running from them and planning my moves to avoid meeting bandits like them! To feel that power, to know that I was no longer their victim was how David must have felt when he defeated Goliath, in the holy book you made me read. But most of all, I was happy to be alive. I was happy that it was them and not me that lay cold in that field. They would have killed me! I know it. I felt that icy fear in my heart when I first heard them; I was held still by it, unable to move, unable to fight, unable to think of a way out! And to be free of this fear was like stepping out of a dungeon and seeing the light of day. To remember that it was men like them that burned down my village and slaughtered my family! To know that after all this time, I may at last have a chance at revenge, at justice! Hear me when I say that come the opportunity, I would take great pleasure and great pride in taking the lives of those who have haunted me since that ungodly day."

Adelaide found that the emotion in her words pushed her to her feet. Quickly sitting back down, she calmed herself and took a long sip from the mug.

"I was younger than you when I had my first kill," Gabriel spoke softly. "It was a prisoner in my King's dungeon. The man was sentenced to death. My father was ordered to carry out the sentence. I was in training at the time and he called me over and handed me his sword. He said that to be a man, to be a soldier, I needed to kill. So I did. I was so nervous that I made a hell of a mess of it too, but once the man was dead my father patted me on the back and said that he was proud. The first kill changes you. It brings out what was always hidden deep in your heart, may it be courage, honour or bloodlust."

"You fear for me? You fear that it was the last… the latter?"

"Not for you, my dear, but for the Gift." With that, he rose to his feet.

"The horse will need hay if we are to keep her," he spoke, leaving the house.

Adelaide sat alone and in silence, pondering Gabriel's words. She could not deny the sick rush that she felt when the bandits lay dead at her feet. Was it evil that had awakened in her? She prayed that it wasn't, not for the sake of the Gift or her training but rather for fear of disappointing her tutor. She could not fail him. She could not bear to see him so full of regret.

The door slowly opened behind her. Adelaide turned to see a face she did not recognise. Jumping to her feet she grabbed a nearby sword. The intruder cowered against the wall, shielding himself with his hands.

"Who are you? Why are you here?" Adelaide yelled at him.

"I saw ye kill those men and leave the village. I followed on my horse."

"And what did you plan to achieve?" Boomed a voice from the door. Gabriel stood there, as hypnotically intimidating as she had ever seen him. He seemed almost calm, but she pitied the man who had to face him as an enemy.

"To… to express my gratitude, I suppose. Those thieves have been terrorising the village for months now. It is good to finally be rid of them," the man spoke, straightening up. In the light, his face appeared more familiar, but Adelaide could not place it.

She turned to Gabriel. He stood leaning gracefully against a wall, silently watching her. This was a test. She was either to kill the intruder or spare this human life, at the risk that he may return home to the village and tell the others about the two swordsmen living in the supposedly abandoned woods. The old man wanted her to make the choice. He had expressed his concern for her vicious soul and lack of compassion but that could have been merely a bluff to find out whether she would spare the stranger to demonstrate mercy or kill him to prove the strength of her character and sense of duty. He did repeat the importance of keeping their home secret mere hours before.

Gabriel could read the thoughts that raced through her head, but remained expressionless, giving her no prompts. Just waiting silently.

He wants me to release the intruder, Adelaide thought, to show that I am kind and forgiving and worthy the carry the God's Rose. Yet her hand remained gripping the sword. To release this man would be suicide. He followed her and lied when asked why. He would surely tell the guards of the murderers that dwell in the woods and there would be an angry mob here before dusk.

Taking a deep breath, she made her decision.

She swung the sword at his throat but a sudden memory twisted her hand. The sword hit the wooden wall right by the stranger's neck. Adelaide leaned on the blade, pinning him against the wall with the sharp metal against his artery.

"I remember you now," she whispered. "So many years ago, in Aeraworth, when I awoke by the carts after the others had abandoned me. T'was my first morning in the city. You gave me a coin for bread."

"Aye," was his quiet reply. "Yer locks are as ashen now as they were then."

The man smiled at her. It was a strangely unnerving smile. Adelaide found she was leaning away from him but with the blade remaining as firmly pressed against his flesh as before.

Surrendering, she lowered the sword.

"Get out. And hear me when I say that if you dare say a word of this place to any man in the village, I will hunt you down like a pig," spoke the girl, moving away from the peculiar intruder.

He rushed towards the door, but hesitated when he met Gabriel's stern gaze. Awkwardly squeezing through the doorframe, the man made it past the ranger, averting his eyes, and sprinted into the woods.

Adelaide had not moved. The blade remained in her hand. Sunlight had cast a shadow across the wall in front of her. The only light that entered the little cabin came in through the doorframe. A grandiose silhouette stirred in the light. Adelaide turned to find empty space where the old man had stood but a moment before.

Questions raced through her head. Was her choice correct? Had she proven herself worthy? Overwhelmed, she collapsed to her knees and twisted around so that she sat with her back against the wall. Only then she realised how exhausted she was.

Through half closed eyes Adelaide looked around the cabin. The high summer sun tinted the room orange. The bright colour cloaked the table and chairs, filled the mugs and chalices and shone off the pile of swords that rested in the corner of the room. One of the swords was dirty and covered in blood. It was not long ago that another man, a thief and bandit, held that sword as his own, wielded the blade against any who had a gold coin in their pocket. Now, he lay lifeless.

Adelaide looked out into the cloudless sky. Birds circled in the distance. Was it those forsaken choughs? Perhaps. Their calls echoed through the woods. Other birds joined them until an eerily mocking choir sounded all around the house. Their sinister song continued for what seemed like an eternity.

Gabriel reappeared in the doorway and the cries of the birds stopped in an instant. The old man walked through the cabin. His heavy boots stomped on the wooden floor. Adelaide's eyes followed his every move. He sat down at the table, looked into one of the chalices, glanced around the room. So calm and authoritative in his entrance, he was now becoming unsettled and fidgety.

"You followed him." It wasn't a question.

Gabriel smiled darkly to himself.

Chapter 25

The Cave

The clacking of swords echoed through the woods. Adelaide held a blade in each hand, her muscles tensed to support their weight, her bare feet digging into the woodland floor as she crouched. Sweat ran from her brow. Her shoulder length hair was pulled back into a bun but locks of it still clung to her face. The bodice of her dress dug into her flesh as she tried to catch her breath, the skirt wrapped itself around her legs, binding her.

She ducked as a sword swung above her head and manoeuvred away. Jumping back towards her opponent, Adelaide struck at him with strength and precision that only he could counter. Before she knew it, one of her swords was knocked from her hand and another held at her throat.

"Good fight!" Gabriel spoke, stepping away.

Adelaide sat down to recover.

"Yet it seems I can never defeat you," she spoke.

"And you never will," he replied nonchalantly. "Rest for now. There is an exciting test awaiting you."

"Another mad life-threatening exercise to supposedly determine my competence as a fighter?" Adelaide shot back.

"Yet another one indeed. Although I am glad to see that in the past six years of training, you have finally rid yourself of that foul dialect and leaned to speak like a woman of class and education."

"Class? Next thing I shall be Lady, nay even Queen Adelaide!" she mused.

"I would worry for the kingdom if that were to become true." Gabriel replied laughing.

He began to walk away and Adelaide stood up and followed. They arrived back at the house and laid down their swords. Adelaide watched the old man carefully, anxiously anticipating her next trial.

"It's best if we eat now," he spoke, rummaging through the shelves.

"This test is going to be a tough one, isn't it?"

"No, you won't be in any... mortal danger, I suppose."

"Great," she sighed.

After eating, Adelaide quickly pulled her boots on and slipped a small dagger into one. Gabriel noticed, but turned away, sniggering to himself.

They left the house and walked through the woods. Spring was in full bloom and young bright leaves covered these ancient trees. The stream sparkled as the cold clear water delicately danced over the pebbles. The grass was reaching up from under the fallen tree branches like an infant reaching for the arms of their mother. The warmth of sunlight caressed the skin of the two rangers who were making their way through the stretching branches, across the meadow and down into the gorge. It was a lake within this same gorge that Gabriel made Adelaide dive into several years before. She remembered it well.

They walked through the valley until they reached a small cave. Ivy surrounded it, stretching up the cliffside, over the large piles of rock on either side of the entrance. A small chough sat atop one of the rocks. Seeing an insect, it hoped onto the ground and into the darkness of the cave.

Gabriel lit a torch and handed it to Adelaide.

"Listen lass, I need you to go in and drink some of the water that runs through the cave."

"Why?" Adelaide looked at him curiously.

"Well, it..."

"Is it magical?" she interrupted. "Like the cave I was in when the hellhound appeared to me?"

"Yes, it's magical," Gabriel condescendingly waved her inside.

Adelaide stepped into the shadows of the cave. Holding the torch close to the walls, she studied the sandstone. A thick layer of moss covered the surface. It was soft to the touch but smelled rather peculiar. The minerals etched incredible, vibrant patterns on the walls. As Adelaide ventured further and further into the cave, the stone formations changed from drapes to pillars to what resembled a waterfall. Droplets of water covered the rock, which sparked in the red light of the torch. Adelaide knelt down by the little stream and filled her cupped hand with the mineral water. Taking a sip from it, she admired the beautiful silence of the cave, where nothing but the soft sound of running water could be heard.

The stone tunnel remained soundless until a loud thud echoed from behind her. Adelaide turned to find that no light could be seen from outside. She rushed out, only to run into a dead end. Placing her hand on the rock, she felt its warmth and knew that it had stood outside, in the sunlight.

"Gabriel, let me out! Let me out this instant!" she called through the rock, but no reply was heard.

So this is the final test. She found, to her surprise, that despite all the reckless and dangerous training, the cruelty of these tests still had the power to frustrate her. Adelaide leaned against the rock, muttering in rage. She turned and looked into the darkness. Hesitantly stepping forwards, she held the torch out as far as she could, but beyond the radius of light, the dense darkness remained still. All these pillars and drapes of sandstone had lost their beauty, appearing more eerie and sinister than before. Using all her moral strength, she continued walking.

A pillar appeared in her path. The cave split into two. Adelaide stood trying to decide which path to take. Both offered an endless tunnel of rock. Surrendering to instinct, she continued down the path to her right. Every breath resonated through her body, every step echoed through these eternal halls.

The silence. It weighed down on her. The girl began humming a song that she remembered from her childhood years, yet the melody that came from her sounded more like the whimper of a frightened child. She was afraid. The realisation struck her like a slap to the face. She was truly overcome by fear, but of what? A shadow? A patch of darkness? A noise in the distance?

Stopping, Adelaide took a deep breath. No. She was no infant. After years and years of training, will her courage fall to the threat of darkness? She could not let that happen. Composing herself, Adelaide persisted through the cave.

The stream that had once sparkled playfully in the light of her torch now flowed lifelessly. Something in the water caught Adelaide's eye. Looking closer, she studied the dark purple vapour that rose from the water. Streaks of this ominous essence lingered above the flow of the stream, seeping deeper into the darkness of the cave. Terror struck her as she remembered when she had seen this before. Looking up, Adelaide witnessed as the darkness thickened and coalesced before her once again. It began to spin and heat filled the cave. Adelaide turned and ran.

She ran and ran, gripping the torch tightly, through the tunnels she came from until the damned dead end appeared in her path. The moist floor of the cave gave no friction as momentum slammed her body into the rock. Adelaide screamed through the blocked entrance, begging Gabriel to let her out but no sound passed through the impenetrable door. She slid to the ground and watched the darkness, waiting for the hell hound to appear at any moment. She waited for it, she braced herself, but it did not come.

After an eternity of waiting, her shaking hands relaxed. Resting her head against the wall, she closed her eyes. Only then she noticed the smell of the cave. It had a thick and musky aroma that emanated from the moss that covered every square inch of rock here, near the entrance. The smell filled her lungs. Feeling light headed, she opened her eyes to look around. The torch she had held lay by her side on the wet floor, drenched and fading out, but there was a light shining above one of the stalagmites like the flame above a candle. Curious, Adelaide crawled towards it. As she got closer, the light expanded until it fully embraced her.

Reaching out cautiously with her hand, she felt cold dry branches at her fingertips. Rising to her feet, she looked around. A dead forest surrounded her. Black tree trunks stretched towards the sky, their branches, like claws, looking for a victim. No bird calls, no animals rustling under the rotten leaves. The edge of the forest was just in her sight and Adelaide snuck quietly out of the woodland cemetery and into the opening.

A tall crooked tower stood menacingly on the edge of a cliff. Very little of it could be seen from this distance, but some flying beasts were circling its roof. They were too big and too grotesque to be birds. Dark clouds hovered in the sky, spiralling over the tower. Adelaide had seen clouds like these before, in Aeraworth. They circled for days and then dispersed.

"It's magic." A raspy voice came from behind her.

Quickly turning, Adelaide found herself facing the old man with a wooden cane; the very same spectre that led her into the enchanted woods.

"It is very powerful magic, like ye hath never seen before," the old man continued, wheezing with every slow breath.

"Who are you? What is this place? Why am I here?" Adelaide yelled at the phantom.

"Could yon questions be any more predictable?" the man scoffed. "Think."

"This is a vision, a dream," Adelaide stated. "Is this my future?"

"Nay. It be a time long gone."

"The air here is warm, even when hidden away from the light of the sun by this forsaken cloud. I can taste the salt from the sea. It lingers on my tongue with every breath I take. This place is far from Starkenhaart."

"When was the last time ye stood by the sea?" the old man asked.

Adelaide watched mesmerised as her vision changed. The dark clouds vanished, replaced by a clear blue sky, the crooked tower crumbled into the ground and the cliff was alive again. Little yellow wildflowers looked up at her from the grass. Now this scene she recognised in an instant. It was a sight she could never forget. The song she was humming in the cave, this was the memory it always brought to her; the happy memory of her home.

Filled with hope, Adelaide turned to the familiar sight of her peaceful little village in the distance. It was intact, with every mud house as perfectly slumped and irregular as she remembered them. People were walking through the streets, shouting to each other, laughing. This was the very place she stood when she watched them die. If only she could go back now, with a sword in her hand and fire in her soul, she could kill the bandits.

A sudden pain filled her heart, pain that spread through her body like a physical injury. It's been years since she thought about this place, since she thought about her parents or Jon, since she recalled the bandit that let her live or the endless exhausting hours that followed. Her brain could no longer reconstruct their faces and she could not distinguish their voices from the hundreds of others that filled her memory.

A chough flew down and landed softly on the grass at her feet. It looked at her with its bright little eyes. The vision faded around it as the grass turned back into the sandstone floor of the dark cave. And yet the little bird remained.

The torch was almost burned out. She wondered how many hours she had slept as hunger was upon her. Sitting up from the moist floor, Adelaide slowly reached into her boot. The knife shined in the dim light. The bird hopped around at her feet, sweetly turning its head to the side. It looked at the girl with eyes full of purity and innocence, eyes that were soon staring aimlessly as the little bird lay dead on the cold floor with a knife ripping through in its flesh.

***

Adelaide threw the grisly remains of the little bird on the floor. Blood covered her face and long red stringy veins hung from her teeth. She struggled to her feet. Every muscle in her body ached, every breath sent her coughing. The girl pushed her tangled knotted hair from her face, smearing blood across her cheek, and held tightly onto the fading torch, hoping to see something in the shadows but the cave was darker and more ghostly than before. Slowly, Adelaide made her way through the tunnel and collapsed at the stream. She drank from it quickly, reluctant to stay this far into the cave for any longer than necessary. The hell hound could return at any time. The water felt cold against her skin and tickled her throat as she drank. Shivering, Adelaide rose to her feet again and scurried back towards the entrance to the cave.

Time passed and she remained in her spot by the entrance. Days must have gone by, but she could not tell. The torch was long extinguished. The clothes she wore were soiled and torn. With no sunlight entering the cave, the temperature dropped and sickness took over Adelaide. The darkness was endless but she was certain she saw flashes and sparks in her peripheral vision. The silence was the hardest to endure. Every time she shifted or moved, it echoed through the stone halls. So she remained motionless. The gentle sound of her breathing bounced around the stone walls and returned to her like a distant thunder. The squelching of her clothes from the movement of her rib cage or from the shifting of her numb muscles made her look around in horror, fearful that someone was approaching in the darkness. The sound of her blood rushing through her veins drove her insane until she clasped her ears with her hands and hummed, rocking back and forth.

Adelaide sat by the moss, leaning her limp body against the moist flora, slowly ripping it from the wall and pulling it into her mouth. By now, she was accustomed to its peculiar taste and even began to enjoy it but, just as she learned to tolerate it, it began to change. With no sunlight, the moss was beginning to die. The metallic taste of blood was constantly on her tongue, from her scratched up fingers and the cracks in her lips.

The heavy humid air infused with the fumes of the decaying vegetation weighed her down and pushed all sense from her head. All she could do was to sit there in the cold wet darkness and wait for the inevitable sweetness of death to finally claim her. This test she could not survive.

How could Gabriel do this to her? Adelaide couldn't decide if she hated that man or missed him. All her thoughts were brought to an abrupt end when she heard the breathing of another person in the darkness.

Adelaide tried to call out a question, but could muster only a croak, followed by a severe and painful cough.

"Ye know who I be, lass," the voice of a man boomed and echoed in the empty tunnel. This voice was familiar.

The man limped towards her, each footstep followed by a little thud, and sat down next to her.

"Been a long time, has it not? And I see ye'd gone to them towns, even though I told ye not to. See where that got ya? Now ye be sitting 'ere eating rotting moss from the walls."

The smell of seawater and rotting wood radiated from the old pirate. A clink was heard and the sound of gulping, followed by the scent of rum.

"Ere lass, ye have some," said Roger, putting the flask in her hand.

Adelaide took a swig and instantly rolled to the side as her stomach emptied its undigested content onto the stone. He took the flask back grumpily.

"I see 'tis not good enough for ye now that ye go around swinging swords and drinking from chalices like noble folk. Stay on this path and being stuck in a cave would seem like child's play. And don't think I haven't noticed ye trying to get yon hands on that rose, and let me tell ya lass, it may look good now but ye'll regret it one day," the old man rumbled on.

"How'd you get in here?" Adelaide croaked quietly.

"I was always here."

"You are not real either, are you? Just another vision."

"Though it'd take ye sooner to figure that out," the man laughed.

"Tell me how to get out," she begged.

"Can't do that I'm afraid."

"Why?" she cried, but raising her voice made her stomach cramp again as more acid and moss spewed onto the rock.

"I do not interfere, I only advise."

"Then advise me."

"My advice is that ye look around."

"Quit your riddles. I can't see shit in this darkness!" Adelaide snapped.

"If ye insist on acting blind then so ye will stay," Roger replied calmly.

"Again, with the riddles! Why must everything come down to riddles and tests?" she exclaimed but the sound of his breathing was gone, as was he.

Adelaide rested her head against the wall again. "Look around." She remembered how the cave looked when she first came in, she could picture it in her head. There was a large stalagmite three steps in front of her and a pillar just a little deeper into the cave, to the right. Sliding up the wall, Adelaide rose to her feet and stumbled through the stone tunnel. The walk was exhausting but she found her steps becoming more balanced. With one hand constantly on the wall, she followed it blindly, occasionally tripping over stalagmites and pieces of rock.

There was water dripping just ahead of her and she ducked, narrowly avoiding a large stalactite. The tapestry of rotting moss has ended and her hand was now tracing smooth cold wet stone. The air was becoming lighter and easier to inhale. It went straight to her head and Adelaide collapsed to the floor. With all her strength she pushed herself up and took a brave step forward, only to walk face first into a pillar. This was the very same pillar that rose in her path before. The path to the right had led her straight to the demon and the path to the left was shrouded in mystery.

Adelaide chose the left tunnel and continued through. She walked and walked but still the dreaded sight appeared before her. The air gradually heated up, until it was glowing red. This is the first light Adelaide has seen in days but it brought her no joy. Yet it also brought her no fear. She stood, supporting herself against the wall, and calmly watched as a burning hellhound emerged from the flames. The heat was surprisingly pleasant and suddenly the whole tunnel was illuminated. The light burned her sore, unused eyes and yet Adelaide could not help but stare with fascination at the beautiful structures formed by these ancient minerals.

The demonic being stood majestically in her path. A rusted steel collar hung around its neck, sharp spikes protruding threateningly from it, and the creature exposed its dagger-like fangs as it growled. There was something about the giant animal that Adelaide hadn't noticed before. Looking into its eyes, she saw the eyes of the angel that had appeared to her first.

"Your deceit will fool me no more, fiend!" Adelaide hissed at the hell hound.

The beast snarled and leaped at her. The girl closed her eyes and shielded her face but a moment later looked up to see the demon gone, leaving nothing but a trail of fire. She stood for a moment, wondering whether to stay by the light or venture further into the cave, back into the darkness. Almost instinctively, her feet began to carry her forward and soon the blackness of the tunnel consumed her once more.

After walking for what seemed like an eternity, skilfully avoiding stalactites, Adelaide began to hear a soft drone. It sounded like a mystical melody, gentle and playful. Hastily, she made her way towards it until a delicate purple glow caught her sight. It seemed to be coming from the rock itself, but as Adelaide got closer, she saw that it was radiating from a large object that rested on the rock. It was wrapped in a hay bag that was now soaked through from the moisture of the cave.

Adelaide removed the bag and stared mesmerised at the beautiful translucent glowing blade of the Dragonslayer. It felt much heavier than she remembered, but she picked it up and with all her might carried it back through the dark cave. Even the walk from the village to Gabriel's cabin did not appear as long as this, but she persisted. She tripped, fell and cut herself on the sword many times, but fatigued and drenched in her own blood she kept walking.

She felt a feather under her foot. This was it; the dead end, the blocked entrance. Adelaide felt the boulder with her hand, then stepped back and smashed the sword against it. The weapon that could cut through anything lived up to its promise, cracking the slab of stone. Several beams of light jumped into the cave. Adelaide struck at it again and again until she found herself walking through the rubble and falling to her knees in the soft green grass. The sun was blinding her but she could make out a figure not far from the cave.

The old man was slumped over in a chair, asleep, with a pile of books and empty bottles at his feet. A burnt-out fire slept by his side. Enraged, Adelaide rushed towards him and kicked the chair over. Gabriel woke up and looked up at her startled. Amusement lit up his face upon recognition.

"Took you long enough to figure it out! If you made it to two weeks, I would have to go in there myself to get you out," he laughed.

In all her fury, Adelaide kicked the man repeatedly until sickness, exhaustion and the sudden outburst of energy took their toll and she collapsed to the ground.

Chapter 26

The Heir

Adelaide opened her eyes. A torch burned in her hand. Cold wet mossy stone surrounded her. Stalagmites rose from the floor of the cave. Adelaide screamed out hysterically and rushed backwards only to be met by more rock. It was as warm with sunlight. Crying, she banged her fists against it.

"Here ye go again, lass." Roger stood just beyond the sphere of light.

His long thin hair was as white as she remembered, and a dark brown leather hat covered his head. He was slumping against the wall, fidgeting and looking uneasy.

"Be careful, lass." He begged, "Soon the wrath of fire will be upon ye. Ye will not feel it, ye will not know it, but the day that it consumes ye will be the day this kingdom falls."

A sudden ringing sounded through Adelaide's head and she doubled over with her eyes tightly shut, covering her ears.

"It's all right." She heard Gabriel's gentle voice.

Adelaide sat up to find herself back at the cabin. Cloths were pinned over the windows, but the bright sunlight still found its way into the house. A warm fire was burning near her. Gabriel handed her a chalice of water and she gulped it down.

Adelaide felt around. She had never been so delighted to feel the rough fur blanket that covered her, the creaky wooden floor and the hot dry stones of the hearth. So overcome by joy, she laughed and laughed like a woman gone mad.

Apart from a throbbing headache and a slight cough, she felt better.

Starving, she started on the basket of apples and berries that Gabriel placed by her side. The anger she felt towards him in the cave was gone, replaced by gratitude and appreciation. When she emptied the basket, she demanded more.

"You've been in that tunnel for eleven turns of the moon and asleep for another two. You need to slow down if you wish to get better," he replied, handing her a bowl of some fragrant herbal remedy.

Adelaide rested for a while, then got up and went down to the stream to bathe and change from her filthy dress. With a fresh one on, she danced back to the cabin but not before taking a moment to admire the blue sky and the grand woodland that surrounded her. How she missed the luxury of sight and sound!

There was so much she never noticed about it; the thick scent of the pines that overlapped the smoke of the fire and the orchestra of sounds that surrounded her. She could hear the stream running over the pebbles, the animals rustling through the leaves. Suddenly, she could distinguish a fox from a hedgehog by the sound of their feet. Everything she heard was clearer and more defined.

"So, you're finally ready," Gabriel spoke, leaning casually on the frame of the door.

Adelaide pondered the statement for a moment. After years and years of training she was both alive and stronger than ever before, she had acquired an education and the skills of swordfight, archery, hunting and many more. She developed courage and perseverance. With her training complete, would she have to leave?

Days passed and Adelaide returned to her full strength. She found herself standing at the edge of a cliff, looking down into the gorge. She could see it now, the tiny pool of water at the bottom. The fear that she suffered several years ago was gone. She was ready. Looking to the old man that stood next to her, Adelaide nodded.

"And... jump!" he commanded.

Together they leaped off the cliff. Adelaide waved her arms around aimlessly at first, then straightened her body and dived down like an eagle towards its prey. She entered the water perfectly, barely making a splash. Climbing out of the tiny lake, she squeezed the water from her hair and clothes and turned proudly to her mentor. He smiled at her but there was so much sadness in his emerald eyes.

They returned to the cabin and feasted on a rabbit that they caught on the way. They sat out by the fire, with a barrel of ale between them as dusk began to set.

"All right, your turn," Gabriel spoke, drunkenly waving a chalice at her, "Most ridiculous merchant you've ever seen."

"Ahh, that one's easy. I was in a city not far from the capital when a man stopped me in the street claiming to be selling the finest elixir to cure any sickness. He gathered a crowd and asked for a sick man to help him with the demonstration. One went up to him and drank the entire bottle. Then he said he felt better and even did a wee jump. The crowd started cheering, folk started demanded the potion. Not a moment later, the constable turned up, demanding to know what's happening. The cured man fell to the ground and the merchant was arrested for trickery and dealing poisons. The crowd all went their way but I stayed, hoping to pick a coin or two from the pockets of the fallen man. Next thing I know, he stood up and grabbed all the remaining bottles of the strange concoction and walked away shouting about how it was the best rum he'd ever tasted!" Adelaide reminisced fondly, "Now, I have a question. What was the biggest beast you have ever slain?"

"A dragon," Gabriel replied nonchalantly.

"A dragon? A real dragon?"

"Aye. The biggest one was in a kingdom far north of here. First time I went in, the beast broke my sword and all but took my life. I returned many months later with the newly crafted Dragonslayer, made purely for that purpose," the old man spoke proudly.

"Who made it?"

"A blacksmith."

"From what?"

"A rare alloy that has never been seen before or since," Gabriel replied, lost in the memory, "crafted by a mad alchemist. By God, you should have seen how that man lived! He was banished to the very edge of his kingdom and lived in an abandoned tower. The sun never shone down on it, the woods died around it, the people stayed away."

The sun had set and the mood turned gloomy. Adelaide was about to speak out about her vision from the cave but Gabriel interrupted her.

"Like many others, he was seeking the Gift. You must know that if you are to inherit it, they will not leave you. The hell hound, the old man with the crooked cane and, God forbid, the alchemist himself will follow you wherever you go. They will torment you for eternity. There is no escaping that. Could you live with it?"

"Aye," Adelaide replied, knowing that she had already become as accustomed to them as one can be.

"This Gift, as much as I try to deny it, is from God. It carries more power than even I know. Use it for good, Adele, for I know good still resides within you."

"You speak as though you fear it will leave me."

"I do. I pray I am wrong."

With that, Gabriel suddenly leaned forward and grabbed her by her left forearm. A cold wind picked up and the night sky darkened until no stars could be seen. Swarms of choughs flew towards the cabin and circled above the two rangers.

The sadness in the old man's eyes struck Adelaide in the heart.

"Six summers ago, I took you in because you reminded me of my daughter, but then I chose you as my protégé. Now, I see you as my friend. My last friend on this earth but one that I must still part with."

"No, Gabriel, what are you talking about?" Adelaide shouted through the sound of the gale that had grown around them.

Silently, he hugged her with one arm, the other still gripping the skin of her left forearm.

"And thank you. For freeing me." The old man spoke in a whisper, releasing her arm and standing up.

Adelaide watched him. Gabriel stood as majestic as ever, dressed simply and with no sword in his belt, no cloak over his shoulders. His greying blonde hair was blown about by the wind, his beard covering his strong jawline. His once youthful green eyes now looked darker, older. Oh, how handsome he must have been at one time.

His muscular arm no longer bore the rose.

With one last smile, Gabriel turned and walked into the woods. Adelaide jumped up and ran after him, begging him to return. She ran around, searched and called, fighting the gale but still she could not find him. It was as if he had just vanished into the night. Adelaide collapsed to her knees in tears. That's when she saw it. On her left forearm, where Gabriel held her, was a small black mark. Looking closely, she realised what it was.

An image of a rose bud.

Part 3

The Bandit

Chapter 27

Evil Unleashed

For days, Adelaide waited, yet her mentor did not return.

It was as if he was never there.

All of his belongings were left behind; the weapons, the clothes, the barrels of ale. He had vanished like a shadow in the night.

The fire had not been lit in days. The logs that lay around it were covered in dew and moss. The rooms were filled with silence. The whole cabin stood abandoned.

Adelaide knew she had to face the reality that he would not return. Wherever she looked reminded her of him; the empty silver chalices on the table, the chair on which he used to sit, the knife that he used for whittling. She knew she had to leave the woods, to hide her sorrows in the hustle of a city.

She dressed warmly, preparing for the days to soon grow darker. Those old fox fur boots, the long skirt that covered her breeches, the leather vest: all crafted right here in the woods. The sleeves of her shirt covered her arms, but through the yellowing fabric, she could see a faint mark on her skin. Tentatively lifting her sleeve, Adelaide studied it closer.

The mark was the same as when she first saw it, a small black bud. It would bloom to be a rose, she knew that, but would it die on her flesh as Gabriel's did? At last, she bore the very Gift that gave him such power.

One thought weighed heavy on her mind: for six years, he taught her in ways of war and scholarly arts. He brought her up as a daughter. Why do that if the rose alone was enough to achieve greatness?

He left so many riddles, so many questions unanswered. Was it due to indifference or his faith in her ability to find the truth?

Adelaide attached a scabbard to her belt and walked slowly over to the weapons rack. There were at least a dozen shiny steel swords but they were not the ones she wished to take. She gently lifted it out; the deadly beauty, the shining masterpiece of craftsmanship, the Dragonslayer.

She had held this sword before, but its majestic grandeur stunned her just as the first time she laid eyes on it. The intricate carvings on the handle told a tale of a fearless knight facing a beast most terrifying. The blade was luminescent, emitting a hypnotic glow that was almost otherworldly. So, this is the only weapon known to pierce the scales of a dragon.

After admiring the weapon for a few moments, Adelaide carefully sheathed it. Gabriel's ruined cloak lay folded over the back of a chair. Lifting it up, she studied the ancient symbols embroidered onto its hem, yet understanding still did not reach her. This language was one that Gabriel had not taught her. The runes were stitched into the moss-green fabric with iridescent golden thread. She placed the cloak over her shoulders, to take with her in memory of that remarkable man.

On her way out, Adelaide attached the quiver to her back with leather straps and put the bow over her shoulder and across her body. The tension in the bow was enough to hold it in place, and the young woman had complete confidence in the durability of the magical tool. Lifting the hood of her cloak, she looked back at the house one last time.

For six whole years, this place was her home and hearth. The burnt-out logs were piled up in the fireplace, the walls of which have turned black from the soot. The table was still littered with empty chalices and dirty bowls as well as knives and shreds of wood. Yet nothing stood on the shelves on the other side of the cabin; Gabriel knew they would not be spending another winter here. The door to the closet was ajar. That little room was once filled with swords and weapons but had later become her private bedroom. It will remain uninhabited for a long time now.

The sun shined in thought the doorway, casting a silhouette that stretched along the wooden floor and far wall. The figure was a grandiose one, a cloaked enigma. Adelaide moved her hand and watched the shadow move, amazed at how much she resembled her mentor. But he was gone, and so she too must go. Turning away from the hushed tranquil stillness of the little cabin, Adelaide made her way past the campfire and, after skilfully leaping onto the horse, through the narrow path and into the fields.

The vast farmland was being tended by the labourers with their horses and dogs. The hounds noticed her departure from the enchanted woods and howled in her direction. A farmer looked up towards her and soon calls of surprise and outrage sounded from all directions. Adelaide turned the horse away from the town and galloped until the farmland was long behind her.

She passed several settlements, but remained on the move until the walls of a large city appeared on the horizon. It had been a long time since she had to pass through a city gate, but still she knew how to enter unnoticed. Yet something inside of her drove her forward, towards the guards. Adelaide walked the horse slowly until she towered before them.

"Remove yon hood, traveller," ordered one of the men as if he had spoken than phrase a thousand times.

Adelaide dauntingly pushed the hood back and met their surprised stares with a glance of superiority.

"I see 'em every now and then, cloaked and equipped for battle, rangers and the like, an' they are never good news, but I 'ent ne'er seen a lass dressed as one," muttered one of the guards.

"Get off the horse, girl, and put them weapons down! We 'ent having this in our city," commanded the other, walking over to her with his hand on the hilt of his sword.

"Step aside!" Adelaide heard herself speak. The power rushed through her, enriching her voice with authority.

The guards froze in place. The one reaching for his weapon began to draw it but stopped when his eyes locked on hers, and released it back into the scabbard. The other glanced rapidly between Adelaide and his associate.

"Step aside," she repeated sternly.

He took a few steps back while the other, still looking between them, began to protest but reluctantly bowed his head and stepped back. Adelaide walked the horse slowly past them, savouring the power she now held. Once within the walls of the city, she jumped off the horse and led it to the nearest stable. The stable boy was paid generously to take good care of the animal, knowing little that the coins given to him were in his own pocket a mere moment before.

As she walked towards the nearest tavern, Adelaide could not deny that she dearly missed this life. As the young ranger made her way through the streets, more and more money just happened to fall into her hand and was soon thrown on the table in exchange for a hot meal and a delicious brew, just as dusk began to conquer the city.

There she was again, after all these years, sitting in a dark corner of a tavern, listening to the drunken rambles of the people around her, waiting for someone to accidently mention any wealth they had come by. Yet now she knew so much more. Every word spoken across the room she could distinguish, every shiny coin she could see. Adelaide was no longer the scavenger, she was the wolf, and her prey was just begging to be caught.

Soon, she found herself following a drunk out into the dark streets. As he walked, blissfully unaware that he was caught in her web, his purse got lighter, a ring disappeared from his finger and even the dagger in his belt was delicately removed. Adelaide was walking away from him, proud of her skill and even a little amazed by how easy it had suddenly become when she stopped and looked over her shoulder.

The man stumbled along, supporting himself against the wall of a house. Such a pitiful sight! He was so worthless, so insignificant and so… vulnerable. She spun around on the heel of her foot. A dark shadow quickly approached him like a black cloud. He was suddenly on his knees coughing and chocking on the blood that ran from his throat. A hooded figure stood over him, watching him die as he reached out for her help and she kicked his hand away. He lay in the dirt motionless but with his eyes wide open, still staring at the horror that had taken his life. Yet she watched in silence as blood poured from his neck and a red pool grew on the dirty street. By the time his body was discovered, she was long gone.

The full moon shined down through the pale wispy clouds as dense smoke from the city ascended into the sky. It was on this calm night that an ancient and powerful darkness rose from its fiery tomb. The image on Adelaide's arm was nothing more than a little bud, but it would soon grow into an unstoppable force that had been imprisoned and governed by the sharpest discipline for so many years and has at last been set free.

Chapter 28

An Introduction

"Adelaide!"

Hearing her name, the girl looked up. Her mother was calling her from the porch of their little mud house. Barefoot, she walked across the dusty little path. The woman before her was angelic, her very skin seemed to emanate light so bright that Adelaide could not even dare to look at her face for fear of being blinded. Instead, she studied the long black hair that escaped from the woman's cotton hat and draped her delicate shoulders. There was a comforting presence about this figure that brought warmth to Adelaide's heart. The voice that she heard was so gentle, so loving but it echoed, as if spoken in the distance and reflected many a time.

"Could ye take these here pots to Geoffrey?" the woman spoke, handing Adelaide three small clay pots.

The girl hugged two of them with one arm and took the third in her other hand. Humming quietly to herself she made her way through the serene undisturbed streets to another little mud hut that stood near the path leading down to the water. She went to knock on the door, but it opened soundlessly of its own accord, revealing a dark empty room. Adelaide stepped inside and looked around.

"He took the fish to the city," the familiar voice made Adelaide jump. "Just leave 'em on the table, he'll be coming back later today."

She delicately placed the pots on a nearby table and walked outside. Jon was standing by the steps, playing with a strand of straw.

"Strange seeing his house so empty, no?"

Adelaide nodded.

They walked along the cliff, looking out into the sea. The winds have changed in the recent weeks, bringing the first sheltering gusts of summer. Adelaide felt the warmth on her face and looked up. What she saw was not the bright afternoon sunshine but, instead, a fire that was dying in the hearth.

She sat up and looked around, finding herself in what appeared to be a room at the inn. The bed was but two steps away, yet she was on the floor, fully clothed and with all her gear still fastened to her body. Two empty bottles were by her side and she had a stale taste of rum on her tongue.

Suddenly, beginning to remember the events of the night before, Adelaide searched around for the dagger. She found it tucked into her belt, still red with blood.

"What have I done?" she whispered in horror, wiping it on the hem of her dark skirt.

Pulling up the sleeve of her shirt, the young swordswoman studied the small black tattoo. It brought her solace to see it there, but something about the little rose bud appeared different. It looked so incredibly real, so alive. Taking a deep breath, Adelaide got up.

Once again, she found herself in a tavern. The voices were hushed, mostly whispering about the criminal that took his first kill the night before. They spoke of a mysterious warrior that rode into the city. Adelaide began to notice every glance in her direction, every gesture towards her cloak or weapons. They knew. They all knew it was her.

Two constables walked in. Adelaide pulled back her hood and quickly removed the bow from her body, laying it across her knees under the table.

The constables glanced at her and mumbled something to each other. The whole room seemed to have gone quiet. The men walked over to her and she placed her hand on the hilt of the Dragonslayer, ready for a fight. They stopped right before her table and looked at her for a moment.

"What's a pretty lass like ye doing 'ere all by y'erself?" one asked, taking a seat in one of the empty chairs.

Adelaide let out a subtle sigh of relief. She noticed the voices of the townspeople were as loud as ever.

"Aye, ye heard about the filthy dog that's been causing trouble last night?" spoke the other constable, sitting down. "They say it was one of the bandits that are hiding out in the woods nearby."

"Bandits?" Adelaide's eyes shot up.

"Aye, but don't ye worry, girl, men like us will protect ye."

"What woods?" she asked sternly.

"Eh?"

"What woods are the said bandits hiding out in?" she demanded with little patience.

"The ones just east of 'ere," the constable replied, a little startled.

"What do ye want to know for?" the other asked.

Adelaide remained silent.

"Do you have a husband... or a father to help take care of them?"

"No, I have no-one," Adelaide replied. She closed her eyes, instantly regretting her mistake.

"Then why such interest? Surely ye're not planning to go out there and investigate it all by yerself?" asked the man, glancing towards the other with a malicious smile.

"No," spoke Adelaide, standing up.

She walked out of the tavern and towards the stables. It was dark inside, hidden from the sunlight by a thin straw roof. Adelaide heard footsteps behind her. Assuming it to be the stable boy she turned around, only to find herself facing the two constables.

"Followed me?" she asked. "That's some poor judgement on your part."

Their hungry grins were wiped from their faces as their heads rolled down into the straw.

Quickly glancing around, Adelaide could not find her horse. She decisively walked towards one of the others; a beautiful cocoa-brown mare with a black mane. Holding out her hand as Gabriel once did, she approached the animal but instead of bowing its head, the horse reared and stomped its hoof. Adelaide tried again, but with a similar result. The animal was not bowing to her power.

After a few moments of struggling, she finally found herself mounted on the horse's back. This animal was as difficult to control as the previous was before Gabriel calmed it. Eventually, Adelaide galloped out of the stables, over the decapitated corpses and through the streets. People were screaming and jumping out of her way. An unlucky few got caught beneath the hooves. Indifferent to their suffering, Adelaide galloped on, leaving a trail of destruction after her. Hearing the commotion, the guards at the gate turned to investigate, only to be rammed to the side by the horse as it ran out of the city and towards the woods.

Adelaide rode east until she reached the woods. Dismounting, she let the animal go and continued by foot. Soon, she heard voices. Sneaking towards them she crouched in the bushes and listened.

"… Twenty-three, twenty-four. Twenty-four coins of gold from the caravan."

"And not to mention the lovely furs…"

"And the meat!"

"Still, starting a fire this close to the edge of the woods was a bad idea."

"But we were so hungry! And if we took the meat back to the camp, we'd have to share it."

Adelaide could see three men. Drawing her bow, she aimed at one of them; a perfect target, sitting by the fire, looking into the flames. The arrow pierced his skull and his lifeless body collapsed into the dirt. The other two jumped up and drew their weapons. In an instant, one took his last breath as a translucent sword pierced his heart and the other was on his knees, disarmed and stunned.

"You will lead me back to your camp, where I will kill every filthy bandit I see," Adelaide hissed at him.

Almost without his own volition the man rose to his feet and walked slowly into the woods. They walked and walked until they reached the camp. There must have been ten men at most. Some were sitting around the large fire, others sharpening swords or carving arrows. Basic tents were placed in a semicircle surrounding the group but one stood out. It was bigger and had a light burning inside. This must be the tent of their leader.

Some of the bandits glanced up. In an instant, weapons were drawn, and the men were on their feet.

Adelaide quickly sliced the throat of her hostage and took out two others with arrows before they got close. The rest she faced with her sword. They struck at her relentlessly but none could even leave a scratch. Her dark cloak moved between the trees like a mythical ghost of death, dancing with the men she knew could not survive her wrath. They fell one by one, mortally wounded, until just three remained. Looking around horrified they backed away from her. Drawing her bow once more, she shot one of them and aimed at the other.

"Stop!" a voice came from the leader's tent. Two men emerged. One walked towards her with his hands held up, surrendering. His greasy long hair was scraped back, revealing a thin face with deep set eyes and high cheekbones.

"Stop this madness. Why do you choose to slaughter my men?" he spoke calmly.

"Why did your men choose to slaughter innocent folk?" Adelaide shot back.

"For fun. For money." The man replied honestly. "Not unlike yourself."

"What?"

"From your skill I suspect it was you who murdered and robbed that man in the city of Gransdew but one moon ago," the man explained eloquently.

Adelaide lowered her bow.

"We are not so different," the leader continued in a calm tone. "Except of course that you are gifted with far greater skill and agility than the rest of us."

"Flattery will not save your life," she replied.

"But I assure you that in sparing our lives you will gain an opportunity."

"What opportunity?"

"To fight alongside an army of others, to cause far more chaos than you can alone."

"What makes you think I want that?"

"I do apologise. It was stupid of me to assume you would. I had not considered that you would much rather waste your skill thieving and murdering an occasional drunken fool," the leader's voice turned sharper as he edged closer to her.

"Enough of this, she killed our men!" protested one of the bandits.

"If one fighter can take out eleven others, they alone are surely far more useful," the leader reasoned.

"What are you offering me?" Adelaide addressed him.

"Travel back with us to our main camp and join us."

"But… but she's a woman!" spoke another bandit. He was instantly silenced by an arrow that pierced his neck.

Lowering her bow once again, Adelaide looked at the remaining three bandits. What did she have to lose?

"You will take me with you," she spoke as power flowed through her, "you will surrender to me and you will accept me as your leader."

Adelaide surprised herself with her words, but that could not match the looks of astonishment on the faces of the bandits. The thin grey face of the leader showed so much more. In his eyes, Adelaide saw admiration. They all nodded, unable to resist her word, but he was the only one to be truly overcome by it.

"My name is Talon," he spoke, bowing.

Chapter 29

The Initiate's Trial

A small wooden caravan was being pulled by a single horse through the planes of Starkenhaart. Adelaide sat on the edge with her feet hanging off, looking out into the distance. It was mid-afternoon and the sun shined brightly over the fields. She pulled her hood up to shield her eyes. It was silent apart from the rhythmic stomping of the horse's hooves and the creaking of the wheels. Two bandits sat at the front, guiding the horse while the other stayed near Adelaide.

"Why do they call you Talon?" she asked him.

"None of the men go by their birth names. It is too dangerous in our business," he replied monotonously.

"Why so?"

"There are many gangs of bandits all across the kingdom. This often leads to conflict."

"And this gang you asked me to join, does it hold much power?" Adelaide wondered.

"We may not be the biggest, but we are strong. We have a special advantage," Talon explained.

The other two bandits turned around hastily and muttered to each other.

"What's this advantage then?" Adelaide asked the leader while cautiously watching the others.

"You'll see when you get there. In fact, in order for you to take control, you'll need to defeat our most powerful warrior. That is our tradition." He hesitated on the last sentence. The other two smiled to each other and turned back around.

Adelaide shifted uncomfortably. She had a terrible feeling that she was walking right into a trap. Yet a smile lit up her face when she remembered that there is no man that can defeat her. If it is a trap they are leading her into, then this trap she will break.

They rode through the day and through the night until they reached a small but well defended settlement. A wooden wall stood around it with guards frequently patrolling the perimeter, yet they were dressed in the clothes of common folk, not the uniforms of the city guard.

Talon stood up. Upon seeing him, the bandits quickly opened the gates and the caravan rode in. Adelaide remained sitting down, preparing herself for a tough battle. The gates were slammed shut behind them.

The three bandits jumped off. Adelaide followed. The horse was led away along with the caravan, leaving Adelaide surrounded by these criminals from all directions. She stood there, her hood over her head, the cloak covering her body. Her feet were wide apart and her hand was hovering over the hilt of her sword. She could hear herself breathing heavily. Now she was beginning to regret her decision for this was the first time since Adelaide was given the Rose that she felt truly frightened.

"I welcome a new member to our… cause," announced Talon in a strong voice that was not new to commanding these men.

Adelaide held her head up high and removed her hood. Taking a deep breath, she prepared herself for the worst. Every moment seemed to drag for days as she looked into the eyes of the men before her. Holding out her arms she slowly spun around, revealing her face to all the bandits that have now gathered around. There were whispers and mutters in the crowd but Adelaide found that she could not concentrate on their words. A man walked up to her from the crowd. He was a little older than her, with a short black beard and sapphire blue eyes. He reached out towards her and she flinched away.

"Welcome to the gang!" he laughed, patting her on the shoulder, "I'm Hunter."

He had a friendly smile and Adelaide nodded back. The others shouted greetings and began to disperse.

"Wait!" commanded Talon. "The girl is not a mere bandit, you see! She is our new leader!"

The men silenced and stared at her with looks that varied from bewilderment to amusement.

"So, she will be put through the initiation," continued he.

"C'mon man, she's just a girl. Ye don't need to do this," Hunter said quietly to his leader.

"At dusk, we travel to the woods!" stated Talon, ignoring the protest.

The men cheered and returned to their posts. Adelaide remained with Talon and Hunter.

"So what's the initiation?" she asked them.

"You'll see. We don't want to spoil the surprise just yet," replied the leader nonchalantly before walking away.

Hunter stepped closer to her.

"Listen lass, ye won't live through this. Come, I'll open the gate for ya. Just don't tell no-one 'bout this place," he whispered.

"No. There is nothing I won't live through." Adelaide remained persistent.

"All right then. Well, there's still time before dusk, so come get some food and drink."

The swordswoman followed him. She sat by the fire with some other bandits, laughing and feasting until the sun began to set.

A young bandit sat across the fire from her. He watched her, listened to her every word. He had a handsome face and a darkly coloured bandana covered his hair.

Talon walked over to her.

"It's time."

Adelaide eagerly jumped to her feet.

"But I must insist that you fight with a different sword," he spoke.

"Why?" she shot back, startled.

"The initiation must be done fairly for everyone who attempts it. We cannot let one have an advantage over another."

"What makes you think my sword will give me an advantage?" Adelaide was becoming agitated.

"It was… brought to my attention."

She had not prepared for this. Breathing slowly, she recalled her years of training. The power and skill came not from the weapon, but from herself.

"Very well," she removed the scabbard from her belt, "but if I find it missing…"

"It will be returned to you should you succeed," Talon took it delicately.

"Take mine, I just had it sharpened," said Hunter, handing her a sword.

Adelaide ran her finger along the blade. It was sharp, she was not deceived. Satisfied, she walked to the woods. All the bandits followed her, splitting up into little groups. They drunkenly shouted, gambled on her outcome and joked about the other unfortunates that had attempted the initiation. The only men to walk in silence were Talon, who was watching her intently, Hunter, who looked sadly towards the ground and the mysterious young bandit who followed her closely.

Upon reaching the woods, Adelaide continued through the bushes until she reached a small opening. The white moon was shining down, but grey clouds stretched across the sky like the crooked fingers of a witch. The woods were dark and the swordswoman could barely see the men that had now quietened and spread around the perimeter of the opening like onlookers of a sport, leaving her in the middle, awaiting her opponent like a gladiator awaiting a lion in a colosseum.

That's when she saw it. A glimmer in the darkness beneath the trees. A reflection of the moonlight in the eyes of a giant beast. It stepped out before her.

Adelaide felt her heart drop. She remembered the first time she saw one of them, when she was still with Gabriel, in the enchanted woods. The creature stood on two feet and towered over her. And there it was, the monster that could kill hundreds with its unstoppable might. A werewolf.

Yet the initial shock quickly faded. This beast was no match for the hellhound that Adelaide had to face since, or the other horrors she had encountered. She found herself forced to accept that Gabriel's deranged training really did work. Adelaide felt no fear.

Holding up her sword she stared into the eyes of the beast. Gasps were heard from the crowd, followed by cheering and laughter which soon quietened as the wolf charged towards her. She knew that she was the first to challenge it so fearlessly. The animal leaped at her, its jaws open, but Adelaide swiftly manoeuvred to the side. It rose to two feet and howled. The sound resonated through the woods like thunder. Birds took off from the nearby trees. This was the werewolf's display of power. Adelaide did not even flinch.

The animal attacked again, grabbing at her with its massive claws but the swordswoman deflected them. Blood splattered onto the grass as her sword scratched its paw. The bandits stood about in mesmerised silence.

The battle continued until Adelaide ducked under the beast and drove her sword through its shoulder. The wolf cried out in pain and took a few quick steps away from her.

"This is where I send you straight to hell, monster!" Adelaide called out with malice as she approached the wolf and raised her sword for one final hit.

"Stop!"

Talon jumped in between her and the beast.

"Stop, you've won. You've won," he seemed genuinely concerned for the animal. "Let him go."

A young woman elbowed her way out from behind the men and ran towards the wounded animal. She was dressed in the simplest attire of an undyed linen dress, much like the clothes worn by poor peasant girls. A grey hat covered her hair.

The werewolf was more than thrice her size, but it collapsed at her feet at if she was a queen. She sat next to him and cradled him in her arms. The wolf transformed back into a human. He had long tangled hair and an unkempt stubble. Even as a man, he was bigger and more muscular than the others, but there he lay on the ground, naked and hurt, desperately gripping his shoulder in an attempt to stop the gushing blood. He was glaring at her with his dark eyes, which then turned apologetically to his leader.

Talon was staring at Adelaide. There was a look of distaste in his eyes and a subtle hint of anger.

"I pass over the leadership to you, Silverblood," he said reluctantly and stormed away.

"Silverblood?" Adelaide asked.

"Aye, for the silver locks in your hair," explained Hunter. He bowed dramatically and laughed. Throwing his arm around her shoulders he led her back to camp.

The bandits followed her, cheering and calling out. The night was spent drinking and celebrating and Adelaide could not help but be grateful for the warm feeling of companionship that she so dearly craved.

Chapter 30

Orientation

"We control the land from here down to Gransdew in the south-east and to Rynell in the west," Talon explained with aid of a map.

"And Ghyrock?" Adelaide asked, pointing to a large city located between this settlement and the capital city of Starkenhaart.

"Just beyond our borders, held by a small group of highly trained men, who were once in the King's guard, but now are just thieves and bandits," Talon explained, leaning over the table.

"They would make useful allies and the city would put us closer to the capital," Adelaide proposed.

"They don't ally with anyone. They see themselves to be greater than the rest of us. Why would you want to be closer to the capital anyway?" The pale man asked.

"I did not become the leader of this group to continue stealing coins from peasant and robbing caravans."

"So what are you planning?"

Adelaide thought for a moment. What was she planning? Her head was full of schemes, her eyes were scanning the map in search of a tactical advantage and her fingers were tapping anxiously on the table. She wanted power. Gold was no longer her goal; it was simply the means of realising her plans. She desired something far greater.

"A rebellion," she whispered.

"You must be mad!" he stuttered. "We can fight, sure, but we stand no chance against the King's knights."

"Not yet we don't," Adelaide gave him a wink and walked out of the large, decorated tent that has now become hers.

She picked up a bottle of rum and took a big gulp.

"Walk me through it. How does this group operate?" she asked Talon.

"We make gold from plunder mostly. We have scouts scattered all around our territory, some in small groups, some alone. They watch out for any rich merchants, messengers and transported goods and either report back here or take it themselves," he explained.

"And the King has done nothing about it?"

"The King does little about anything. Everything is run by Darius, the royal advisor. The kingdom would be in ruins without him. We have a contact within the King's castle, a brother of one of our men, he reports to us if there are any patrols sent out or any changes that would concern us. He works willingly with us... sometimes."

"I see. Bribery."

"Bribery or beatings. Either way, we know all that happens in the castle."

Adelaide nodded, looking around at her subjects.

"They are just sitting around, doing nothing," she pointed out.

"More and more men have been joining over the past few summers. If we send out any more, the King's knights are bound to come investigating," Talon spoke, scraping his hand back through his dark hair.

"What if we were to attack another gang rather than the civilians?" Adelaide suggested.

He considered it for a moment.

"I suppose there is less danger in that," he agreed. "Darius is hardly likely to act if a few known bandits were to turn up dead."

"How many are we bordering?

"Three. The Ghyrock bandits, the group controlling Avenstead in the west and a small group in the south."

"How many men do we have in Rynell, that town between our camp and Avenstead.?"

"A dozen as far as I can recall."

"Send an order for them to begin investigating enemy territory. We will seize Avenstead." Adelaide commanded. "Now the settlement in the south; it is little more than just empty woodland so I doubt we will meet much resistance. Half a dozen men will suffice. If we begin to capture the territories and eliminate other bandit troops, we will soon be able to push the King's guard out of the cities and replace them with our own."

"You plan to steal the kingdom from right under his nose," Talon spoke with admiration, gazing at her with his dark eyes.

"Aye. Now I doubt we will receive any support from the common folk, but if we control the cities, there is little they can do against us," Adelaide mumbled to herself.

Hunter jogged up to her. His round face was lit up as usual.

"The men wish to meet their new leader!" he said, grinning happily.

Adelaide followed him towards the group of bandits that were sitting on the dusty ground, sharpening swords and drinking. She walked with her back straight and her head held up high, as a figure of authority should. Standing in the middle of the group she turned around, looking carefully at each dirty bearded face that was now turned towards her.

"Silverblood is the name I have been given. It is not the name I relate to or even the name I would have chosen for myself, but it is a name that will be celebrated in songs and tales from hereon after as the name of the thief that changed a kingdom! I was born a daughter of a poor man, uneducated and plain, but through the years I have acquired a Gift that cannot be matched nor bettered. I have proven myself worthy to lead you and I tell you now, I will lead you to greatness! No longer will we settle for picking pennies out of pockets and tricking a coin or two from a foolish peasant! No longer will we kill and plunder those that have little to offer for their lives! We will gain land! We will gain power! We will gain more than a mere handful of coins! We will rise and we will fight until the King himself bows to our wrath!"

The men cheered and stomped their feet. They were in the palm of her hand. Adelaide stood wrapped in the warm blanket of arrogance and superiority as they gazed at her the way mortals would gaze at a goddess. How easy they were to manipulate! Even the wary devious eyes of Talon, that had previously glared with resentment that he so desperately tried to hide, were now full of awe and acceptance.

Once the bandits quietened and resumed their duties, Adelaide picked up another bottle and took a long swig.

"Quite a speech," a soft deep voice sounded near her.

She looked over to meet the face of the man who had been silently watching her from the moment she arrived. His bandana was still on his head and he wore a dark blue tunic to match, looking as if he made an effort to appeal to her eye. Adelaide nodded in response.

"I am glad ye survived the fight."

"As am I. Did Talon defeat the beast when he took leadership?" she asked.

"There was no leadership to take. Talon assembled us, found us thieving and offered us a place here. Had it not been for him, many of us would have been caught by the guards and hanged or just murdered by other bandits. He is the one who found Bertrand in the woods. Bertrand has always hated himself for what he is and was near ready to leave this world when Talon saved him. Not one man can match his other form... or at least so we thought. Talon never made Bert fight for him, it was always his choice and he always chose to stand up for his leader. Hence Talon remained at the top. Ye can always rely on a wolf; they are loyal," the man explained.

They had wandered away from the larger group of people and were now sitting with their backs against the wooden wall of the settlement, sharing a bottle of rum.

"Bertrand? I thought the bandits never used their true names?" Adelaide asked.

"Ye've seen him. There's only one nickname we could give him, and no-one dares use it. Hunter jested about it once. Only once."

"I see. And the girl? Who is she?"

"Daisy. She feeds us and cares for our wounds. She's like a sister to us all. But don't let her skinny build fool ye, she can scare the hell out of ya if ya get her angry," he laughed. "Her and Bertie fell in love over the years, they were even goin' to get married. But he couldn't make a vow to God because of what he is; he didn't think himself worthy of her. I think he still doesn't."

"How romantic," Adelaide commented dispassionately. She stood up, brushing the dirt from her skirt.

"I believe the men here need more training if we are to advance in our cause. I want sparring to be taking place constantly for those that remain in this camp and archery targets to be set up just beyond the wall. A seasonal tournament would also serve well in motivating the men," she faced her companion but spoke mostly to herself.

"Sparring, eh?" he said, standing up. "Then why not start now? I challenge ya."

He drew his sword with a smile on his face. Startled, Adelaide mimicked him. She once again wielded the Dragonslayer and her opponent's eyes lingered in fascination on the translucent blade. Throwing back her cloak, Adelaide took a fighting stance. There was little room to fight here as they were surrounded by small tents made from whatever material the bandits could gather, be it leather or cheap rough fabric, but she scanned around searching for the best direction to manoeuvre.

He fought well, blocking her strikes and pushing her off balance but he was no match for her. The others heard the clashing of the swords and gathered around to watch, but it was not long before the handsome young man was disarmed and on the ground. Adelaide sheathed her sword and held out her hand.

"Good fight, you!" she said, helping him up.

"The name's Morrihold," he replied smiling.

Chapter 31

The Conquerors Ride Out at Dawn!

Weeks had passed since Adelaide took leadership of the clan. Now she sat with five others in a small tavern in the city of Rynell. The room was full of smoke and the smell of cheap ale. The loud voices of the people drowned out the quiet conversation the bandits were having, as they leaned in close and discussed their plans.

"There are four camps surrounding Avenstead with no more than ten men at each," spoke a man dressed in the clothes of a farmer.

"Are you sure?" Adelaide asked.

"Aye! We have been scouting the area for weeks and we could not find any others. Now come, we can't talk 'bout it 'ere!"

Adelaide got up and followed the man as he scurried out of the tavern door. In the eyes of the bandits, they owned the territory around this city but to the King's guard they were just criminals and would be hanged immediately if found out. She tensed up uncomfortably at the realisation of how little power they truly held. Covering her scabbard with the runed cloak, she followed the informant through the streets. Despite her recently earned position she could not restrain herself from picking a few pockets on the way.

The man led them to a building that looked like an ordinary, if a little rundown, family home. Boots stomped on the old wooden floor as the bandits entered the house. Inside, a large group of men were sitting around a table, who all looked up anxiously to meet Adelaide.

"What is this place?" she asked, removing her cloak.

"My house," one of them shouted out. "I worked in this city a few years ago, then I joined the gang. These bastards haven't left my house since!"

"This is our camp, in a way, so we don't have to hide out in taverns and inns," explained the disguised bandit that led them here.

"Not that it keeps them from the taverns!" complained a plump, simply dressed woman as she walked in carrying a large bowl of stew. "I married a good, hardworking man! Then he decides to join this bunch of criminals. I spend every day cooking and cleaning after them and still they turn up drunk and dirty!"

Adelaide watched the woman with amusement. The local bandits moved around to make space for their leader and she accepted it with a nod of gratitude. She took a seat at the table, as did Talon and Morrihold who came with her to Rynell.

"Now back to the matters of Avenstead," she resumed.

"Aye, the camps are on each corner of the city," explained one of the local bandits, "we can take them out one by one."

"How close are they to the city wall?" asked Talon.

"Just far enough so the guards don't see 'em from the towers."

"Very well," Adelaide spoke, "we will ride to each camp. Those there who wish to join us may do so…"

"They won't want to join us," someone called out.

"I can be very persuasive," she replied, glancing at those who have already succumbed to her voice.

"And those who refuse, we kill!" cheered the men.

Adelaide woke up the next morning on the floor of the little house, which was barely big enough for one family but now served as a resting place for eighteen people, who huddled together much like the homeless folk she met shortly after taking her first steps into a city. The window shutters were closed but light was creeping in through the cracks. It was early and the air in the poorly insulted house was moist. A chill ran through Adelaide's body and she pulled her cloak tighter around herself. She sat up and looked around. The side of her face was hurting from using the arrow quiver as a pillow but she couldn't help but giggle quietly at how uncomfortable the others looked. Morrihold had awakened too and was lying next to her, staring at the ceiling. Adelaide nudged him and gestured towards the door. The two got up and quietly snuck past their sleeping accomplices.

"So, we're still doing this then?" he spoke as they stepped outside.

"Aye. We are taking the city. Today." Adelaide replied.

"Damn. I need a drink," he announced and headed towards a tavern.

Adelaide followed him and together they sat and drank until the others awoke. Talon was the last to join them.

"The south-eastern camp is nearest to us," he said, passing Adelaide her bow.

She traced her fingers over the metal pattern. How desperately she yearned to use it! It had been weeks since she had participated in a real fight and her heart hungered for blood and murder.

"Then we ride there!"

Soon, eighteen horses were galloping across the border of the two territories and over the hills of this new region. Mountains rose first in the south, then stretching to the west, enclosing the fields of Avenstead like a wall. Snow cloaked their peaks, some of which disappeared into the dark clouds that loomed over the land. Cold droplets of rain began to fall and an icy wind bit at Adelaide's face and neck, tugging at her cloak, pulling her hood from her head. The cloak twisted around the bow that Adelaide placed across her shoulders, pulling at it with force, but its wielder was certain that it would not break.

The stone walls of Avenstead appeared over the horizon and the riders changed their direction and galloped south. The farmers' fields were dead and empty this time of year as the soil was flooded from the constant rains. Mud splashed up from the horses' hooves, splattering the riders behind.

A small camp came into view in the distance. There was no wall surrounding it, just a few tents with a burnt-out fire in the middle. Upon hearing the sound of the horses, the local bandits emerged from cover with their swords drawn. Expecting to face the King's guard of Avenstead, they were surprised by the darkly cloaked riders.

The horses halted and Adelaide walked hers further so that she stood ahead of the rest, right before the startled crooks. Gingerly wiping the mud from her face, she addressed them.

"Standing before you now, is Silverblood of the Rynell bandits," she announced. They held up their swords but she continued, "I urge you to surrender your weapons and your land to our cause. If you refuse, you will face certain death."

The Rynell bandits jumped down from their horses and drew their weapons. The Avenstead gang looked bewildered, first staring at Adelaide, then the men that stood behind her. One of them dropped his sword and held up his hands.

"Never!" shouted one of the others, an elderly man, and in his fury drove a sword through his cowardly accomplice.

The others stepped away from the body that collapsed onto the wet grass. The old man yelled and rallied them to fight, charging towards Adelaide. A moment later, he fell to the ground as an arrow pierced his gut. He wiggled in pain, gasping for help. One bandit took a step towards him but backed away as Adelaide took another arrow from her quiver.

"He will die slowly and suffer a lot of pain. Would anyone wish to join him?" she called out against the ringing winds.

The bandits dropped their swords. Adelaide called Talon closer.

"I need you and four others to stay behind to secure the camp and ensure they keep their loyalty," she said from her horse. "I will ride to the south-western camp with the others."

He nodded and proceeded to carry out her orders.

Before the day was over, Adelaide captured the other three camps and sat with Talon and Morrihold in a tavern in their newly conquered city.

"Remarkable!" said Talon with a grin while shaking the rainwater from his long black hair.

"A cheer to new land and the first of many conquests!" called Adelaide, raising her mug.

Joyful clinks and resounding calls of celebration sounded through the tavern. Over the voices and conversations, the gentle patter of rain on the roof and windows could still be heard.

"What next? Ghyrock? Tarrynsdew?" Talon inquired excitedly.

"We will discuss that tomorrow, for tonight, we rejoice!" she replied, emptying her mug of its contents.

They drank and danced and laughed until the curfew bells sounded, then they left the city and stumbled to the nearest camp, where they drank and danced and laughed some more.

Chapter 32

Divine Purpose

Several days later, Adelaide rode back to what had become known as the Silverblood camp, where she was greeted like a hero. With her, came some of the bandits that rode with them from Rynell as well as those that had joined her in Avenstead. Orders were sent for old, trusted members of the group to ride out to the new land to oversee the camps until the recruits gain her trust.

Once Adelaide dismounted her horse, Hunter approached her with his usual cheerful stride. He bowed dramatically and lifted his hat in the manner of a jester.

"I have heard of yon great successes in the west," he spoke, parodying a court official.

"T'was a great success indeed," Adelaide replied, carrying on the formal impersonation. "And how are matters in the south?"

"The woods are ours!" he yelled excitedly, "scouts have been sent out further, around the mountains of Avenstead and towards the enchanted forest."

"The enchanted forest?" Adelaide's smile dropped as grief reignited inside her.

"Do ye wish me to call them back?" Hunter asked, wary of her response.

"We will find nothing in the forest." She said, composing herself. "Command them to go west."

"Aye." He nodded and hurried away.

As Adelaide walked through the camp, she noticed a change in it.

The bandits were no longer sitting around preparing for fights they would never have. Instead, they were training. It was just as she envisioned it; swords were clashing all around her, cheers were heard from beyond the wall as archers challenged one another to more difficult targets and voices were heard eagerly discussing their next quest. Adelaide approached one of the little tents and peered inside.

Bertrand was sitting cross legged, hiding from the noise. His massive body was slouched to fit into the tiny space, yet his head still brushed the planks of wood used to hold up the sloping roof. He looked irritated, wincing every time another bandit shouted or cheered. Adelaide entered the tent and sat next to him as he glared at her from under his long honey blonde mane of hair. He wore breeches and a dirty old shirt that was too big even for him.

"I see your shoulder's healed." Adelaide pointed out. He offered the response of silence.

"Forgive me, I believe we got off on the wrong foot," she tried again.

"This is not your group to command," he snarled, "they may cheer for ya, but I will not be so easily fooled by a few lucky tricks."

"Luck? It was not luck that conquered Avenstead…" her voice grew harsher with offense.

"No, it was that wicked magic of yours."

"How do you know? And how did you know about my sword, back when I first arrived? Yes, I know it was you who warned Talon."

"I am a creature of evil. I can sense others like me," he replied with a voice full of self-disgust.

"No. What you sense in me is the gift of God. And you fear it. A vile beast like you would resent the power of light," her voice rang with that same familiar influence that had conquered others.

She could see a battle in his heart between the rage at her words and the surrender to the influence of the Gift. He clenched his fist and closed his eyes, stuck in the middle of a struggle that would determine his allegiance. Taking a deep breath, he relaxed and looked back towards her. He supposedly spoke of himself as less foolish than the others, but even he could not stand against the strength of her power. He was at her disposal, just like the rest of them.

"We were met with little resistance so far," Adelaide spoke sternly to him, "but once we venture further north, the larger clans will begin to pose more of a threat. That's when we'll need you to fight. And you'll do it. You'll do it, or you will die."

With that, she stepped out of the tent leaving him staring sorrowfully into space. He did not deserve it. He did not deserve to be forced to fight, to be forced to kill. None of them did. But Adelaide knew that war was inevitable; it was her mission, her purpose to change the fate of the kingdom, it was the reason she was granted her power. It took her so long to realise it but now she knew, and she was more determined than ever to fulfil her place in this colossal puzzle, to play her role in this game. Many would die by her hand or her order but those are the sacrifices that have to be made for the greater good.

As Adelaide paced around the camp, lost in a delusion of her divine purpose, an old hooded man with a crooked wooden cane watched her. His withered wrinkled face stretched into a wide smile, revealing a set of black rotten teeth. He knew of her role and he watched as she gave a perfect performance. A little chough landed on his shoulder. He petted the bird and fed it a wiggling maggot that somehow emerged from the folds of his cloak. His fingers were twisted and dirt was clumped in the wrinkles of his knuckles and under his long yellow nails that curved at the ends like the claws of an animal. The bird flapped its wings and took off from the shoulder that had vanished like a cloud of smoke on a dark night. It flew over the heads on the two bandits that were heading towards Adelaide.

"Where did all these damn crows come from?" complained Morrihold, shooing the little bird away.

"It's a chough, lad," commented Hunter.

"How can ya tell?

"Different colour beaks. Seen hundreds of 'em down south, near the enchanted woods," explained the bearded man.

"You hunted there?" asked the younger bandit excitedly.

"No, my father did. He was the only one from Gransdew who did. Then one day he returned home, looking terrified, wouldn't say why either. After that, we left the town, travelled around, got poor," for the first time, Hunter's voice lost its usual merriment.

"You two, follow me!" Adelaide strode past them, still transfixed by her psychotic ambition.

She led them hurriedly to the main tent and pointed to the tattered map that rested on a wide wooden table that took up most of the already limited room.

"This!" her hand shook as she traced her fingers along the badly drawn river, "who owns this land?"

The two men uncomfortably watched their erratic leader as she twitched and shook.

"Whose is it?" she screamed, slamming the palm of her hand against the table.

"Stormhawk's," replied Hunter nervously, "they're the biggest gang in the kingdom. They will refuse to join us."

"Then they will die," she hissed in response.

"Going against them will start a war for sure!" Morrihold protested. "The King's knights will be sent out."

"They too will die."

"We can't face both Stormhawk and the King in battle. Not yet," the young bandit persisted.

"Then we ride to Ghyrock and recruit the rogue knights," Adelaide stared at the drawing of the city on the map.

"From there, we ride to the capital," added Talon as he confidently entered the tent.

The other two turned to him in surprise.

"You support this mad idea?" Hunter asked quietly.

"Do you have no faith in your leader?" the tall man replied sternly as he walked towards the map.

"Why the capital?" Adelaide looked at him curiously, the way a child looks at a parent that just presented them with a puzzle.

"There is somebody there I need you to meet." Talon replied smiling.

Chapter 33

The Legend of Eylrissen Mountain

The wolf fur draped across Adelaide's shoulders was wet from the rain the moment she emerged from her tent. Her cloak tattered in the wind that almost pushed her from her feet. The cold air tickled her lungs. Still, she wiped her long wet hair from her face and pulled the hood of her cloak further over her head. She could barely see the tent next to her through the fog, but she stumbled towards the main gate of the camp in near blindness. Ten horses stood just beyond the wall with their riders ready and waiting.

"Must I come?" called Bertrand from his horse.

Adelaide ignored him as she struggled to climb up onto her mount. The skirt of her dress was wet and clung to her skin. Frustrated and barely able to walk, she pulled out a knife and put several slits in the fabric. The men ogled at her bare legs as she silently got on her horse and lead the way.

The ride was a long and difficult one. A gale raged around them and keeping the right direction was a struggle. Soon the fields ended and the bandits entered the woods. They rode one behind the other down a narrow path, shielded from the storm by the trees. The horses were walked in order to rest them before commencing the gallop upon leaving the shelter of the wooden sentinels.

The grand stone wall of the city came into view through the dense fog. Adelaide glanced around, trying to find Talon but the bandits were indistinguishable in their cloaks and hoods so she continued towards the city gate. As they got closer, they could make out that it was locked shut.

The horses halted just in front of the gates.

The men looked at her expectantly as Adelaide desperately searched for another way in.

"Those craven ill-bred halfwits! What kind of man would fear a little storm?" she screamed out in rage and then upon composing herself continued, "no, no, this is an advantage. With no men on guard no-one will know who enters the city."

"And how do ye plan on entering the city?" called out one of the bandits.

Adelaide flashed a smile and jumped off her horse. She struggled against the wind towards the thick wooden gates.

"They are impenetrable." She heard from behind.

Grinning to herself, she drew the Dragonslayer and with all her strength drove it in-between the doors of the gate. The wooden bar on the other side almost broke and as Adelaide raised the sword for another strike, it gave way under the immense force of the wind and the gates swung open, knocking Adelaide back. Just like the entrance of the cave she was trapped in before, these gates too could not withstand the power of the magical sword.

Getting back up, Adelaide walked into the magnificent city of Ghyrock and the others followed on horseback. The streets were mostly empty and even the citizens who witnessed her entrance would not have seen her face. The bandits jumped from their horses and walked through the vacated streets.

"This clan, they are not like the other bandits," spoke Talon, "they do not hide out in camps, out of sight of the city guards. They operate in plain sight, but not one man dares to stand up to them. They rule this city, and they know it. We need to be prepared for a fight."

"Where can I find them?" Adelaide interrupted.

"This way," he said submissively.

The houses were sealed off from the weather, with every door locked and every shutter closed. Smoke rose from the few houses that boasted their own chimneys. The bandits approached a large two-storey house.

"Here?" Adelaide asked, surprised. "This house looks as if it should belong to a well-off merchant or a court official."

There was no castle in Ghyrock, but this building was the closest thing to it.

"We will enter," Talon said to the others, "you wait out here and listen out for trouble."

The men groaned discontentedly and sat down in the wet mud against the wall of the house, desperate for even a little cover from the storm.

Adelaide knocked on the thick wooden door. A few moments later, it was opened by a small elderly man dressed in a plain but neat fashion. Adelaide unceremoniously barged in, pushing him to the side. Talon followed, giving the old man an apologetic nod. Shaking his head in disapproval, the servant closed the door. Instantly, the house quietened, sealed from the gale. It was very dark inside, with nothing but a small candle held by the old man to illuminate the corridor. The walls were decorated with swords and mounted deer heads. Despite being much larger and much neater, this house reminded Adelaide of Gabriel's. It was the house of a warrior. The room they were led to by the elderly servant was much brighter and warmer than the rest of the house. A fire was burning in the hearth and a cushioned wooden chair was positioned near it, facing away from the door. A well-built man was lounging in the chair, lost in a book he held in his left hand, resting his chin on the other.

Adelaide cleared her throat. Sighing in an irritated manner, the man slammed the book shut and turned his head without bothering to stand up. With his hand, he gestured for the visitors to approach. Talon obeyed and Adelaide reluctantly followed. The man studied Adelaide with a puzzled look as his eyes traced over her fancy cloak, cut-up filthy skirt and the weapons that she carried. He was most fascinated by the latter.

"You I know," he spoke to Talon in a deep hypnotic voice, "but who is this?"

"Silverblood, leader of the southern bandits," she introduced herself proudly.

"So you succumbed to a woman?" the man purred.

"She is not an easy woman to stand against," Talon replied with a smirk.

Excitement sparked in the knight's eye.

"And how did your animal fair against her?" he asked.

"Bertrand was defeated." Talon replied, tensing his hands, then with a taunting smile added, "may I remind you that not even you or your fellow brave knights could stand against a werewolf."

Feeling mocked, the man jumped to his feet. He was the same height as Talon but much broader and his shadow towered over Adelaide as he stood before the fire. She instinctively reached for her sword, drawing it slightly from its sheath. The pale purple glow of the blade was just visible enough to attract attention. The knight's eyes were transfixed on it in a flash.

"The Dragonslayer!" he croaked in amazement.

Stepping back defensively, Adelaide drew the sword fully and held it at him.

"How do you know of it?"

"It's an old legend. Can this truly be the mythical Dragonslayer? Can it truly... pierce the scales of a dragon?" the man's voice softened in admiration.

"Yes." Adelaide replied after a moment of hesitation.

"This weapon is not from this land. Where did you find it?" By now, his voice was almost a whisper.

"That is none of your concern. What more do you know about it?" She held the weapon firmly.

The knight backed away and lit a candle from the hearth fire. He walked to the other side of the room, pouring candlelight over the giant bookcase that took up the entire wall. He traced his finger across the numerous volumes, muttering to himself, then threw his hands up in joy and pulled a very delicate old tome from the shelf. Adelaide reached out her hand and he passed it over. The letters were in a foreign language but she recognised them.

"The tale of the Eylrissen Mountain?" she looked up, brows raised.

"You read their tongue?"

"Aye, and many others," Adelaide muttered smugly.

"Well, the legend goes that the Eylrissen Mountain harboured a dragon that no man could defeat. His scales were as red as fire and his skin was made of solid rock. Few knights attempted to face him, and even fewer lived to tell the tale. But there was one knight of unmatched strength and valour who forged this sword from solid magic itself and defeated the dragon."

"Who was this knight?" Adelaide struggled to hold back her tears.

"No-one remembers his name," the man replied sadly. "Are you his descendant?"

"I am his heir," she replied, stifling a sob.

"This explains a lot," mumbled Talon.

"If you truly possess his skill in battle, I will not dare to stand against you. I am Sir Hansfell of the Ghyrock knights, and you have my sword at your command." He bowed.

"Your real name?"

"My family name. It gives us authority over the common folk of this city," he explained.

"You carry your former title?" Talon asked in a contemptuous tone.

"Former?" Adelaide turned questioningly towards their host.

"Aye. It is said that all three of the men now known as the Ghyrock bandits had their knighthoods stripped," Talon continued, merely amused by Hansfell's loathing glare. "They were disloyal to the King, exploited their authority and carried out their duties with a revolting degree of cruelty."

The knight breathed heavily through his teeth, desperately restraining himself from punching the taunting bandit in the face. He stared Adelaide in the eye and she stared back, ignoring Talon's mocking babbling. The man that stood before her was the only one she had ever met who knew of the Dragonslayer. He understood her and he could help her learn more about the sword and the magical legends that surround it. Adelaide needed him.

"Then you will be the perfect men for our fight against the King," she spoke unfalteringly. "Summon your associates. And for the love of God, let our men inside the house."

Hansfell nodded and called for his servant. The old man walked slowly into the room, leaving plenty of time for Hansfell to awkwardly try to ignore Talon's stare. The bandit would not normally dare show such open disdain towards a knight, but he knew that while Adelaide was present, the knight was powerless to fight back. Like a Yorkshire Terrier barking ferociously at a Doberman from the safety of his master's skirts, Talon continued to stare at Hansfell with a disturbingly cheerful smile on his face.

Chapter 34

Local Informant

Once the alliance was established and the storm died down to a gentle drizzle, Adelaide rode for the capital. With her came a few of the bandits and Sir Hansfell, while the others stayed behind to secure the city. They journeyed for three days, camping in woods or near small villages in the nights, and resuming at the crack of dawn. Small hills spanned the land and the rain-soaked soil that covered them splashed up from the horses' hooves. The sun emerged from the dark clouds and streaks of light were seen reaching down to earth in the horizon. The view of the cold winter countryside was strangely breath-taking as the hills gave way to the woods and distant mountains rose into the skies. Adelaide turned and flashed a smile at the dirty mud-covered faces behind her. Morrihold smiled back and Hunter called out laughing and galloped faster. His horse overtook Adelaide's and he cheered as he raced ahead. Not willing to let him win, Adelaide leaned down and dug her heels into her own beast. The others followed and the horses raced through the fields. They were forced into single file by a narrow bridge but resumed the race immediately after and galloped towards the grand city that was beginning to creep over the horizon.

She had dreamt of this moment for as long as she could remember, but Adelaide could never imagine that this would be how she would enter the capital city of Starkenhaart; with a powerful weapon in her hands and loyal friends by her side, with an ambition that will one day make this city hers to command.

The horses slowed to a walk as the riders approached the city. The grand stone walls were colossal in height and the magnificent castle overlooked the whole kingdom from deep within the heart of the city. Six huge stone towers rose from the walls, equipped with ballistae and armed soldiers. Smaller wooden guard posts were frequent in between the towers. The city was an impenetrable fortress.

The mighty gate was made from reinforced tree trucks secured together into panels. The entrance to the city was patrolled by a dozen armed guards, who inspected every cart and caravan that entered the capital. Adelaide and the riders joined the queue and while most of them pulled up their hoods and covered their faces, their leader made no effort to disguise herself or her weapons. When confronted by the guards she diffused their suspicions with a few well-chosen words.

The city was full of life, from the loud merchants that urged people to their stalls, to the delightful street performers. Adelaide jumped from her horse and disappeared into the crowd that surrounded them, fascinated by fire dancers and magicians. A lively minstrel played a melody on his lute as he walked around, dancing from one side of his makeshift stage to the other, serenading the wealthy citizens in the crowd as they stood around in their fur cloaks. His voice resonated over the sounds of the city as he sung the words of his ballad.

All hail the great king!
All hail the great queen!
Our hearts are untroubled,
And our sorrows unseen.
The kingdom is rich
In spirit and gold
But in shadows of wealth
There are stories untold.
King speaks of protecting,
Of guarding the folk,
But the bandits ride in;
Sharp sword and black cloak.

Adelaide felt a hand on her shoulder and was quickly pulled out from the crowd.

"Come, we have business to attend to," Talon spoke with urgency.

The bandits made their way through the busy streets with their heads bowed, averting their eyes from the guards that regularly patrolled the city. Adelaide would often stop and stare up towards the grandiose castle or closely study the intricate little brooches at the market stalls. At times, the bandits would fight through a heavily crowded street only to discover that they had lost Adelaide on the way and were forced to return and pull her away from the distractions. As they entered the poorer, emptier region of the city, they turned back to find her admiring a beautiful silver-emerald trinket that she swiped on the way. With a cheeky smile she hid it in a pouch on her belt and caught up to them.

They passed the castle and entered the back alleys, which were lined with pig pens and chicken coops. This was far from the glamour and excitement of the main city centre, the noise of which could still be heard in the distance. The animals moved around, snorting and cooing, and dirty men coughed as they sat leaning against the cold wall with pipes in their twitching hands.

Adelaide was quite a sight in her beautiful dark cloak as she wafted away the feathers from the coops and covered her face from the stench. Yet their walk through the filthy streets soon came to an end when they approached a man in a guard's uniform as he stood leaning nonchalantly on one of the coops. He was young and his shoulder length ash-blonde hair was partially tied back with a ribbon. Although he had a look of boisterous confidence, he flinched slightly when Talon got close.

"So, you received my letter," the former leader announced.

"Aye. And I expect full pay this time," the young guard replied, straightening up.

Talon merely grinned and turned to introduce Adelaide; "This is our... informant, James. He will be of great use to us, if we can persuade him to cooperate."

Hunter's laughter boomed through the little alley. Several menacing sniggers were heard from the other bandits. James suddenly began to look very uncomfortable.

"Listen, this time, if ye dare touch me, I'll fight!" he spoke nervously, drawing a sword.

Still amused, Talon grabbed James's dominant hand, pulled him close and punched him hard in the face. The young man fell against the wall but quickly straightened himself up, miserably holding his bleeding nose.

"And we can always persuade him," Talon added, grinning.

"So, any news from the castle?" Morrihold spoke, holding out a small bag of coins. James reached out to grab it, but Morrihold quickly pulled it back, shaking his head.

"There's a wizard at the castle," James replied with a sigh.

There was a silence among the men.

"Now, I don't want any more of your lies, you lousy halfwit," Hunter rushed towards him.

"No, no, there really is a wizard at the castle!" James jumped back.

"A wizard? What does he look like?" asked Morrihold curiously.

"I only ever saw him once, but he had a hood and a long green robe."

"What's he doing here?" the young bandit was still more fascinated by the wizard than the implications of his visit.

James reached out his blood covered hand towards the bag of gold. Morrihold tossed it over.

"I don't know," James replied with a smirk and turned to go back into the castle.

Talon dashed forwards and pinned him by the neck against the wall.

"You lying swine," he hissed, punching the blonde man again.

Adelaide rested her hand on the angry bandit's shoulder and gently pulled him back. Talon obeyed, releasing the guard. James was accustomed to them taking turns to deliver their beatings and held his head up, challenging Adelaide to do her worst. Yet she did not raise a hand. She stood relaxed and stared him down with a look that bore deep into his mind. The guard was beginning to look uneasy, averting his eyes and fidgeting, but still he stood strong. She took a step closer. He tried to step back but was met with the cold stone wall behind him. Adelaide reached out and gently caressed his cheek. A look of confusion ran across his face, but he did not move. Leaning close to him, Adelaide whispered,

"You will tell me everything you know."

There was so much power in her quiet words that James instantly felt compelled to obey. Yet he resisted it. He squeezed his lips shut and took a deep breath but his resistance was beginning to turn into physical pain. His face turned red and his body began to shake until he collapsed to his knees. Still, he refused to answer.

"Tell me," she whispered again.

"Darius summoned him!" James hissed, exhaling deeply. "I don't know why, but he arrived from the neighbouring kingdom a fortnight ago. Ask me, it has something to do with Avenstead. Yes, Darius knows something's been happening there. But he 'ent sent the knights yet, he can't without the King's orders and the King don't believe there's anything to worry about so ye are all safe for now."

"How did he find out?" Adelaide was becoming concerned.

"Well, I heard him talking to the constables, who reported to him that more and more carts have been arriving safely from that direction, without being raided. The constables were happy and he was too. But then I suppose he realised something must be stirring. So it was ye who started all this?"

"Yes, it was me," Adelaide replied absentmindedly. Distracted by the calculating schemes that were now flying about in her head, she turned and walked slowly in the direction they came from. The other bandits watched her, awaiting orders.

"I don't know what magic you used on me, witch," James shouted after her, "but you'll suffer for it!"

Adelaide merely smiled at his angry words. Her wandering steps turned into confident strides and she began to hurry towards the castle. Glancing at each other, the bandits moved to follow, leaving James slumped in the alleyway, clutching the little bag of gold that was catching the blood dripping from his face into its fabric. He silently watched them retreat, still trying to figure out just what it was that he encountered.

"Where are you going?" one of her bandits shouted after Adelaide.

"We have ourselves a wizard to find," she called back.

Chapter 35

Archaius

A noblewoman entered the castle, an aristocrat from a distant land. She wore a dark red gown of astounding beauty, made with golden thread and jewels that sparkled in the light of the fires. A dark green cloak was placed over her shoulders, the hem of which bore runes known only to the northern kings. Her long ebony-black hair was done up the way a duchess would wear it, with a delicate silver circlet that looked as if it had melted and ran through her locks, so brightly shone her white curls. Even her walk radiated grandiosity, with her head held up high and her hands tightly clutching a small gem-encrusted purse. The mysterious woman conversed with other members of the nobility with such eloquence and wisdom that no-one dared question her stature.

It took Adelaide all the self-restraint she could muster to stop herself from looking around the castle in pure amazement. The building was even more magnificent on the inside. Bulky metal candle holders were secured against the walls and three iron chandeliers hung from the ceiling, illuminating the entire reception hall. The rugs beneath her feet were each worth more gold than all the trinkets and jewels she had stolen in all her life and the long wooden tables struggled under the weight of the mountain of delicious food.

"Good evening." Adelaide heard from behind and turned to face the man she had been trying to avoid. "I did not mean to startle you," he continued with a polite smile, "I do believe I have not yet had the pleasure of being introduced to you."

Adelaide's heart began to race, but she took a deep breath and smiled back.

"Lady Adele of the house Silverblood," she replied with a nod.

"I am afraid you are the first of your house to visit our kingdom," he spoke, struggling to hide his suspicion.

"And you are Lord Darius."

He bowed in response.

"What brings you here from Haarsten?" he probed further.

"Haarsten?"

"Forgive me if I am mistaken, but the runes on your cloak are of the language commonly spoken there. I only presumed…"

"Yes, of course," she quickly interrupted him, "it is simply that you are the first to recognise them."

Darius smiled to himself and nodded slowly. He had a perfectly upright posture, holding his hands behind his back and his shoulders loose. His clothes were not those of a Lord; he wore no jewels and no fur, but rather a modestly designed well-crafted tunic made from expensive burgundy fabric and boots, breeches and shirt of the same colour. His skin was dark, even in this cold winter and his black hair was tied back. The King's advisor excused himself and walked slowly through the crowd, as not to arise concern but once he was out of sight for most of the noble guests, he dashed towards one of the guards. Adelaide watched as the guard listened to Darius's urgent words and obediently disappeared into one of the side rooms. Darius resumed his composed posture and returned to the conversations, yet his eyes would still occasionally pan the room for the mysterious Silverblood woman.

Adelaide knew she had little time. Desperately searching the reception hall for the wizard, she found him entertaining the mesmerised crowd by producing a small flame in the palm of his hand by merely clicking his fingers. Next to him stood another man, who was leaning lazily against the wall. He looked almost bored, despite the women that surrounded him, giggling and batting their eyes. As well as being extraordinarily handsome, he was also dressed like a prince, with a long cloak made from wolf fur and a stunning black tunic with a pattern sewn in silver thread. Long, raven-black hair reached past his shoulders and seemed to fuse with his clothes. Only the wizard seemed to interest him, as he would quickly look up whenever another little flame was produced with eyes of such brilliant blue as can only be compared to a lapis gemstone. Something about this man was familiar.

The wizard's handsome dark friend finally got so bored that he fought his way through his undesired harem and went out to seek more wine, leaving the mage by himself. Adelaide joined the excited crowd and quickly turned around to see whether more guards have been summoned. Happy to discover that there were none, she turned back to find the wizard frozen in place, staring intently at her cloak. Adelaide had long pondered on how to pull him away from the safety of the castle but an easy answer quickly arrived. He was a young man, but there was more knowledge in his hazel eyes than she had ever seen in anyone else and she knew that he too recognised the runes, but was struggling to remember them. A sudden insight struck him and he reached out to her. Adelaide quickly manoeuvred through the nobility and hurried out of the castle, knowing that he would follow. She led him to the dirty back alleys behind the castle wall and turned to confront him.

"Do you know where this cloak is from?" he asked in a concerned tone. His voice was softly melodic.

"The kingdom of Haarsten," she answered loudly.

"There is no such a place," he replied, puzzled.

That was Darius's trap! Half the kingdom will be after her as soon as the nobility take to their beds. The King's advisor would not compromise the merriment of the upper classes for the capture of one con-artist but once they find the mage missing, the guards will tear through the city in search of him.

Night has fallen over the capital but not even the moon could light up the streets as a swirling black cloud hovered over the castle, plunging the city into darkness. From the shadows stepped out the other bandits and Morrihold passed Adelaide a steel sword. She could not allow the wizard to see the Dragonslayer, at least not until he was captured.

"Did you steal it?" the wizard demanded. "Did you steal the cloak? Where is its owner?"

"Why are you so concerned about it?" asked Talon.

The mage did not reply.

"We offer ye an exchange," spoke Morrihold, taking advantage of the situation, "information about your connection to Darius for information about the cloak."

The mage remained silent.

"So he refuses to cooperate?" called out Hunter as his usual grin somehow turned menacing. "Let's beat some sense into him!"

With that, the bandit went to attack the wizard. The young mage quickly raised his hand and a strong current of air blasted towards Hunter, who went flying back into the chicken coops, dropping his sword on the way. The wizard jumped forward and picked it up. He looked uncomfortable taking a fighting stance in his long laurel-green robes but, as the bandits went to attack him, he fought them off effortlessly. In skill and agility, he almost matched Adelaide and he had the advantage of shooting fire or currents of air against his opponents. The wizard defeated the thugs but never killed them, even if given the opportunity, instead knocking them unconscious. As the battle progressed, only he and Adelaide remained standing. They circled each other, threatening and taunting until Adelaide leaped forward. The fight was fast, each of them moving with incredible speed, manoeuvring swiftly away from the other's strike and retaliating instantly. With sudden realisation, the wizard stopped.

"There are few people in the world that can fight this way," he called out.

She nodded, amazed by his ability.

"You are not... You couldn't be..." He stuttered. "Do you bear the Rose?"

"How do you know about the Rose?" Adelaide was defensive, but at the same time felt incredible joy to meet someone who knew of the Gift.

"I am a mage. It is only expected of me to know about magic, is it not?" he replied with a fresh look of recognition and joy. "Let me see it."

Adelaide cut a slit through the sleeve of her dress and held out her arm. Upon seeing the tattoo, he dropped his sword and rushed over to study it. Only when looking closely did Adelaide notice that the rose had aged and was beginning to bloom.

"I surrender," the wizard said softly, still not letting go of her arm. "I will tell you all you want to know."

"How do you know Darius?" Adelaide asked after a pause.

"We met in the kingdom of Mortendenn. There was an uprising there of an unusual nature," he explained quickly, focusing all his energy on the tattoo.

"Rebels, bandits…?"

"The undead."

Adelaide simply stared at the wizard.

"But Darius put an end to it," he continued, "with my magical assistance and the intellect of my friend. You really should let me introduce you to him."

With that, he suddenly stopped talking and looked Adelaide in the eye. There was pity in his face and an overwhelming sadness.

"Actually, perhaps I better spare you that fate. Tell me, what's your name?"

"Adelaide," she found herself unable to lie, "and yours?"

"I have many names. You may address me as Archaius."

The other bandits were beginning to awaken. Adelaide quickly hid her torn sleeve under her cloak and helped some of them to their feet. Soon, James came sprinting through the narrow alleyway. Upon reaching Adelaide, he leaned on a chicken coop to catch his breath.

"The guards have been sent out in search of you! Leave the city. Leave now!" he croaked before doubling over in a coughing fit.

Adelaide looked towards her newfound wizard and he nodded, reinforcing his surrender. Together with the bandits he fled the capital.

Chapter 36

The Expanse

Five days later the group found themselves sitting around the fire at the Silverblood camp. The logs they sat on were moist from the melted snow and little puddles of muddy water formed within the reach of the flame's warmth.

"Was all this of your doing?" Adelaide addressed Sir Hansfell as she sat on the ground still dressed in her fine stolen frock.

"Indeed, we brought some Ghyrock to this camp. The walls are being expanded and rebuilt from stone. The logs are being reused for the construction of houses. Soon, this little camp will stand as strong as any of the King's forts," he replied, pouring himself another chalice of ale from the barrel. Adelaide insisted that chalices are to be used for drinking instead of mugs as her personal silent commemoration to Gabriel. Archaius held them with unease, preferring to drink from the bottles.

"You must stay cautious. This camp is better off undiscovered by Darius. He is already searching for you. I suggest you pray to every God you know that he does not find you here as then no wall of stone will save you," the wizard spoke forebodingly.

"Aye," nodded James, who had followed them for reasons no one was entirely sure of, "there have been whispers of a rising army."

"If it is an army they fear, then an army we will summon!" Adelaide spoke, raising her chalice. The others cheered and drank.

"Damn, when you first slaughtered all my men outside Gransdew I never would have thought that I would find myself by your side, leading a rebellion," Talon shook his head drunkenly.

"I'll take any reason to cut some throats!" called out Hunter, brushing the snow from his hat.

"And how exactly do you plan on summoning this army?" mumbled Bertrand. He sat away from the group but still listened in. "We may have a wizard here but I fear ye can't rely on him to conjure ye up a single man."

"The citizens of Ghyrock and Avenstead will have to be recruited," Adelaide spoke with determination.

"They will not go willingly," Bertrand objected.

"They will be given no choice," was the leader's definitive answer.

"That will only attract more attention from the King's advisor," pointed out Morrihold. He wore a hat over his bandana in this cold weather, the wide brim of which sloped under its own weight. "If we take all the men to fight for us, there will be none left to tend the farms in summer. Hundreds will die. The King will surely take action then."

"We will be prepared for that," Adelaide responded without any idea as to how. "Besides, if we rise up and fully take over the operations of the cities, the tax and the food will go to us, thereby draining the King's resources."

"Then he will turn to Stormhawk," Talon thoughtfully intervened. "Believe you me, he will see gain in siding with the monarchy, he will exploit them."

"We have to act quickly. If we claim some of his land before the alliance is forged, we will weaken them both," she persisted.

"It is a hasty decision but I concur," Sir Hansfell added, "we have been holding Ghyrock against his men for long enough. It is time we push them back."

"If you insist on pursuing this madness," Talon spoke with a sigh, "Tarrynsdew would be a good place to start."

Adelaide nodded, "It is a coastal city and rich with resources, bordered by our land on one side and the sea on the other."

"Go east and take Tarrynsdew, but Stormhawk will strike in the west," Bertrand complained. "They have already tried to claim Ghyrock, no? This will only trigger them to mount a full attack."

"That could be used to our advantage," Hansfell said, downing his chalice in one and wiping the drink from his face. "If they send their strongest force against Ghyrock and we defeat them, they will be left weakened and short on men."

"Then they too will start recruiting common folk. Men who would otherwise be gathering food or crafting or trading." Morrihold resumed his dark line of thought, "What will that do to the people? They will oppose our rebellion and stay loyal to the King."

"The concerns of the commoners will have no effect on the forthcoming war," Adelaide replied heartlessly.

"That is until they start dying of starvation as we exhaust their supplies." The young bandit continued, "in the end we are still bandits, criminals. Once our men take control of the cities they will tear through, robbing and killing. How many sacrifices have to be made for us to win this war? How many innocent lives have to be taken? It will be young men, boys we have to recruit into the army and train them up to be vicious dogs. And once we win, we will have nothing but dry empty fields and piles of corpses to rule over."

With that Morrihold rose to his feet and stormed away from the group. The others were left sitting in a sombre silence. Talon stared into the fire with absolute acceptance of this fate. He was prepared to kill thousands of men without a single guilty thought. Hunter, James and Hansfell were looking to Adelaide for a response. They would follow her to hell and back and if she persisted with this recklessly brave ambition, they would not protest. Archaius glanced behind into the snowy mist that the young bandit disappeared into. The mage forced himself to lounge nonchalantly on the rough ground but he was still uneasy. He looked up at Adelaide with melancholy wisdom, with knowledge of what was to come but spoke nothing. Bertrand got up and followed the only other humane bandit. Adelaide cleared her throat and spoke with a sharp voice.

"Archaius, how powerful is your magic? Would you be able to hold a city against a siege?"

"I'm afraid that you have already seen all there is," his voice was tense and his hazel eyes darted around.

"I heard that wizards could bring down whole castles or alter time or cast powerful curses on their enemies," Hunter mocked.

"If I could," Archaius turned to the bearded bandit, "you'd be the first to know."

"Very well." Adelaide took a commanding tone, "We will have to fight the old-fashioned way. Hansfell, you and the knights will return to Ghyrock, recruit at least four hundred men and begin training. Expect an attack in two months. Talon, ride to Rynell, then Avenstead, recruit five hundred men and lead them to Ghyrock to join the training. Hunter, wait here for the current bandits to complete the reinforcement of the camp, give them five weeks at most, then travel through Rynell to Avenstead. Kill the King's guards and plunder the cities, then recruit and train any men that are left and prepare for an attack from the King. I will travel to Tarrynsdew with Bertrand and Archaius. I believe each of their unique skills will be most useful to me. There, we will destroy Stormhawk's men and kill the King's guards, taking over the city. And lastly, James, I need you to return to the castle and monitor the movement of soldiers, report back to me with any information."

Orders given, Adelaide rose to her feet and went after Morrihold. Wherever she looked she could not find him. Bertrand squeezed between one of the yet unfinished sections of the stone wall and upon seeing Adelaide nodded towards the nearby woods.

"He took a bottle of rum and went off. The boy doesn't like killing. And ya should really listen to him, if you stop now, the King's advisor will likely leave ya alone," Bertrand tried to reason with her.

Adelaide merely shook her head and walked past him into the woods. The snow was thick and white, recently fallen. She followed the two sets of foots prints leading away from the camp. Then one of them stopped and turned back. The other continued further. The trees shielded her from most of the snowfall and the mist lessened. So beautiful was the forest in winter! The strong brown tree trunks towered all around her and every branch of every bush was covered in a layer of fluffy snow. Still, the forest was alive. Red berries were peeking out from their white blankets, squirrels scurried around the branches and birds nested in the tree tops. Briefly mesmerised by the stunning surroundings, Adelaide almost didn't notice the bandit sitting under one of the trees.

Morrihold wrapped himself in his cloak and took a big gulp from his bottle. He heard her approaching but did not look up.

"I grew up in Aeraworth," he slurred, having already began to experience the effect of the rum. "My father owned sheep and my mother made woollen clothes. I helped them sell the clothes at the market. It was a simple life, but a happy one. I don't know why, but I chose to leave it all behind. The appeal of the dangerous, exciting life of a bandit drew me away, into one of the gangs. I stole, I plundered and I killed.

"The first life I took was a lad two years younger than me. I tried to steal from him and he caught me. I was scared so I drew my sword. Damn, I barely knew how to use the thing! And then I drove it through his stomach. Then I held him as he died. I couldn't tell you how long it took, I couldn't tell you anything that happened during the time that I watched my little brother leave me. He was so surprised at first. But I think he forgave me. I sure hope he did. He did not say a word, but he just... he just squeezed my hand like he knew." With that, Morrihold held up his hand and stared at it as if seeing something else, and smiled. "If only I had known it was him! If only I could have seen his face before I reached for my sword!"

His face was expressionless, but his voice rang with anger. He paused, shook his head and took another long gulp. Pulling his hat and bandana from his head he threw them into the snow in rage. Adelaide sat opposite him and silently waited for him to continue.

"My name was Duncan until only a few summers ago, when I abandoned my clan and went out searching for a better life. I was in the city of Morrihold when I met Talon and Hunter. I was reluctant to join the bandits again but there was no other life for me, nothing else I knew how to do. That city had become my namesake since."

He put the bottle down and moved closer to Adelaide, taking her hands into his. His skin was ice cold but he was not even shivering. Looking down, she saw the entire bottle of rum was emptied.

"I don't want this war. I don't want all this death. But I can't refuse ya. I see the way they all listen to you, I know that there's some powerful magic in your heart that bends their thoughts, but I feel it not. It has no hold on me. Yet, I follow ya nonetheless; just to be near you, to see you, to hear your voice. I love you, Silverblood! Hell, I don't even know your real name, but if it is conquest you wish for, then I will fight by your side till the end!"

"Adelaide," she spoke softly, caressing his stubbled cheek, "my name is Adelaide."

She took his face in her hands and pressed her lips against his.

Chapter 37

The Fire of Tarrynsdew

The romantic moment they shared was brief, as Duncan soon emptied his stomach and passed out in the snow. Adelaide sat by his side for a while, contemplating his words, then woke him up with a gentle slap and helped him back to the camp. Upon seeing them, Hunter ran over and laughed loudly at his half-conscious friend, pointing like a child the whole time. They then debated what to do with him and decided to simply put him into the nearest tent. By the time the displeased owner of the tent returned, they were long gone.

As the day drew to an end, preparations were being made for the departures in the morning. Bread was packed for the journey, clothes were repaired and weapons were sharpened. The camp was hectic with everyone running from one tent to another and shouts were heard from all directions. Yet there was a gloomy mood among the men. An aura of nervous anxiety surrounded even the most optimistic of bandits.

"Ay, Silverblood." Hunter walked over to her. Despite the chaos, he still smiled brightly.

"Evening."

"This… killing the guards business… this is it, isn't it? This is war?" his voice trembled beneath his cocky facade.

Adelaide thought for a moment as she watched the men in the camp. They were scared, all of them. And they had every right to be. Should she fail in her quest, they will all end up with swords through their stomachs or a noose around their necks. Her entire life was spent hiding in the shadows but at last it was time to come out and fight. This is what everything has been building up to.

"Yes," was her quiet reply.

Hunter nodded bravely but his hands would not stop fidgeting. He breathed in as if to speak, then bowed his head and awkwardly walked away. Adelaide remained standing by her tent, looking at her army. Her arms were crossed and her fingers dug into her sleeves. She breathed heavily to calm the nerves that were tearing her apart on the inside, yet she wore the expressionless face of a cold-blooded killer. Once the sun had set, she took to her tent in hopes of resting well before they ride out, but no sleep came to her that night.

The next morning, Adelaide stepped out of her tent ready for battle. Thick leather boots stretched up to her knees and leather pads were strapped over her breeches. The once stunning red gown was torn and cut apart at the skirt with long slits running through all the layers of fabric for the fast mounting and dismounting of horses. Her upper half was covered with more thick leather armour but on her head rested the silver circlet she stole from the markets in the capital. She stood dressed as both a soldier and a princess. Soft fur padded her armour and the mysterious northern cloak still rested upon her shoulders. It was unlikely to win her as many favours with the common folk of Tarrynsdew as with the educated nobility of the capital yet she dare not take it off. The Dragonslayer was firmly attached to her belt and a quiver with thirty steel tipped arrows to her back.

Adelaide walked over to her horse and secured the bow to the saddle. The horses were uneasy, rearing and stomping their hooves. Bertrand stood by his, trying to calm it down.

"This is your doing!" he called out accusingly. "They can sense your magic!"

"They are just fine with my magic! It's you they are scared of!" she called back.

"Aren't wizards gifted with the art of taming animals?" Bertrand gestured towards Archaius, who was struggling with keeping his own horse still. The animal reared and he was pulled off his feet, still holding onto the reins. He looked as uncomfortable in his long wizardly robes as he did outside the King's castle, but still refused to don the armour, claiming that he would not be needing it since he refused to fight. For the first time, Adelaide and Bertrand shared a mutual amusement.

She mounted her horse and looked back at the camp. Some parts of the stone wall were already finished, mostly around the gate, while wooden scaffolding was still exposed further in. The wall was made of beautiful well-cut stone and further decorations were added to make it resemble the walls of a castle.

"By God, Hansfell sure went all out on this. I don't remember those at Ghyrock," Adelaide muttered to Bertrand, pointing at a stone figure that was mounted on top of the wall.

The gargoyle was in the shape of a four-legged winged creature, the size of a large dog, with long sharp claws that appeared to be digging into the stone. Its head had bulging round eyes, ears like those of a long-eared owl and a gaping mouth with sharp teeth and an extended tongue that reached down past its chin.

"How did they even make it so quickly?" Adelaide wondered.

To her astonishment, the creature retracted its tongue and opened its wings. Its stone body came to life as it took off from the battlements, flew down to the ground and landed near Archaius with unexpected grace. The reins of his horse broke from his hands and the animal galloped away. Sighing he turned, only to find the gargoyle behind him.

"Limestone!" He fell to his knees before the creature and threw his arms around it. The gargoyle pressed its face into the wizard's shoulder and moved the way a happy dog does when reunited with its owner.

"What in hell...?" mumbled Bertrand as he and Adelaide sat on their horses, watching in wonder.

"Limestone is coming to Tarrynsdew with us," announced Archaius.

"Very well... I suppose," Adelaide replied, still not fully comprehending the events that were occurring before her, "the more the merrier."

"He follows me everywhere, you see," the mage explained. "Except he left me to go to the capital by myself. There was a man there that he is not very fond of."

Archaius found another horse and soon they were on their way to battle and conquer, with the gargoyle following them in the skies. For two days they rode until a town appeared in the distance. They stopped their horses and looked out towards their goal.

"You are certain we do not need an army? If we ride back now, some of the men will still be back at camp," Bertrand spoke with caution.

"We are not going back. We will fight today and we will take Tarrynsdew today," still she stood determined.

"It would be better to wait for the moon to rise," Archaius pointed out. "Our friend here will need it. And considering our gifts, we will not be as disadvantaged by the dark as the guards."

With a mutual consensus, the trio rested. They did not start a fire for fear of the townspeople seeing the smoke but Archaius would occasionally conjure a flame in the palm of his hand and watch it dance. He was leaning leisurely against a rock, with his hood hiding the caramel hair that somehow still fell in his face. He was young and handsome, with a small nose and hazel eyes that stared intensely at the little trick of magic. Limestone sat near him and froze into the shape Adelaide first saw it in, as the cold stone it was made from solidified once again.

Bertrand laid down some distance away from them and closed his eyes. Wearing nothing but a shirt and breeches he seemed untroubled by the cold air or the thin layer of frost that covered the ground. He awoke when the first rays of moonlight touched his skin.

Adelaide and Archaius rose to their feet, both watching him cautiously. The werewolf's eyes shined white.

"It's time," he hissed urgently, dreading the upcoming violence.

"Go," she commanded.

His body twisted and deformed. He fell his knees and dug his fingers into the ground as they elongated and sharp claws ripped through his nails. Long rough fur broke through his skin and his jaw stretched. After a few agonising moments, Bertrand stood fully transformed into a being half human half wolf. Adelaide nodded and he sprinted towards the town on all fours.

The other two jumped onto their horses and rode until they were closer to the town. Screams could already be heard and people were waking up and running from their houses with any weapon they could find. To Adelaide, it was a sick reminder of the awful day when her own village was brought to the ground. The people were terrified, the children were crying, the civilians were desperately trying to defend their lives with any household object they could find; fire pokers, knives, rakes.

Archaius jumped from his horse.

"I'm not much of a rider," he explained, "and the animal would only get spooked."

Letting his horse run free, he was about to run towards Bertrand when Adelaide grabbed him by his robe and pulled him back.

"Burn them," she urged. "Burn them all. Burn the houses, burn the people; the guards, the Stormhawk bandits, the civilians! If you refuse, you will not hear another word from me about the Rose or its former master."

He stared at her for a moment with a look of revulsion in his eyes, then nodded and ran towards the town.

Adelaide rode closer to the city and jumped up, standing with her feet on the saddle. She aimed the bow and began shooting, each time hitting one of the men that were circling Bertrand. He was magnificent, swiping several people off their feet in one go, tearing them to pieces before any of them could even strike at him. Archers climbed up to the roofs of the houses and aimed their bows but they were quickly brought to the ground by Adelaide's arrows. One managed to shoot in time, hitting the werewolf in the back. Bertrand howled in pain, then ripped the arrow from his flesh and continued fighting. The gargoyle swooped down from the skies and carried men away, tearing them apart in the air and letting their bloody remains fall onto the heads of their families.

In the hysteria, no one could tell who was a guard and who was a bandit. The whole population was united in taking down the monstrosity that had invaded their home. The criminals were protecting the soldiers and the civilians were taking the fallen into their homes and tending to their wounds. In the middle of this turmoil, the people had found this strangely beautiful harmony.

Yet the houses that had become safe refuges for the injured were now engulfed in flames. The whole town was made from wood and straw and the flames spread quickly in the wind. Archaius had vanished from the scene. Once her quiver was emptied, she joined Bertrand and together they fought; two unlikely allies together side by side in a battlefield. Hundreds fell before them. The blood ran through the streets and endless corpses covered the ground. Fire rose towards the skies and the town burned like a bonfire on that dreadful night.

They battled on until every man, woman and child lay lifeless. Adelaide pulled her sword from the chest of another victim and ran through the streets in search for more. The fire reached towards her from every direction but still she persisted, so great was her psychotic desire to end the lives of all those who lived here. Yet in the flames between the houses she saw a familiar figure. He stood there, indifferent to the inferno raging around him; the old man with the crooked cane. Adelaide froze in place, staring in horror at the apparition.

A hand grabbed her arm and dragged her out of the burning town. Upon reaching the outskirts she saw Bertrand up on the hill, still in his wolf form, as he sat and stared at the distant mountains. She then looked towards her rescuer.

"It's done," said Archaius, releasing her left arm. He was biting back his guilt.

"We had to kill them all," Adelaide tried to explain. "They would send message to Stormhawk."

"He will know within a few days anyway." The wizard turned away from her, bowing his head.

"And we have no men to hold this land, so he would only come back and reclaim it. Now, he will see no gain in doing so."

"No gain at all," Archaius agreed gravely.

Chapter 38

Utopia

Candlelight shone softly from the beautifully crafted golden candleholders on the walls of the room of the small council.

"You urged me to welcome your beloved guests here and now this!" King Bohemond raged, pacing the small room.

"I am sure it was not his intention to be captured so cruelly by the bandits. If you would allow me to send the order for the knights," Darius pleaded.

"No such order is to be sent! We cannot risk it!" the King's deep voice boomed through the room.

"But they are growing stronger with every day. First the violence in Avenstead and now their control has stretched to the capital!" Darius was starting to lose his composure.

"Do we have any solid evidence that they have taken Avenstead from the other scum that resided there? And if they have, what difference does it make? Half the kingdom is terrorised by one bandit clan or another." The King's heavy body collapsed into a cushioned chair in defeat.

The advisor glanced around the room, carefully choosing his next words.

"There was never talk of a rebellion before," he spoke delicately.

"There will be no rebellion! The people will not side with these criminals."

"The people may not be given the liberty of choice," Darius approached his King, "they may be forced into service to this Silverblood clan, as they have chosen to call themselves."

"And you let their spy waltz straight into the castle!" Bohemond snarled.

"I admit my fault, but if we stop them now, we may yet recover the wizard!"

"And what is it that you expect of him? What did he do in Mortendenn that was so damned heroic? Him and this alchemist of yours."

"He helped me fight brutality with knowledge," Darius spoke softly. "If we apply the same measures here, we can find the source of their strength and weaken them. The people despise them. They can be united by the knights into a crude yet large army. That will provide at least some resistance to their conquest."

"Do not dare speak of their looting as a conquest!" the King shouted in anger.

"But that is how they see it." Darius was once again calm. His voice rang with wisdom, "Let me send a messenger to Stormhawk. We can bribe them into an allegiance, at least for a short time."

Sighing, the King waved his hand in submission. Darius left the room and hurried to his quarters.

The servants had already lit the fires and the small room was bathed in a warm orange glow. Tapestries hung from his walls, showing legendary heroes from his native land surrounded by exotic animals and trees that would not bear the cold winters of Starkenhaart. Darius sat at his writing desk and prepared the parchment when he heard the door open behind him.

He glanced up and instantly put down his quill.

A beautiful young woman quickly slipped into the room and quietly shut the door. Her pale lilac dress sparkled with jewels and long blonde hair was draped over her shoulders. Darius quickly got up and almost ran to embrace her.

"We don't have long, my love," she spoke with an angelically sweet voice.

"We never do," Darius replied, caressing her face, "my Queen."

***

Adelaide and Archaius sat in the dirt by a fire. There were no longer any people to see the smoke. Limestone loyally took his place by his master's side and solidified once again. The mage lovingly wiped the blood from the fangs of his pet.

"How did such a creature come to be? What sorcery breathed life into it?" Adelaide asked, fascinated.

"I never asked," Archaius spoke, thinking back to the time he first met the gargoyle.

"Was it not wizards like you that made it?"

"No, it was… an experiment of some sort. Unlike many others, this one went right. By God, you should have seen some of the abominations that were created there! Monsters ten times the size of a werewolf. Beings half human half beast. That was not a place of magic."

"Where was this?" Adelaide's curiosity grew.

"A distant land. One full of dragons and creatures neither human nor animal." There were so many memories in the mage's mind, he could barely pick which to tell. "We heard so many rumours about that place, so many stories about a kingdom cursed with eternal darkness. Of course not the whole kingdom was affected, just the land around that one tower. It was as if sunlight itself refused to touch it. An old and crooked building it was…"

"Surrounded by dead woods?" Adelaide asked, remembering in horror of the visions she saw in the cave.

"You have heard of it?" He smiled, "I suspected as much."

"What happened there?"

Archaius opened his mouth to speak but Bertrand returned to them, wearing his rags, and demanded to leave at once. It pained him greatly to look upon the remnants of the city. They had no horses and so began the long trek to the west, hoping to pass a village or a settlement on the way.

"You did not think this through," Bertrand stated.

"No." Adelaide could feel his burning hatred. "No, I did not."

"We would have plenty of horses, if you didn't command this fool to burn the whole city to ash," he continued.

Archaius glanced up in offence but remained silent.

"I would not advise you to question my judgement, dog," Adelaide snapped at the werewolf.

Bertrand stopped and tensed his hands into fists.

"Do you need to be reminded of who it is that commands you now?" she snarled at him. "Well, I would be delighted to."

She drew her sword and twisted it tauntingly in her hands.

"So you carry the Dragonslayer too?" Archaius mumbled. "I did not notice that in the fight. And you never did tell me how you acquired the cloak."

His attempt at distracting her from her rage worked and she commenced the walk, with Bertrand following reluctantly behind.

"I suspected that you would know of the sword. I was trained by a man named Gabriel, a righteous and brave ranger, if a little eccentric," Adelaide spoke fondly. The mage listened intently to her words.

"He taught me to fight and to read but never spoke much of himself or how he came to have the things he had. And then one day he told me I had finished training and then he took my arm. It was as if the dead rose on his arm became mine, only it was renewed and replenished. After that, he just vanished."

"The rose he had was dead?" Archaius asked in surprise.

"Yes."

He contemplated on that.

"It appears a lot of mystery surrounds this mentor of yours."

"Yes. I wish I knew more."

"As do I."

They walked and walked through the empty land. It was strangely peaceful to be in such complete isolation from the world; away from the fights, away from the deaths. Her companions were savouring this moment of uninterrupted tranquillity and even the fire that burned so wildly inside Adelaide was beginning to subside. It gave them a chance to calm their nerves.

They hiked up a hill and paused for a moment, admiring the view. The gentle light of the rising sun painted the sky a soft blue and fluffy white clouds were slowly continuing their pilgrimage up above. Fields stretched before them, covered by a white blanket of snow. Hoof prints were scattered across it from the woods to a small settlement that was tucked away under a hill. The cave that sheltered it was wide but did not stretch far into the ground, perfect for a few small houses.

They entered the little village and not even Adelaide could raise a sword to the peaceful people who lived there. They welcomed the strangers into their homes and offered them food and drink. The hosts showed such generosity, such kindness as Adelaide had never seen before. These people have lived under this hill their whole lives, supporting anyone who wished to join them, never travelling to the city, never being corrupted by greed or envy. This little settlement was a utopia.

The travellers ate and warmed up by the fires. The villagers surrounded them, mystified by their weapons and attire. A little girl ran up to Adelaide and sat near her. So trusting was this child, so unaware of the dangers of this world. She reached out and touched the circlet on Adelaide's head, then quickly pulled her hand back and giggled. Adelaide took it off and placed in on the girl's hair.

"You are as beautiful as a princess," she said softly. The little girl jumped up and ran to show off the present to her friends.

Archaius was watching her with a smile.

"It's surprising to see kindness in you," he said.

She smiled in return, "Show them some magic!"

A crowd gathered to watch as the wizard stepped out from the cave and filled his hands with snow, then returned and held it out in front of him. A little flame began to dance right atop the snow, but it did not melt. Children shrieked with joy and adults stood bewildered. The little flame danced and flickered. Archaius then went over to a little boy.

"Hold out your hands," he said playfully.

The boy obeyed and then giggled excitedly as the mage placed the burning snow into his hands. Holding his palm over it, Archaius made the flame stretch into a long column that twisted and turned. He whispered a few magical words and the colour of the flame turned purple with a flash. Gasps were heard all around. Taking the snow from the boy's hands, he threw it up and it exploded in the air, lighting up the cave like a magical chandelier. And there it vanished. People clapped and cheered.

If only there was any way for Adelaide to thank them for their hospitality. Kindness was their gold, love was their silver. No material goods were as valuable to them. Such untainted purity!

The trio rested and amused the villagers with their tales of adventure and magic until a horse was seen approaching from a distance. A lone rider galloped towards the settlement and hurriedly dismounted. He begged the villagers for information of any travellers that may have passed and was soon shown to Adelaide.

"Morrihold?" she stood up to greet him.

He bowed. His black cloak was covered in snow and a linen mask shielded his face from the icy air but Adelaide knew him by his soft brown eyes that shined from under his hat. He reached out, took her by the hand and led her away from the others.

Together they ended up walking out from under the cover of the cave and into the frozen fields. The sun was high above them now and the snow sparked in the light like a million tiny diamonds.

"How did you find us?" Adelaide asked.

"I've searched everywhere from the camp to Tarrynsdew, then back through those woods," he admitted. "Did you take the city?"

Adelaide thought for a moment.

"It is of no use to us. But it's of no use to Stormhawk either so I would say our quest was a success."

"I see." Duncan was too distracted by other thoughts to feel upset at the destruction. "I apologise for my drunken behaviour in those woods. But not for my words."

With that he stopped and took her hands.

"With the war just beginning, I thought this would not be the right time, but now I think there will never be a better moment. As our clan grew under you rule, so has my love for you. Now that we are limitless and unstoppable, I feel that so are you and I. And with that, for every victory, for every success, future and past, for every word you speak, for every breath we take, will you accept me as yours and be my wife?"

With that he fell to his knee before her.

Chapter 39

And Her Words Fell on Deaf Ears

"We will continue to push north. The rogue knights and the bandits should be able to hold our land against the inevitable attacks. Stormhawk resides in the city of Farendale but another major sea port lies between us and them. It borders the mouth of the river and is far better defended so will not be as easy to take as Tarrynsdew. We will need men and supplies, but until then, we can infiltrate the city and see what can be discovered about their operations and influence over the surrounding territory. By now, there is no doubt that Darius has established an alliance with Stormhawk so we have to be very careful in his territory."

Adelaide stood by a map that was laid out against a rock and held in place as best it could against the strong wind. This was not a good time to leave the safety of the cave but after resting there for three days and celebrating the recent engagement with their generous hosts they felt obliged to move on. The villagers had only a few horses and after the kindness already shown by them to Adelaide, she could not take them.

They hiked for a week through the snow, which to them was no longer a soft and glistening blanket, but rather an icy marshland that slowed them and drained them of strength. In the nights, they would take shelter under hills or in woodlands, if they could find any, then start a fire and eat what they could hunt. Limestone would often fly away and loyally return to his master with a gift of a bird or a rabbit. The cold could not damage his stone skin, and neither could the teeth of the wolves that frequently passed them. Yet they did not attack, but rather stared at the travellers with their yellow eyes. Bertrand would often stare back with both aggression and heart-breaking longing for a loyal pack of his own. Being by far the biggest of them, he often went first, ploughing a path through the snow, entirely unperturbed by the frost that covered every inch of his skin.

The same could not be said for Archaius. The mage was of small build and certainly better accustomed to a warmer climate. Whenever possible, he would conjure a small flame to warm his hands. In the worst of blizzards, he cloaked himself in fire but that quickly tired him out and he fell behind the others.

Adelaide and Morrihold walked together, pulling each other out of the snow and, when the winds quietened, discussing the arrangements for their wedding.

At last, the frozen river could be seen in the distance, with a small coastal village right on its bank. The villagers most likely made their money by taking travellers across the wide mouth of the river, but in this weather, they must be struggling and desperate for work. Adelaide saw an opportunity.

They entered the village and gathered what citizens they could by the docks. Adelaide climbed up onto the hull of a small, beached rowboat and addressed the crowd before her. She held her back as straight as the immense force of the wind would allow, with her cloak dancing wildly in the gale, pulling her one way or another but still she held on, gripping the weathered wood with her numb fingers. Her hypnotic words boomed through the storm with the eloquent power of a true leader, summoning the men to her side.

"Hear me now, as I stand before you, that no greater glory may come to any man than to one who fights under my name. This cursed bitter cold is the work of the demons, a failed attempt to weaken us, to bring us to our knees. But still we stand! We stand in the face of this wretched weather! We stand in the face of our enemies! So stand with us! Do not fall, do not fail, do not surrender! Cross this river with me and help us in our fight against the beasts that have been terrorising your land! Ally with us and you will find greater riches than you could ever have dreamt of! "

She was not prepared for the response her words received. The villagers muttered among themselves for a moment.

"We are good, hardworking people," a woman spoke from the crowd. "Why should we let our sons and husbands go out fighting for ye? Ye don't look like a messenger from the King or a fancy knight. So I think we'll all stay right 'ere and wait for the winter to pass."

The crowd agreed. Adelaide watched them for a moment. Why were they immune to her power? Humiliated, she climbed down from the boat and stood in the snow.

"Nice work," was Bertrand's sneering remark.

Confusion quickly turning into anger, Adelaide strode over to Archaius and grabbed him by the collar of his robe.

"You know about this magic," she hissed quietly. "Explain this!"

"Some people are not affected by the power of your Gift," he stuttered.

"Well, I can see that much! How do I make them succumb?"

The mage only shrugged.

The crowd dispersed and feeling defeated, Adelaide was preparing to undertake the long walk to the city of Marrynport with no supplies or reinforcements.

One of the men from the crowd, a blacksmith, walked back to his shop and quickly shut his door to shield his home from the snowstorm. The wooden door refused to stay shut and after slamming it repeatedly with no success, he propped a chair against the handle. Letting out a long sigh he brushed the snow from his coat and walked through his house. It was a small building with a very low ceiling and a dirty wooden floor that creaked loudly under his every step. Standing in the poorly furnished room he called out to his wife and children but the house stood silent, except for the whistling of the wind in the walls and roof. Suddenly the storm pushed the door open once again, sending the chair flying through the room. The powerful weather screamed through the house and a strong current of air slammed into the blacksmith with force, knocking him to the ground. Struggling to stand up, he fought his way against the wind to the door. Slamming it again, he leaned his back against it and gasped for breath. The cold air stung his throat and chest and he coughed, doubling over in agony. Looking up, he saw his whole house covered in snow. Every surface, every wall and even the ceiling were white. The push of the wind on the door was increasing with every moment and it took the man all of his strength to hold it shut. Then it came. That horrific sound. Like the howl of a banshee it resonated through his house. The door pushed and pushed until he could hold it no longer. A small gap opened up between the door and the frame. Through it, crept in four long crooked yellow fingers.

***

Adelaide stood on the thick sheet of ice that covered the river. Hopping up and down, she tested the strength of the ice.

"It will hold!" she called out to her companions.

Bertrand and Archaius nodded and stepped out onto the river.

They waited for Morrihold to return. He had disappeared into the crowd after Adelaide's disastrous speech. The village looked so small, so quiet yet the people who lived in these miniature stone houses could withstand a magical force that brought down numerous gangs of bandits. Their flat roofs were covered in a thick layer of snow which was being fed by the ever-growing storm. At times, the heavy load would break off the edges of the roofs and pile up by the walls and doors, trapping the citizens inside. Straining to see into the distance, Adelaide noticed the mountains that rose to the west. Their majestic forms stood white, like ancient greying elders of the earth. In contrast to their profile rose a dark stone tower. It must have stood in the centre of the settlement and reached up towards the sky, crowning itself the tallest building in the village. The masonry was impeccable and the craftsmanship could easily surpass any edifice in the western side of the kingdom. The tower was very narrow, allowing but one person to stand on the uppermost floor but its needle-like structure would not give in to the wild fiendish forces of nature. Adelaide wondered if it drew strength from the ground and the sky and the living souls of this village and concentrated it in the large golden crucifix that shone like a star from its pinnacle.

She was pulled away from her daydream by the return of her beloved. With him, he led two horses.

"Nobody even dares to look out from their house in this weather. They won't notice these beauties gone," he said with a smirk.

Quickly jumping on, he pulled Adelaide up behind him.

"But we should really get going!" he called out to the other two.

Bertrand and Archaius both stood facing the horse.

"You bloody better be musing..." Bertrand complained.

"Come on!" Adelaide shouted back as her and Morrihold giggled quietly together.

The huge man climbed up onto the horse and waited.

"Oh, the humiliation," Archaius mumbled and struggled onto the horse behind him, holding awkwardly onto the rider.

Just as they were about to set off, a man came sprinting towards them through the storm. He desperately called for them to wait. Upon approaching the riders, he was confronted with swords.

"I tell you now, if you value your life, you will not demand the horses back!" Morrihold threatened.

"I am not here for the horses." The man's skin was almost grey. Dark black rings surrounded his eyes, which were so bloodshot that barely any white could still be visible. "The others... they do not see your power, your glory as I do. I am forever your loyal servant. And although I am nothing but a humble blacksmith, I am sworn to you, now and forever, my liege. I can gather others. We may not be strong enough to stand beside you in a field of battle but we are good tradesmen and any armour or swords that you wish for will be made as quickly as resources allow. Forgive me, my noble mistress that I can offer nothing more."

Adelaide glanced at the others, as surprised as they were at the sudden declaration of servitude. There was great worry and unease in the wizard's eyes.

The riders were soon on their way, galloping across the frozen river. They rode in silence as the storm raged around them but Adelaide could feel the mage's gaze on her back. He knew no more than her about the mystical Gift she possessed, although it was almost as if he had seen it in action before. Adelaide must find a way to convince him to disclose his knowledge, but that was a challenge for another time as the towers of Marrynport soon revealed themselves through the falling snow.

The ice beneath their hooves had turned into land and they slowed the horses, approaching the grand city gates. The guards merely watched as the enigmatic riders entered the city, powerless to stop them. Once in the stables, Bertrand and Archaius hastily jumped from their horse and stood some steps away from one another.

"Go and see what information you can uncover about Stormhawk's control and tactics. Speak to the guards, the merchants and any men of power you can find. I will see what is hidden in the walls of the castle," Adelaide instructed.

"Word is, it's not much of castle," Bertrand mumbled.

"Still, there will be some knowledge inside."

With that she left them, somewhat excited to once again revisit her true art. The small fort was truly inferior to the grand castle of the capital city but its stone walls still stood strong and windows were nothing but small slits. This was a powerful and well defended military base. Ballistae and trebuchets were mounted on an elevated hill near the castle, facing out to sea. If an armada came to attack the port, they would inevitably be sunk. Adelaide cautiously made her way past the fort and towards the servants' quarters. Disguising herself as one would be an easy way into the castle, but it would not allow her passage into the military rooms. Alas, she could no longer fight the yearning to become the master thief she once was, even for a short while.

The servants were busy, rushing through the corridors, crowding in the kitchens, completely oblivious to the dark figure that brushed past them like a ghost. At last, she found the stairs leading up to the main halls. Unseen, she slithered through the garrison and into the chambers of the lord. A young servant girl was just leaving the room when she took one last glance back. In a moment she witnessed the cloaked silhouette move quickly towards her. A scream froze in her throat and her blood-covered body was kicked unceremoniously under the lord's bed.

Chapter 40

The Castle Guard

James was resting his head on the rough fabric of his pillow. Facing the wall, he stared tiredly at the dark wooden panels that spanned the sleeping chambers of the barracks and shielded them from the cold stone from which the castle was constructed. His eyes emptily focused on a nail that was hammered in by an amateur, most likely a guard, when this section of the castle was rebuilt a few centuries before. The young man's straw-coloured hair fell into his eyes and he brushed it away, turning onto his back to stare at a different architectural finesse of the room; the ceiling. It much resembled the wall.

The other guards were engrossed in a game of Cheat, throwing playing cards into the middle of the small rickety wooden table and shoving each other away as they tried to get a better look at the faces of their opponents. Suddenly a roar of profanities broke out and the men called and pointed to one another, accusations flying around the room.

Growing frustrated, James rose abruptly from his low-sitting bed and strode out into the hall. Laugher boomed from behind him as he slammed the door shut. Sighing deeply and brushing his hair back with his hands he tried to understand why he felt so ill at ease. There was a nervous knot in his chest ever since he returned to the castle. His absence was questioned of course, by the captain of the guard, but he manoeuvred through the interrogation swiftly and got off with no harsher punishment than a few additional "voluntary" latrine cleaning duties. Yet he remained extremely uncomfortable within these walls.

He wandered down the corridor, noticing how much colder the air was, until he reached a thick wooden door that marked the exit of the barracks. Quietly pushing it open he entered a much larger castle hallway. It was beautifully decorated, with expertly woven tapestries reaching all the way to the high grey-stone ceiling and cabinets set up along the walls with intricately crafted baskets placed on display. There were furs and exotic fruit laid about for all eyes to see. James walked indifferently past all these wonders, sick of gazing upon the precious ornaments that he had to guard in silence day in day out. He was desperate the leave the castle, to taste the sweet cold air of the night. There were other guards positioned at intervals down the long corridor. The King and the foreign dignitaries rarely found themselves in this part of the castle, so the common folk and the servants were permitted to scurry about in these halls. Coming to an intersection, James glanced curiously into another adjoining hall, this one reserved for people of high class. Swallowing envy, he slipped out of a side door into the street.

The hens were asleep in their coops and a few pigs still wondered sleepily in their pens. Trying not to take deep breaths of the putrid smell that lingered like a cloud between the castle and the city wall, James rushed to a stone that was well known to him and a few of the other adventurous guards. Pushing at the stone fiercely, the young man felt it slide through the wall and a moment later it fell into the dirt on the other side. Crawling through the narrow passageway he made his way out of the city unnoticed. Cautiously replacing the stone, he turned and took a long deep breath of long-awaited freedom.

Whether due to the icy night-time mist or the excitement that now overshadowed his anxiety, his body shivered with a spasm. His bright eyes sparkled with energy and without purpose or reason he broke into a sprint. His legs carried him through the farmers' fields and towards a small hut in the distance. The cold air burned at his lungs but he ran on, feeding on the ecstasy of a liberated body. The wind hit him hard, stinging his face and grasping at his loose-fitting clothes but he did not halt. Energy pulsed through his veins, thought the nerves in his brain. He had never felt more alive than in that moment. Eventually, slowing down, he doubled over, placing his hands on his knees and gasping for breath. Laughing hysterically, the guard ignored the fluids that flowed from his mouth and nose and dripped onto the cold soil in front of him. From his chest erupted an unprecedented scream that rang through the fields and seemed to echo in the distant woodland. It may well had been heard at the castle but he cared little for the sleep of those in there. Releasing the last of his energy in this incomparable outburst, James straightened up, still laughing, and wiped his face.

The young man walked around the farmers' abandoned little hut and looked out into the distance, savouring the silent beauty of Starkenhaart in this late hour. Turning back, he looked up at the castle. Light shined from a few windows at the top of the structure. He wondered what it must be like, to sleep in a room with a window, to look out at the stars from your very bed during times when sleep was reluctant to come. He wished to sleep inside a room like that, just once.

As James pondered his melancholy thoughts, a leather-gloved hand grabbed him by the collar of his brown shirt. Instinctively breaking away from the grasp, the young man jumped back and faced his attacker. Reaching for his sword, James found only an empty belt where the scabbard was secured only a few hours before. Regretting his choice of attire, he shot a look at the castle, calculating if he could outrun the assailant and get through the tunnel in the wall before he was grabbed again. Seeing no other way to escape, he was ready to take his chance but with a final fleeting look towards the man behind the hut, he stopped in his tracks.

"It's been a long time, little Jimmy," the man spoke as he leisurely strolled out from of his cover. "Surely ye aren't running away from me just yet."

"Dear brother," James sneered in acknowledgment.

"Ye have met our new lady in command," the older man stated with a hint of condescension.

James only nodded.

"And ye have agreed to provide any information she desires." Another mocking statement.

The young guard resented the man that stood before him. Bullied and beaten from childhood, he now stood before the initiator of his torment. And when at last he thought he had escaped the iron grasp of this blood bond, when he joined the guard and was trained in the art of swordfight, he discovered that his hopes of freedom were tragically misplaced. Abused into submission, he was forced to give up his knowledge of the King and the castle. Hunted down and made to betray his protector caused more pain to him than any wound they inflicted. Eventually, his righteous mind was torn apart and he consented to bribery to escape the physical torture. Yet that only lessened their violence, never ending it completely.

"I have nothing new to give you," James hissed bitterly.

"Oh, dear brother, must we play these games each time?"

The elder of the two drew a knife from his belt. The blade scraped against a metal buckle, resonating a teeth-grinding sound.

"I have been to your camp!" James announced, "the Silverblood camp, I've heard it called. I know it's exact location. Lay one hand on me and the captain of the guard will know."

Taken aback by this revelation, the elder brother lowered his weapon. A dark thought passed across his face and in an instant, he rushed towards his sibling and grabbed him by the back of the head, digging the blade into the skin just below his jaw. With added menace in his voice he yelled right into James's ear.

"Do ye think I will be commanded by a wench and blackmailed by a dirty cur in the same day? I should slit your little throat right now!"

James stopped fighting and relaxed his body. In absolute silence he stared into the eyes of his brother.

"What're ye looking at? What is it, ya little swine?"

James just continued to stare. He was fascinated by Adelaide and her magic when they first met and later, upon visiting the camp and seeing how she spoke and held herself around the other bandits, he was fascinated further still. A woman who could easily defeat any of them in battle was not using force against them. Her intimidating aura that commanded their obedience was less violent and yet somehow more unnervingly frightening. Like the calm air before a storm. With that knowledge, he continued to stare into the eyes of his demon.

Each moment dragged for an eternity and the hard face of the elder weakened. He threw his brother to the ground.

"I will return in a fortnight. Ye better have something then."

With that he kicked dirt towards the younger man and walked off into the night. James jumped to his feet and scurried back towards the castle. Two intelligent eyes watched him from the dark face of a slender figure who stood by one of those lit up windows in the highest towers of the castle.

"Treason is a crime punishable by death," Darius recited and he turned his black eyes back towards their original subject, the sparkling stars in the moonlit sky. The King recently welcomed a guest to the castle, a man who had a remarkable degree of knowledge about the stars. And just about everything else. That guest had departed since, and the wizard that travelled with him from Mortendenn had been claimed by the bandits. Darius wondered if his dear friend was still alive and safe in their dwelling.

"They will use him against the King," the royal advisor thought to himself, placing his elbow against the windowsill and burying his face in his arm. The heavy plum coloured curtains danced gently in the wind, brushing against his side. The man turned and looked around his chamber.

A fire burned intensely in a large stone hearth to his left. Above it hung a painting of the King. Darius studied the canvas. The brushwork was impeccable and the resemblance to the monarch was uncanny. A young king looked down at him with the brave noble eyes of a lion. Darius was presented with this picture when he first rose to the title of the King's advisor, against the wishes of the small council. Those greedy power-hungry harpies wanted the title for themselves but Bohemond learned to trust Darius after a series of difficult decisions that lead to new laws and more secure international relations. The people warned the King not to take a bastard son of a dignitary from a southern land as his close companion, but the monarch defied them, seeing the intelligence and strategic talent in the young foreigner. If only the King could maintain his faith now. Darius's loyalty to the crown was boundless and his head was full with ideas to end the rising rebellion and stabilise the kingdom, returning it to order and righteousness. But the ruler would not listen.

The advisor turned his gaze to a wide desk that stood against the wall to his right. He remembered back to all the letters he had written at that desk, the orders he had signed, the little secret notes he scrawled for the eyes of the woman he loved. Above the table hung a weapon display. In the case, against the red fabric lining, was placed a sword. A gift from the king of Mortendenn and a symbol of his gratitude. Darius was never a lover of brute force but he valued the weapon and looked to it when the strain of the current political situation overwhelmed him. He had been taught to fight but as he looked at himself in the light of the fire now, he could see why his greatest strength was his mind. His tunic was undone from the collar and the white shirt underneath hung open, revealing the bony chest of a very delicate body.

Sighing, he looked up. A large oak bed stood against the back wall, the cover of which was decorated with intricate embroidery in green and yellow thread, similar in colour to the tapestry that hung above it. In his heart, he knew that the one woman he would give his life to share it with would never be his. Yet their endless love held them together, driving them to sin and to commit the greatest crime in the kingdom.

Treason. He thought again. The word sat bitterly on his tongue.

Chapter 41

The Heart of Battle

A young servant girl made her way through the stone corridors of the Marrynport strategic tower. In her hands, she carried a small linen handkerchief, winding it nervously around her fingers. The girl made her way into the kitchen and looked around like a new-born cub looking for its mother. A stout cook was rushing through the kitchen, knocking pans off the table in her gaucheness and screaming at the hectic kitchen maids to pick them up.

"Ma'am?" the nervous young maid called out.

The cook continued in her duties without lifting an eye. The girl called out again.

"What? What is it that you want? What could you possibly desire of me in this time? Right before the main luncheon is to be served to the generals? Do you wish to volunteer to be the one to tell them that the stew is not ready? Is that what you wish for? Well, in that case, be my guest! But if you are here for any other reason, you can go to hell and leave me be!"

"Please, ma'am," the young girl pleaded, "I am new here and I don't know where to go or what to do."

"Well, I don't care for the duties of a lady's maid but I can tell ya, you won't find any corsets to tie or jewels to polish down here!" the fat woman called out.

"If you would only allow me to change my frock and serve the lunch to the generals as a humble kitchen maid, I would be ever so grateful."

The kitchen staff paused in the work and looked at her as if she had said something ridiculous. The cook threw a cloth down onto the table and leaned on it with her fist, her other hand placed in frustration on her hip.

"I don't know where they find them! Ya wish to serve food to the generals? Have you ever been in a kitchen before, lass? The maids don't serve luncheon to the generals! They don't want to look at our tired grey faces! We don't show ourselves in the upper floors of the castle! The ladies' maids go wherever they please so you think ye can just come down here and prance about like a bloody princess? Get out of my sight!"

The young girl stopped fidgeting with the cloth and straightened up. Her face contorted from the look of innocence to a cold violent profile. She moved slowly past the counters and the tables, her pace steady and tense, like a lioness about to sprint after her prey. Moving the cloth swiftly between her hands, she locked eyes with the cook and glared with a look so menacing the old woman recoiled and backed away.

"Get back to your duties!" the girl commanded to the other servants, turning her head slightly and speaking sternly over her shoulder, never taking her eyes off the cook.

The old woman was backed against a cupboard. She glanced around nervously, trying to avoid meeting the gaze of her opponent, who was now inches away from her.

The woman in the lady's maid frock stopped and leaned closer. The other servants were moving around but did not make a single sound, whether for fear or curiosity. In the apparent silence of the room, the hostile newcomer spoke with a discomforting gentleness.

"My dear, hardworking, honest companion. Do you turn away every young soul that asks for your assistance and advice? How could you be so cruel, dear woman? I cannot return to the duties of a lady's maid yet. Not just yet." Her voice lingered softly on the repetition. "Although I will require to pass into the generals' hall."

"They are presently in the northern command tower. Soon they will take their lunch in the grand hall, with the Duke of Sumerfyn," the cook whimpered.

The other maids watched as the cook gave up this information, which she was never meant to know in the first place. Some moved to protest, but their steps were slowed by a force they could not understand.

The air around this stranger was so intimidating, so commanding that they dare not confront her. Yet their fascination held their sheep-like eyes locked on her. The cook took shallow breaths, feeling like her chest was constricted by a heavy chain. She watched the lips of the woman before her form shapes as the gentle words that were emitted by them passed through her skull and twisted the vines of her mind.

With the necessary information obtained, Adelaide left the kitchen with feigned grandeur. Since she entered the fort, plan after plan fell apart right before her. Her lack of knowledge about the structure and order of the servants in the castle left her looking like a fool. A lady's maid! That servant was nothing more. Adelaide inwardly raged at the pretentious maids who dress differently based on the floor upon which they are permitted to walk while being kept from the sight of the upper classes like dirty dogs for fear of offending the gentility with their brutish ways.

As Adelaide furiously stormed down the narrow stone corridor of the servants' halls, she found herself glancing around at the half-dozen wooden doors that reached from the dusty floor to the low ceiling. No torches or lamps illuminated the passageway and the staircase that this dishevelled new servant had walked down only moments before was nowhere to be seen. Stopping in her tracks, Adelaide looked back. The kitchen maids had gathered at the entrance to the corridor and were watching her like woodland animals watch a retreating wildfire. To turn back now would be shameful so instead Adelaide forced open a nearby door only to be confronted with a cramped, poorly furnished room that resembled a prison cell, albeit in better upkeep, with three low set beds covered in rough fabric and straw and a tiny barred window on the wall opposite the door.

One of the kitchen maids has snuck closer, alarmed by the intrusion to what appeared to be her dorm. Adelaide, who's temper by now was reaching its peak, turned back with a look of blind aggression and grabbed the young girl by the white linen hat on her head and a handful of hair underneath. The maid squealed in pain and twisted her body towards the assailant to lessen the tug on her hair. There was a surprised murmur among the others watching and Adelaide knew that she was running out of time. Violently pulling the girl closer, she hissed a command into her ears, splashing her face with droplets of spit. The girl moved down the corridor, leading her captor to her goal.

***

The generals gathered around an octagonal table upon which sat a tactical map. There were five people in the small dark room, a young blonde man who stood by the tiny slit of a window idly watching the port, a bearded general who leaned on the table, swaying slightly and glaring down at the map with his fierce eyes, an armed man with a multitude of medals who placed his elbow on the back a large ornate oaken chair upon which rested an old obese man who's costume was similar to that of a court official. The last commander paced around the room in frustration. With the lack of natural light, the chamber was illuminated almost entirely by candlelight from the small lamps that hung from the walls, next to intricately detailed maps of different lands and sketches of battle strategies. Curtains and tapestries decorated the walls, so that the cold intimidating slabs of stone underneath were hidden from the eyes, replaced by ornaments that gave the little hole of a room an aura of confidence and power.

The door creaked ajar and the men turned in alarm to see who would dare intrude on the council. After a long moment, a young servant girl stumbled into the room, falling to the floor some distance in, as if she was pushed into the room with a strong force. The hat on her head was slipping off and her hair was falling messily down her face. Her cheeks burned red and tears streamed down her innocent face. Mortified and frightened, she rushed out of the room, tripping over her skirt and falling again before she could make her escape.

In silence, the armoured man walked hastily to the door and shut it gently behind her.

"One of the lads in the castle was probably trying to have his way with her, thought this room to be empty," he tried to explain.

The generals looked to one another, startled by such an interruption. The first thought that passed through the minds of all five was the fear of an enemy spy and they glanced around the room, searching for anything suspicious. In the dim light, they did not see a tapestry move slightly behind the ornate chair, as if shifted by a gentle breeze. All the while their eyes were turned towards one girl dressed as a servant, another one dexterously slipped into the room.

Walking over to the table, the armoured man looked down, trying to turn his focus back to their task.

"The King's message has reached that bandit up north," the old Duke called from his chair.

"This is madness!" returned the man pacing in frustration. Tugging incessantly at his sleek black hair, he continued ranting. "To fight one enemy by willingly throwing your body onto the sword of another. Does the King believe that this bastard will not exploit him and turn against him at the first opportunity?"

"It's that foreigner he lets whisper in his ear, it's all his idea. Treason is what I call it!" the Duke added.

"But I have heard word from Mortendenn," the armoured man protested. "And they say that the rebellion was dissolved and everything is back to normal there. The monarchy of Mortendenn are eternally grateful to Lord Darius."

"I heard it was all sorcery," the bearded man joined in with a maniacal smile, tracing his finger over the lines of the map.

"If the current relations between Starkenhaart and Mortendenn are so strong, why does the King not contact them for support?" asked the young blonde man delicately, still staring out of the window. "I am certain they would not refuse to return the favour of silencing a rebellion."

"They have just survived one war, I doubt they would be so eager to get involved in another," the armoured general responded. "And even if they were willing, what can they do? Send troops? We have troops here, but the King is reluctant to send them out for fear of starting a war."

"The war has already begun. It started at Avenstead," the bearded man hauntingly added, still grinning down at the map in an unnerving manner.

"I agree with Henry," the black-haired man with an ill temper shouted, waving his arms theatrically. "The war has started without us. It will not finish that way. I will take a small group of men and travel down towards Tarrynsdew in order to assess the situation in the south, closer to what we believe to be their stronghold. I would be surprised if the locals have not formed a militia of some nature by now."

The bearded man finally tore his eyes from the map to glance at this ally. His psychotic stare panned the room, studying the men that surrounded him as if he had only just met them. When his gaze had reached the Duke, he straightened up with the look of worry that reached past the old man and his courtly chair and stopped in the shadows behind.

"It would be wise for us to depart this chamber now," Henry spoke, still staring into the darkness, "I am certain the feast we were promised would be ready by now."

***

In the sunlit streets of Marrynport, the bandit assembly reunited.

"Any news from the castle?" Morrihold inquired.

"It was far too much danger with far too little a reward," Adelaide proclaimed dejectedly. "All I could gather from the generals was that they are conflicted in their support for the actions of the King, but this could be expected. Darius is pulling all the strings at the capital, but he is receiving resistance from the King and some of the generals, who still foolishly believe that a war can be avoided. I think it best to leave them to this belief. One of the generals is travelling down towards Tarrynsdew, if we could ambush him there, we could extract more information, as well as eliminate one of the powerful players on their side."

"There are a lot of soldiers in the castle," Archaius quietly chipped in, "yet they all wear different crests. Each of the generals must have brought a small group with them."

"Have you found out who is the main captain of this fortress?" Bertrand asked more out of curiosity than desire to participate.

"No, although I know that the Duke of Sumerfyn was present. I gather he is an old and stout man?" Adelaide questioned.

The others looked at her blankly, clearly having as little knowledge about the dukes and lords of Starkenhaart as Adelaide did herself.

"The traders are becoming worried about the lack of imports from Tarrynsdew," Morrihold informed the others, "but for now, they are content blaming it in the incompetence of the southern folk and the laziness of the villagers at the crossing."

"It is only a matter of time before they discover otherwise," decided their leader, still shaken by her recent failings. "And frankly, I find this city very unsettling. We shall return to Tarrynsdew and prepare an ambush. How many men will he bring?"

"I could not know which crest belongs to which general. Anywhere between five and thirty," the wizard shrugged.

***

The quartet arrived at the ruins of the city they had destroyed. Adelaide once again regretted her hasty decision to burn down the houses and wipe out the entire population. She remembered back to the heroic unity that was forged by her fire in the hearts of the people: bandits, soldiers and civilians working together to fight the plague of violence that has invaded their homes. Some retreated and abandoned their friends and families, but they could not make it far through the snow with no fur or leather to warm their bodies, which now lay blue beneath the deadly white blanket. Yet still, Adelaide convinced herself that her decision was righteous and if the citizens were granted their lives, they would rush to Marrynport telling stories of a bandit clan with werewolves and wizards. Information such as this must be kept from the authorities for as long as this war would allow.

Archaius and Bertrand averted their eyes from the blackened ruins which now supported a layer of sparkling fluffy snow. Morrihold climbed between the fallen beams, mesmerised by the carnage yet appalled by the pure fury that had caused it. He glanced back at his beloved, looking from under the brim of his hat with eyes that were full of pain and pity. He was aware that it was a monster he had fallen in love with, yet he was helpless to stop himself from admiring her, even at times when she resembled the devil incarnate.

They waited in the maze of wooden planks and beams that still stood broken and cracked. With every step they lifted the snow from the ground, revealing the ashen remains beneath. No words were uttered except an occasional whispered prayer that resonated from Morrihold's bowed head. From Bertrand, Adelaide received glares of hatred, but he spewed no accusations. The snow was uneven, raised in places by the fallen buildings but spread out in every direction were small mounts that were even more haunting. Their size and shape made them unmistakable. There were so many of them. The sight of dozens of these dead bodies buried in the ice struck Adelaide's heart with regret. At last, she began to see the horror of her actions; the nightmare she had brought onto the people. There was no smell of decay, no maggots, no flesh being torn from the corpses by starving animals. No, this death was like nothing she had seen in the cities, it was graceful, it was beautiful. Awe inspired, she placed her hand on her forearm, over the Rose that was growing beneath her sleeve.

"I have a Gift," she thought to herself. "A Gift from God. I cannot be a sinner, I cannot kill. I only grant salvation. I am their saviour."

***

It was the vibration of the ground that tore Adelaide's mind from its shelter of pride and delusion. The hooves echoed like a thunder in the distance. And there she was again, a lost scared child, running for her life through the empty dead fields, abandoning that piece of heaven she once called home. The horse was right behind her and the rider drew his sword. Then he stood before her, his long, crooked fingers digging into her shoulders, his yellow nails piercing her flesh like the talons of a hawk. His face was a mask of black smoke that swirled and coalesced into the shape of hellish hound in the stone tunnels beneath the enchanted woods. Adelaide felt a touch on her shoulder and with a frightened shriek she spun towards the assailant, taking a step back and drawing her sword in a flash. Morrihold instantly pulled back his hand and moved away, watching her with a look of worry and fear. Sheathing the translucent blade, the bandit leader regained her breath and shook her head apologetically at the man who's neck she nearly separated from his body in a fit of panic.

"The enemy army is approaching," he spoke coldly, averting his gaze.

"Army?" Archaius jumped to his feet, "all of the soldiers at the castle? That is more than twice the number of trained swordsmen that were here when we first arrived."

Bertrand climbed up unto a fallen rooftop and standing on the wooden spine that ran along the top he focused his eyes into the distance. Uncertain, he climbed back down and cleared a small patch of snow, placing his ear to the ground. With closed eyes and slow breathing, he listened to the sounds that pulsed through the earth like ripples on water. The others watched him expectantly, Morrihold and Archaius growing increasingly tense as the advancing attackers approached.

"About two dozen," Bertrand stated at last, drawing a sigh of relief from the mage.

"Archaius, head to the east and bring forth some fire."

"In God's name, woman, there is nothing left to burn!" the wizard cried out.

"The soldiers will make for nice kindling," Adelaide shot back cruelly. "Morri, take to the west. Try to stay out of sight and attack only the ones who are on the ground and isolated from the others."

"I may not be a wizard or a werewolf but I can fight!" he protested like an offended child.

"Not twenty men at once. I will face them head on, halt them in their tracks. I am sure they don't fully know who they are expecting to find here and the surprise should offer us a window of opportunity. And lastly, Bertrand, I need you to circle around and stop them turning back. Can you frighten the horses, make them throw their riders?"

"It's the middle of day," he responded passionlessly.

"Well, can't you just—you know—make do?" Adelaide approached more delicately than usual, suspecting that he was pushed to the edge and was waiting for an opportunity to abandon the entire scheme.

"Oh, of course I can! There is nothing I enjoy more than to consciously terrorise villagers and murder the innocent," he spoke bitterly, walking away from the burned down city. "I'll do what I can, ya villainous hag."

Startled by his open contempt, Adelaide thought of calling him back to remind him of the power he was standing up to but more important matters quickly conquered her mind. Retreating into the shadows of the fallen buildings she crouched in the snow, briefly reappearing into the sunlight to ensure that her accomplices were also hidden.

The hill rose up in the distance, separating Adelaide and her men from the oncoming attack. She knew what they would see upon arriving; the black graveyard of collapsed buildings and a sea of corpses that littered these snowy fields. She would emerge from the ashes not like a phoenix but like a ghastly shadow of death, weapons in her hands and warm fur against her skin, prepared to fight until the blood of her enemies tainted the white snow and seeped into icy soil beneath and their bodies lay unburied and dishonoured, with the expressions of pain and anguish frozen onto their faces until the warm winds of spring bring about the life that will feed on their remains and decay their flesh! A manic grin exposed her teeth. She will walk away victorious, wearing upon her brow a new silver circlet that would shine in the sunlight like it was made from the very snow that has been turbulent and unforgiving this winter.

Snow. With horror, Adelaide noticed one fatal flaw in her plan. Four sets of footprints lay exposed, leading from the charred city to the hill, from behind which the general's armies were just about to emerge. They must have seen the footprints by now, she was certain. They knew only that four pilgrims have traversed this land since the last storm, they would never suspect that the city now lay faded and lifeless and a powerful ambush was brewing within its corpse.

At last the army emerged. They stood grandiosely upon the hill, watching from a distance, careful to approach. Only six sat on horseback, but two were at the front, leading the whole ensemble. The horses walked slowly down the mild incline, their riders mortified by the sight before them.

"Now we know why they have not been trading," one of the leaders called out, following the remark with a cruel laugh that seemed to linger in the air, intensified by the silence of the others.

Adelaide recognised his voice as one of the men from Marrynport's defence tower. This was the bearded man named Henry. He must have agreed to venture out here with his ally. The bandit leader wondered why they would let a man this unstable anywhere near a sword, let alone an entire army. Yet she could sense opportunity in this. Instead of incapacitating one of the main generals of the King's army, she could now get her hands on two of them. This, surely, will cause more than a little distress to the all-beloved Darius. As the army approached the ruins of the city, Adelaide stepped out of her hiding spot.

The horses halted and the men looked at her with cautious curiosity. The armoured woman leisurely strolled over towards them. Her dark green cloak offered such contrast to the whiteness of the surroundings yet such similarity to the cold embers of the city, as if she had just risen from the very ashes at her feet. She stood before them with the posture of a goddess, fearless and frightening yet she shivered like a mortal in the cold winds.

Henry looked at her with familiarity.

"That's the face I saw in the shadows," he stated with awe.

"The spy?" his easily-agitated companion replied.

"The ghost," Henry corrected, not taking his eyes off her.

Adelaide was caught off guard. She did not anticipate them recognising her. Taking a deep breath, she stopped herself from calling for Archaius. With feigned confidence she stepped closer to the men on horseback.

"Yet, you are surprised to find me here," the bandit addressed the generals before her.

"We are hereby placing you under arrest," the jittery man began coldly, unsettled by the events.

"What for?" Adelaide returned, her voice smooth and deep, digging into his mind.

"For conspiring against His Majesty—our royal—Great King Bohemond the Merciful," the nervous man finished, his voice breaking towards the final words.

Henry watched the exchange with fascination and then leaped from his horse to stand before her.

"Surrender now, mage!" he said almost playfully.

"I am no mage," she turned her power to him yet he stood unaffected.

"No?"

"No. And I will not surrender."

She drew her sword, savouring the sharp sound of the blade against its sheathe. The man before her moved back and gestured for the footmen to attack. Raising the Dragonslayer into the sky, she let out a battle cry and unleashed the full force of her Gift on the unfortunate ones. Warm blood from their ravaged bodied spilled onto the white ground, dripping from her blade and staining her furs. Taking a moment to wipe it from her cheek, she looked down at the red liquid that glistened on her skin, feeling nothing but satisfaction in extracting in from those who dared to challenge her. The pity and remorse that she may have felt at one time had now all but vanished, leaving a merciless and bloodthirsty husk in its place.

The horses reared and threw their riders, galloping wildly away from her but they were caught and herded by the well-built man in rags, who led them away from the fight and calmed them as they struggled to free themselves. He stood there watching the fight from a distance, swearing to himself over and over again that this is the last battle he would have to partake in. After this, he would return to the camp, grab Daisy and carry her as far away from the turmoil and bloodshed as he could. They would go to a different kingdom, they would start a new life there, and he would not fight under this witch a day longer than he must.

Adelaide saw him standing there and grinned to herself knowing full well that one word from her and he would once again fall before the power of the Rose. Seeing her psychotic smile, he turned away to face the distant planes. A flash of fire to her right startled her and she turned to see foot soldiers rolling in the snow, desperately trying to extinguish the flames from their leather armour. Walking menacingly over to them, the cruel bandit drove her sword into their necks one by one. Archaius stood by the burned timbers, looking at his feet. Not even he would meet her gaze.

Shaking off the disgust they must feel for her, Adelaide turned back towards the battlefield only to find it still and lifeless apart from the bearded general who stood on the other side of the red pool, calm and thoughtful, not once having drawn his weapon. Clashing of swords sounded from under the charred beams and Adelaide rushed over to find her beloved in a battle to the death with the other general. For the first time, she was genuinely concerned for the life of another human being and in a flash, she appeared behind the general, driving her bloody blade into the back of his knee.

The man yelped in agony and collapsed to the ground. Adelaide grabbed him by the collar and dragged him through the snow into the sunlight as he choked and struggled. Morrihold emerged from the shadows just after her, struggling to catch his breath.

The injured man glared up towards this friend with a piercing look of betrayal but Henry was oblivious to his suffering, instead watching Adelaide's sword with childlike curiosity.

"The military commander of Marrynport, who is it?" she demanded with fierce energy.

The general who lay bleeding in the snow before her had strangely recovered his nerves and calmly tried to stop the blood that was flowing from his leg. He seemed tranquil and turned his newly empowered eyes towards the woman. Silently, he smiled, his mouth moving slowly, numbed by the cold, revealing teeth that were coated in red. Impatiently, Adelaide hit him hard in the jaw with the hilt of her sword, demanding an answer.

"Look at you now," he croaked in response, "so strong, so courageous. Do you truly believe that the cause you are fighting for is the righteous one or do you simply enjoy the chaos? Either way, the blood that flows through your veins will be tainted by the murders. The mind that was once so solid will collapse into shambles. War. It changes one. Be it man or woman, swordsman or mage. It will destroy you. It will become your addiction. You will flee from your family, you will abandon your faith. Your skin will tighten around you, suffocating you until the only place you feel safe is on the battlefield. You may not drive your sword through the hearts of those men but if you were the one to speak the command, then their blood will always stain your hands. It will pour into yon glass in place of wine. It will soak into the canvas of every painting you lay eyes on. It will flow from the flesh of your children when they fall and scrape their knees."

Morrihold listened to the man, captivated by his words. He had hated to kill for those very reasons. Seeing this man take a calm breath only when he was wounded condensed his every fear into a caged panic in his chest. Pulling down the brim of his hat, he closed his eyes and prayed to God that this uprising would be over soon, knowing full well that this prayer would go unanswered. He prayed for Adelaide, for her goodness and mercy, for her sanity, yet he feared that it was already too late.

Archaius was also drawn closer by the words of the injured general. He had seen this so often. When a man spends his life in battle, he could return each time in perfect health yet his heart would not follow him home. Educated and intelligent, these men spoke many languages but violence was the only one they truly heard.

Adelaide, at whom this warning was targeted, was more than a little moved by it. Seeing the reflection in herself of the twisted and bloodthirsty killers that he was describing sent an uncomfortable tension up her spine and through her jaw. At that moment a cold revelation came to her, of what others see in her commands and her actions. At last, she could understand their repulsion. Amazed by Morrihold's continued loyalty and faith in her despite the brutality was heart-warming. Yet, the foretold demise of her sanity did not frighten her. It intrigued her. It allured her. With a sly smile she changed the hold on her sword and lowered the blade with force into the other leg of the bleeding general. His scream echoed through the snowy valley. The others turned their faces from her.

"The military commander of Marrynport," the bandit stated her demand.

"Sir Mark Varshaw. A young blonde man," was the strained reply.

Adelaide's hard-set demands continued until she exhausted the entire supply of knowledge from the dying man. For his co-operation she rewarded him generously with a quick death.

The bearded man named Henry stood by and watched the demise of his friend with a warm detachment. He was a prime example of the severe emotional damage described by the other general and he was aware of that, if not of anything else. Yet, he seemed to carry a sixth sense, emphasised by his childlike curiosity and fascination with the world. Adelaide knew that he could be of use to her, if not on the battlefield then at least as consolation that she was not alone in her state. She asked him sternly if he would join the bandits or die right there, to the surprise of her companions. As sick and unstable as this soldier was, he was resolved on upholding his loyalty to King and country. Knowing his fate, he spoke one last aimless prayer and dramatically stretched out his arms, baring his chest. Asking only for a quick death he looked at Adelaide with understanding and forgiveness. With a hand more gentle than ever, she raised the sword and placed it to his ribs. Kind words of apology were exchanged and, in a moment, he fell peacefully to the ground. The three stood around him, looking down first at the peculiar yet remarkable man and then to his knowledgeable and insightful friend. With silent prayers, the three departed from the battlefield. Adelaide sheathed the blade, knowing that although it was named the Dragonslayer, that day it had slayed two heroes.

Chapter 42

'Til Death Do Us Part

Many weeks had passed and the trio returned to the Silverblood camp, Morrihold choosing to gallop back to the village on the riverbank. Yet it seemed that "camp" was no longer a fitting word for the settlement, as the now-expanded fort stretched far beyond the old wooden fence that previously bordered it. The thick stone wall was now completed, with watchtowers peaking evenly throughout the perimeter. A thick wooden gate was locked shut, much like the gates of major cities, and bandits were positioned outside. Upon seeing their mistress return, they jumped up from the wet ground that was slowly awakening from its winter slumber and ran towards her with cheers and merriment.

Seated grandiosely upon her horse Adelaide bowed her head and waved her hand at them, as a king would towards his peasants. These bandits were not dressed how she remembered them. Over their simple clothing they now wore thick leather armour that looked as if it was crafted by a skilled hand. One arm of each man was placed through two leather straps of a wooden shield with steel lining and reinforcement. Adelaide queried them on their newfound equipment, but they only beckoned her inside the fort.

Behind the wall now rose a town that she could barely recognise. The tents were replaced with small but solid huts made from wood and stone. They were not scattered throughout the open space but organised into sections. Great planning had been put into erecting this miniature city. Walking the horse to the centre of the fort, Adelaide then jumped down and looked around in awe. Dirt roads stretched outwards, cutting cleanly between the different sections of the town. The layout was perfectly symmetrical, with a guard tower at the end of each road, which split up into smaller capillaries that weaved between the huts.

"Hansfell, you have truly outdone yourself, old friend," Adelaide spoke aloud.

"Why thank you," he returned, striding towards her.

Turning to face him, she remembered her instruction with growing concern.

"You are here! But then who is at Ghyrock and Avenstead? What if the King was to attack?"

Hansfell placed his hands on her shoulders and looked at her comfortingly.

"Worry not, my future Queen," he spoke, "Talon is set up at Ghyrock, we have ensured that it is in best military condition with the walls reinforced and the citizens terrorised into submission. Hunter has succeeded in taking over Rynell and Avenstead! The soldiers are dead and their King is enraged! Although the army may require a little more training, they should hold against a moderate attack."

"Good," Adelaide replied thoughtfully, still trying to comprehend their lucky successes.

"Now you three travellers go and rest, I will show you to your new quarters. And where is the young Morrihold? Not lost in battle I hope?"

"God no!" Adelaide exclaimed. "He left on personal errands but should return shortly. You see, we are to be wed soon." With that she extended her hand to reveal the promise ring upon her finger. Sir Hansfell congratulated her fiercely and wished them the greatest of happiness and begged to attend the ceremony.

He led her through the streets and towards a grand house, much like the houses that he and his fellow rogue knights occupied in Ghyrock. It towered over the settlement and although it was crafted from the same wood and stone as the other buildings, it carried that intimidating aura of a castle. Adelaide exclaimed with joy upon seeing it and after venturing inside found the interior most delightful.

The following days were spent discussing military tactics and Adelaide informing Hansfell and the others of the two generals that had been ambushed at Tarrynsdew. The three others who had attended the tactical meeting at Marrynport were identified and the threat from each landowner was assessed in full. Keeping the location of the Silverblood fort a secret was of utmost importance and further reinforcement of the walls was to take priority.

James had arrived at the bandit settlement and took great interest in studying the walls and structure of the fort. He investigated the guard towers and counted the number of men positioned there at various times of day. He stood on the battlements and looked out into the emptiness. His brother insisted that James was to be kept from the tactical command rooms and Adelaide did not need much persuasion.

The bandit queen was eventually introduced to the master blacksmith who was behind the craftsmanship of the weapons and armour. She stepped through the low doorway of the smithy to see a familiar face.

"How did you find us?" she asked after a pause.

The old man shook his head, keeping his eyes fixed on the ground, and placed his trembling hand against the stones of the forge for support. His skin has a peculiar tint of yellow and his aging yet muscular arms were covered in long red streaks from where the flesh had been cut. Had he injured himself on his tools, Adelaide wondered.

"I had to come." At last, the blacksmith replied, "I had to come. I had to leave the village and come. I had to."

He let out a whimper and backed against the forge.

"It is you who summons him," the blacksmith grew hysterical.

"Summons whom?" Adelaide inquired.

He looked at her now, revealing eyes that were so bloodshot, no white could be seen, with large purple bags of skin hanging beneath them.

"The hermit," was the simple reply. Then he continued, speaking mostly to himself, "It was so long ago. I was young, I was foolish and I made one mistake. And now he has taken hold of my soul. Now I am his slave."

Archaius had been hovering by the door, listening. Upon sensing his presence, Adelaide shook off the power of the unsettling words and commanded the old man to make armour for her. Then, leaving the smithy as nonchalantly at she could muster, she nodded at the mage in passing and continued to walk, knowing not where to. When she was some distance away, the wizard slipped through the low doorway to speak to the old man.

Adelaide walked and walked until she arrived at the gate of the fort, where she explained her desire to see the wall from the outside. The bandits guarding the entrance offered to go with her to introduce her to how it had all been built but she politely yet decisively declined and left the fort by herself. She made some distance between herself and the wall before stopping and looking back. Her ribcage expanded, pulling a large volume of air into her lungs as if she had just stepped out of a stuffy tavern cellar into the fresh outdoor air. Oxygen rushed to her head and she sat down on the wet grass and admired her capital. Limestone was circling above the grand stone battlements like a seagull above a port. For once, Adelaide's mind was at peace, resting from the stress of new revelations. She could not bring herself to question the blacksmith but she was once again surprised by how little knowledge she had of the mysterious Gift she harboured. The hermit was the old man with the crooked cane, the spectre that she had seen so often, she was certain of that. Yet, the question of who he was haunting was one she could not answer.

Adelaide brushed her hand over the strands of grass, pulling them from the ground and ripping them in her fingers, the way a child does in summer. The thin green stands began to quiver and the ground shook slightly from the stomping hooves that were galloping towards the fort from the distance. Adelaide looked up to see two riders approaching from the northeast. As they got close, she stood up to greet her beloved. The second horse carried a priest.

***

The ceremony was to begin. The ensemble of spectators was small, only a few of the bandits were stationed at the camp. A few small bouquets of field flowers were placed around the main square of the fort, where the dirt roads intersected and the buildings stood tall like those in the cities. A stone well served as the centre of the square and the priest stood by it, looking around nervously. The skies had begun to colour, with splashes of orange tinting the horizon, feeding this simple wedding set up with natural serene beauty. The bandits stood calm, held transfixed by the tranquil surroundings and the emotional suspense.

Morrihold walked slowly over to the priest and spoke quiet words to him, in his usual delicate manner. Yet the feigned composure still betrayed his underlying nervousness through the tapping of the foot and the continuous fidgeting of the fingers. He wore his best tunic, one of a dark clay colour with leather boots from which he had scrubbed all the dirt and blood that had previously accumulated on them. Yet still he fussed. Brushing back his short mahogany-brown hair with his fingers, then placing a brown hat on his head. Then changing his mind again and removing it, holding it uncertainly in his hands.

The priest walked carefully over to him the way a child approaches a large dog.

"I have come here on a favour, young man. Once the ceremony is complete, I demand to be returned home safely," he spoke with assertion.

"I have given you my word," the handsome bandit responded. "A ceremony cannot be carried out by a man who has committed murder. Yet each man at this camp is guilty of that. We have blood on our hands. We need an innocent man, a man of God for this marriage to be true and pure."

"And I would not object to the joining of two people in love. Among your kind, family values are not held by many. And may this one righteous deed help you see the light of good and turn you from your wicked ways."

"You have our gratitude. You are welcome to stay and attend the celebrations," Morrihold offered. The priest promptly declined.

Soon, Adelaide emerged onto the scene. She wore a dress of simple pale cloth that hugged her figure and her hair was plaited with small blue flowers. Gabriel's green cloak still rested on her shoulders, padded with wolf fur. The merciless bandit queen now stood unarmed and undefended. Childlike excitement radiated from her flushed cheeks and she moved with feminine grace that only slightly resembled the steady stalk of a thief.

Morrihold dropped his hat to the ground and stared at his lover with heartfelt awe. He moved hypnotically to his position to the left of the priest. The clergyman also assumed his place yet he now looked at the young bride with disbelief. This was not the face of a woman who raised an army, slaughtered thousands and challenged the King. This was the face of a maiden, a girl ready to become a wife and a mother.

Sir Hansfell took the role of her father. Arm in arm they walked past the astounded bandits, taking delicate steps to protect her skirt from the sludge of the roads. A gentle breeze moved her raven black hair over the fabric of the cloak. As they walked, one pearl-white snowflake sunk through the air before them. This little intruder was soon accompanied by many others. White snow landed on her shoulders and hair, invisible against the unpigmented locks that framed her face.

The groom pressed his hand to his mouth, trying to contain an overpowering emotion. When she had completed her slow parade, tears had welled in her eyes and she reached out towards him. Instantly he caught her arm and pulled her closer and together they stood holding onto each other, both overwhelmed with love.

The priest had begun the ceremony. His voice was strong and the words carried power through the respectful silence of the crowd. Sir Hansfell stood to the side and watched the wedding with affectionate fondness. Archaius observed it all with a melancholy thoughtfulness. Daisy and Bertrand stood some distance away, her small frame hidden from the cold in his embrace. She pressed her forehead against his chest and watched the wedding with curious eyes while his were full of envy of the ceremony he could not share with the woman he dearly loved.

The priest revealed the true names of the bride and groom, drawing a gasp from the crowd, and pronounced them man and wife. The newlyweds threw themselves into a passionate kiss and tears of incomparable joy streamed down Adelaide's face.

With the ceremony complete, the priest departed, accompanied by a bandit who swore to deliver him safely to his village. As for the rest of the attendees, they drank and danced for days on end. The wedded couple excused themselves from the party early to continue their celebrations in the privacy of their home.

No festival could compare to the joy of that day. Mead flowed freely, food was plentiful, and songs of praise were belted loudly by the bandits.

**

Across the self-established bandit border, in the northern city of Farendale, a man rose from his throne. The throne did not stand in a castle, but rather in the old abandoned dungeon which had since been converted into an underground fortress for the most notorious bandit organisation in Starkenhaart, an organisation that has been pinched and taunted for years by the "Silverblood bandits" and forced into an alliance with the self-righteous manipulative advisor to the King.

This man was long past his prime, but his body was strong and his mind was sharp. Greying auburn hair hung in tangled clusters from his head. Thick leather clothed him. Ruthless killers averted their eyes from his terrifying gaze. This was Stormhawk. And he was ready for the hunt.

Part 4

The Queen

Chapter 43

The Years That Passed

Four years had passed since the day of the wedding. The warm winds of spring have once again begun their invasion of the Starkenhaart meadows. The Silverblood fortress was beautiful this time of year, surrounded by undisturbed fields and a woodland to the north which, although small in area, still provided the bandits with plentiful game and fresh water. The stone wall of the fort had stood strong against the continuous attacks, repaired time after time as Stormhawk's troops advanced through the countryside and retreated again to the north, each time unable to hold a prolonged siege. Over the years, Darius had succeeded in convincing the King to involve the royal army to suppress the rebellion and Adelaide was facing constant force from the capital. Hunter and Talon had remained at their bases in Ghyrock and Avenstead and held their posts against the pressure of the trained soldiers. To succeed they had to compromise the lives of the citizens, arming the able to join the rebellion and sending the weaker into the fields to farm the depleted soil for whatever crops they could grow, which were then ripped from their hands and fed to the rebel soldiers. This regime had stolen the lives of hundreds of undertrained militants and an even greater number of peasants. Famine and starvation gripped the kingdom in its claws and the prospect of victory was the only release. Darius was more determined than ever to send out the knights yet the King was reluctant, held timid by Stormhawk's influence. The King's slow response also prevented the cooperation of the neighbouring territories that his competent advisor would otherwise, no doubt, have secured.

Adelaide held more land and power than ever before. Her troops had by now occupied the central and southern regions of the realm. Major cities and military forts were overrun by her soldiers, bandits and otherwise, with any available structures of strategic advantage being manned by the rebels. Their skill improved as rapidly as their bloodlust. As predicted, the Silverblood queen had created an army of vicious hounds, cruel and ruthless in their methods. Merciless in their victory.

Her delusional ideals had not faltered. In her own eyes, she was a saint, a prophet of the Lord, sent to earth with her righteous Gift, honourable and brave, to cleanse the land of the heretic King and his army. Only she carried God's true mark. Only she had been trusted to enforce his word. Drunk on power and success, her closest advisors spoke nothing in contradiction. They were more grounded than her, yet even they found their weaknesses in gold and pride. Twisted and corrupted by the world their whole lives, plunged into the harshness and danger of this earth from a young age, they killed and plundered long before her arrival and now at last they had the right and liberty to do so in the open and without the fear of eternal damnation, allowing themselves to be guided by her narcissistic blasphemous insanity to their own imagined salvation.

Even Morrihold, the one man not influenced by her power, had accepted the war and taken his place by her side, renouncing the authority that a man would normally hold over his wife out of both love and fear. Together they remained at their established capital, along with Sir Hansfell, to reinforce and defend it as the headquarters of her operations.

Yet those stone walls guarded something far more precious than the heart of her militant activity as now, four years after their marriage, Adelaide and Duncan had two beautiful little children. The patter of tiny feet on the wooden floor of their house was the older, a black-haired young menace named Rupert, born in the autumn after the wedding. The younger, only three months of age was Edith, adored by all and cradled all through the day. Sir Hansfell was particularly fond of her, spending many evenings reading her legends of heroes long gone.

Archaius would often remove himself from the fortress, only to return a few weeks later. He watched the infants with wonder, sometimes studying their plump little arms closely for any markings, curious to see if the Rose would spread its power through blood. Alas, nothing showed, and their skin stayed as pink as a healthy child's should. There was a sadness in the way he looked at them which almost resembled pity. The mage could not stand Hansfell's tales, disappearing at the first mention of dragons and knights yet he often lingered by the blacksmith, speaking to him in hushed tones, begging him to leave, to return to his village, to resist the Hermit. Unnoticed by most, the spectre showed itself to Archaius openly, holding to the connection between magic and phantoms. The old man with the crooked cane reminded the blacksmith of his debt and repelled the young mage with threats and warnings.

The wizard would take a bottle of rum and hide away at the stables, remembering back to his first journey to Starkenhaart. He had known Darius for many years and greatly admired the man for his intelligence and loyalty. He could not have suspected to find himself on the other side of the war. His personal allegiance lied with Darius but the fascination with the Rose bound him to Adelaide. This was much more than a mortal war. He knew the power of the Gift and watched idly as it destroyed both the carrier and the kingdom, knowing full well that he did not harbour the level of magic needed to stop it. This was not magic as it has ever been seen before. If only the others knew of that.

The leadership of a powerful female bandit attracted a lot of women to fight by her side, offering them more protection and respect from the men than any other army ever would. They were often young women, defiant and headstrong, those who refused to be given away like cattle by their fathers. They, like all voluntary fighters, were the dreamers, the mislead opportunists. As for the soldiers who did not offer up their contribution without some forceful encouragement, they too would quickly become consumed by the war, by the rush of cruel satisfaction that ran through their veins as blood ran from their swords. Others were horrified by the events unfolding before them. They were forced to take the lives of their neighbours, their fellow countrymen. After a while, some chose to take their own lives too.

The bandit women swarmed around the handsome young mage and he did not refuse their advances, searching desperately for a cure to his loneliness. In his desolate drunken states, he would ramble of the times long gone and every now and then a song would escape his lips which to

Adelaide sounded oddly familiar.

One fine spring morning, a messenger arrived breathless to Adelaide's door. Holding tiny Edith in her arms, the bandit leaned her shoulder on the mahogany door frame and listened with the calmness of a resting lioness. Although unarmed, she stood aware and alert, prompting the nervous horseman with knowledgeable nods. She wore the bodice of a simple dress but the skirt had been cut into slits and reinforced with an outer layer of thin leather that was as misshapen and distorted as the fabric underneath. It was both a mother's dress and a soldier's tunic in one.

"They be rioting in the north of the border!" the messenger blurted out enthusiastically. "The people are in hysterics. They demand to know why the King had not taken action. The region is in chaos."

"Those who keep a cool head in times of chaos do often find in them an opportunity," Adelaide quoted the teachings of her former mentor.

"The city of Morrihold had seen the worst of the rioting," the man continued, "I have heard rumours that the common folk had overturned the cart of a southern merchant and looted the goods. Right outside the lord's house too. And that city is right between Farendale and the capital. If the panic spreads either way, we will see gain."

The leader listened patiently to the messenger and invited him into the military quarters of her house, instructing him to write down his account. Orders given, she returned to the large open hall where a fire was blazing fiercely in the colossal stone hearth. At the far end of the room stood an oaken table that seated two dozen men. Many feasts had been held in this room celebrating the victories and commemorating the fallen, but now only two silhouettes moved in the light. Sitting on the bench was Duncan, his dark-brown hair longer and more dishevelled, smiling as he reached out towards the energetic three-year-old that bounded about the room. The father grasped the youngster in his arms and sat back down, cradling him despite the child's struggles.

"An ironic namesake, Morrihold," Adelaide spoke, standing by her husband.

"Why so?" he asked looking up towards her with gentle brown eyes while trying to prevent the little one from wiggling out of his arms.

"Riots, violence, chaos. And here you are, an advocate of love and peace," she spoke with a hint of bitterness. As strong as their love was, he never understood her, never shared her vision.

"I think we have enough chaos in this house alone," he joked, at last releasing his captive, who then galloped across the hall towards the door.

"No!" they screamed after him in unison and defeated, Rupert collapsed to the floor and picked up a corner of a rough woven rug, plucking at the thick threads.

Adelaide seated herself next to her beloved, rocking little Edith in her arms.

"I'll need to teach him to read."

"It would be a miracle to get him to sit still for long enough," Duncan spoke, looking lovingly towards the older child.

"Then we better hope he'll turn out to be good with a sword," Adelaide said coldly. Her children were her legacy and Rupert, being the elder of the two, must eventually inherit not only her kingdom, but also a Gift of a very different nature. A Gift that was now nearing full bloom on the skin of her arm. A secret of her family, known only to a select few.

Chapter 44

Royal council

James stood in a castle corridor, back straight, hand on sword, eyes coldly forward. Another guard stood in the same position in a different corner across the hall. Foreign dignitaries had long ceased to visit this ruin of a kingdom so the long rooms and reception halls of the magnificent building were now filled with military leaders; generals and lords, eager to contribute their efforts and experience to the recovery of their land. Some had turned from their King, disgusted by his reluctance to act. Yet they still communicated with Darius, fully aware that he was the only member of the small council courageous enough to challenge the monarch's decision. Although in these dark times, even his defiance did not produce fruitful results.

The man himself walked past James at this moment, pausing in his conversation with Sir Mark Varshaw, a young land owner and commander of the Marrynport fortress, to steal a glance at the guard, running his eyes over the armour and weaponry, lingering on the soldier's bruised hands. James stared ahead as any guard who knew his place would, yet his hand twitched slightly under the scrutinising eyes of the royal advisor. Rolling his fingers over the hilt of the sword he took a subtle but deep breath. Many soldiers and guards felt nervous around members of higher authority, especially those of such close connection to the King himself but Darius, already certain in his suspicions, noted the discomfort of the young man, mentally expanding on his readily formulated plans.

He continued down the corridor with Sir Varshaw, discussing the plans of defence. Marrynport was under heavy attacks from the bandits, who have become more organised than Darius could have anticipated. He underestimated his enemy, this enigmatic and seemingly all-powerful warlord that terrorised the kingdom and kidnapped his friend. The wizard he knew as a close friend had not returned to him in over four years and he was certain that those barbarians had destroyed him. Back in Mortendenn, Darius had seen the wizard fight and knew for certain that it would take a herculean champion to defeat him but alone, against those vicious hordes, even a master swordsman would be forced to his knees.

"They have attempted a siege on multiple occasions," Varshaw went on, "time and time again holding us for days, bombarding the walls with trebuchets."

"Trebuchets? My God!" Darius had not thought they possessed any advanced technology.

"The tower will not withstand much more. Hundreds of men have been lost. The city is filled with bandits and scoundrels. Worse still, they have blocked our access to the river. Civilians had long ago abandoned the surrounding area and now the soldiers are getting massacred or starved out. The city is a battlefield. Every day and every night," the young landowner spoke. Horrifying as his words were, his voice carried little emotion. He was distant to everything around him and not with the carefully crafted illusion of composure, that the royal advisor was a master of, but rather with genuine apathy. For a man who had lost so much land and witnessed the deaths of so many of his subjects, he seemed exceedingly indifferent.

Darius listened to the account in grave silence, keeping track of every important shred of information, organising it in his head and building up on the existing knowledge. The army had been pushing the rebels back from the capital towards Avenstead for a long time now with no real success. The advisor knew that a change of strategy was necessary and redirecting the troops to Marrynport appeared hopeful. The key was to protect the northern and north-eastern segments of the kingdom as those were the few locations where civilians were still safe to work the farms. The competition for land and jobs had become chaotic and the depleted soil produced poor quality crops. If they were to reach out across the sea to foreign lands, supplies could be delivered safely to

Aeraworth, the neighbour to the northern docks, from where a passage for provisions and possibly even reinforcements would be secured.

The northern land was still under the control of Stormhawk, so whatever was imported to Aeraworth could then be transported to the capital with relatively few delays. Stormhawk was reluctant to share the crops grown on his soil with the King's army unless they were willing to pay his exploitative prices.

"If we send more troops towards Marrynport, what defence would we have at the capital?" Darius asked himself out loud.

"We must begin to use their tactics against them," boomed a voice from the hallway ahead of them. A well build, armoured man strode towards the advisor, who hurried forward, ensuring that their conversation was out of James's earshot.

"Mark," the general nodded towards the landowner.

"Sir Randall of Hovenshire," Mark Varshaw responded in his typical monotone.

"Mark, Darius, it has been four years since Henry and Rufus were murdered in the ruins of Tarrynsdew and since then no progress had been made from our side. If they burn down every settlement that they capture but cannot hold, then so must we. I propose we burn everything from the capital to Ghyrock. The trip from there to the capital must be a week by horse. If they were to carry full supplies with them, they would be putting more weight on the horses and lengthening their journey. If they run out of supplies, they will starve in the ashes."

"But what of the civilians? There are small settlements still present there," Darius protested.

"They can't withstand much more. I suggest we relocate the people to the western shore of the capital, so that they are protected," Randall explained.

"There is but a thin strip of land..." Darius raised.

"And water. Fish, mineral-rich soil. And it's still owned by the King, with no influence of either bandit clans." Randall's dislike of Stormhawk was no lesser than the advisor's and in that they both found comfort.

"I will raise this proposition to the King," Darius stated.

At this point Randall grabbed him by the elbow and dragged him with a moderate force to a secluded corner of the castle. Mark followed closely behind, looking around for the guards. For the first time his face showed lines of anxiety. The advisor, although startled, did not resist.

"Listen," the armoured man began, "we can no longer rely on the King. The kingdom is at war and we are losing more and more each day. More men, more territory and more power. We need to pull this back, to restore the might of this land, to end this ridiculous ordeal. These are our goals. Our loyalty lies with the kingdom. With that in mind, please consider the persistent idleness of Kind Bohemond and our desperation to change the course of this war, to bring it to an end." Mark was nodding the entire time as Randall spoke, still keeping a lookout. "Suppose, if we were to proceed without the approval of our beloved King? To take this war into our own hands. Why bother him with these minor propositions?"

Darius stared at the two men before him with a mixture of surprise and understanding.

"You are suggesting we go behind the King's back?" he asked at last, not out of confusion but more as a voiced thought.

"That's rather a harsh way of putting it," the young landowner intervened.

"That's the honest way," the loyal advisor retorted. "What you are proposing is treachery!"

"As is your relationship with Queen Lylith," Randall snarled. "She is with child now, is she not? Would be a shame if this whole 'affair' was to be made public at such a happy time."

Darius froze in place. A cold sensation shot through his muscles, covering his skin in a layer of sweat. Those words ripped a gaping hole in his heart and he twisted slightly under the physical pain. A bitter taste filed his mouth as his last meal rose up from his stomach. The feeling of utter terror that filled every inch of his body now was incomparable. Thousands of questions ran through his mind; how did they know, who else knew, what if the guards heard, what if Bohemond were to find out? What was most horrific to him was the notion that the Queen would be beheaded without trial. His own life came as a secondary priority, with her wellbeing and safety being the first and ultimate goal. Knowing that, he steadied his breathing in an attempt to slow his panicked heartbeat, and raised his dark determined eyes towards the faces of his blackmailers. Forcefully pushing Randall away, he straightened up, miraculously recovering his signature composure, and nodded affirmatively.

The three then proceeded to hold council with the King, knowing that none would speak one word of their plans. The courtroom was intimidating in size, with large stone blocks making up the walls, as in the rest of castle, but there were no tapestries large enough to shield the full area of the exposed structure. The chandeliers were unlit and the only illumination came from four huge metal wood burners that stood by each corner of the table, spitting embers and sending torrents of ashy smoke towards the blackened ceiling. The whole room had a raw atmosphere, enough to bring discomfort to even the most self-assured visitors and fuel the King with a feeling of strength and empowerment. He may not have been decisive in nature but he more than made up for it in commanding authority.

Seated at the head of the tall oaken table, King Bohemond addressed the elder man who expressed his influence by leaning tauntingly across the table. Darius slowed his pace upon seeing Stormhawk, unaware that he was in council with the monarch. The King gestured lazily for the three to sit down and they reluctantly obeyed, Mark and Randall each taking seats on either side of their companion. Sensing the momentary hesitation in the advisor, Stormhawk leapt at the opportunity.

"My Liege," he spoke slyly, "why must we fight each other when we have a shared enemy in the south? You seek to stop the Silverblood woman, which your advisor has taken his sweet time doing, and I humbly wish to assist you, to prove my worth, so that this alliance may last beyond our undoubted victory. Our interests meet on many points. I ask for only one thing; grant me the rightful ownership of the land which is, and has long been, manned by my soldiers. The regions from Farendale to Morrihold. Then, transportation would be much cheaper and delivering supplies to your royal army would be more efficient, removing the necessity for our current... steep prices."

Darius nearly leaped from his chair in rage at this proposition. Overwhelmed by all the emotion of the day, he dug his fingers into the arms of his chair and worked to steady his flood of panic once more. The King, noticing Darius's reaction leaned back into his intricately carved throne, resting his forehead in his fingers. His eyes remained on his advisor. Darius, upon collecting himself stared at the King with determined opposition. Bohemond pondered the situation for some time as the others sat around him in tense silence. He remembered back to when he first took on his young but brilliant advisor, how the others urged him not to trust a man of darker skin, a man of much lower class but the King defied them, believing in the boy. He wondered now when that faith faded. Yet seeing him so absolutely resolved on preventing Stormhawk from clawing his way into the royal council, the King softened towards him once more.

"You will not be granted this favour," he spoke sternly. "Remove yourself from my sight at once!"

Darius sunk back with relief. The old bandit glared at the advisor as he left.

"With your permission," interjected Mark Varshaw, "we now have another matter to discuss."

"Speak," the King commanded with a sigh.

"The Marrynport fortress is under constant attack. We propose that five hundred of the men that are currently protecting the capital be redirected there to push back the rebels once and for all. As of a week ago, they outnumber us three to one, we must send reinforcements. In place of these men, to protect the capital, we send out the knights towards Ghyrock and Avenstead to destroy these major Silverblood settlements and from there, advance towards what we believe to be their central headquarters east of Rynell."

The young fair-haired man then watched the King expectantly. Darius and Randall looked at him in wonder, impressed by his logical and well organised argument. The royal advisor had long been trying to convince the King to send out the knights, each time meeting rejection. Struck now with a hint of jealousy, he reminded himself that regardless of who persuaded Bohemond to send the order, what remains most important is that it is sent. The King again watched the men before him with a thoughtful pondering gaze. Sir Mark Varshaw, a methodical tactician who ascended to a position of military power shortly after inheriting the Marrynport fortress and its surrounding land. His father had met an untimely death, sending rumours that Mark invested more heart in ambition than in the lives of his family. These rumours were extinguished as quickly as the mystery surrounding his father's death. Lord Darius, a reliable commander and once-treasured friend to the King. Sir Randall of Hovenshire, who had proven himself to be a warrior without equal and who should have been named the commander of the royal knights long before, had he not been so lacking in political tact. Combined, these three bettered the King in knowledge, initiative and physical prowess. Bohemond had grown bitter of that truth as he slumped in his cushioned throne, his royal gown scrunched and stained. But he knew that they spoke sense and that personal issues must wait until he had the head of that bandit bitch on a stake.

"It is decided," he spoke at last, "Darius, send the knights."

Chapter 45

Be Wary of the Mighty Spirit

Adelaide sat at a small wooden writing desk in the command room of her house. A fire was raging in the hearth to her side, flooding the vast room in orange light. She was leaning onto the inclined table with her entire arm, curling her fingers over the edge and with the other hand she held down a yellowed page against the surface, stretching her fingers to keep the document flat. She twisted over it like an old woman, studying the words with careful precision. Sir Hansfell rested comfortably in a luxurious armchair on the other side of the room with a book in his hands. He brought hundreds of them with him from Ghyrock and Adelaide adopted the majority into her house, fascinated by the old legends, knowing full well who the main protagonist in them was. Reading them painted scenes in her head of ancient wars and battles, and unimaginable fiends which were destroyed by a fearless and powerful knight. She found herself holding onto those scenes, becoming more and more invested in them.

Hansfell glanced over the top of his book.

"What is it? You've been staring at that same scrap of paper for days now," he called to her.

Remaining silent for a few moments, Adelaide eventually shifted her arms and responded coldly:

"A deed."

Unsatisfied with her irritated reply, he pestered her again.

"Thinking of investing in some property?"

"Looking into the laws of this kingdom." She was not in the mood for his humour. "The King owns all the land in Starkenhaart."

"That's right. Even the landowners are nothing but tenants, who charge smaller tenants for the right to work the soil."

"What of water?"

"Water?" Hansfell struggled to follow her trail of thought.

"Would the waters surrounding the kingdom also belong to the King?" she persisted.

"Yes. But to what distance from the shore I can't say."

"Damn!" Adelaide rose from the little padded stool in frustration.

"I would not put it past the King to blur the borders but Darius would have corrected this soon after he rose to his post. You will find no ambiguity there now."

"All right then. Well, you were close to the King in another life, can you think of any way we can declare even a small space under the sun to be truly ours to own?" she insisted.

"Under the sun, perhaps, but you will need to sail a long way to get there."

Adelaide stared into the fire for some time, then as if suddenly coming to life, she bounded across the room to the detailed map of the known world that spanned the full width of the wall. Tracing her fingers along the lines, with her face nearly pressed to the chart, she bounced a little with excitement. Gesturing for her advisor to approach she pointed enthusiastically to one part of the map. The aging man, startled by her unexpected change of heart looked at the section which brought her so much happiness, only to find an empty stretch of coastline west of the capital. With a questioning gaze he prompted her for an explanation.

"Water! The wall of the city nearly meets the western cliff. To push on from the south and the east is proving ineffective and the northern regions are protected by that insolent son-of-a-bitch Stormhawk. What if we attack the castle from the sea? Surely there must be pirates amongst our bandit ranks, ones who would know how to sail a ship."

Her mind brought back the visions of the old pirate she once saw in her moments of sickness. Roger. Maybe this was his purpose all along, to show her the way to her goal. This was a sign; she was suddenly certain of it. This is how it was meant to end! The illusion of destiny brewed rapidly in her head, only to be rudely interrupted by her companion.

"We appear to be missing one vital factor. A sailboat. Or a few dozen of them. Ones that won't sink under a small catapult or ballista."

"So we need a woodcutter and a carpenter."

"And someone who knows how to build a boat! Are you truly considering this insanity?"

"Yes! And I know who would help!"

With this she dashed out of the house and hurried through the town and out of the gate, nearly pushing the guard from his feet. Energized and breathing rapidly she spun around in place before stopping with her eyes focused on the woodland. Taking a chance, Adelaide broke into a sprint towards the trees. Upon reaching the shelter of their thick branches she wandered and waited, hoping that her saviour would come. Not long passed before he revealed himself.

"Greetings, child," the vision spoke from the shadows.

"Hermit," she addressed the well-known spectre.

"I shall permit thee to call me that. Thou search for me with a purpose?"

"Yes. You have given my men the gift of protection by bringing the old blacksmith to us. I must now ask you for a gift far greater. I aim to destroy the unworthy King from the sea. I know this is a path that God himself has chosen for me. And I know that you are his earthly servant as much as I am myself. So I ask this of you, bring me men who can craft sturdy ships. We can access the sea from Marrynport. We could sail north, past Aeraworth and around the northernmost peak, beyond which we shall return down the western side of the kingdom and take the castle by surprise."

"This is truly a great thing thou ask of me. I cannot provide thee so much. But think back to the wonder thee found at the castle. Who knows how many other treasures are hidden away behind those stone walls?" the crooked old man responded.

"I will insist that James investigates the castle for a master builder. As for the craftsmen..."

"Thou carry the greatest of gifts on thy very flesh. Use the power that thou hath been granted. The royal advisor is powerful opponent, but he is a mere mortal man. Thou will always be greater."

Nodding energetically, Adelaide was a puppet on his strings, willing to loyally carry out any command he should speak. To her he was a prophet, wisdom itself bound in this earthly attire of flesh and cloth. The words that left his lips pinned themselves to every idea, every scheme in her mind, growing and twisting their vines through the folds of her brain. She had stood against him once, fearful and doubting but reason had long since left her, replaced over time by his whispers. Her words commanded hundreds. His words commanded her.

Adelaide left her mythical mentor and returned to the camp, only to be greeted with the news that Talon and Hunter had returned. The other bandits were in a panic, rushing around in search of scribes, beckoning her hurriedly towards her house. Half the residents of the camp were present inside, gathering in the main entrance hall, with little Rupert dashing between them. As soon as Adelaide stepped through the threshold hands reached out towards her, pulling her into the central headquarters. Shouts erupted from all directions, some of worry, some of fear, some demanding that she deals with this unexplained issue at once. Growing irate, she stopped in the door of the command centre and turned her savage gaze at her soldiers.

"Get lost!" she screamed. "If I see one of your ugly faces in my house when I step out of this room, I swear I will cut your hearts from your bodies and feed them to you whole!"

Entering the military office, she found all of her generals seated about the room, arguing intensely.

"Explain your return!" she commanded.

"That bastard sent the knights at last," Talon spat with rage, "four to Ghyrock, four to Avenstead. And a hundred men with each. We regrouped at Rynell and retreated. They near wiped out our armies."

The room was then filled with a long chilling silence as her subjects looked to her for a solution. Hunter stood by one of the small barred windows, dirty bandana on his head and bloody rags wrapped tightly around his left leg. As animated and lively as he had always been, at a time like this his face sunk with more dismal sorrow than anyone else. Talon leaned against the fireplace, uninjured but clearly frightened. Watching Adelaide slaughter all his men during their first encounter did not compare to this. He could not bargain for his life this time. Watching the knights lead their hundreds was like watching a storm, an uncontrollable destructive force of nature and that was enough to frighten even him.

Bertrand glared at her from his little chair in the corner with accusing eyes, blaming her for the deaths of their men, for provoking Darius. She had poked a sleeping bear one too many times and he came after her soldiers.

"There is more," Talon raged on. "Oh, there is more! They liked your trick up in Tarrynsdew. So they adopted it! All the soil, from Avenstead to the capital wall was burned to ashes! We will not be returning that way for sure."

Archaius cocked his head to the side, listening carefully to the bandit's account. A smirk appeared on his lips.

"Wondrous," he stated quietly. "Just like in Mortendenn."

Hunter pounced at him from across the room, a knife striking for the mage's throat but the young wizard brushed him off effortlessly, sending the bandit crashing into a cabinet. Growling with pain Hunter rose to his feet to attack him once more but Adelaide held him in place, telling him gently to seek out Daisy and ask for a fresh bandage. Murmuring insults under his breath, he obeyed. Turning her full force to the wizard, she began the interrogation.

"How wondrous indeed. Your old friend used your methods against us."

"Those methods were not mine," Archaius retaliated. "I did not choose to burn down that town. That was your command, my mighty leader."

"Is that why you told him of our locations?"

"They would have known that you held the towns east of here for years! The whole damned kingdom knows! For a master thief you truly do lack subtlety."

"So you deny the accusations of being their informant?" she continued coldly.

"Absolutely. They did not need an informant."

"And of advising them to send out the knights?"

"I am surprised it took them this long," he stated confidently.

"So where do you travel when you leave our camp? Please don't think we haven't observed your absences."

"Limestone does not like it here. He does not like you."

"I am heartbroken," she retorted sarcastically. "Where do you travel?"

"To search the enchanted woods." He was beginning to sound hesitant.

"For what?"

"For knowledge." His eyes filled with passionate meaning that bore into her soul and it was then that she realised that he knew just as little about her magic as she did herself. He was searching for Gabriel. He was searching for answers.

"You are granted a chance to redeem yourself, to prove your innocence and fight among us in the field of battle. The knights will need to be defeated. Talon, are they based at the capital or have they established a temporary settlement close by?"

"I know not," he responded.

"Then find out! The burning of the land is as much an inconvenience to them as to us. If we push them back now, they will starve in the ashes of their own schemes."

***

Adelaide, Talon and Archaius crouched in the brush encircling a small tented camp just east of Rynell.

"Remember, you two are here in case things get nasty. Otherwise, stay put," she whispered to them. Both men nodded in agreement.

'Subtlety', she thought to herself, 'I'll show them subtlety!' The King's soldiers slept in their tents, with no more than twenty men patrolling the base. They had recovered their strength in the days since the fight but they were tired from the late hour and the nervous suspense that hung about the place like a dense fog. The whole kingdom has heard of Adelaide's triumphs and many of the King's men feared to tread on the soil that has long ago become hers. Stormhawk's troops were tougher and not as easily intimidated but, fortunately, none were present here. Creeping stealthily through the camp, Adelaide decided then to fully formulate her plan, realising that she was moving on an impulse. Yet this was an impulse that had never betrayed her before. In the blackness of the night, her face lit up with a smile as she thought up an homage to a trick that was used by her mentor. May the spirit of the woods haunt them all!

At last she had arrived at the tent occupied by the leader of this ensemble, one of the royal knights. These soldiers were fierce in battle, unmatched by most, fearless and swift but that was not all. They had an aura about them that made the common folk avert their eyes. They were legendary heroes in the minds of the citizens, master swordsmen brought out to fight only the most macabre of monsters. Adelaide pondered the parallel between herself and them. Would they have welcomed her into their ranks had she chosen to join them rather than the bandits? Of course not, yet there was an advantage to that. Their minds are fabled to be as powerful as their bodies and her unnatural magic would not have bent their wills as it had done with the weaker men. Had she chosen that path, she may have been a knight, but she would not become the queen that she was truly destined to be.

With those thoughts rushing through her head, she slipped silently into the tent. The knight was sleeping before her; so peaceful, so... vulnerable! Unarmed and undefended. In a flash she was standing by the bed, a crude iron dagger in her hand, hovering over him like a ghost from a nightmare. He took a deep breath in his sleep, his muscular chest moving heavily, as if his lungs were plagued by an infection. Then he slowly breathed out. Then he jerked awake and tried to cry out as her blade pierced his throat but his voice was instead replaced with desperate gurgling. Blood splashed up from his mouth and flowed down his windpipe, filling his lungs. Several violent spasms later, he lay still as his sheets glistened with an expanding viscous pool.

With a harlequin grin she knelt by his bed and drove the bloody dagger into the soil, inscribing a message to those who will find the body.

Be wary of the mighty spirit

Whose land you've turned to ash

His vengeance knows no bounds

Your throats he will gash

After that, she moved swiftly from tent to tent, slicing the throats of over seventy soldiers. Adelaide chose to let the others live, to let them run, to let them spread rumours.

Chapter 46

Flightless Hawk

"Magnificent success!" James enthused as he bounded up towards his leader.

Surprised at his genuine commendation, Adelaide inquired to the state of affairs at the castle.

"They are more frightened than ever been before, milady; your name is spoken in hushed tones, for fear of summoning the spirit of the ashes as they have started to call it. That was a clever trick of yours, was it not? There is no such spirit really, right?"

"I've been wondering that myself for many years, James," she replied thoughtfully.

Praise flowed towards her from every corner of the settlement as even the bandits themselves spread whispered rumours of her magical power. To them, she was truly the goddess she perceived herself to be. Only the small group of her generals did not fall to their knees as she walked grandiosely through her fort.

***

"There is no such spirit really, damn it!" Sir Randall of Hovenshire yelled as he stood before his fellow knights.

The mid-morning sun was blinding as the generals and accomplished swordsmen gathered in the military training court. Darius had wandered some distance away from the others and stood in solemn silence in the shadow of the great castle wall. With one arm across his lower chest and the elbow of the other leaning on it as if for support, he held his right hand up to his mouth, biting at the nail of his thumb as he pondered the situation. His eyes rested vaguely on the cobbled ground as schemes collapsed in his mind like great towers after an earth-shattering quake.

"Will it all be well for us?" a gentle voice sounded near him.

Looking up with a start, he met the eyes of the beautiful queen of Starkenhaart. Her hair was tidied into a headdress but it shone in the sunlight like the wings of an angel in a painted masterpiece. Her delicate frame was ever so slightly contorted under the weight of her maternal illness. Steadying his breath, the advisor replied;

"Of course, Your Majesty. No need to worry. This is nothing but superstition."

"I had hoped so." Queen Lylith stepped into the shadows closer to him. Darius cast a cautious eye around the court before confiding in her.

"I believe it will not be long now," he spoke with playful exaggeration, "until two of this great kingdom's problems are extinguished together."

***

"I believe it will not be long now," Stormhawk spoke to Sir Mark Varshaw as he paced the strategic tower of Marrynport, "before we wipe out that bitch for good. But an open attack? No! He is being reckless!"

"Those are Lord Darius's specific instructions," Sir Mark murmured while nonchalantly looking out of the window.

"But why must this be led by my troops?" the old bandit demanded.

"That, I know not. All I can say is, Darius is the main obstacle between you and the title which you so desperately desire. You may try and destroy him but I assure you, that will gain you no support from the other officials or from the King. Your best option, my dear Stormhawk, is to befriend him, obey him and gain his trust. He is a more powerful ally than you appear to realise, and that misjudgement may one day cost you dearly."

"When did a young lad like you gain such insight, huh?" the bandit king scoffed in reply.

"Also, if I lead the attack from here to the bandit camp and you lead your men from Morrihold to Ghyrock and then onto their camp from the north, then we can push for a double siege of their fortress," Varshaw spoke with as little spirit as ever.

"That is true," the elder man responded while studying the map. "I suppose this is his plan then."

***

"This is my plan!" Adelaide announced proudly. The generals gathered around her in the command room of her house. "I take seven hundred men and move from here to Marrynport, cutting between the mountain ranges. The terrain will be difficult to pass through and may delay our army by a few days but we will acquire the element of surprise. From Marrynport we move directly towards Farendale and capture Stormhawk's capital! Talon, Bertrand and Archaius will come with me while Hunter, Duncan and Hansfell hold the city with the remaining men."

"I don't mean to sound pessimistic," Talon offered, "but I really don't think we have seven hundred men left."

"How many then?" Adelaide demanded.

"Five, five and a half hundred at most," the long-haired man replied uncertainly.

"Damn!" she hissed, slamming her palms against the wooded table. The noise woke the baby and she hurriedly and apologetically took Edith into her arms, rocking her back to sleep.

"All right then," the bandit queen spoke in almost a whisper, "we take three hundred and recruit more on the way."

"The people up that way were more than a little defiant last time," the mage stated.

"Yes, and I never discovered why," their leader was almost hesitant. "Well, I suppose if we can't persuade them, we must intimidate them into submission. Threaten them, tell them stories of magical ghosts, that sort of thing."

"You really think that'd work?" Hunter asked, limping closer to the rest of the group while his walking stick produced little thuds against the floor. "This is an open attack, you cannot just set out with a few men and hope for the best."

"The good Lord guides me, dear soldier. Fortune will meet us on the way."

"So you're a prophet now too?" Bertrand growled from his corner.

Ignoring the snide remark, Adelaide laid out her plan before her friends.

***

"May the good Lord guide us into battle!" Sir Varshaw called out to his troops as they took formation at the foot of the valley. The mountains rose into the skies both to the east and the west as the river ran towards them from the southern peaks. The bandit army was advancing from the same direction. Unfortunately, Varshaw and his troops discovered that too late, after they had moved towards the remnants of Tarrynsdew and had to turn back.

The battle lasted for many days and the blood of hundreds flowed into the cold water of the river. Varshaw's soldiers had the pleasure of bearing witness to the most magnificent feats of magic and wonder. A beautiful bloody festival for which the price was far too high. The last thing they saw before their eyes closed for eternity was the grotesquely magnificent shape of the werewolf as it reached towards them with its massive paws. Claws like daggers cutting into their flesh. Fangs like spears digging into their throats. The crude steel armour on their bodies could not withstand the pure force of this beast. Those who stood back from the fiend firing arrows, desperately trying to protect their brothers in arms were rewarded for their dedication with a storm of fire that picked up suddenly, as if summoned from the ground itself. The gates of hell swung open, swallowing up the soldiers, burning the wooden longbows in their very hands, melting the metal armour while it still hung from their bodies. Yet the fires did not last long. The wizard collapsed from exhaustion each time, tears of guilt and horror flowing down his round cheeks as his sobs were drowned out by the screaming on the battlefield.

The demon that forced him to commit such vicious crimes was also his protector. She fought armoured in the toughest of steel, the mystical green cloak draped from her shoulders like some fairy-tale heroine, a translucent sword wielded by her hands. She was Adelaide, the Queen of bandits, the Bringer of suffering, the Keeper of ancient secrets. The mage knelt weeping behind her as she fought a dozen men at once, decapitating them, wounding them, tearing their limbs from their bodies. A second great warrior fought by her side, his greasy long hair swinging around his aging face. Talon held a sword in each hand, using them for both attack and defence.

In the beginning, Varshaw's army outnumbered the bandits by three to one yet the soldiers could not withstand the chaotic destructive force of this woman and after days of fighting, the King's army collapsed under her power. Sir Mark Varshaw escaped, abandoning the remaining men and galloped for the shore, hoping to flee overseas, knowing that his treachery would cost him his head. Just under a hundred men were taken prisoner by the bandits and forced to fight for the rebel queen as she hoped to make up the losses to her ranks. Nonetheless, the size of her army now was half that with which she had set out from her base and measly in comparison to the troops awaiting them at Farendale.

"I urge you to reconsider!" Talon begged her as the bandits were setting up a temporary camp, "we cannot hope to take a city with the numbers we have now!"

"We had extracted hundreds from Rynell, Avenstead and Ghyrock. This city is greater in population than all three put together! Once we take it, we can recover and expand our army almost immediately if we recruit the citizens," she responded while wiping the blood from her sword.

"You're avoiding the vital flaw in this plan! We can't recover our army because we will have no army to recover if we go against the city like this! How do you propose we break through the city wall?"

"There is advantage in small numbers, dear friend." A cruel smirk twisted her mouth.

"If you are proposing infiltration, then please explain what makes you believe that Farendale hasn't already got its defences up? They will question every man and woman entering the city."

"There are farms and crop fields surrounding the city. Workers have to leave and enter through the gates at dawn and dusk. Some will remain in the farmhouses, but most will stay in the bunkhouses overnight, which are located within the walls."

"So what, you're going to send the lad with the flames to sneak in dressed as a farmer and burn the city down from the inside?"

"No, no, no! We can't afford to burn those men alive! We need to keep them this time." Adelaide sat on the ground by the fire, holding her hands over the flames. "I will enter myself and use the power that only I have been granted. I will turn them against their officials. I will lead them to riot!"

"You would be exposing yourself in doing that. And what if they resist? What then?" Talon spoke as he knelt by her side.

"Worst comes to worst, I will kill the guards and Stormhawk's bandits right there."

"A one-woman army, huh? That will not do. I have a better plan," her right-hand man said with sincere confidence.

***

"An order from Stormhawk!" a young messenger ran up towards the group of bandits that remained in Farendale when the rest set off south. They waited in a private room of a small tavern for orders from their leader.

"Who the hell are you?" one of the men put down his flagon and stood up to face the youngster.

"A new recruit," the bandit stuttered in response. "Stormhawk sent orders! They have captured the Silverblood fortress! It is finally time to turn against the King himself. He demands that we slaughter the guards of the city. There are not many left as most have been pulled to the capital to join the army. There are enough for us to take them on. He will ride towards the King's castle and lead a full attack."

"How the hell do we know ya ain't lying?" the man standing took an imposing step towards the young messenger.

"Stormhawk's stamp is on the letter!"

The bandits looked at the page for some time.

"All right then lads. We got ourselves some guards to kill!"

They scattered to find armour and weapons. The young messenger stood alone in the private room of the tavern. Hearing their voices through the window he leaned against the wooden frame, watching them disappear into the crowds of the street. Reaching into his pocket he removed the stamp with Stormhawk's crest and let it rest in the palm of his hand. It was magnificent, how easily his queen had stolen it from Stormhawk's former quarters.

***

"That witch! That fiendish whore!" Stormhawk raged as he paced outside the stone walls of the Silverblood camp.

"Milord, I am certain that if we ask Lord Darius for assistance, he will provide troops to defend Farendale," a fellow bandit pleaded with his leader.

"Goddamn it, he ain't going to do a damn thing! That Varshaw kid from Marrynport was due to join the siege before the end of last week! When he didn't arrive, I gathered that she got him on the way. I sent message after message to the castle and got nothing back! And now my own damn city is in chaos and I bet you, that's her doing! Her and that wicked magic!"

The men stood in silence for a while, listening to the trebuchets launching their artillery at the stone walls of the fortress. Soldiers were screaming as arrows flew from the battlements like a rain of steel and wood. Corpses piled up under the wall.

"There are barely any men inside. We have an advantage here," the bandit began cautiously.

"That doesn't matter. I have my own land to protect. Fuck the advisor and fuck the title." Stormhawk looked at the wall for a moment, revealing the frustration on his face. In a bitter tone, he spoke the inevitable command, "Retreat! Retreat from here at once!"

***

"Well, would you look at that! This plan of yours has gone smoothly, Lord Talon. I commend you," Adelaide spoke slyly as she stood by a window in a fortified tower within the walls of Farendale.

The enemy bandits killed the guards and the citizens in turn rose against the bandits. No reinforcements have arrived from the King. It's like he abandoned the city altogether, letting the dogs fight over it.

Talon sat in the darkness of the room, gazing at the dirty floor. His leader turned to face him now, her profile illuminated by the distant fires. Dark hair rested untamed on her shoulders, dirty as the fur that padded her armour. The future queen was savagely majestic.

"It's your turn now," he spoke drily. "Our men are still stationed some distance from the city. If Stormhawk returns now, they will be vulnerable. We need to get them inside the city walls."

"Then let me speak the word of God to these people," Adelaide spoke grandiosely, holding her head up high as she watched the streets below. "Let me show them the righteous way!"

***

Stormhawk's army returned a week later to find their own city armed against them. The people, in their rage and fear had forgotten their values and held on with all they had to the mysterious cloaked southerner. Not once had she stated who she was, but some had learned of her nature and history. Yet they did not rebel, they did not run. They were broken and frightened and, in an attempt to protect their families, they joined her, knowing that she was rising, that she will win in the end and they wanted a share in that glory, in that comfort. Many did not know who it was that stood before them now, but they had previously accepted Stormhawk and his merry band of criminals. What's one charismatic bandit leader over another?

The battle lasted for two weeks straight, with Stormhawk pushing his men to the limit. Yet he did not stand a chance. In this battle they were outnumbered and although the new enemy recruits were nothing more than simple peasants with spears, they were protected by the city defences that Stormhawk himself had long ago erected. Adelaide showed her face on the battlements every now and then as if taunting the enemy troops. Burning arrows were sent towards the advancing soldiers and a mote of fire was created by the magic of the wizard.

Stormhawk sat on horseback and watched his men die. As the days passed, he began to realise his fate. With nothing more than a few muttered curses, he turned his horse and galloped away.

***

"I beg you, allow me council with the King!" the elderly bandit leader pleaded with the castle guard at the capital.

"That won't be necessary," came the all-too-familiar voice.

Stormhawk turned to face his nemesis. Darius strolled into the room with an uncharacteristic swagger. Standing right before him, he gestured almost comically as he spoke, yet his tone remained as cold as ever.

"It appears that during your absence, some information has been uncovered."

"What are you doing?" the former bandit king screamed as he drew his sword and was immediately restrained by the nearby guards. "I have no army! I have no castle! I have nothing left!"

"Correct. Nothing to hide behind. Now you will face the consequences of your crimes," the advisor continued. "Are you aware, that during you rein as the "Bandit King" as your men call it, you have committed at least eight hundred recorded acts of crime, and possibly countless more, ranging from theft to genocide?"

"No! No, that wasn't me!" the old man protested desperately.

"Of course not. It was your bandit soldiers who committed the said crimes. But we have recently been able to prove that the initial order always came down from you. With this knowledge, I have no choice but to sentence you to death."

Chapter 47

Price of Silence

An order was sent down south to appoint Sir Hansfell as the lead commander of the Silverblood fortress. He was to restore the damaged wall and defend the city against all further attacks in whichever way he saw fit. Morrihold and the children were summoned to Farendale to join the rising queen at their newly established base in the north. Talon and Archaius remained with her to witness her power over the citizens of the city. The force within her radiated authority, bending the wills of the people and robbing them of their personal morals. They stood before her like a crowd of puppets.

Standing bent over a map, Adelaide traced her finger along the very same lines as she did all those months ago in the command room of her southern home.

"Sir Hansfell doubted my schemes," she spoke with a smirk, addressing her two subordinates. "What are your thoughts?"

The bandit and the mage stood on either side of her, studying the faded lines with a mixture of curiosity and hesitation. Leaning on the table with both hands, Talon pondered her proposal and shook his head, clearly locked in a silent internal debate. Archaius delicately held his hand to his chin and studied the area of the map surrounding Starkenhaart. His eyes kept finding their way to the nearby kingdom of Mortendenn.

"I suppose it'd work," Talon spoke at last.

"Reassuring words," Adelaide purred facetiously.

"Well it is one hell of a gamble," her elder companion retaliated. "I can see why Hans would not be eager to engage in this. But with the support of the people of this city… I think we may have a chance."

"You understand that this is not the sole front of attack. But we will stand a better chance against the capital if we come at them from both land and sea," the leader explained her plan further.

"I reckon we could get Hunter to lead the boats. I heard he had some experience with sails right before he joined us."

"So there we go!" she responded enthusiastically, "we seek out some skilled—volunteers—here and send them to our base in Marrynport."

"We don't have a base in Marrynport," Talon complained with a note of frustration. "You are rushing into this without thinking it through!"

"Nonsense! I hereby appoint you as the commander of Marrynport. Take some soldiers and establish a base there. Then once everything is set up, summon Hunter to be your hand and recruit some locals to travel west and collect the necessary wood from the forest at the base of the mountains. Send for the builders when you are ready and get them working. I am giving you one year."

"You want me to build a fleet in one year? From nothing?" Talon had abandoned his frustration only to have it replaced with mere amusement.

"It is a coastal city. They've been building boats there since before the Rynell dynasty took the throne."

"Yes, fishing boats! Trade vessels! Not goddamn war-ships!"

"Well, my dear commander, I have faith in your leadership. You'll have me a few boats in no time," she spoke with a childish giggle and galloped to the other end of the room, glancing out of the window towards the battlements. "If you struggle motivating the men, then I might make an appearance and encourage them to work their hardest! But now, how about we all go from tavern to tavern and celebrate our prospects!"

"Insolent girl," Talon teased playfully under his breath as he followed her out of the room. Yet the schemes fell together in his head. Calculating the number of soldiers they could place on each ship, and considering how much weaponry they would require, he knew that Adelaide was expecting nothing more than five or six boats. This was to serve mostly as a distraction for the King's army, a surprise attack to get them to scatter about the castle and protect the western walls, which would allow an opportunity for the main gate in the east to be taken down by the ground troops.

To support a trebuchet, the sails would have to be removed while the ship is anchored right outside the castle, else they would be torn down by the force of the heavy artillery. Yet if that is done, the boat would undoubtedly capsize once the trebuchet is released. No, trebuchets and catapults were out of the question. Those would be left to the ground soldiers. Although, artillery of a lighter kind would be more easily supported. Ballistae could be placed like giant crossbows on one side of the vessel and although their wooden bolts would do little damage to their stone target, they would also double up as a thick wooden shield for archers to stand behind, leaving the bandits covered from the attacks of the King's guards, who would undoubtedly be commanded to take their fatal positions on the battlements.

The boats would most likely be made unusable during the battle and many of them would sink. Hunter and the other sailors would need to be protected, God forbid he agrees to this suicidal mission. There is no doubt that Darius would command the western troops to use flaming arrows to burn down the sails and the wooden vessels. Although, considering the vertical angle at which the ballistae are to be mounted, the ships would not necessarily need to be stationed far from the wall. This would allow for any soldiers whose boat has taken damage to swim ashore. The overhanging cliff at the base of the city wall will provide them with shelter from the King's archers and a support to cling to so that the exhaustion does not pull them underwater. All this relies on the assumption that they will be able to safely swim through a bombardment of arrows that will rain down on them from the battlements.

Talon stopped in his tracks and considered a sudden new thought in stillness. Sensing the change, Adelaide too halted her step and stood ahead of him, watching his plan come together. When the elder man at last focused his eyes and raised them to hers, he was met with an expression not that of a playful child but rather a conspirator of a masterfully deceitful nature.

"That's your plan. To send them into a panicked frenzy," the bandit confirmed with his ruler.

Once again returning to the mischievous facade, the future Queen smiled like a youngster that had devised an elaborate prank and strolled to a nearby tavern with a light step.

Upon entering the pub, the three commanders were greeted with cheers from their troops and recently recruited supporters. Talon stealthily retreated to a private chamber with a bottle of wine and the company of a handsome male recruit while the others rejoiced with the crowds. Archaius drank and sang and danced with the rest but every now and then his gaze would linger on some distant object and a dark grief would cast its ugly shadow over his youthful face. Seeing Adelaide taking a rest on a nearby stool, he joined her at the same elevated table. The surface had supported many flagons and was wearing down from the layer of moisture on the unpolished wooden panels. With a repulsed grimace, the mage lifted his gloved hand from the table in the manner of a self-important nobleman and, holding onto his mug with both hands, he turned drunkenly to his leader.

"You've stuck with me in hopes of finding Gabriel?" Adelaide addressed him before he got a chance to speak.

Archaius only nodded.

"You said you met Darius in Mortendenn. You also know Gabriel. Yet you yourself look no older than twenty years of age. Does this mean that Gabriel was in Mortendenn too? Did he know Darius?"

The wizard smirked.

"Never thought of that. There is almost no chance of those two becoming acquainted, I can tell you that much. But I suppose Gabriel must have passed through there at some time. Yet that is not where I met him."

"Where then?" the woman persisted.

"In a tower."

"The crooked one, near a dead woodland?"

The wizard produced a strained laugh. "The visions. The old man. The crooked tower and the crooked cane."

Adelaide was starting to turn hostile.

"What are you not telling me? What did Gabriel not tell me?" she demanded.

"If you have not discovered it for yourself, then you are not fit to know yet. But don't worry girl, you have a long time to figure it all out. I can assure you of that."

"Even as a parting gift, you cannot tell me?" she spoke dryly, looking into the mug of ale that sat in her hands. The fluid appeared black in the dim light of the tavern yet thick in consistency as it clung to the clay surrounding it. The young man bowed his head, a drunken smile contorting his face.

"I am half expecting you to draw your sword and remove my head for treachery."

"You are free to leave." Her tone was commanding yet gentle, like a mother scolding a child, "But first you must tell me why."

"I respected Gabriel too much to abandon an opportunity to find him, yet I respect Darius too much to go into a battle against him directly."

"Fair answer."

They both sat in grim silence for a long while, listening to the joyous calls of the surrounding folk. Adelaide tore her stare from the black liquid and turned her face closer to the mage.

"I don't know what happened to my mentor. I don't know where he is. I don't know if he is alive or dead. For this honesty at least, you must give me some clue. You owe me that much now."

"Dearest Rose-bearer," he replied standing up, "if only you knew how much I have done for you with my silence."

With those words, Archaius the wizard finished his ale in one gulp, gave her one last charming grin and swaggered from the tavern. As she watched him leave, Adelaide wondered what great plains of knowledge were still beyond her grasp.

***

James, having returned to the King's castle, stood by a window in one of the corridors, trying to ease the boredom of his job by watching the sparrows outside. Further down the hallway, another guard straightened up and looked dead ahead, pulled out of his relaxed stance by some noise that had not reached James just yet. Eventually he too heard the rapidly approaching footsteps and assumed the designated position of a castle guard. The source of the footsteps was revealed to be Darius himself, striding down the corridor as two soldiers hurried after him like loyal hounds. Walking past the other guard, Darius paused momentarily, just long enough to authoritatively gesture with his index finger for the guard to follow. Obediently, the man broke his stance and fell in line with the other two soldiers.

Darius continued the parade down the hallway. James took a deep breath, expecting to be recruited with the others as the advisor carried on his way. Yet when the tanned man stopped before him, the index finger of his slim long hand did not summon the guard but instead pointed at him in cold accusation.

"Seize the traitor." Darius's expressionless gaze rested on the young man. After a brief hesitation the three soldiers pounced on James and took him by the upper arms, removing the sword from this belt in the process.

The King's advisor then spun on his heel and lead the party back through the stone halls, deeper and deeper into the dark bowels of the castle. James tried desperately to gain his footing but was forced to move at an unnatural angle, having his feet dragged along the rough floor. He submitted initially, hoping to cooperate and talk his way out of this situation but as they passed the barracks, he began to grow increasingly nervous.

Once the gate to the dungeon fell into his sight, James began kicking and fighting, struggling to free himself from their grasp only to receive a sharp hit on the top of his head. Momentarily paralysed by the sudden shock, he could only watch as blood ran down the straw-coloured hair that hung in front of his face.

Once inside the dungeons, Darius's steady pace slowed and he manoeuvred to the side as the soldiers threw the young spy into one of the cells. Dried blood stained the stone walls and torture apparatus of the most horrifying nature stood right outside the metal bars. There was another man now with Darius. This one was armoured from neck to toe in the most expensive metal plating. In a dazed confusion, it took James a while to recognise his own commander, Sir Randall of Hovenshire.

"This is the one working with the Silverblood girl?" Randall demanded with a note of pity in his voice.

"No doubt about it." Was Darius's ice-cold reply.

Chapter 48

Secret

Morrihold and the kids had finally arrived at the castle, accompanied by a fair number of other bandits from the old fort, hoping to establish themselves as trusted leaders, having heard that Adelaide is recruiting untrained and undisciplined townsfolk who will need to be supervised. Duncan dismounted his horse and reached back to pick up little Rupert from the saddle, who was previously clinging desperately to his father. Yet the curious dark eyes of the boy shot up as soon as his feet touched the ground, eager to study the new city. The Farendale castle towered before them like a colossal mound, with guard posts ascending over the battlements at regular intervals like stone titans tasked with protecting the city.

Rupert stared at the magnificent structure before him with silent wonder, fearless as he was, and swaying slightly from looking upwards at the dizzyingly tall towers. Duncan held him by the hand to stop the youngster from falling over yet he mirrored his son as he too looked up in awe. For a few brief moments they stood together side by side and studied the edifice of their new home.

Daisy rode in on a pale brown mare and halted the horse by the others. She had a wide green cloth tied diagonally across her torso, creating a portable cradle for little Edith, who was fast asleep on her back, seemingly rocked into calmness by the jerking movement of the galloping horse. Daisy jumped down and joined the others in gawking at the castle before them. A few locals snuck up to the bandits, as if they were afraid to make the slightest noise that would irritate their new residents, and led the horses to a nearby stable.

Bertrand was the first to come bounding towards the new arrivals. A rare warm expression befell his features upon seeing his lover's face. The girl threw her small frame into his arms and he returned the gentlest embrace, careful not to place his hands over the baby, afraid that one touch from him would crush the tiny sleeping body. He had always taken great care to escape the presence of Adelaide's children and viewed them with distant pity, knowing full well what path in life their mother would force them into. Yet some hope remained for them as Morrihold was a man with whom Bertrand shared a mindset and respected deeply, which had led the two to become good friends.

Daisy removed the child from the cloth and handed her to her father, leaving the green pouch hanging loosely from her shoulder. With her hands on her hips, Daisy interrogated her beloved for all the news about the rebellion. Adelaide too soon emerged from the castle and greeted her family with genuine affection, cuddling the baby girl and crouching down to speak to the elder son, nodding knowingly at his half comprehensible sentences.

All the bandits were led into the castle to enjoy a feast unlike any other. The long wooden table seated the whole clan and they cheered and called at one another over the mountain of food that was laid out before them. Many of these bandits started off in life struggling for scraps of bread in the streets of big cities and here they were now: powerful beasts that had led an uprising against the royal advisor himself, challenging the undefeatable knights and conquering the land, city by city. When their fingers first curled around the hilt of a sword, all those years ago, they never would have known that a life this good could come to them, and it never would have done, was it not for one courageous woman. In their cheers they called the name Silverblood as if the word itself was made of gold. Their loyalty grew with every victory, with every violent miracle she performed and now, seated in a castle they sang of devotion beyond the realms of faith. She was their goddess. A vain mortal goddess for vain mortal souls.

Steam rose from the spit as a sizzling boar was removed and served before the bandits. Flagons and mugs clanked and ale sloshed from large wooden barrels. Adelaide herself, seated at the head of the table, raised her chalice with the cheers and laughed along with her men. A smile of genuine happiness was engraved upon her face and as her elder child climbed up onto the back of her decorated throne, giggling and clinging to her shoulders, she picked him up and flipped him onto her lap, tickling the little boy as he squealed and kicked playfully.

The celebrations lasted for days but every feast must eventually end. Word was received that Morrihold, a city just west of Farendale was willing to surrender. Leaving the army in the trusted hands of her loyal commander Talon, Adelaide gathered Duncan and Bertrand and set out with them. Seizing this city would certainly offer her an advantage, considering its proximity to the capital and the bandit queen was eager to occupy it under her banner. Upon arrival, the trio discovered that they had not been deceived. The King's guards had abandoned the town, having been summoned to assist in the south. Liberated from Stormhawk's occupation, the city folk were willing to bend the knee to any leader that came their way and soon Adelaide was walking through the streets of yet another source of soldiers. By now, word of her successes had spread among the people and many doubted the King's persistence in standing against her, believing her to be a true deity. The woman found herself smiling at the thought of bandits, who have been terrorising the citizens of this country for centuries, being now seen as their saviours. They had fallen in love with their captor, and with her rumoured mystical power.

"I suppose I have no need to retain you here," she spoke to the werewolf.

Happy to return to his woman, he hurried away, lingering momentarily near the stables. His sharp ears curiously monitored the conversation behind him.

"So this is the city from which you draw your nickname?" Adelaide said gently to her husband.

"Morrihold," he carefully pronounced every syllable of the word, "it's not the nicest sounding of names."

They both laughed. The sun shone down brightly, blinding them slightly as they strolled arm in arm through the city. In the bright light, Duncan's dark hair revealed strands of golden brown as it fell into his eyes in the breeze. Tucking it under his blue bandana, he picked a wide brimmed hat from the head of a nearby peasant and took it for himself, leaving the man looking helplessly angry behind him. Wrapping his arm around Adelaide's shoulders he pulled her into him, shielding her from the sunlight. Resting her head in the curve of his neck she closed her eyes, enjoying the calm simplicity of the day.

"So tell me, how did you end up here? All those years ago when you first met Talon," the wife said sweetly.

"I was only a young kid back then," Morrihold replied with a sigh, "on the run from my past and looking for something to do with my life. I was sticking to petty thieving back then. Can't say I was ever too good at it, got myself caught every now and then. It's a bloody miracle that I still have both my hands. Then Talon came in with his troupe. Looked like the sort'a man that's got his gang under control. Bertie was there too, scared the shit out of me at first, the way he towered over the rest. More I got to know him, more I found out he's actually a decent man."

"I can't say I agree," Adelaide murmured.

"He just don't like fighting, that's all."

"That doesn't make him a very good soldier."

"Has he been a bad soldier?" Morrihold asked with a smirk.

"I suppose not. He's useful on the battlefield, I'll give him that."

"And he is loyal. He would follow Talon to hell and back. Even you tamed him eventually, with all that magic of yours. Tell me, what does that Rose really mean?"

Adelaide glanced around cautiously before replying in a hushed tone, "A Gift."

"So you've said before. But from whom?"

"From God."

"Do you truly believe that?"

"Of course."

"Then why does it only affect those with no faith of their own?"

The bandit queen stopped in her tracks and looked at him quizzically, demanding an explanation.

"You must have noticed. It is bandits that follow you most unquestioningly; criminals, murderers, thieves and such. Also, men that have lost faith in their King and their own freedom. Bertrand fell under because of his nature. James, because of his avarice. Yet, do you remember that little village by the river, on the opposite bank to Marrynport? The folk there ignored your every demand. And did you see the spire of the church that towered over the whole place? I think that's why they turned away from you."

Adelaide was lost for words. Even Archaius could not explain what happened that day yet Morrihold knew all along. She couldn't deny the accuracy of his observations either. Only then she finally realised that she had been looking for answers in all the wrong places.

"But, all that time ago," she addressed him with desperation, "that time in the woods, when you said that it had no effect on you, is that still true?"

"I think so, but does a man ever know when he's under a spell?"

"How could you resist it? You are a bandit too!"

"I hadn't given up my faith. Can't say I'm a follower of God, but I believe in doing what's right. I would not wield a sword at an innocent like many of the others have."

"I know I have," she replied quietly. Then, with a surge of empowerment, "Then that's it! I am their saviour! I unite the corrupt and the fallen and give them a purpose. I am the path to their eternal salvation."

Morrihold smiled gently, not entirely convinced by her words.

"You said you were on the run from your past," his wife continued inquisitively, trying to uncover the source of his resistance, "you were a bandit before too. Were you working under Stormhawk?"

"No, not Stormhawk. Just a small gang. We were on our own. Last I heard they disbanded a long time ago."

"Why leave them and join Talon?"

"Because I couldn't stand to see the slaughter in the northern villages!" he replied passionately, then his eyes widened as if he had spoken a secret.

Adelaide drew back. A cold sweat broke out on her skin. Her heart pounded fiercely in her chest, sending jolts through her whole body.

"What villages?" she whispered.

Morrihold stared at the ground with a look of horror. His fists clenched, he rotated as if to turn away but then returned, uncertain of how to proceed. Opening his lips, he went to speak but could find no words.

"That dark hair, those dark eyes," Adelaide recalled, "it was you. All that time ago… It was you!"

The long-suppressed memories came flooding back. That day of terror. The cliff, the childhood companion, the violence and murder, the blood in the dirt, the children forced to watch as their parents were killed, the run, the chase, the horse, the man. Those cold cruel eyes haunted her for years afterwards.

Adelaide stumbled away from him, lightheaded and gasping for breath.

Chapter 49

War of Vengeance

Her legs carried her far out of town, but Adelaide kept sprinting until she collapsed to the ground. Shaking her head, she curled up and let the heart-shattering sobs break through from her chess. Hysterical, she rocked back and forth in the long grass. Hearing movement behind her, the woman jumped to her feet and drew her sword. Morrihold had come running after her and now stood with his hands held up before him. At last those dark eyes were on her and they were desperate. Still, his wife held the blade firmly pointed at him.

Tears streamed down her face and she clung to the weapon yet her stance was not one she used to fight. Holding onto the hilt with both hands and stretching her arms out straight in front of her, the queen was not threatening to fight him but rather warning her husband to stay back, which he soundlessly obeyed, keeping the palms of his hands out in front of his chest, gesturing gently downwards in an attempt to calm her down. Eventually Adelaide lowered the blade and looked down, her shoulders still shaking with silent sobs. Dropping to the ground, she sat among the long grass, crying quietly. Morrihold dared to take but one step towards her and knelt in the grass, watching her with heart-breaking guilt.

The sun was only just beginning its descent towards the horizon, still sending out currents of warm yellow light that bathed the field and embraced each strand of grass that rocked in the gentle breeze. The couple sat some distance apart yet just close enough to see each other through the flora. After a long while, Adelaide finally spoke.

"You let me live," she whispered.

Morrihold nodded.

"Why did you let me live?" she continued.

"I couldn't kill you." Was the simple answer.

"Why?"

"I don't know. I couldn't bring a sword down onto an innocent."

"Did you kill other people in that village?" she persisted.

Her husband winced and replied, "Those that fought, yes."

"They were innocent too."

He remained silent.

"You've known it was me all this time," she stated.

"I recognised the white locks in your hair the moment you rode in with Talon."

"And you said nothing," she began to raise her voice. "You slaughtered my village, my family and then you let me befriend you, you let me fall in love with you and you said nothing!"

Morrihold bowed his head. All this time, he watched her reign terror through the kingdom, he watched her commit war crimes one after another and yet he could not perceive her as the monster he knew she was. All because of that day, the day that he looked down from his horse into the eyes of an innocent child, knowing that it was he who had taken that innocence from her.

The tears had dried on her cheeks and she finally looked up at him. Yet, the creature sitting in the grass now was no longer his heartbroken wife. It was a thirsty sadistic look that she wore now, ruthless eyes boring into his soul, a crooked grin twisting her face. Her fingers curled around the hilt of the sword and she raised it with a loose wrist, waving it before her.

"How many were there?" Adelaide hissed.

"From what I recall there were three dozen."

"You say they've disbanded, they must still be around somewhere! We have wiped out all other bandit clans. Are any of them within our ranks?"

"I think so."

"Lead me to them," was her command.

"Addie…" Morrihold started.

"Lead me to them!"

Together the two returned to Farendale and after much searching, they finally found a man Morrihold could identify as one of the bandits with whom he raided the northern villages. They watched him for a while. A big man he was, loud and boastful, loved his drink. Deep scars covered his right arm, evidently battle wounds. Adelaide could not recognise him as one of her own but she never really did pay much attention to anyone but her commanders. He walked through the night-time streets with a bottle in his hand, calling out obscenities at every woman he saw.

Adelaide rotated a thin metal lockpick in her hands, hoping to stalk him into his very home but a more creative idea occurred to her. As the bandit took a turn down a dark side street, Adelaide pushed past Morrihold and flew through the darkness like a ghost. Her target would be found in that same street the following morning, with a lockpick embedded at an angle into the base of his skull, having pierced upwards through his brain.

Over the following days more and more bandits were brutally murdered, sending a wave of panic through the city. Tension grew between the invaders and the locals who invited them in, with accusations flying from one to the other. The people were starting to regret the decision to accept the fighters, although there was no choice for them now but to avert their eyes and deny the accusations as best they could. The military commanders of the city were investigating every suspicion, every superstition that was provided for them but could detect no pattern, other than the savage mutilation of the deceased. The rebel soldiers who were killed were often disliked by the others, but every man in that profession would claim to dislike any other when the circumstances got suspicious. Bertrand was of the few who saw no danger to their own lives, but he did show unexpected curiosity in the cases, each time hovering over the corpse as if sniffing the air around it and each time turning away with a knowing look. Normally a man to use his brute strength and natural talents in combat, he now kept himself equipped with a steel sword at all times, searching the streets for the trail of the killer. With a dark smile, he shook his head when informed that the queen and her husband had left the city. The murders stopped that very day.

**

For months, the couple travelled to every bandit settlement in the kingdom and unleashed the wrath of vengeance upon the chosen few. Indifferent to weather and the terrain, Adelaide pushed on, guided by the inferno of rage that burned in her chest. They crossed rivers and streams, scaled one mountain after another and camped in the woods instead of seeking shelter within towns. Morrihold followed her loyally and informed her of any men he recognised, pained to be the one to seal their fate yet unfalteringly dedicated to regaining the trust of his beloved. It was on one of those nights that Adelaide rested her head on the trunk of a fallen tree and looked up through the thick canopies. The night was dark and hundreds of stars sparkled gently above her. So cold they seemed, so distant. She reached out towards the sky and held her arm still for a few moments, trying to count how many of those little twinkling lights would fit onto her fingernail. With a slow deep laugh, she watched them as they mocked her from their celestial pedestals. Her fingers moved to the right, into the rising smoke of the fire, creating new eddies and vortices in the opaque grey fluid. Stretching, she rolled to the side and looked into the fire. The hot air blinded her and burned her skin so she rotated away to end up lying on her belly with her arms crossed over the tree trunk to form a soft rest for her chin. Morrihold sat before her, absentmindedly poking the fire with a charred stick.

"Where shall we go next, dear husband?" she asked in an unnervingly childlike tone.

"Seems like we've been to every bandit camp in the country by now," he replied sleepily.

"We truly have. Talon's boats will be ready soon, the preparations are nearly over. This little personal errand of ours must come to a finish now if we don't want to delay the conquest," her voice was sly and haunting.

"Yes."

"We must have killed most of the surviving bandits from your old band by now, don't you think?"

"Yes."

"Of course we will always be one short," she began to sound more maniacal than ever before. Duncan glanced at her quickly, the stick frozen still in his hand.

Adelaide rolled back and looked at the stars once more. The branches waved slowly in the cool, late-night breeze.

"You know, I was once taught to speak with the spirit of the woods; to feel the movement of air around me, to feel the presence of every bird in the branches above me, every woodlouse in the fallen trunks, every little crawler under the leaves," she whispered.

"Sounds like pagan nonsense to me," was Duncan's guarded response.

"Perhaps, but there is something pagan, magical about being in the woods at night, wouldn't you say? It is as if you can feel the presence of the earth herself, the mother, the giver, the guardian. She warns us when there is trouble nearby, she whispers her soft words of warning and the trees pass the alarm onto us, conveying her omniscient knowledge with the rustling of their leaves."

Before Duncan could question her intensions and sanity, she contorted and reached into her boot to pull out a thin dagger, launching it with full force into the shadows beyond the light of their campfire. With one arm still resting on the tree, she sat up to see if she had hit her target. A scream erupted from the darkness and three men emerged into the light. They were dressed in dirty rags but wore leather hilts at their belts, all of which were empty as the rogue bandits charged armed and angry at the couple. Duncan, being the nearest to them, was their prime target as they were still unaware of quite how the flying dagger killed their fourth companion. Scrambling for his sword, Morrihold could barely rise to his feet when the first strike came. With lighting fast reflexes, the future queen shielded her husband with her translucent blade, which had somehow appeared in her hands. Kicking the opponent away, Adelaide swirled past his sword and drove her weapon into his neck. With a sadistic grin, she gave it one firm push and the head separated from its body, showering the ground in blood, and rolled towards the exposed roots of some nearby trees.

The two remaining rogues honoured their fallen brother with one glance, and then forgot him in order to focus on preserving their own lives. Duncan had at last managed to find and unsheathe his sword and now went for the attack. The enemy blocked his strike and shoved him away as the other circled around to capture him from behind. Caught off balance and stumbling backwards, the Silverblood lieutenant fell into the trap and one enemy surged forward as his companion went to attack from behind.

Using the momentum of his attacker, Duncan caught the sword of the advancing man onto his own and rolled backwards, giving into the strength of the opponent and flipping him over with his feet, thereby sending him flying into the man who in that moment started to question his sneaky plan of attack. They could not recover quickly enough and Morrihold effortlessly took both of their lives.

Standing over them with blood and sweat dripping from his dark hair, the victor was joined by his wife who placed a proud hand on his shoulder. As he looked at the faces on the men he murdered, the bandit forced his mind to cloud in order to recall a distant memory. Ah yes! With recognition came a melancholy smile.

"That one." He pointed to one of the bloody corpses with his foot. "He was up north too."

"Wonderful!" Adelaide exclaimed. "Well, this has been some joyous marital bonding!"

Chapter 50

From One to Another

The sun hovered high over the woods, diving down through the canopies with every ray, roaming happily across the sky in the brief absence of the dark clouds that often intruded on this realm. Duncan and Adelaide had not left the woods after their encounter with the rogues, instead wandering deeper into their embrace. Waltzing on ahead, Adelaide was humming a sweet song, one that she often sang to her kids, while caressing the nearby flora with the lightest touch. Her movements were like those of a young girl, delicate yet a little clumsy, contrasting her fiercely armed attire. The rose on her arm was practically shining from its canvass as if fuelled by the warmth of the light. Duncan pondered over it with both wonder and doubt as he morosely followed his joyful wife.

"It's done, it's done, it's done!" Adelaide suddenly announced. "I can feel it in my soul. My people are avenged."

Duncan could only nod. Guilt flowed through his veins, convulsing his heart every time it dared to beat, yet he wondered if he was more tormented by the memories of running with the northern clan or his actions since. Pained by the recollections, he stopped against an old oak and let his head rest against its bark. Looking up, he squinted in the light and closed his eyes, watching the sunshine paint rapid colourful pictures through his eyelids.

Two hands pressed to his chest and he lowered his head to meet Adelaide as she gently gripped his tunic with her fingers to raise herself to her toes and locked her lips to his.

***

Deep beneath the King's castle, within the walls of the dungeon where many men had met their fate, now sat the former guard. The weeks he spent in this vast stone chamber consisted of continuous torture, the only release from which was his time in the shackles that hung just the right distance from the floor that he could neither sit nor stand, dangling helplessly as the weight of his starved body pulled at the joints in his shoulders. He got to sit at last, in the iron chair the executioner kindly provided. Sharp round spikes stuck out of the metal, digging into his bruised, infected flesh. His wrists were bound to the arms of the chair with thick coarse rope that also wrapped around his ribs and ankles, binding him securely to his place. The executioner stood by the door without his black mask, revealing his cold cruel eyes. Beside him was the torturer, James's only companion for most days. Every feature of his old face; every scar, every wrinkle, every wart had now engraved itself into the young man's brain. It was all he saw when he was given the privilege of closing his eyes.

Just then another friend made his reappearance. Darius squeezed into the dungeon, struggling to heave open the thick iron door. He was more energised than before, almost excited yet his face momentarily contorted with horror and pity upon catching a glimpse of the young guard. Hastily recovering and averting his eyes, the advisor began to question the torturer.

"I have been informed that you have news," he stated formally but with a warm tone of hope.

"Aye!" croaked the old man, drizzling spit as he tried to speak through the five teeth he equipped, "but it be just crazy babble, milord."

"Best you tell me, anyway. What has the prisoner said?"

"He better tell ye himself, the Lord wouldn't believe it if little old me was to tell it," the torturer spoke with an amused grin.

"Would you please just…" Darius began, but seeing the sadistic amusement of the old man he gave up and waved towards the prisoner with his hand, turning his ear towards the chair and firmly shutting his eyes.

The creep scurried towards his toy and lifted James's chin with his dirty fingers. His claw-like nails were black from the dried blood that was caked beneath them.

"Now tell our Lord what ye told me, lad," he said into his prisoner's ear, spewing saliva onto his yellowing cheek.

The voice of his tormentor sent James into a frenzy as he tried to turn his head away and struggled against the ropes. The spikes ripped at his body as he shifted in place. With a yelp he froze in place, his head dropping loosely to his chest. The once straw-yellow hair was now stained a dark brown from the blood, dirt and mould that covered every inch of the dungeon. Tears fell onto his thigh and he twitched as the salty fluid stung his open wounds.

"Boy doesn't want to talk, milord," the torturer announced.

By this point Darius has raised his trembling hand, shielding his face from the terrible spectacle.

"What did he say? Why did you tell the guards he spoke? What information did he provide?" the advisor screamed in rage, "why the hell did you drag me in here?"

"I didn't ask ye to come, milord," the fiendish man giggled.

Darius dropped his hand and glared at the madman before him. With rapid breaths he turned and rushed towards the door, shoving the executioner out of the way.

"But since ye already be here, ye might as well stay and listen," the torturer called after him.

With his forearm pressed to the door, the advisor stopped in his escape and buried his face in his shoulder, the other hand held to his stomach to fight the nausea. Having recovered his spectator, the cruel old man carried on the performance. Screams echoed through the vast stone room and Darius slid down the door, still facing away from the chair and curled up on the ground with his arms pressed to his ears.

Eventually the young bandit cracked.

"A werewolf!" he yelled sobbing, "a werewolf, a werewolf, a werewolf. That's her weapon."

"A werewolf now, is it lad? T'was a wizard last time," the torturer hissed.

"Yes! A wizard and a wolf," James spoke weeping.

"So ye see, milord, nothing but crazy talk. The boy's no use," the old man addressed the advisor, who had leapt to his feet and was now stood facing the prisoner with his eyes wide open.

Darius couldn't believe what he was hearing. Breathing faster and faster he started to pace in front of the door, whispering to himself and moving the fingers of his right hand as if calculating something.

"The wizard, what was his name?" he demanded. James replied with silence. "Oh, what am I saying, how many wizards are there in this kingdom? It has to be him. Yes, it must be him. But why? Why would he betray me so? Why would he save one kingdom only to destroy another? She must have captured him, forced him to cooperate."

"He looked pretty damn happy to me," James croaked mockingly, satisfied to see someone other than himself in pain.

"I thought she had killed him," Darius spoke with poorly-disguised relief. Whether his old friend betrayed him or not, Darius was pleased to hear of his survival. "You were the one who informed them of his visit, were you not?"

James only grinned in return, revealing empty gums from which his teeth were pulled long ago.

"Oh, it all makes sense now," the advisor mumbled to himself. "Tarrynsdew. He burned it to ash under her order. Tell me, young man, do you know how many people inhabited that city? No? Nor do I. But I know how many remain. Not a single one. All those lives lost and for what? To have the kingdom fall into the hands of a maniac?"

"From one to another," James croaked.

"Treachery!" the advisor chastised. "How dare you speak of your King in such a way!"

"At least I'm not fucking his wife." Was the reply.

The room fell into silence. Darius stood limp, stripped of his rage. The cold emotionless eyes of the executioner were almost animated while his lower face twisted into a perverted smile. The torturer was nearly bouncing off the walls, pressing his wrinkled hand to his mouth to hide the laughter that was moments from erupting out loud.

"What ya going to do, little traitor?" James continued, "have me executed publicly or strangle me right here? I sure can't wait to find out."

Darius closed his eyes. It looked as if a thousand thoughts were running through his head at once. Steadying his breath, he looked up once again. Those fierce dark eyes burned with resolve. There he stood as composed and grand as ever. It was a clash of willpower between the two men.

"We've wasted enough time," Darius announced clearly, "now we shall return to our previous discussion. You say it was a werewolf that aided the rebel army?"

***

Adelaide stood with her back pressed to that same oak tree. Duncan leaned over her, one hand against the bark and the one holding her exposed thigh to his waist. They were both sweating and out of breath but satisfied. Letting go of her leg, he gently brushed her hair from her face, caressing her cheek, and pressed his forehead to hers. They stood holding each other for a long time, bathed in the warm rays of the sinking sun.

"Let us head back now," spoke Duncan, stepping away and securing his belt. "We'll see how far Talon and Hunter progressed with the ships."

Adelaide stood silent, her arms dangling loosely by her sides, looking into the distance with a kind of sadness. Her husband lovingly placed his hand on her shoulder and ran it down her arm to take her hand.

"It's done now," he said quietly.

Her lips remained sealed.

"They are all gone," Morrihold tried again.

"All but one." Was her sudden reply.

Before he could react, she pulled him closer by his hand and drove a dagger into his chest. As he collapsed to his knees, desperately clutching at the weapon, she looked down with the same cold menacing expression that Duncan wore when he had let her live seventeen years before.

Chapter 51

The Siege: Part 1

In a small townhouse near the vast harbour of Marrynport, Hunter sat across the table from his rebel queen. His right arm was outstretched with compassion over the chipped wood, reaching towards his old friend. Talon stood behind her, his hand resting on her shoulder.

"It was awful," Adelaide sobbed, removing a tear-soaked cloth from her red eyes. "My beloved... my dear husband..."

She could muster no more before breaking down into more hysterical sobbing.

"How..." Hunter began delicately, "how did this happen? We saw you fight Bertie all that time ago, I would have thought a bear would be an easy kill."

"I went to look at the traps we had laid out for the hares," Adelaide squeaked. "The beast must have sniffed us out. When I returned to the campfire, he was... There was so much blood... It was awful!"

"Did you find any hares?" Bertrand called coldly from across the room. The other two men stared at him in outrage. With his brows low over his eyes, he continued, "Hares have a certain scent about them, as do bears. It lingers on the one who caught them. And their blood, it smells different to that of a human."

From her puffy cheeks, Adelaide's eyes sparkled with malicious excitement.

"What were you doing in those woods, my queen?" Bertrand continued the interrogation. "I wouldn't have thought there would be any bandits there."

"Bandits?" Talon and Hunter asked in unison.

"Yes," Adelaide hastily jumped in, "we were looking for some additional recruits in anticipation of the upcoming battle."

"Did you find any?" her companions asked.

"None that were willing to join us," replied Adelaide with a well-disguised grin.

"As for the upcoming battle," Talon spoke, taking a seat next to his leader, "I know this is a hard time for you, but we cannot delay any further. Our informant within the castle has not been seen in months now and the ships are ready. We have to assume that the advisor now knows of our plans and we have to mount the ballistae and begin the sailboat journey."

"My children…"

"Rupert and Edith are safe within the walls of Farendale. They are being cared for by some local women our boys befriended."

"Don't tell me you left my children in the hands of whores!"

"The best thing about whores is that their loyalty is easy to buy."

"Christ, Talon! Well, I suppose we'd better start. Send messengers to our generals in Farendale, Ghyrock and Avenstead. I expect that by now the full reinforcements of the Silverblood camp must be completed, so send a rider south with the order for Hansfell to lead whatever men he can to join his peers in Ghyrock. We will aim to have all three armies join up to the southeast of the capital. At this point, Hans, along with the other knights and Bertrand will separate off as the elite fighters, leaving all the troops under the command of the other generals. Talon, you will in turn command them.

"Hunter, I will need you to sail over the northern point of the kingdom and down the western side, as planned. This will take you two months at most. We will position scouts in the King's Woods, north of the capital. Once you reach the castle, fire the ballistae at will. Aim not for the walls but for the archers on the battlements. The trebuchets will be brought by the land troops when we launch the attack from the southeast. This should take them by surprise and leave the east conveniently undefended. We'll send a few hundred ahead to distract the archers. After that, the elites will move in. Bertrand, we need you to break down the gate. Once inside, we kill every man we see."

***

Two months had passed. Hunter stood at the bow of one of five small sailboats. The captain told him they were approaching the castle. One arm leaning on the moist wooden beams and the other firmly gripping a metal-cased eye glass, the bandit lieutenant once again impatiently looked through it at the woods. No movement could be seen in the brush. He was certain that the scouts were instructed to send a light signal upon seeing the boats, but this did not come. Turning back and leaning against the side of the boat, Hunter looked at his men. Four soldiers, four sailors, two ballistae per boat. One flaming arrow from an enemy and the whole thing would sink. Bracing himself for the biggest battle of his life, the bandit looked to the other end of the boat to see the captain standing still by the wheel, looking ahead with fear and regret. With trembling hands Hunter raised the glass to his eye, yet he already knew that this time he would see the stone peak of the King's castle stretching up over the canopies.

***

Within the walls of that very castle, chaos was moments from breaking out. Six bandits were kneeling before the throne. Their hands were bound and blood ran from their broken flesh. The King sat with little comfort in his grand chair, his eyes watching not the spies but his advisor who paced rapidly behind the six accused. Soldiers filled the room and two knights stood by the game they caught during their patrol of the northern forest. The King silently looked to one of his trusted heroes and gestured downwards with one finger. Drawing his sword, the knight stabbed one of the bandits through the chest. The other five whimpered as their friend gargled, choked and died. Darius stopped pacing, his hands clenched before him.

"Now," King Bohemond spoke in a sombre tone, "will you continue your treason? Will you stay silent when your king commands you to speak?"

The five did not utter a word. Another gesture from the ruler and another man fell dead onto the floor. The remaining four still refused to talk. The soldiers surrounding them watched with hatred as a third man fell. Darius was ready to bury his face in his hands, barely maintaining his composure in front of his monarch. To his relief, one of the spies finally cracked.

"We were watching for boats!" he screamed. The other two averted their eyes from the traitor.

"The Silverblood bitch is sending boats from the north?" the King pushed.

"There are no bandit settlements directly north of here," announced Sir Randall.

"There must be one that we were not aware of."

At this moment, the door burst open and a soldier ran in. Confronted with a few dozen angry eyes, he stopped in his tracks, bowed, nearly falling from his feet and loudly announced that boats were seen approaching from the north bearing an unknown flag and mounted with weapons. The King all but leapt from the throne and his advisor shuddered. The three bandits smirked yet their joy was short-lived as they realised that their queen will not be informed of Hunter's arrival at the castle. They were not given much time to entertain their sorrow as Randall rapidly cut their throats and strode from the hall, breaking into a sprint towards the battlements as soon as he was out of his King's sight. Darius was desperately trying to calm his nerves. Upon receiving a nod from Bohemond, he followed the knight, along with the other generals.

The men ran up the stone steps, tripping in their haste, yelling at one another in frustration. Eventually the dim candlelight of the spiral staircase gave way to the pale twilight. Iron cage lanterns stood intermittently on the battlements, some extinguished by the coastal winds. Moist salty air weighed heavily upon the strained lungs of the generals and their calls were lost in the sound of the waves that crashed against the crumbling cliff. Rushing towards the stone wall, Darius scanned the horizon. A nearby guard sheepishly offered him an eyeglass and the advisor snatched it from his hands. Leaning onto the rough stone, Darius looked in the direction the guards were pointing to see the badly magnified image of a group of small ships. They appeared to be approaching the castle head on.

"How many?" he demanded.

"Five." Was the unified response from the soldiers.

Lowering the glass, he looked towards Randall. The general met his gaze with the same panicked look. They both knew that this was greatly unexpected. There were no known nations across the sea so the west was lightly defended. The peasants who were re-homed to this thin strip of land just before the burning of the south-eastern fields were quickly catching on to the commotion in the battlements above them. Some looked up to their grand castle, some looked out into the sea. The sharper-eyed children noticed the ships too. Many minutes passed in uncertainty but panic soon ensued as rakes and hoes were thrown onto the ground and the farmers started running for their lives. Yet one stayed behind, standing close to the castle wall so as to remain unseen from above. Leaning his weary old body against the castle, he watched the ships with a smile. Ripped black garments hung from his skeletal form yet he lifted his crooked staff with surprising strength, waving it as a conductor waves his baton. The soil that the farmers worked so hard seemed to dry beneath his feet, turning to dust and rising up in the air currents. With it, almost as if materialising from beneath his dirty cloak, a flock of red-billed choughs soared into the sky.

They flew upwards towards the receding clouds, beautifully performing their intricate tricks over the cliffs of Starkenhaart. Such delicate grace to welcome such horrifying bloodshed.

Darius stood with his head bowed, the eye glass held loosely in his hand. Yet his face was not of a man who was defeated. A fire grew hotter in his heart, a desperate defiant strength burst forth from his soul. That same strength with which he had put down the rebel armies of Mortendenn. But this was different. This was his kingdom. This was his home. This was his solemn duty.

"Why are they sailing directly towards us?" he called out sternly over the noise of the sea. "What damage can a ship do from the front?"

"These boats don't look like they can support a lot of heavy artillery," Randall replied, still studying the attackers. "The ballistae they are carrying don't have a long range. My guess is that they will continue to approach the cliff."

"They can't get too close. The ballistae can't shoot directly upwards," Darius spoke his thoughts aloud. "They must remain far enough away to shoot comfortably. Can you approximate the distance they will stop at?"

"Yes."

"Then organise your archers. Use flaming arrows."

"Flaming?" Randall appeared momentarily hesitant, "not the special arrows we had prepared?"

"No. Those will be used to defend the east. Look at those ships, they can hardly support her entire army. In addition, they are sailing right towards a cliff. I suspect they are merely a distraction and the main force will attack from the east. Try to burn these down as quickly as you can, then join us by the main city gates. I expect her to strike there directly."

Randall nodded and called for his archers to equip. His commanding voice boomed over the battlements with overpowering authority and the soldiers quickly scurried away in search of cloth and rope to soak in oil. Randall's ever-armoured fist rested on the stone as his heartbeat slowed in his chest. Initially outraged by the treacherous tenacity of the Silverblood army, he was growing calmer with every passing moment as his conditioned fighting instincts took over. Looking back over the battlements he saw the small cloaked figure of Darius hurrying in the distance. With a smirk, the general admired how such a feeble frame could possess the courage of such calibre.

***

Adelaide sat on a rock some distance from the castle gate. Her army was spread out before her, hidden from the view of the city soldiers by a hill. Awkward jokes and nervous laughter sounded around her as the rebel troops tried to ward away the tense silence, but their hands trembled nonetheless. Only Adelaide sat in perfect stillness, her hair plaited back and her beautiful gown replaced with thick cloth and steel armour. Only the rune-inscribed green cloak remained, swaying around her in the warm wind. With her elbows on her knees and chin resting against her fists, the rebel queen stared at the men gathered before her, waiting for the scouts to return. In her mind she worked through every step, every possible move that Darius could make, yet her concentration was broken whenever she met the eyes of her werewolf. In them, she saw such fierce hatred and shameless accusation. Adelaide watched in silence as Bertrand barged through the crowd and grabbed Talon by the elbow, pulling him up with undisguised urgency. Talon was nearly lifted from the ground but broke free and refused to listen to the words his oldest friend whispered in his ear, shaking his head, waving Bertrand away as if to say that gossip could wait until after the battle was won. Daisy soon arrived at her lover's side. She, and a number of other women, set up tents behind this same hill to treat the wounded and her small form was struggling under the weight of several knapsacks and satchels. She leaned around Bertrand, holding onto him to stop herself from being pushed to the ground as others moved past her, and spoke to Talon with what appeared to be an expression of warning. So she knew Adelaide's secret too. That was hardly a surprise, Bertrand was bound to share his suspicions with her before anyone else. Adelaide could feel the power emanating from the Dragonslayer as it rested within its scabbard. Before this battle ends, it will draw the blood of two lovers. Wouldn't want them to spread their lies. It was simply a necessity to maintain the morale of the group.

A sinister smile brought Adelaide's stone face to life. Yet she sensed the all-too-familiar presence nearby. Turning her head upwards, she witnessed a flock of choughs make their way from the west, barely visible against the dark cloudless sky. Realisation struck her like a bolt of lightning. Jumping to her feet she paused for one breathless moment as all faces turned to her. Then sounded the inevitable command.

"Attack!"

Her voice seemed to echo through the surrounding land and the soldiers sprang into action. The first infantry group ran ahead, horses pulled the colossal trebuchets uphill, Bertrand moved against his own will, rapidly changing his form. A cry of pain burst through from his mouth as the bones in his body broke and reshaped themselves. It sounded over the commotion, over the clanking swords and panicked chatter. Daisy hovered next to him, desperately looking for a way to ease his suffering but the yellow eyes of the monster had awaked in his skull. On all fours, he leaped over the men rushing towards the hill.

Adelaide herself, mounted on horseback, galloped past her troops, leading the advancing army towards their goal with a look of grandiose heroism, directing them with the Dragonslayer. Also on horseback were her elites: Sir Hansfell and the four other rogue knights who had spent years awaiting an opportunity to destroy the King that stripped them of their titles. Their excitement was evident and genuine, as opposed to the fearful squeaking of the foot-soldiers, poorly disguised as battle cries.

Chapter 52

The Siege: Part 2

There it was. The army approaching from the southeast of the castle. More and more bandits spilled over the hilltop, crudely organised into groups. Trebuchets moved steadily closer and cartsful of heavy artillery followed suit. Darius knew at once where the Silverblood queen was, so great was her pulsing power. On this scale maybe it truly was a gift from God, but it sure as hell wasn't being used in His name. She kept her distance, riding from one group of soldiers to another, staying out of range.

Royal archers increased in number and the commanding knight barked at them to get in formation. Darius himself could only watch as rebel troops swarmed towards the wall, and the bloodthirsty rogues he hoped to never set eyes on again were riding proudly among the rest, as if taunting the soldiers to come out. Rushing to the other side of the wall, the advisor watched as the King's guards collected before the gates, waiting for the wall to surrender her city. Some prayed, some simply stared ahead in sombre silence.

Returning to his previous post, Darius awaited the impossible. The traitor was lying, he was certain of it. Yet he himself had witnessed the horrors that can exist in this world. He had befriended a wizard and brought down an unimaginable evil. His fear was soon confirmed. There it was. The beast itself. Running through the burnt soil faster than a horse could, his giant paws landing heavily under his weight. Yet he avoided the foot soldiers with surprising dexterity. In all his monstrosity, there was a certain grotesque beauty. Gathering his senses, Darius ran to the knight commander and told him to equip his men with the arrows they had prepared some time before.

A tremor shook the wall. The stones shifted and small rocks crumbled onto the King's soldiers. The men on the battlements dropped their bows and crouched in fear. Darius found himself clinging to the fellow commander with his thin trembling hands. The enemy was at the gate.

Another tremor. The advisor detached himself from the knight and cautiously manoeuvred towards the edge. Looking down he saw the werewolf retreat slightly from the wall and then sprint towards it again, crashing his colossal form against the wooden beams. This third tremor would have shaken the advisor from the battlements had he not leaped back in time.

"Raise your weapons, men! Arm your bows!" he found himself calling out. "We must stop the monster! We must protect the city! We must protect her people! Your wives and children, your friends and allies, your King and guardian, today we fight for them!" Then turning to the knight, he confronted the panic in his eyes, "These are your men! Overcome your hesitation and command them to glory!"

Several sharp knocks were heard across the wall as crudely made wooden ladders, held together by rope, hit the outer face of the wall, just out of reach for the archers who immediately tried to push them away. The enemy was ascending. To protect the ladders from falling, the beast stopped charging the gate and, knowing that he had already greatly damaged the wall, started clawing at the hinges of the doors. The wood was thick, fashioned from many tree trucks bound together, yet it could put up little resistance against his unnatural claws. All the while, bandit archers assembled in formation and were steadily approaching the city. The foot soldiers had yet to reach the top of their ladders and defenders were leaning over the battlements aiming their bows downwards as best they could. Taking this opportunity, the green cloaked rider raised her translucent weapon and called out and order. A shower of arrows came towards the battlements. Some archers were hit but most threw themselves on the ground in time, pulling the advisor down with them. The arrows scraped just past them and rained down onto the city. Commotion ensued as the King's guard suffered damage but it took mere moments for the well-trained men to resume their ranks.

Rising from the floor, Darius gestured towards his commander, who gave the order to ready aim and fire on the bandits in retaliation. He knew they desperately needed the silver tipped arrows or the gate would fall. He was growing impatient.

The climbers were half way up their ladders. They were going to reach their goal soon. The archers on the battlements were not equipped with full sized fighting swords and were at a disadvantage in close combat. Aware of that, Darius abandoned his post on the frontline in search of the commander of the ground troops. Calling some of the archers to retreat with him, he led them across the wall and down a stone staircase. Running as fast as his legs would carry him, he had at last reached his target. Demanding to take a large group of soldiers to the top of the wall to defend it from the bandits who have by now likely engaged the archers in hand to hand combat, he offered the group currently following him in exchange for when the gate falls. Finally, he ordered one of the soldiers to find the oil used to make flaming arrows and bring it to the top of the eastern wall. Fearing it may be too late to tackle the ladders, the advisor was nonetheless undeterred.

**

A flash of light shot by. Hunter had been expecting it. The sails of the boat behind his own caught the projectile. They tensely waited to see if the moist ocean air would extinguish it, alas the sail soon went up in flames that spread rapidly to the wooden mast. Terrified bandits shook off their leather and dived into the water, some swimming towards the other boats and some heading straight for the shore. Hunter looked up towards the western battlements. Dozens of men stood in line, flaming arrows aimed at the ships. Another order was given. More fire. The sailors stood in silence, knowing they could not prevent their fate. The flames passed overhead. The four remaining ships were safe while the fifth was quickly becoming a waterborne inferno.

In contrast to the fiery rage of mortal men, the grand ocean stood tranquil, barely swaying in the wind, broken only by the frantic splashing of drowning men. The weather truly was lovely that day. The shimmering waves stretched into the horizon. Seagulls would have been soaring above these waters had it not been for the aerial assault on the miniature fleet. The dark blue sky guided thin distant clouds to the east, away from the glow of the waxing gibbous moon.

An eastern wind! Hunter started. His heart began to beat more fiercely, to break through the hopeless despair.

"Aim the ballistae!" Was his order.

The sharp assertive command sparked up the bandits and they adjusted the heavy wooden machines to aim towards the top of the battlements. Arrows loaded, they looked towards their leader.

"Fire at will! Break their ranks!"

The men obeyed and a barrage of heavy arrows soared upward with the wind. They may not have been flaming, they may not even have had steel tips and they were certainly not great in number, but although their mass caused them to sink in the skies, breaking against the stone wall of the capital, they caused the archers to flinch, to hesitate for a moment.

"Keep firing! Keep them distracted!" Hunter knew his job was not to cause destruction, but rather to keep the archers occupied for as long as his ships would hold out so that his queen could make her move in the south east. His loyalty soared towards the east alongside his arrows, but it pierced through the city like a beam of promise though the shadows of fear.

***

Darius's suspicions have been confirmed. The bandits scampered onto the battlements like rats, forcing the archers into a hasty retreat. The advisor had arrived just in time and with a wordless gesture, sent the soldiers to push back. The men were disorganised, pulled unexpectedly from their posts and their general but they ran ahead with raw spirit and clashed with the rebels. The clanking of swords sounded like a bell announcing the start of battle. It probably echoed through the surrounding hills but the screams of the wounded drowned out any other sound. The soldiers were stronger and better equipped than the bandit troops and were able to push them back further and further. The enemies climbing the ladders were trapped, unable to get onto the battlement due to the density of close fighting and unable to climb back down due to the number of people on each ladder.

Soldiers sent to fetch the oil had now returned, carrying large wooden barrels, two men for each. Darius watched the battle intently, waiting for an opportunity. Although the soldiers he brought were successful in their pushback, the bandits moved along the other side of the battlements, over the northern curve of the wall and were advancing fast.

"Are they within range?" he asked a nearby archer, a member of the group that had retreated from their post above the gate.

"Aye Sir, just about, I'd say."

"Then strike them down. As for the frontline," he addressed the exhausted oil barrel carriers, "as soon as an opening appears, alight the oil and pour over the ladders."

The men nodded, one nearest to the staircase disappeared in search of a torch.

Soon afterwards, Darius's fateful weapon arrived.

***

Adelaide sat majestically on horseback behind her archers. The city wall looked impenetrable from there, rising grandiosely into the moonlit skies. The peak of the castle could be seen just beyond it. Her army was spread out before her, following the tactics drawn up during meetings with Hansfell and his knights. Archers were positioned further back, inevitably disadvantaged by the altitude of their capital counterparts. Bertrand was up in front, tearing down the gate and the disposables were making their way over the wall. Watching the commotion, she could see them engaged in battle, some being pushed off the battlements and sent screaming towards the ground.

Let them die. Use them to force more and more of the King's soldiers to assemble above the gate. The trebuchets will be operational shortly and then will destroy the front face of the wall and all the men who stand upon it. When the bandits were pushed back and the entire front battlement appeared to be covered in city armour, the soldiers suddenly retreated and four barrels of burning oil were poured over the edge. Three were aimed directly at ladders, igniting their wooden steps and the bandits who clung to them. Burning bodies were crashing into the ground, piling up and forcing back the surrounding infantry. The fourth barrel was only half emptied onto the last ladder, destroying it but causing less damage than to the others. The remaining oil was thrown in front of the gate, showering the werewolf in flames. The creature howled in agony, its fur burning from its back, fat bubbling from cracks in its charring skin. Yet it did not give up. Scratching away at the gate it finally broke through.

Soldiers from inside poured out, immediately striking the frontline bandit troops. Bertrand was in a feral state, more powerful and more terrifying than ever before, he fell victim to his animal side.

The rebel queen leaped up and positioned her feet on the saddle, crouching for balance. When ready, she stood up straight and aimed her bow. With inhuman precision, the future queen fired an arrow, piercing through several of the Kings soldiers. Her next one was aimed at the back of the wolf's head. His job was done now.

Before she could release it, a shining light flew down from above, and embedded itself in Bertrand's flesh. She at once recognised the timbre of his screams. It was shortly after she met Gabriel, Adelaide recalled, when he confronted those werewolves in the woods, he scratched one with the Dragonslayer and it howled like a banshee.

"Silver! They're using silver tipped arrows. That brilliant devil Darius," she mumbled to herself.

More and more of these shining lights raining down onto the creature. It was instantly weakened and fell to the swarm of soldiers cutting at him from all directions. The poor being collapsed into a pool of its own blood.

Adelaide heard a shrill yell behind her. Carefully looking back without losing her balance, she watched as Daisy — having witnessed the fall of her beloved — ran past her out into the battlefield. Her tiny form seemed to dodge the solders with sheer force of will and she quickly arrived at the gate, to her lover's side. Shoving through the soldiers, she embraced the dying beast and clung to his broken body with all her might as life escaped him. Surrounded by enemy soldiers, it did not take long for her to be cut down alongside him.

Chapter 53

The Three Commanders

The aura of suspense and horror that had previously lingered over the battlefield was burned to ash as the soldiers clashed. The south-eastern side of the capital was engulfed in blood and violence, men from both sides cutting and slicing at one another. Battle cries were joined in a sickening harmony by the screams of the wounded, the number of which soared by the second. Metal struck metal, releasing that ungodly sound that sends a shiver down the spine of whoever hears it. It is merely an innate human instinct to shudder away from such a sound, to fear it. And fear it did those who were positioned further from the frontline, the archers and the commanders, as the ones engaged in fighting were in no position to ponder the horror of their actions. Those hundreds of men on either side, each came to this battle for a reason of his own, some were there to fight for glory, some for loyalty, some for gold and jewel, those were all reasons that brought the soldiers to this place but they were no longer the goals that guided them. Out here, in the centre of it all, none of that mattered. They fought simply to survive. As grotesque as these monstrous acts of violence were, there was a certain raw power to them, the stunning display of man's will that hovered somewhere between courage and desperation.

So beautiful was the night-time sky above them, that immortal observer who remains idle through all human folly. So gentle was the glowing moon as it trekked far above, peaceful and uncaring. So free was the salty sea air that was brought from the western walls by its currents. No minds were there to admire it, no eyes could notice the tiny specs of still glowing embers that now joined those very same currents. They seemed to act like the transition between the distant tranquillity of the skies and the onslaught going on the ground. We are bound to this ground, these petty vain gods that we are, and in our greed we disfigure the face of the life-bearing Earth beneath our feet.

High above the rest, seated upon their strong steeds were the five great men of the bandit queen's army. Sir Hansfell was their undisputed leader, his steel armour shining beautifully in the still-burning pools of oil as he now joined the front-line battle. Galloping past the King's soldiers, he swiftly took heads from their bodies with nothing more than a swipe of the blade. He has missed this, the thrill of the fight, the danger and, above all, the hot red blood that still squirted from the ravaged bodies of the men at the hooves of his horse. He had often been accused of unnecessary cruelty and a ruthless approach during his time as a royal knight, those very same accusations being the catalyst of his demotion, but he could never bring himself to deny them. He was a man who killed and raped and destroyed and nothing in the world could bring him more joy.

There, up high on the battlements, were the cold judgemental eyes of the man who took Hansfell's title from him. That filthy foreigner who played the King's otherwise idle hand. The great merciful Bohemond would not have bothered with it, indeed would not have noticed it, had it not been for his self-righteous fool of an advisor. He then recruited knights that were supposedly better suited for the job. Those were the men Hansfell was searching for and he did not have to look far. It seemed that their objective was similar to his own. This was the inevitable outcome of this battle; the new against the old, the loyal against the treacherous and, perhaps, in the end it really was as simple as the good against the evil.

The King's knights were also mounted on steeds and riding in haste towards Hansfell and his elite team. Sword in hand and fire in soul, Hansfell urged his horse on, towards his rivals. His journey was cut short because before he knew it, his horse was cut down from beneath him by a foot soldier and the rogue knight was sent flying to the ground. The still twitching corpse of the horse landed onto his left leg, crushing the bone under its weight. He could feel the tendon holding his kneecap rip under the tension. That same foot soldier now came for him, bringing his blade down with unhesitating determination towards the trapped bandit lieutenant.

"This son-of-a-bitch would get one hell of a promotion if he takes me down like this," Hansfell mused to himself right before he deflected the attack and allowed the soldier's own momentum to send him falling onto the knight's sword.

Wasting no time, the bandit commander shifted along the ground and dragged his broken leg out from under the fallen horse. Leaning onto his sword, he raised himself up and looked around. The other members of the Ghyrock clan were engaged in fierce battle against the royal knights, displaying quite the spectacle of power. Heavy artillery smashed into the wall, shattering the thick rock and sending huge stone fragments speeding towards the ground. Not far from him was the burning corpse of Bertrand. Hansfell could not help but find it amusing that this dead creature had previously been the only reason Talon's bandit gang were safe from Ghyrock's invasion and here they all were now, fighting the same battle under the command of the same queen.

That queen of theirs was as inhumanly destructive as ever. Those noble knights that could so easily take out hundreds of bandits and turn the tide of this war were sent crashing off their horses by nothing more than a single arrow from her bow. There she stood, feet firmly on the saddle of her unnaturally still horse, drawing the magical weapon with herculean strength, the purple light from its metal body reflecting in the black pupils of her unblinking eyes. Another arrow was fired and in an instant a royal knight collapsed into the crowd of swordsmen, his horse going berserk and breaking through the swarm of men in its escape.

Hansfell's expertly adapted fighting instincts warned him of a nearby threat. Turning to the north he caught the blade of a royal soldier onto his own and pushed the man back. Staggering slightly, the soldier bounced back and came in for another attack. In his right hand was a sword, a crude yet efficient steel tool commonly used by the King's guards. In his left was a shield made from an iron frame that joined in the centre like the wheel of a cart. Thick wooden planks filled the space in between. By this phase of the battle, the wood was worn and soaked in blood. From the centre of the shield, the iron extended outwards to form a thick long spike.

The bandit knight fought against his opponent tirelessly. Normally, a simple foot soldier would pose no threat, but with the injuries already sustained, Hansfell had to put in his best effort just to stay alive. An attack came and, in an attempt to deliver a fatal retaliation, Hansfell manoeuvred with great agility, or at least what would have been great agility had both of his legs still been functioning. Instead, thrown off balance, he fell forward and was met with the spike of the shield. His metal helmet protected his nose and the sides of his head but could do nothing against the iron that now entered his face just below his right eye, shattering his cheekbone. The steel of his helmet bent in slightly during the impact but, fortunately, prevented the spike from travelling too far into Hansfell's head. Because of this, his brain remained undamaged, but the soldier pushed the shield upwards, ripping through the knight's flesh. Shards of skull embedded into his right eyeball and the pressure squeezed it until it burst, sending the inner fluids to join the torrent of blood that now ran down the bandit's face.

Certain of his victory, the royal soldier failed to notice the knight's blade as it broke through his ribcage. The man collapsed, gasping for air to fill his pierced lung, taking the shield down with him. A fountain of blood erupted from Hansfell's open wound as soon as the iron spike departed and he doubled over with his hands over the right side of his face, trying desperately to slow the bleeding. Through the whole event he remained unfalteringly calm and logical in every move he made. This is what made him such a useful member of Adelaide's army; it wasn't purely the immense physical strength he carried or the intelligence that helped him rise to such authority, it was the cool temper and sadistic love of violence of this psychopathic bandit that made him a force of nature.

Hansfell heard a familiar voice nearby. Squinting up with his left eye, he saw one of his fellow rogues galloping towards him on horseback, calling out his name. This Ghyrock knight carried a worried expression and upon reaching Hansfell, quickly pulled him up onto the horse and rode away from the wall, towards the bandits' temporary camp.

The leader of the knights was placed horizontally across the front of the saddle. One of his legs dangled uncontrollably on one side of the horse and his hands shielded his head wound on the other. Yet even still, the cries of the battlefield sounded lovelier to his ears than the gentlest of lullabies.

***

Bandit forces were making progress. Only one of the royal knights remained and he had retreated behind the wall after watching his companions shot down. Many foot soldiers were also taking refuge inside the walls of the capital, walls that were being rapidly weakened by trebuchets. Archers could no longer be positioned on the battlements so they were hastily arranged along the wide stone staircases on the southern and northern inner faces of the wall, awaiting the bandit troops that would inevitably break through the defences and enter the city.

Darius stood behind the archers, watching in horror as the bandit queen herself took to the frontlines and effortlessly massacred dozens of royal soldiers. In addition to her brute strength, it appeared as if she was radiating some sort of magic that sent nearby bandits into a bloodthirsty rage. She took the sea of emotions that they were feeling; the agitation, the fear, the anger; and morphed them into something demonic.

Covered head to toe in beautifully crafted steel armour that remained to this point without a single scratch, she abandoned her horse and went ahead on foot, revelling in the satisfaction of obliterating the enemy herself. Darius commanded the archers to aim for her. Hundreds of arrows were sent flying, some hitting the men around her, both royal and bandit, some heading straight for her body.

There she was again, a child in a meadow, rocks hitting her from all direction. Stop. Listen. Feel the vibrations in the air. Trust in the spirit of the woods.

Metal arrowheads smashed into the translucent blade of the Dragonslayer as Adelaide rotated it through the air with speed a weapon that heavy should not be able to move, forming a momentary impenetrable shield around herself. Hers was the sort of power that was repeated in legends since a time long forgotten.

Darius was starting to accept the inevitability of this battle. No number of soldiers could defeat her. Nothing they did would bring an end to her reign. As soon as this bandit queen took a step onto the battlefield,

342

it was over. With a heavy heart, Darius abandoned his post and rushed towards the castle.

Alongside his queen was her right-hand man, Talon, himself a powerful fiend. As well armoured as the knights, he carried a sword in each hand, which by now were both dripping with blood. His armour was certainly damaged, inevitably so for a foot soldier who carried no shield. The leather straps that bound his left gauntlet were ripping under the tension. He stalked along the southernmost wall while the queen took to the north. Separating from her was a mistake on his part as shortly after, three soldiers went for a joined attack against him. He overpowered them, of course, but lost the gauntlet of his left arm in the clash.

He was scratched up, beaten and bruised, his armour had bent inwards in places, digging into his flesh, and blood ran down the steel from those small exposed locations in-between the metal plates. He was not much younger than Hansfell but with far less physical training, and the continuous fighting was taking a toll on his body. Fatigue was starting to set in and his lungs cried out from breathing in the dust of the collapsing wall. Sweat tickled his brow as it ran down into his eye. Talon attempted to wipe it off but the steel helmet he wore was too restricting. Although, he certainly didn't regret wearing it as it had saved his life countless times in this battle.

Another attack, this time from the direction of the castle. The bandit lieutenant wielded his swords with skilful precision and powered on ahead towards their ultimate goal. A shower of arrows rained down onto him but not before he got hold of a nearby bandit ally and callously used his body as a meat shield, dropping him onto the ground afterwards and walking away without a backward glance. The mighty walls of the castle could be seen over the rooftops and served as a motivating factor in the invasion.

A group of young royal soldiers emerged from the crowd and surrounded him with their shields up and their swords at the ready. Talon stopped and waited for the first to strike. The fool must have been a recent recruit, as no experienced soldier would break such an advantageous formation. His body collapsed at the feet of his friends. The position where he stood was now empty and Talon didn't hesitate to slither into it and cut down the soldiers on other side, one blade in each. The remaining men fell out of rank and attempted to overwhelm him with a combined attack. Talon went for a defensive manoeuvre designed to push them back by spanning the space before him with both swords. To his surprise, the weapon in his left hand was caught by a solder between his armour and his shield, forcing the bandit to surrender either the blade or his arm. Quickly dropping the sword, Talon withdrew from the soldiers but the others had now seized the opportunity to attack. He cut down two of them, but the remaining men kept coming.

An attack from the left and the right together. On the right, he deflected the enemy's blade with his own but, on the left, he was vulnerable. The attacker was going for his neck. With no other option, Talon raised his unarmed left forearm and caught the sword into his flesh, rapidly twisting his arm so that the weapon would pass through his muscle rather than shatter the bone underneath. Carrying his sword around with all his strength, Talon took down both men. The move only cost him his left arm.

The bandit was briefly isolated from the battle and took a moment to rip the fabric from the surrounding corpses and bind his wound. At last he surrendered his technique and finally accepted the use of a shield, which he took from the fallen soldiers and bound awkwardly to his left bicep.

Bertrand, his dear old friend, had died a painful death in this battle. Talon would not let that sacrifice be in vain.

***

There were fewer and fewer archers on the western side of the battlements as Randall received a continuous influx of urgent messages demanding that troops be relocated to the east. He now stood next to just ten men. Their flaming arrows had expired. But that no longer bothered this commander, as his duty was done. The bandit ships burned on the water. Men jumped into the waves, desperate to extinguish the flames on their hair and clothing and swim away from the torched vessels.

Hunter was among them. The scene around him was like something out of a nightmare. Sails burning in the wind, sending hot embers towards the shore like a plague of locusts that destroyed everything they touched.

Columns of black smoke rose into the sky. How beautifully blue that sky once was. Now it looked as if sunlight may never again strike these waters.

The archers had not relented. They continued to fire at the retreating bandits, hunting them down like fish in a barrel before they reach the shore. Planks of wood floated in the waves alongside dead bodies but holding onto them made one an easy target so Hunter, like many others, took as deep a breath as he could and dived underwater, his position disguised from the archers by the shimmers.

The soldiers continued to fire from above. Arrows pierced through the water. Some painted the waves red on impact. Those bandits who escaped early were now starting to reach the shore. The cliff face was weathered away by the constant attacks from the seawater but it appeared as though it has recently crumbled, with lots of crooks and ledges that made it easy to climb. Grass and earth hung from the top of the cliff, dangling by interconnected roots.

Hunter hurried along, constantly looking up from the water to check his direction and judge the distance. Not far now, he repeated in his head, not far now and I'll be safe.

Arrows fired again. Hunter felt a piercing pain in his leg and splashed about, losing his aquatic stride. Struggling to look down through the water, the bandit could only see that no arrow had been embedded into him. In fact, it just barely scratched his ankle. Resuming haste, he continued his journey towards the shore. A couple more bombardments followed before he reached safety but none of these landed a single hit on him.

Grabbing onto the earth, he pulled himself from the water and onto a dent in the cliff. Leaning back against the rock he took a moment to catch his breath. He was the last one to make it to shore, no more movement could be seen in the waters. The ships still burned in the distance. Dust fell onto him from above as bandits were making their way up the cliff and onto flat land.

Hunter had shed all his armour and nearly all his clothing before jumping into the water and now sat in breeches and a shirt, water dripping from his dark hair and beard. Contorting slightly, he brought his leg up to his side and assessed the wound. It was bleeding rather profusely still as the submersion in water made it difficult for blood to clot, but the scratch was not deep and would recover quickly. Assertively he stood up, intending to climb up the cliff, assuming that the archers would by now have joined the eastern side of the battle. James had once conveyed rumours that a secret exit from the castle was positioned not far from this spot. Hunter was determined to seek it out and enter the King's residence unnoticed, earning commendation from his great queen.

Before he could make a move, flames of incomparable tenacity spread out over the cliff edge. Bandits were screaming and their charred corpses fell past Hunter into the water. These were not the same flames that were used to sink the ships but they certainly were ones this bandit recognised. These flames were magic. And there was only one wizard in this part of the world.

Chapter 54

The Bandit Queen

Darius ran back to the castle as fast as his legs would carry him, praying that it was not too late. Soldiers rushed past in the other direction but civilians, desperate to take refuge within the sturdy walls of the fortress, ran alongside him. Anyone who was able to fight was recruited for this battle, the only ones left to flee their homes were women, who pressed their infants to their chests to shield them from the commotion, the hysterical children, who gripped the skirts of their mothers with their tiny hands and were pulled into the retreating stream of people, and the elderly, who did not have the strength to run but were incessantly urged to by their families. These people appeared to be wearing upon their bodies all the clothes they owned and some even had the determination to try and drag a sack of their possessions through the crowd. They had expected this outcome. Yet the King did not order an evacuation prior to this battle as he refused to believe that the bandit bitch and her army of criminals would be able to tear down the city gate. Nor did he believe the rumours of magic and werewolves that spread like wildfire through the dwellers of the castle.

A boy in his early teenage years looked up at Darius. He was old enough to recognise him yet still foolish enough to shout to his mother:

"Look, it's the King's advisor!"

Within a moment, chaos erupted.

"He's retreating too!"

"The bandits will take the city!"

"God save us all!"

Darius ignored their cries and pushed on ahead. Soon, he entered the main hall of the castle with the civilians. A small number of low-ranking soldiers were scattered around, hurriedly guiding the townsfolk into various passages in an attempt to spread them out through the castle. The fewer get in the way of the bandits, the more would survive.

The main hall looked desolate. It was a grand open space that was once covered in lavish carpets and tapestries. A banquet table formally stood in the centre that served endless delicacies to local lords and foreign dignitaries alike. Now, the room stood barren, large grey rectangular stones were the only texture to the walls and the floor. The colossal chandeliers that had once bathed the room in candlelight now hung cold and lifeless; what light seeped in through stained-glass windows allowed their iron skeletons to cast eerie shadows upon the walls.

The King sat upon his throne. He slouched silently, one hand supporting his chin and the other loosely holding a long-unused sword. The furs that draped his stout body revealed steel armour underneath. Darius slowed his pace. His King looked up, as if sensing his oldest friend's presence. He met Darius's gaze with a melancholy stare. They both knew that before dawn, their kingdom would fall.

After a moment of hesitation, Darius moved towards a certain spiral staircase and pushed his way past the civilians without turning his back. The King watched him as he left the hall.

The staircase was narrow and Darius had to try and manoeuvre up the inner side past the civilians, where each worn stone step was barely wide enough to place the toe of a shoe. Taking two or three steps at a time, and slipping every now and then, he managed to very quickly make his way to the top level, where he broke into a sprint down the hallway. This part of the castle was not stripped of its prizes; thick red carpets still adorned the floors and curtains were drawn back with little silken ribbons. The civilians had not yet made their way here so the corridor was empty of people yet the walls trembled as a result of the chaos going on outside.

At last, Darius reached the room that held what was most precious to him. Opening the door unceremoniously, the advisor barged in. Lylith, the queen of Starkenhaart, jumped to her feet, holding her screaming infant close to her. She was terrified and seeing the urgency in her lover's eyes only sent her further into a panic.

"That sound..." she sobbed with tears streaming down her face.

"The bandits were firing trebuchets. They overran the city, the castle will fall soon. We have to go now!"

With that, he grabbed her by the hand and dragged her out of the room and down the corridor, towards that same staircase. Both the woman and the child were hysterical and Darius stopped and took a brief moment to embrace them both.

"There is another way out of the castle. I arranged for a boat to be waiting there just in case. We'll make it out alive, I promise," he said as softly as his shaking voice would allow.

Taking the baby into his arms, he once again resumed haste and soon they were rushing down the steps, pushing the gawking civilians out of the way.

***

Sir Randall of Hovenshire stood like a monument in front of the castle doors. He seemed to have embellished himself in even more armour than he naturally wore. One side of his body was hidden behind a heavy shield that stretched from his face to his ankles. The steel was shining brightly in the moonlight and the design on the face of the shield was exquisite. It was foreign, acquired from the eastern smiths perhaps, and certainly unlike anything used by the common Starkenhaart guards. In his right hand, Randall held an unsheathed blade. Once again, the weapon looked unusual, heavier than standard military blades. In weight, it was similar to the Dragonslayer yet the metal from which it was forged was nothing more than common steel. Not that this was a fair reason not to admire the expert craftsmanship.

Before him stood the Queen of the bandits. Whilst protected by armour, she carried no shield. Even the metal bow that exterminated hundreds of enemy soldiers was left behind outside the city gates. There was nothing to her other than that fatal sword and the raw power that possessed her. Randall felt uneasy standing in front of her, as if she was leaching his courage. From the slits in the helmet, her unblinking eyes stared him down, seeking to intimidate and weaken her prey before going in for the kill. They were quite the contrast; one so heavily defended, so tall and broad and the other quite small in comparison, with cloth showing in the joints of her armour and a single tool at her disposal. The bandit had an occasional splash of blood here and there on the outside of her steel plate mail but both fighters were themselves unharmed. That mere knowledge struck fear into Randall as he had been protected on the battlements, away from the melee, while she had walked straight through the frontlines.

Talon, despite his injuries, closely followed his leader, taking on the foot soldiers behind her so that she may engage Randall in one-on-one combat. Her closest commander's left arm was by now useful for nothing other than to attach his shield to but fighting one handed appeared to pose him little challenge.

Randall made the first move, bringing his sword down heavily onto the bandit Queen. A sharp sound resonated as the blade struck the pebbles on the ground beneath. She stood mere inches to the side, still staring, but now with the addition of a disturbing grin. She was toying with him.

Bringing the blade up and to the side, the knight twisted his wrist so that the side of the sword was coming directly towards the bandit's torso. She could not dodge this one. But she could feel those same vibrations that she felt when guided by the spirit of the woods. It was that same disturbance in the air, that moment of anticipation.

The woman caught his sword onto hers directly, holding the Dragonslayer vertically downwards with both hands on the hilt. For her to be able to hold against an attack like that, her strength must be truly god-like. That was her tactic, first to test his brute force and then demonstrate her own. That was the way to frighten someone who was very confident in their own ability.

Randall hit her with his shield, pushing her back, but when he withdrew his sword to go in for another attack, he noticed a chip on the blade in the place where it clashed with the Dragonslayer. Even as a defensive mechanism, that magical blade did more damage than expected. Of course Randall, being an educated man, had been told stories of that legendary weapon that took down an ancient dragon but he would not let himself believe that such a powerful tool would fall into the hands of a bandit like her.

They fought and fought by the castle doors, each proving themselves to be a fierce opponent, but there was only one outcome to this match. Randall collapsed to the ground, bleeding profusely from a gash in his neck. His shield, still attached to his arm, weighed it down and he ended up sprawled out, clasping at the cut, struggling to shift around. Adelaide walked over, herself having suffered a few hits, exhausted yet victorious. Out of respect, she chose not to toy with him further. Studying his helmet, she estimated where it would be thinnest and brought the Dragonslayer down with full force. As expected, the sword that could cut through anything, cut through steel like it was paper. Randall twitched for a little and then his body relaxed. Adelaide found it rather ironic that the man who loved armour died the moment she cut through it.

***

King Bohemond of Starkenhaart remained unmoving on his throne, watching the door. The clashing of swords that sounded so close was suddenly silenced. The King dared not hope that Randall had won the battle, knowing that it was far too late to stop this demonic force that tore through the capital city. Those few moments of silence dragged on for what felt like an eternity.

The heavy door was locked shut under his command as soon as Darius disappeared up the staircase, leaving only the knight outside. Whatever number of civilians were able to gather inside were the number saved, the others had perished beyond the walls, cut apart by the bandits. The guards ordered to defend the royal hall had finished escorting those few lucky citizens into various nooks and crannies and took up their positions around the King. All of the royal knights had now fallen, and these men would soon fall too.

Then it came. That unimaginable sound. The thick wooden gate trembled and creaked open; those beautiful gold-plated locks holding it shut crumbled under the power of the unstoppable blade. A single figure stepped inside, her armour glistening in the moonlight that now poured into the reception hall. She paused, looking around, her movements slow and relaxed, the sword now by her side. This figure looked almost angelic, bathed in gentle white light. She stepped further in, deliberately pulling the doors open, revealing the army of bandits that had gathered behind her. To her right stood Talon, blood pouring onto the ground from underneath the shield on his injured arm.

Adelaide began her walk towards the King, rapidly picking up pace. Soldiers darted in front of her, trying desperately to halt her assault but they were cut down like flies. One of them rushed towards Talon, who took the hit onto his shield yet so exhausted was he from his battle and loss of blood that he stumbled back, weary and clinging onto consciousness. Before the King's soldier could attack again, he found his head separated from the neck. The quick-acting saviour collapsed to the ground, unable to halt his own momentum due to an inability to use his left leg. Shards of steel from his helmet were still embedded in his face, covered by layer upon layer of bandages but his other eye was as sharp as ever, and no number of injuries could stop Sir Hansfell from returning to a battle that brought him so much excitement. He was picked off the floor and held upright by the surrounding bandits and exchanged a look of understanding and mutual joy with his former nemesis. How bitterly they once fought over their border and how strong they were in their union! Talon and Hansfell held onto each other, supporting one another, and hobbled into the castle hall, watching as their Queen raged through, impatiently approaching the King.

Bohemond had finally roused himself from his sloth and from beneath the folds of his cloak he brought forth a weapon of recent invention. An automated bow, small in size and packing far more strain in its drawn position, a crossbow was not commonly seen in these parts aside from the market stalls of travelling weapon smiths. The bolt was in place and the tension in the string was at its fullest. At close range, such a weapon may even be strong enough to pierce through the rebel Queen's steel breastplate.

It was at this moment that Darius emerged from the staircase, holding the infant prince in one arm and pulling Lylith by the hand with the other. He looked in horror at the fury being unleashed by the bandit leader as men fell in her path, leaving a trail of corpses. Darius rushed past the throne, fully engaging the King with a stern and non-apologetic gaze and hurried towards a hallway on the other side of the vast room.

King Bohemond gripped the crossbow tighter in his left hand and pondered his choices. The approaching beast was near indestructible and even if she were to fall, her soldiers remained great in number, while his own had all but perished. In addition, punishment for treachery was far more inviting. Raising his left arm out horizontally, he squeezed the trigger. The mechanism operated and the bolt shot out. It flew through the stale air of the castle, creating vortices in the particles that were suspended in its fluid, and struck Queen Lylith right between her spine and the base of her right shoulder plate, piercing her lung.

The woman fell and blood started to pour out from her lips as she gasped for breath. Each time the muscle in her ribcage contracted, blood would squirt out, staining her light pink dress a much darker colour. Darius, crouching by her body and holding the screaming baby prince to his chest, held his trembling hand out to her, not knowing what to do. Just a moment before, that same hand touched the skin of the woman he had loved his whole life and now she was dying an agonising death right before his eyes. He wept, babbling incoherently as grief tore apart his heart. Lylith raised her dying eyes to him one last time and in them, he saw acceptance. She was no longer afraid. The hysteria that gripped her during their escape had dissipated and her last wish escaped as a whisper from her lips.

"Save my son."

Darius nodded, sobbing, and rose upright. Turning away from the dying woman, he ran into the passage through which he had hoped to take her.

King Bohemond released the crossbow from his hand and its wooden frame hit the stone floor by the throne. His face wore no expression. The murder of his cheating wife brought him neither grief nor the joy that he had hoped for. She began her final convulsions, drowning in her own blood and the King simply watched, unfeeling.

Adelaide was now mere steps away from him and despite his attempt to use his long-untrained fighting skill he soon found the Dragonslayer slicing through his breastplate and breaking his ribcage. The sword had cut him open and he fell to the floor. Adelaide pulled off her helmet, throwing it down the hall, and placed the golden crown from the head of the fallen King onto her own. Gripping him by his hair, she sawed at the now-dead King's neck until his body fell to the ground, leaving a bloody head in her hand. Holding up her trophy with the vicious laugh, Adelaide crowned herself the new sovereign of the kingdom of Starkenhaart and collapsed happily into her throne, placing the decapitated head on an armrest. Blood flowed down the mahogany legs of the throne and soon joined the red pool forming around the body, once again fusing with its own self. The bandits cheered and threw their helmets up towards the ceiling. The merriment was picked up by those who heard it outside and it wasn't long before the entire capital was celebrating the coronation. Talon and Hansfell limped over and were the first to kneel before her throne. The others quickly followed and Adelaide had the pleasure of seeing her rebel army pouring into the reception hall to honour her.

***

Hunter, having finally gathered the courage to climb further up the cliff, had now reached the top. Peeking over the edge, he could see nothing but the wall of the capital rising out of empty land. Right before he pulled himself up fully onto horizontal ground, he heard voices, and civilians emerged from a passage in the wall. The first few were cautious, they moved slowly and looked around with curiosity. The ones behind them walked faster, shouting about the bandits entering the castle. The ones that followed moved hurriedly as if they were being pushed and lastly ran out King Bohemond's royal advisor himself, carrying an infant in his arms and cursing the King in full voice. The advisor looked around, seeking the contact he prayed had come.

Hunter watched this whole scene unfold while hanging from the cliff. His arms were starting to ache but he dug his feet further into the crumbling soil of the cliff-face and kept watching.

Darius spun around, panic rapidly growing inside him and then suddenly stopped in his tracks, looking in wonder at the familiar face that emerged from the brush.

"There you are!" cried Hunter's former ally. "Once I heard what you were hatching, I knew I had to come myself. Now, follow me, I have a boat waiting for us."

"Mimiral…" Darius whispered, "you burned down Tarrynsdew. You worked with the Silverblood clan. How can I trust that you will not betray me now?"

The wizard's hazel eyes looked at his old friend with the warmest expression. After all this time, he still looked as if he was barely out of boyhood, not a wrinkle on his skin, not a strand of grey in his chestnut hair.

"I cannot ask for your forgiveness," the wizard spoke, "but allow me to at least begin my redemption by saving you this time. Come now, we must hurry."

"Where are you taking me?"

Mimiral smirked.

"Back to Mortennden of course."

Epilogue

First of Her Name

It had been a year since that fateful day when the Silverblood dynasty took its roots. The dust had settled on the kingdom of Starkenhaart yet many still trembled at the memory of the violence they had witnessed. To the citizens of the north, who welcomed the bandit troops into Farendale, this was a joyful time. The trade that had once passed through these lands from the northern ports was no longer flowing due to the Queen's undiplomatic take on international relations; however, many jobs opened up in assisting the war effort. Farmers had been assigned to land and taxed a lower rate as long as half of their produce went to the growing military. The demand for blacksmiths and carpenters rose as more recruits were trained and more ships were crafted. Former bandits who fought alongside Adelaide during her rise to power were now treated like war heroes, given shelter in official barracks that had started to emerge in every major city, provided with moderate rations and were free of taxation. Being a soldier was made to be the most inviting profession.

The eastern midlands also reaped these benefits. Marrynport not only had a major river flowing through its surrounding land, but was also an old and well-fortified city that was just a short stretch of water away from the neighbouring kingdom of Mynellia. It quickly became the prime location for the royal navy to grow and develop. The little village to the south of it that at one time had the courage and willpower to stand against Adelaide's demands was to meet its destruction shortly after her coronation and would forever after lay in ruin. Tarrynsdew was never rebuilt after its grand fire, but its charred remains became a place of refuge for those who had their livelihoods ripped from their hands.

The Silver City, as the old Silverblood camp became known, prospered and thrived! Sir Hansfell's construction of its grand wall and ordered layout made it a comfortable and well defended military fort. Avenstead, Rynell and Ghyrock suffered greatly during the years leading up to the siege but little investment was made to help them recover. The citizens lived simple lives and took what mother nature provided for them in the surrounding woodland.

For the south, the situation was dire. The population had always been scarce and after all of their able-bodied men were recruited by the bandits during the rebellion, the remaining folk migrated north in search of jobs. Within the first year of Queen Adelaide's rule, this mountainous region became barren, a perfect stretch of isolation that separated the Enchanted Forest from the rest of the world.

Prince Rupert was to be educated by the most knowledgeable scholars in the kingdom and treated as any royal heir would. Princess Edith was showered with attention by her governesses and servants. At just over two years old, she was a precious and beloved member of the Queen's family.

Talon went on to become Adelaide's trusted advisor. Hunter and Hansfell served as members of her council, along with any bandits who distinguished themselves during the siege. Two of King Bohemond's council members were willing to serve the new monarch to protect their status and income. All the rest were swiftly executed.

James was found in the dungeon after the city was taken by the bandits. Adelaide was made aware of his treachery in revealing knowledge of the werewolf to Darius. However, Bertrand's death served in Adelaide's favour so she commanded James's wounds to be tended to and left his life to the will of God. Miraculously, the young spy survived and after several months of bed rest was able to walk once more. The injuries he had sustained during his months of torture made him physically unable to fight in battle so he remained within the walls of the capital, serving as Adelaide's assistant. His loyalty to her had grown, nurtured by his freedom and her mercy.

***

Many hundreds of thousands of miles east, within the castle walls of the now peaceful kingdom of Mortendenn, the former royal advisor of Starkenhaart sat by the light of a single candle. Those black eyes stared emptily into the walls of his chamber, which although modest in size was well decorated and contained a decent sized hearth that now stood unused even on the coldest winter nights. The intelligence that brought him such high status played strongly in his head, pulling together characteristically intricate schemes. He had somehow lost even more weight from his already small frame and these long skeletal fingers tapped rhythmically on the small table upon which the candle stood, sending shivers through the faint light that landed on the walls of the room. It has been one full year now since Lylith was struck down before his very eyes. Her infant son slept peacefully in a cradle on the other side of the room. Bohemond's son.

The tapping against the table rose in volume. Kind Bohemond, whom Darius served since his teenage years, was dead and gone, but the son-of-a-bitch just had to take Lylith with him. And it was his son sleeping next to Darius now. The man turned to look at the child. The little boy bore a strong resemblance to his father. The father whom Darius cursed every day since his death. The tapping became stronger. The rightful heir to King Bohemond's throne. King Bohemond's successor. That's who the boy was. Darius lingered on the dark thoughts that often plagued him. That worthless king does not deserve a successor.